He took her mouth with his, and Merilee knew she belonged to him now, whatever he wanted, however he wanted to take her. As she went completely limp in his arms, Jake broke away from the mind-altering kiss and stared at her with those stormy gray-blue eyes she absolutely couldn't look away from. They flickered to gold, then back to gray-blue, making her heart stutter. His lips pulled back and his skin shimmered from tanned to pearl as his fangs flashed in and out of existence.

"Do you really want me?" he asked, his voice so low, so ominous that delicious chills charged all over her skin. "If you say yes, I won't stop."

Jake's eyes flashed golden. Merilee's breath caught painfully in her chest, but she absolutely could not deny the raging want, the need, that filled her.

"Yes," she whispered.

Also by Anna Windsor

Bound by Shadow
Bound by Flame

BOUND BY LIGHT

A NOVEL OF THE DARK CRESCENT SISTERHOOD

ANNA WINDSOR

BALLANTINE BOOKS • NEW YORK

A Ballantine Books Mass Market Original

Published in the United States by Ballantine Books, an imprint of The Random House Publishing Group, a division of Random House, Inc., New York.

ISBN 978-0-345-49855-7

Printed in the United States of America

www.ballantinebooks.com

OPM 9 8 7 6 5 4 3 2 1

For Nancy Yost,
who keeps me laughing

(prologue)

May, fourteen months after the Battle of Motherhouse Ireland

Jake Lowell stared at the woman on the crystal balcony across from his own.

A cool mountain breeze stirred her short blond hair as she moved through the training patterns of an ancient form of *tai chi chuan,* and she opened her long arms to welcome the wind. Stretched into it. Took the energy inside her and let it go, moving with the air, rhythmic, easy, and absolutely fluid.

Jake's blade-sharp senses registered every detail of her appearance, from her lean, curvaceous shape to the light tint of her olive skin to her soft, ethereal scent of white tea and honey. When she opened her eyes, he saw the same deep, startling blue of the nearby Mediterranean Sea. She looked at home here on the hidden slope of Áno Ólimbos, upper Mount Olympus, near Litochoro, Greece—the City of Gods—in this crystalline palace where villagers once assumed Zeus and Apollo resided.

The woman could be a goddess. Aphrodite, with beauty beyond comparison, or wise Athena, or Hera, the queen of Olympus. Artemis, goddess of the hunt, might be appropriate, too, since she was unwaveringly accurate with her bow and arrows. Most of these women, though, would claim lineage to Hecate, the formidable three-faced goddess who predated Zeus.

A woman so fierce even the king of the gods feared her and treated her with respect.

The woman on the balcony was that fierce, and Jake knew her name.

Merilee Alexander.

Angelic—and as deadly as a Greek horn-nosed viper.

Merilee might look supple and giving, the epitome of everything gentle and female, but Jake knew her secret. Merilee was a Sibyl, one of the Dark Crescent Sisterhood. She was a warrior bearing the mark of the Dark Goddess—a tattoo of a mortar, pestle, and broom in triangular points around a dark crescent moon—and groomed for combat since she first learned to walk. She could kill with her arrows or her elemental control over wind and the movements of air. If she had to, she could snap a man's neck with her well-trained hands.

He responded to her beauty *and* the danger of being near her, as he had the first time he saw her two years ago, when she was standing next to his twin brothers, Nick and Creed, both cops with New York City's almost-secret Occult Crimes Unit. How could he forget her? After all, Jake had been sent on a mission to murder one of her best friends.

His blood pumped hot, and he tightened his fists. Jake set his jaw and worked to tolerate the painful pulse in his hard cock.

Merilee had distracted him that day, the force of his attraction giving him strength he needed to fight the curse laid upon him by his very creation. She had been a fantasy, a beautiful dream.

But now . . .

The sight of her, the raging heat he felt at her presence, only reminded Jake of what he was, and what he might never be. If the Greek Mothers couldn't help him, he didn't know what he was going to do.

When he looked down at his own body, he saw nothing at all.

He was invisible.

No one could see his blond hair or his bare feet pressed firmly against the white crystal of his balcony. No one could target the hated talisman around his neck or snatch it from him. He raised one hand and squeezed the chain and ring that could be used to control his every thought and action.

"You surprise me, Jake," said a musical voice from the room behind him. "I sense you out on that balcony—but in all the months you've been with us, I never took you for a voyeur."

Jake let go of his talisman, tore his eyes from the tempting sight across from him, and strode back into his large, bright room of crystal, ivory, and white granite. Wind became music in this place, playing softly around each corner and angle, through each piece of intricate latticework. Jake thought Motherhouse Greece had probably been designed to make the air sing. As he passed through the curtains surrounding his doorway, he let his emotions flow with the music, then marshaled his energy and focused on becoming visible and . . . and human.

Mother Anemone waited, her blue robes pulled around her tall frame. Her ash blond hair had been swept back and fastened atop her head, no doubt a defense against the ceaseless wind. Jake was uncomfortably aware of the older woman's misty green eyes fixed on him as he transitioned from nothingness into a creature with white hair, golden eyes, translucent pearly skin, fangs, claws, and a double set of huge leathery wings.

A monster.

I'm no better than a gargoyle, and she knows it.

Yet Mother Anemone did not move her hands closer to the two gold-handled *falcata* swords belted about her waist. She just stood there and watched him. Studied him like an unusual circus attraction.

Rage bubbled through Jake's very essence, but he didn't lose sight of the fact that Mother Anemone was trying to help him. She, the other Greek Mothers, and many adepts had been searching week after week to find solutions to his dilemma, even though the other two Motherhouses in Russia and Ireland had already concluded that it was impossible. The earth Sibyls and the fire Sibyls had sent Jake on his way quickly, unable to grant his request. The air Sibyls, though, were archivists, record keepers. They had stores of books and scrolls the other two Motherhouses did not possess. Some forgotten bit of text might exist, some lost practice or ceremony. The air Sibyls, at least, had given Jake hope.

He forced himself to concentrate on pulling in his wings, and they vanished with hardly a stir of air. Jake sank into the heavy feel of gravity. Twinges pinched along his spine as his muscles bulked out and squeezed into more compact shapes. His body adjusted and accommodated, shifting to a height more like a normal human male, a little over six feet tall. His skin darkened to a golden tan, his hair shortened and became blond, and his eyes shifted from golden to blue.

A brief, hot sensation gripped him, like standing in a shooting flame—but everything happened faster now, without as much pain, since he spent so much time in this shape. Even the jeans and white sleeveless T-shirt came easily, reconstituting, as real and tangible as before Jake had given up his corporeal form to take a better look at Merilee's workout. Some aspects of his identity and appearance, like his lack of wings, his clothing, and his surname, came from conscious choice. His height, his shape, his hair and eye and skin color—this was more mysterious to him, since he never chose these traits, but more or less flowed into being with them the first time he moved from invisible to visible.

To the waiting Mother he said, "You seem shocked I'd watch a beautiful woman. All men are voyeurs at heart.

Didn't you know?" When he gave her a purposely wicked wink, her dazzling smile flared.

A surge of hope claimed Jake, chasing out some of the despair at his center, even raising the hairs on his arms and across the back of his neck. "Did you find something?" he asked, but faltered as Mother Anemone's smile quickly faded.

Her eyes darkened with a sadness that seemed to weight her supple frame and reveal her great age.

Everything inside Jake sank at the sight.

"We've spent many hours delving through archives. Only a few of us speak the languages necessary to read some of the books. Tomes so old the pages threaten to turn to dust when we move them. We read them all. Every possible source—and we can find no ritual to reverse the process that changed you into an Astaroth demon."

Jake's gut knotted. His breath jammed in his chest. Fresh rage rushed the length of his body, his trunk, tightening every muscle until he thought he would snap in half. "There must be a way. Some book you haven't discovered."

Mother Anemone shook her head.

Jake's essence shimmered. His human form tattered at the edges. He fought an urge to turn his head from Mother Anemone, to see if Merilee still occupied the balcony across from his. The sight of Merilee might calm him, but it might shred his insides, too.

Mother Anemone moved to stand directly in front of him. She placed a long-fingered hand on his forearm and squeezed, as if to battle the storm of misery breaking across his soul.

"I'm sorry, Jake. You cannot be human again."

He didn't respond. He had no more ability to speak.

It was all Jake could do to remain a solid, tangible

presence in the room. His last hope scattered on the breezes of Mount Olympus, destroyed with her simple words, no matter how softly she spoke them.

He pushed off Mother Anemone's hand and turned from her, desperate for something, anything outside the darkness threatening to shroud his being.

The balcony across from his was empty.

Jake closed his eyes.

Most of his mind wanted to surrender, to give himself over to invisibility and the teasing call of the mountain winds. He could fly to some obscure place, never return, never expose himself to companionship—or the risk of capture—again. Or he could deny what Mother Anemone told him. He could force himself to stay in his corporeal form. Longer this time, until he couldn't attain invisibility, or release his human body. He had already discovered that the longer he stayed present, the harder it was to disappear. He could be human in practice if not in fact, damnit.

He could do *something*.

Jake turned back to Mother Anemone.

She was trying to smile again. He knew she wanted to soothe him, but he didn't think he would ever be soothed.

"After experiencing the freedom of invisibility and flight," she said, "after touching the wisdom of centuries of memories shared by those of your species, could you truly limit yourself to human flesh and human ignorance?"

Jake pulled the chain and ring over his head and held it out to the side, as far from his heart as he could get it without letting it go. "If this is the price of that so-called freedom, then hell yes, I'll give it up. Just tell me how, or help me destroy this fucking thing."

Mother Anemone shook her head. "The writings have been clear on that point. If you destroy your talisman, you destroy yourself. When that chain and ring cease to exist, so do you." She gestured to the talisman. "Put it back on, *agapitos*. Keep it close to you at all times."

"I'd rather die," he growled in spite of her term of endearment, and wondered how far it was to the forbidden heights of Káto Ólimbos, lower Olympus, where he had heard the Keres, a bunch of carnivorous winged death spirits, resided. Hadn't he signed an agreement not to go there when he arrived at Motherhouse Greece? To honor and respect a no-contact treaty held by both races?

Well, fuck that.

Jake bet the death spirits could handle him, talisman and all.

Mother Anemone seemed to read his thoughts. In a lightning-fast yet gentle motion, she plucked the talisman from Jake's fingers.

He lurched from the shock of her fingers pressing on his inner being, yet her touch was not intrusive or demanding, nothing like he had experienced before when someone else was in control of his talisman.

It was . . . not completely unpleasant.

A surprise.

He blinked at her, unmoving, eyes pasted to the talisman now lying across her open palm. She could take the thing and force him to do whatever she wanted, whatever she desired. He knew he could resist people who commanded his talisman for a short time—he had done it before—but the agony . . . God, he didn't know if he could go through that again.

And yet he couldn't grab the chain and ring back from her.

His arms wouldn't lift. His muscles wouldn't obey his commands to do that. Either she gave it back to him, or he retrieved it when she died. No other way to regain possession of it, and control of his own will.

The thought made him boil inside.

Jake felt like an active volcano, ready to explode.

"You haven't spent months poring over the vestigial memories of your species, learning and growing into one of the most intelligent beings I have ever known, only to kill yourself." Mother Anemone moved with graceful deliberation, letting the talisman drift up on a breeze she controlled, moving it toward him, then settling the chain over his head. The ring pressed against his chest once more, and she withdrew her hand and the well-controlled wind, giving up her power over him as easily as letting out a breath. "You're bound by the light inside you. It must shine. *You* must shine. A man who wants to perish doesn't boldly march into all three Sibyl Motherhouses and demand a solution to his problems."

"I'm not a man," he reminded her through his teeth, shaking from the relief of having the talisman back again. If anyone else had done that to him, he might have torn off their head.

"You're as much man as any male I've ever met, *agapitos*. And in your heart, better than most of them." She placed her palm on his chest, next to the talisman. "You would be a valuable warrior in our fight against the Legion. With the terrible battles ahead—and we sense them coming—we can scarcely afford to lose such a brave and powerful leader."

Mother Anemone's gaze drifted to the side, and he knew she was looking at the balcony where Merilee had been. "There are men and women who can interact with you without subjecting you to abuse and control, Jake. Your brothers and the Sibyls amongst them." Her eyes shifted back to his and blazed with certainty as she added, "There are people who will respect you, accept you, even love you for *all* you are, if you'll allow that."

He let out a slow breath, trying to rein in his temper, out of respect for Mother Anemone and her efforts to assist him. He moved away from her instead of knocking her hand off his chest. "Don't worry. I would never let that happen."

"You mistake my meaning." She was smiling again, this time for real. "I'm not worried about your interest in Merilee. I'm intrigued. Merilee is a special woman, perhaps one of the most gifted Sibyls I've had the pleasure to train. In my opinion, no man on Earth has been good enough for her, or strong enough to make her take the personal aspects of her life a bit more seriously, experience them more deeply—until now. She's very important to me. I trust you will look after her, when she needs looking after."

Jake found himself speechless again, only this time, it had nothing to do with his talisman. A few moments of uncomfortable silence passed before he nodded, retrieved his duffel from its spot on the crystal floor at the foot of his bed, and began to pack his few belongings.

Another quiet minute passed before Mother Anemone asked, "For now, where will you go?"

Jake bit back sarcastic responses. "Since the Sibyls can't help me become human again, or rid me of this talisman, seems I've got two choices left."

Mother Anemone waited without interrupting.

Jake grabbed a last shirt from the dresser nearest his bed, then turned to face the Mother again. "It's either a visit with your neighbors the Keres, or the Police Academy."

Mother Anemone had shivered at the mention of the death spirits, but Jake's mention of the Police Academy made her smile bright enough to lighten the room. "I'll get in touch with Captain Freeman. He'll be glad to have you, Jake. And your brothers, too. They're both fine officers. Married to Sibyls at that. Merilee's triad sisters."

She sounded way too delighted, and pleased with the

situation and the possibilities. Again, out of respect, Jake didn't dash the woman's hopes as she left his room.

He'd look after Merilee as Mother Anemone wished. And he'd do this thing the Mother suggested, try being a warrior in the fight against the twisted Legion cult that stole his humanity and created him—but he would *not* mix that closely with people other than his brothers, Sibyls or no.

Jake shouldered his duffel.

His free hand drifted to his talisman, which he tucked inside his T-shirt, out of sight.

Mother Anemone was a brilliant woman, but too kind. She was able to look away from the terrible things Jake had done when others controlled the bit of jewelry now concealed beneath a layer of white cotton.

As he left the safety and peace of Motherhouse Greece, Jake knew that no matter what, he couldn't lose sight of his crimes, of his potential for evil and devastation. That would be far too convenient—and far too dangerous for everyone involved.

Even for Merilee.

He grimaced as he walked out of his room and into the long crystalline hallway.

Make that *especially* for Merilee.

Sunlight blazed through the wide room's crystal columns as Merilee folded three new pairs of hand-tooled battle leathers one at a time, then fit them into her travel bag.

Beside her, Mother Anemone settled herself on the white silk bedspread and gazed at her. As always, a soft breeze, as gentle and sweet as a baby's breath, flowed off the older woman's shoulders. She smelled like lilacs.

Merilee smiled.

Mother Anemone had always smelled like lilacs. It was one of her earliest memories.

"Have you truly rested enough?" The Mother's concern showed in every tight line of her aged, but still beautiful face. "Your burdens in New York City will only increase when you return."

Merilee closed the bag and zipped it. "I don't want to stay away any longer. My triad needs me—and I miss them."

Mother Anemone sighed, stirring the light wind in the room until it sang through the columns and carved abutments. "And the dreams?"

The bag in Merilee's hands slipped through her fingers and landed on the polished crystal and ivory floor with a soft *whump*. She shivered and snatched it back up, hoping Mother Anemone didn't notice—but knowing that she did. "I've had a respite while I've been here. Maybe the nightmares won't come back when I leave. They're not too frequent, anyway. I only came to tell you about them because they involved the Keres."

Both women looked out the bedroom's arched window, in the direction of the low, misty mountain where the death spirits had resided since time before time. The carnivorous monsters remained on Káto Ólimbos because of an ancient treaty with the Dark Crescent Sisterhood.

Merilee's muscles tightened as her mind faded back to her sixth year.

Clear as if it had happened a few minutes ago, she saw herself climbing out this very bedroom window to feel a storm rolling across the sea, to touch the rushing wind, so cool, so salty and fresh and powerful.

She remembered how she sat on the wide stone cornice, soaking up the manic breeze, watching the clouds chase across the bright full moon.

And then . . . *them*.

Black shapes whirling off Káto Ólimbos, reeling into the sky.

Merilee's hands twitched and she almost covered her ears as she remembered the pain of those shrieks.

A stench like blood and rot . . . and one vulture shape breaking toward her, coming, coming, howling like an underworld demon—

Merilee swallowed and closed her eyes to stop the images. She touched the small scar that ran between her right ear and jaw. Just a thin white line nobody could see, but she always knew it was there. The reminder of what it felt like to fall off the Motherhouse roof and crash into a stone terrace.

The other adepts had laughed at her. They had called her a coward. Which, she supposed, she had been. All of that stuff about the death spirits—that had been a vision. It couldn't have been anything else, and she acted a fool and freaked out, jumped off a building, busted her chin and jaw, and knocked out the rest of her baby teeth.

Idiot.

Merilee opened her eyes and took in the gentle curl of the faraway mists.

Nothing terrifying now.

Just fog and clouds and mountain.

The Keres kept to themselves.

She tried to let go of some of the tension that had knotted her shoulders, and she dismissed the tingle along the hidden scar on her jaw.

It was a long time ago, and I'm a warrior now, not a little coward who jumps off roofs.

Besides, her nightmares were totally different, not memories at all. "I think my bad dreams are just metaphors. I think maybe I'll be facing some losses soon, and I need to get ready."

Mother Anemone was silent for a time, and the two of them remained still, listening to the beautiful movement of the wind through Motherhouse Greece.

Then Mother Anemone stood and put her hands on

Merilee's arms. "Your life needs to be about more than worry and work and duty, my love."

Merilee gazed at the woman who had always been both Mother *and* mother to her, emotionally. "Worry and work and duty *are* life. I'm a broom, remember? With *my* triad, there's always a mess to clean up."

"That, I cannot argue." Mother Anemone squeezed Merilee's arms and turned her loose. "But we'll discuss this again."

Merilee frowned and leaned toward Mother Anemone, almost touching her nose to nose. "Okay, now wait. I've seen that gleam in your eyes before. What are you planning?"

The Mother's smile was far too innocent as she moved back and swept her arms wide, as if to embrace all the mischief in the known universe. "I never plan, my love. I *arrange*. Now come. Share some tea with me before you go."

Still frowning, Merilee followed Mother Anemone out of her bedroom into the shining crystal hallways.

Arrange.

Yeah.

Her shoulders knotted all over again, a little more with each step.

Why do I have a feeling my nightmares just became the least of my problems?

1

April, twenty-five months after the Battle of Motherhouse Ireland

There were some situations where violence and sarcasm just weren't appropriate.

For the life of her, Merilee couldn't think of a single one of them, especially not at three in the morning, confronting a naked demon in her bathroom, *after* her leather jumpsuit had been burned off from the waist down.

Thank you, Cynda, my dear, sweet triad sister. I so love night patrol with a psychotic pregnant fire Sibyl.

If it hadn't been for her friend Andy's relatively new elemental control over water, Merilee might have lost the top half of her jumpsuit to Cynda's hormonal outburst, along with everything else. No more patrols for Cynda—not until the fire Sibyl delivered her little spawn of Satan and settled down again. Well, as settled down as fire Sibyls ever got.

Merilee leaned past the door she had just opened and glared at the tall figure partially hidden by billowing mists from the dripping shower. "Hey. Surfer boy. Get away from my tub before I shoot holes in all your wings—and a few things you don't want to talk about."

For a long moment, the demon didn't move, keeping his well-defined back to her. Beads of water formed across his muscled shoulders and slipped down perfect, touchable skin. Merilee caught a delicious, exotic scent, something spicy and unique, almost Caribbean.

Her heart rate increased.

Not familiar.

But then again, she was exhausted, singed, and pissed off, so she couldn't really count on her memory.

Which Astaroth was this? They all looked alike when they deigned to be visible. They all acted alike, too. Arrogant, a little flighty and airheaded, and entitled.

Damn it, whichever demon this was, he knew better than to use her bathroom. The winged surfer boys preferred the fourth floor of the large townhouse on New York's Upper East Side just as she did, because it was brighter and more open, with plenty of windows and terrace doors to access the sky and open air.

Only, Merilee lived here in "Head Case Quarters," the combination OCU headquarters and boardinghouse. These Astaroth visions of perfection just passed through after getting rescued and regaining their talismans, until OCU processed their paperwork and they found housing.

They ought to show a little respect. Which, of course, they never do.

Still keeping his back to her, the demon reached a tanned, sculpted arm to his left and grabbed her favorite fluffy yellow towel off the rack.

Merilee stared at the darkened skin.

What the hell?

Were those faint lines scars?

They were . . . and becoming more visible by the moment.

But Astaroths never had scars. And Astaroths were always pale. They never stayed visible or solid long enough to get tanned. Even when they took solid form, they retained that translucent, pearl-white quality—which this one didn't seem to have. But he had the height and build, and the dead-giveaway blond hair they all seemed to manifest in human form, and he was wearing a thick gold chain around his neck. Not to mention the fact that his presence made her Sibyl tattoo tingle along the inside of her right forearm and her instincts shout *demon* so intensely the sensation used up what little energy she had left.

Yep.

Tanned and scarred or not, the trespasser was an Astaroth.

And now he was wrapping her towel around his tapered waist, covering powerful thighs and a rock-hard ass any woman would die to squeeze.

Maybe it was the yummy Caribbean smell or the tan, or the fact that nightmares, pregnant triad sisters, patrols, and emergencies wrecked her sleep on a regular basis, but Merilee barely contained an urge to let loose a little burst of wind. Aimed just right, she could flap the towel and get a second look at that fine behind.

She actually lifted her hands and stretched her fingers through the doorway before she caught herself and rubbed her temples instead. With a sigh, she said, "You're probably new, and I know you're drawn to the windows and light, but the library and hall bathroom up here are mine during night hours. Visiting Astaroth demons stay on the second or third floor. We've got lots of empty rooms—with their very own bathrooms."

The Astaroth turned to face her.

Merilee, who had been about to ask him less politely to get out of her space, clamped her teeth together.

She drank in the sight, from his damp, close-cropped hair to his slick, unbelievably chiseled chest and the talisman necklace and ring hanging in plain view. More scars covered his chest—wounds from what, she didn't know, but she could tell they would have hurt like everloving hell.

Her eyes drifted lower. To the way that towel barely clung to his waist, tempting her yet again to use her elemental powers to move the cloth. Droplets of water slipped into the trace of blond curls just above the towel's edge, and Merilee couldn't help seeing herself pressing her lips against his tight abs, licking him dry.

Her entire body shuddered with the force of that image.

He folded his arms and studied her with eyes unlike any demon's she had ever seen. Brighter, yet also serious, with traces of something like sadness—and the *color*. A pastel indigo, almost gray, like storm clouds rolling across a bright sky.

Steam flowed around Merilee's face.

Thank the goddesses of Olympus, one and all.

Otherwise, the supernaturally handsome Astaroth might have noticed when her cheeks flushed red-hot.

As it was, he surveyed Merilee's burned, crumbling jumpsuit top, the remnants of the pashmina shawl she used to conceal her weapons, her yellow lace panties, and her bare, soot-streaked legs. The demon didn't seem at all concerned about the olivewood reflex bow and quiver full of arrows still slung over her shoulders, visible because the shawl had been so singed and melted.

His gaze held her so deeply, so totally, he might have been appraising her body, her soul, hell, maybe even her DNA.

Her skin tingled everywhere he looked, but he didn't smirk or grin, even though he had to have seen the effect his presence had on her.

After a pause sufficient to allow Merilee's heart to tap-dance along her ribs, the demon said, "Jake Lowell. I took the last name of my brothers."

His deep, sexy voice reminded her of wind rushing through mountains—and sounded familiar enough to make her process what he said.

Jake.

Jake Lowell.

As in, younger brother to Creed Lowell and Nick Lowell. The half-demon cops who just happened to be married to Riana and Cynda, her triad sisters.

As in, Jake Lowell, the Astaroth who had once been ordered to murder Cynda—and who damned near carried out those orders.

Merilee's mouth went dry, and her jaw tightened for entirely new reasons. She had to force her muscles to cooperate long enough to say, "I—I thought you were abroad. Or in school. Or . . . somewhere else." As the steam in the bathroom slowly dissipated, she eyed the talisman around his neck, trepidation edging out the magnetic shock of his presence. Her fingers curled. Primal instincts demanded that she grab her bow and nock an arrow. Maybe shoot him once for good measure. After all, she was the broom of her triad. She glanced at the tattoo on her forearm, focusing on the broom etched into her flesh. Wasn't it her job to sweep up all the messes?

But in the end, Jake hadn't killed Cynda. He had done everything in his power to save her, and now he had his talisman back. Nobody could use that necklace or signet ring to order him to kill.

Unless he loses it again . . .

"I got back to Manhattan this evening." Jake glanced around the bathroom, then down to the yellow towel barely covering his manhood. "Sorry. My brothers told me to shower up here."

Merilee bit back a few choice swearwords for the twins. Nick and Creed knew she had a hair trigger right now, with both her triad sisters out of sorts and now officially out of commission, and so much happening in the city. She could easily imagine the mirror-image bastards sending their younger brother straight into her line of fire, just for kicks.

"They must have thought you'd be out longer," Jake added with a frown.

"I'll just bet they did." Merilee relaxed her arms and felt a flash of pity for Jake, who, all that murdering-Cynda stuff aside, seemed too serious and quiet to be related to either of his jerk-monkey brothers. "Well, no harm done. And I guess we never really met when you were around before. I'm Merilee."

Jake's unnerving eyes shifted back to that stormy gray intensity. The force of his gaze touched Merilee directly in the center of her being, setting off shivers that only doubled when he said, "I know who you are."

Her body vibrated with each rumbling word, and her mind instantly blew through several hundred interpretations of that comment.

Get a grip. He means he saw you when he was around two years ago—and Nick and Creed probably filled in the details.

From seemingly a great distance away, Jake asked, "Any skirmishes with the Legion while you were on patrol?"

"No, it was just Satan tonight." Merilee couldn't quit staring at the man. *Demon. He's a demon who almost murdered my triad sister.* She made herself breathe, then realized what she had just said. "I mean, three satanic cultists. They were trying to summon the Prince of Darkness to help their candidate win the presidential election in November."

The sadness edged out of Jake's expression and his whole body seemed to relax. His eyes never left Merilee's, but now she saw sharp intrigue instead of storm clouds.

Jake gripped her yellow towel with one hand, keeping it firmly in place. "Do you believe the biblical devil exists?"

Merilee's response, like her response to all theoretical or academic questions, came easily and quickly. "Mythic monsters are always part fact, part fear-based storytelling. I've got nine research volumes in my library supporting Mephistopheles, and twice that many disproving all things Beelzebub. Which translates into, we've got no idea, but my triad's not about to take chances and find out."

"Have you read Wray and Mobley's *Birth of Satan*?" Jake kept hold of the towel as he spoke. "I liked the balanced Catholic and Protestant take on our need for a cosmic scapegoat."

Merilee's senses slipped off alert as her brain clicked into full action mode. She almost gave a complex, studious answer before she remembered she was talking to a gorgeous, half-naked, wet Astaroth demon in her bathroom doorway, at three in the morning—while she wasn't wearing pants.

And the Astaroth had just referenced a book she hadn't even finished reading.

A smile tugged at her lips as she looked at Jake's intelligent, interested expression—and tried to keep her eyes away from the muscled arm and hand holding the yellow towel. "You're . . . not a surfer boy, are you?"

Confusion flickered across Jake's handsome features. "I'm a police officer. Just hired by the NYPD."

"What?" Merilee propped a hand on her hip. "Since when does the force allow demon cops—well, ones they know about on the front end, anyway?"

"Since Sal Freeman wrote my letter of recommendation and asked for me." Jake's voice and gaze remained steady, though he looked disappointed, like he really had wanted to debate the existence of Satan. "That's why I got the off-season hire, too."

Merilee let out a breath, barely able to grasp the fact that Jake might not be a transient presence in her life, or the townhouse, even if he did stop using her bathroom.

That thought unsettled her at bedrock levels, and caused little jets of air to swirl around her ankles and elbows.

A small gust struck Jake in the chest and face, ruffling his short, damp hair and rushing the last drops of water still finding their way to the towel.

His mouth twitched, like he might be about to smile.

Annoyed with herself, Merilee pulled in her wind energy and covered her discomfort as quickly as she could. "You're a Lowell. Of course you're a cop. What else was I expecting?" She finally managed to pull her eyes off the demon-man and studied a spot on the wall somewhere over his left shoulder. "We need all the manpower we can get right now, with the Legion going insane and all the political rallies and protests. Crowds suck in supernatural terrorists like big cosmic magnets."

"The Legion's taking more chances," he said more as a statement of fact than a question.

"Hell, yes." Merilee figured Jake's brothers had briefed him on the massive increase in Legion activity over the past twelve weeks. "They took as big a hit as we did in the Battle of Motherhouse Ireland, but they're more in our face than ever, and our numbers suck—OCU and Sibyls alike. Which you probably know."

Jake's expression turned dark, along with his eyes, which seemed to reflect every nuance of his mood. "We have to stop them, numbers or not."

"Really? No kidding. I thought we were just supposed to pick our noses on night patrol." Merilee gripped the doorframe with one hand and dug her nails into the wood.

Jake looked confused all over again, and Merilee realized he didn't completely follow sarcasm.

Give him time. If he sticks around this place, he'll learn or die.

Understanding dawned across Jake's perfect face,

faster than Merilee expected. "I'm sorry," he said. "No offense intended."

Merilee relaxed her grip on the door.

Just like that he apologizes?

She narrowed her eyes. "Are you sure you're related to Creed and Nick Lowell?"

Jake shrugged. "Scholars of demon creation could debate that point."

Under the force of his gaze, Merilee's nipples tightened, distracting her beyond measure.

Hecate's torch, she needed a good night's sleep. Without an Astaroth in her bed.

And without nightmares of a man who seemed to be carved out of stone, or the abominable Keres, either. Those black faceless monsters with their creepy feathered wings and longs fangs terrified her like she was a little girl hearing horror stories from adepts at the Motherhouse.

More jets of wind slipped from her control.

Jake's yellow towel flapped, and Merilee's entire body flushed hot scarlet in response to her sudden glimpse of paradise.

Jake glanced down at his settling towel, then at Merilee again.

This time the bastard did smile.

He looked on the verge of asking her something, but Merilee panicked before he could say a word. "I really need a shower so I can crash. Can you—uh, shove off now?"

Once more, Jake seemed disappointed, but she didn't see any hint of anger or annoyance as he started toward her. She also didn't see any of the arrogance or cockiness she expected. Overall, Jake Lowell appeared to have more humility and self-control than his brothers, and he was tons harder to read than any Astaroth she had met so far.

His talisman necklace gleamed in the bathroom lights as he drew even with her in the doorway, paused, and gazed down at her with those heart-grabbing eyes. His unusual Caribbean scent washed over her, along with the heat of his nearness.

Her breath jerked and stuttered like the inner wind she was trying to suppress.

She mentally grabbed hold of buzzing emotions and gave herself a forceful inner shake. *If a bad guy takes control of that necklace, you could wake up and find Jake Lowell ready to eat you for breakfast.*

If you wake up at all.

She stepped aside to let Jake pass, heart thumping so hard she was pretty sure he could hear the *pound-pound-pound.*

He kept his eyes on her for a few more agonizing seconds, heating the wind inside Merilee until it became a sirocco.

Then he walked past her without making a sound and without looking back. Seconds later, he vanished from view, heading down the stairs.

Merilee leaned against the bathroom door and tried to gather herself. She had experienced powerful initial physical attractions before—but that—that—

Damn.

That wasn't natural.

Eyes closed, she rubbed the sides of her head, trying to chase off a dull, tired throb and the hazy stupor of Jake's presence.

There had to be an explanation for her over-the-top response to him.

Like, way too long since she'd been to the gym and picked herself up a fine boy toy for a night of recreation.

Or, not enough time for deep yoga and more meditative workouts.

He's a demon, *for the sake of Olympus.*

Hmm. Maybe Astaroths had hidden powers when it came to sexual attraction.

Maybe a person could be allergic to a demon presence, and manifest that allergy with mindless lust.

In this crazy world, anything was possible.

Right?

Merilee opened her eyes and glanced toward the door of her large combination library-bedroom, at the end of the hall on the right. She'd have to drag out all the papers and research info on Astaroths and make sure she hadn't missed anything.

Some of those documents were so dry and boring, they ought to help her fall asleep in a hurry. That would be a plus.

As she closed the bathroom door, Merilee couldn't take her eyes off the spot where she had last seen Jake on the townhouse stairs.

"At least I might not have nightmares tonight," she muttered to herself. "I could *definitely* handle a juicy erotic fantasy for a change."

2

Bartholomew August preferred the dark. The modern world always seemed cleaner in the soft yellow glow of streetlamps, or the silver shine of the moon.

He stood on the dock and took a long, slow breath of night air, tainted by brine and rot and pollutants, but oddly satisfying nonetheless.

August's first and truest home was darker than night itself, and cool, and deadly, a place where the slightest traces of scent drifted for miles unaided. He had just departed from that home without making a sound, reached this gods-forsaken spot, and assumed his alternate shape as fluidly as a magician closing his fist to complete some mystical transformation.

One moment, August was nothing—and the next, a man.

Tonight as he shifted, he chose black silk for his suit and light overcoat, not unlike Armani signature pieces. Once he settled into the human world, into his human surroundings, he would gather real garments—or rather have the woman and the boy gather clothing for him. Granted, the boy was mostly useless, but August *had* fathered him many years ago, and the boy had the lightest touch of August's formidable gifts. Time and poor habits had ravaged the boy and the woman, but by his own choice August himself had remained unchanged in both appearance and attitude.

New York City stretched before him, a festival of glaring lights, activity, and absolute disorder. The stench of human life surrounded him, assailed him, and he hated it, and he hated the dilapidated abandoned dock creaking beneath his feet. Human waste. So prevalent and pathetic. The chilly spring air pushed at his skin and bones, and his ears ached from the grating noise of traffic and music and the chaos that was Hell's Kitchen and its Hudson River boundary.

He had no place here.

He had no place anywhere.

August worked his newly solidified jaw and walked off the dock, trying not to stare into the black pit of loneliness that always waited, no matter where he went or what form he took. His all-too-human hands shook from the power of that awful, dark hole in his mind. He wanted to tear out his hair to make the sensation of loneliness stop. He would rip off his fingers or chew through his own feet if he thought it would help the pain in his now-beating heart.

But it wouldn't.

For now, he'd just have to endure it as he had so very many times before.

"You're later than what you said," said the gnarled, rheumy-eyed woman as she stepped from the shadows of the gray warehouse looming on his right. "But that's nothing new, now is it?"

The sound of that unmistakable Irish brogue, the ring of that never-ending defiance, dragged August from his despair. His acute senses registered garlic, cooked meat, and yeast as he appraised the wizened creature standing before him. Thin. Wrinkled. Hair whiter than cotton, combed into a frizzled bun. All of this he saw in the partial light of one flickering streetlamp, because the rest of the bulbs had exploded upon his arrival, before he placed barriers around his energy.

His human-looking skin crawled with the realization that this woman's spotted, lumpy hands had once touched him with a supple, fiery grace. Those wrinkled lips had once kissed his own, and driven back the raging emptiness and loss inside him, at least for a few days, a few years—seconds, really, in the span of his life. His gut ached from the memory, and from the weight of his own disgust.

Never again.

But he had vowed that before about relationships with humans, only to surrender to need, to natural desire. A night's pleasure or a month's satisfaction—anything but return to his home alone. Always alone.

"Where's the boy?" August asked without preamble or apology. He owed this woman no special treatment for her recent infiltration of his enemy's strongholds—nothing but perhaps a peaceful death, which would come soon enough.

The woman grunted. Her expression seemed grim, frightened, a little angry and worried, but she gestured toward the shadows from whence she came.

A tall, thin, scarred boy—in human terms, a man, though August couldn't see him that way—with raggedy blond hair stepped forward. He had on a blue suit and the odor of cigarette smoke clung to the cheap cotton—but for once, August didn't detect the reek of marijuana, hashish, heroin, crack cocaine, or any other substance he had forbidden the boy to touch on penalty of tortures only August could provide.

"Good," he said, hoping his approval would mean something to his son, though he knew that even with decent mental barriers in place, his natural energy was churning through the boy and the woman, too. "I'd prefer you give up tobacco. Bad for the body and in the end, the mind. If you treat yourself well, more of my gifts—the gifts that set you apart, raise you above—might make themselves manifest."

"Cigarettes won't send me back to jail." Color rose to the boy's pallid cheeks as he spoke in the same brogue as his mother. His dull blue eyes showed a smidgen of the defiance so characteristic of his mother, of his species, but his voice issued forth in its typical whine as he looked away.

August thought of his other children in cities all over the surface of this planet, and how none of them whined as insistently as this one. The boy couldn't help his defiance, his quarrelsomeness, what with August so physically close to him, of course. August knew his energy engendered such behavior. He forced himself to ignore the smoke-smell and his own irritation, and he ruffled the boy's greasy hair with something like affection.

Then his hand paused at the boy's crown and he squeezed, feeling the pitiful, weak bone beneath his fingers. Human bone. To August, little better than a brittle paste made of twigs and toothpicks.

The boy groaned, but made no effort to physically fight his father. August knew that after these many years, the boy realized such a battle would be not only pointless, but fatal.

He does learn from some past mistakes. I could crush his skull to powder, and he would allow it rather than face my wrath.

If the boy chose to destroy the powers inside him with his drug use, so be it, but he would at least remain as well trained and loyal as any street mutt—or August would put him down.

"Stop," the woman said from beside him. "I told you if you hurt the boy, I'll see you dead."

August let go of the boy, turned toward the woman, and smiled as he imagined human parents smiled at wayward children. "I understand that my presence stirs rage and discord, but don't think to threaten me."

"You promised never to raise a hand against him." The woman didn't whine like the boy. Her voice had the sharpened edge of a lifelong felon, a con accustomed to getting what she wanted, when she wanted it. "You promised—"

August kept up his smile, but let loose the slightest bit of his power to scold her for her impudence.

The woman fell back as if slapped, clawed at her throat and burst into tears. She dropped to her knees, then rolled on the ground, sobbing and gasping "No" again and again.

August felt the flick of the boy's fist against his cheek.

"Let her be!" the boy yelled. "I'll—you—you let her alone!"

Another brush of knuckles, this time against August's gut.

The woman's agony didn't stir August on any level, and the boy's punches had no effect. Human strength—like butterfly wings. Yet he was pleased, and he stopped sending the woman visions of their son's bloody, mangled corpse.

"Good." August gave his wretched offspring a pat on the shoulder. "I'm proud of you for defending your mother."

He tried not to notice how the boy glared at him, or how the old woman cursed him as she rose. They weren't worth much, these two. Perhaps the worst of his many poor choices in moments of desperation, before he fully accepted he could not restore his race by interbreeding with inferior stock. Yet these two had their practical uses, and he rather enjoyed the woman's larcenous spirit in her younger years.

All in all, August preferred their company to being alone.

"I have business in the city, with the Sibyls—perhaps for the last time," August told them. "You'll spend time with me and see to my needs, and continue your work observing my enemies as well—until I release you." His gaze traveled from the boy to the woman. "Both of you."

He hoped his meaning was clear.

From the downcast looks they gave him, he was certain he had made his point. If either made him unhappy, he would visit his displeasure on the other.

August shared little with humans, but he understood their need for attachment, for love from their family, and to protect their own. If any of *his* own still survived, the true kind, the pure-blooded kind, he would move the moon and stars to ensure their comfort and safety, to win them to him and hold them close forever. As it was, he was doing everything within his considerable power to bring them back into existence.

He was close now.

Closer than he had ever been.

Somewhere in this region, the right genetic combinations existed. August sensed them when he had reached out to select candidates to re-form his near-broken Legion. Now he felt them with a deep certainty. Not just one woman—but several who were decidedly *not* inferior. He would find them and introduce them to a destiny greater than they could imagine.

As the boy and the woman hung their heads and skulked into the night, August drank their despair and unrest like nectar. Feeding on that energy, his human shape became more real, more believable, more comfortable, as he imagined the misery and, ultimately, the deaths of all the filthy, useless people in New York City. All the filthy, useless people in the wider world beyond.

Soon, they'll be gone, and I'll keep only the best for my purposes.

Soon, I won't be alone anymore.

3

"These first few days at headquarters have been interesting," Jake admitted to his new captain, though Sal Freeman wasn't a new acquaintance. They had been communicating the entire time Jake was training, at first by e-mail, then by phone, then in person.

If I'm hiring a demon on purpose, Freeman had told him, *I'm goddamned gonna know him first.*

Jake respected Freeman's position on that subject—and appreciated the chance the man took, arguing for Jake's acceptance in the NYPD and giving him a position with the OCU. Freeman had a knack for weaving things together, making fits out of mismatches, improbable combinations, and unlikely candidates.

Jake glanced around the paper-clogged room, realizing the talent extended into the physical world, too. He was still amazed that Freeman had managed to cram a desk, a couple of cabinets, two chairs, and a truckload of files and folios into such a tiny space. The space was almost as messy as Merilee's archival area in the fourth-floor library.

Jake's mouth twitched.

Almost.

He had decided her unrepentant sloppy housekeeping was her one rebellion against being a broom. She swept up other people's messes all day long. Screw her own—or something like that.

As for Freeman, the man didn't have any more time than Merilee did to worry about cleaning house.

Freeman was about the same age as Jake's older

brothers, but bigger, like walking-mountain bigger. He looked like he could lift two or three cops and pitch them out a back window if he chose to.

Had Freeman had ever done that?

It wouldn't surprise Jake at all.

Since Freeman was still quiet, Jake figured he was supposed to say something else. "The old home place is a shitload busier than when I was here . . . uh, before."

Freeman leaned back in his rolling chair, dwarfing its wooden slats. He studied Jake from behind his desk, with a gaze so intense Jake worried that his wings or fangs were showing. He shifted in his own chair—the plastic kind—and had to fight not to lift his fingers to check his mouth. He tested his teeth with his tongue instead.

No sharp points.

That's a plus, at least.

Freeman's face, shadowed in the room's poor lighting, remained tense and serious, but concern sparked in his night-black eyes. "Is it too much for you, coming back here?"

For a moment, Jake didn't respond.

The truth lay between him and his captain in the silence, the reality of the fact that Jake Lowell—or the child he once was—had been murdered in the basement of this townhouse on New York's Upper East Side.

The transformed servants' cupboard Freeman used for a captain's lair was one floor up, directly over the spot where Jake died.

Directly over the spot where he awoke, reborn as a demon. An Astaroth. A monster.

Jake's muscles tensed against the weight of the talisman around his neck and he had to swallow to keep bile from rising up his throat.

This is hell, Freeman. Thanks for asking.

Out loud, Jake said, "It's not too much."

Freeman's dark brows pulled together. "The other demons giving you shit?"

Jake forced himself to relax in the plastic chair, to the best of his ability. "No. A couple expressed surprise about my career choice, but most of them took it in stride."

Sal eased off on his intense scrutiny, and his expression shifted from concern to worry. "How many Astaroths do we have in residence right now, other than yourself?"

"Five, but two are leaving tomorrow." Jake quickly ran through his recent memory of memos, notes, and overhead conversations. "None due to arrive that I know of. That could change any second—but you know we're a finite resource. Kind of . . . costly and dangerous to our makers. I'm not sure there are that many more Astaroths to find or liberate."

Freeman frowned. "We had twenty demons at the townhouse a month ago. We could *use* twenty now, damn it. Do you think you can persuade the last three to stick around for a while?"

Jake's insides hardened at the thought of interacting with his own kind, with those mirrors of what he didn't want to be. But this was his captain asking, a man who had taken a major risk to give him a shot at a normal human life. A man who had already become a friend to him, as close if not closer than his own brothers.

What could he say?

"I'll try."

"Good, thanks." Freeman scrubbed a hand over his chin. "I know you don't—that you're, well, more like us. A real man. Like a human man, I mean. But I need you to take the lead with them, and with any other Astaroth who passes through here. They're highly useful in fights, but they won't listen to me about tactics or training. I don't think I've ever earned their respect. Maybe you can."

Jake doubted that, but he meant what he said. He'd try. He owed Freeman that much, and a lot more.

Freeman leaned back in his chair again, and this time Jake could see fatigue shoving out all other emotion and expression. "You've already seen what we're up against. Multiple hot spots across all hours, all boroughs. The Legion—and whatever other crazy shit's starting to happen around New York City—it's running the OCU to death. Hell, right now, I'd welcome an army of Astaroths. I pray for shit like that every night."

A knock on the door made them both look toward the sound.

Andrea Myles, the OCU's second in command, stuck her head inside and said, "Hey." The word came out sounding like *ha-ay*. Her red curls hung damp and loose around her face, and the wet hair was a perpetual feature from what Jake could tell—as natural for her as the Southern twang.

Freeman surprised Jake by straightening in his chair, yet at the same time going soft around the edges. His expression turned nervous, halfway to goofy in Jake's book, but Andy didn't seem to think so. She smoothed her water-flecked jeans and blouse and smiled at Freeman, oblivious to Jake's presence.

When she did notice Jake, her cheeks flushed and the rest of her message came out in a Southern-fried rush. "Y'all need to finish up. A couple of fire Sibyls want a word with you upstairs in Cynda's room, Sal. Then it'll be time for evening meeting."

Somehow, dreamy gaze and all, Freeman managed to nod before Andy left, closing the door behind her.

"She's—" He broke off, then seemed to catch himself. He tried to regain his professional demeanor, but failed.

After a second he shook his head. "Guess that was pretty obvious."

"Way past." Jake didn't smile, but he almost broke his lips keeping them straight across his face.

Freeman didn't smile either. He pulled at his already open collar. "Do you think it's obvious to *her*?"

Jake shrugged and did his best to come off completely no-big-deal. "She'd have to be pretty thick to miss it, and I don't think she's thick."

Freeman pulled at his collar again. "She *works* for me, for shit's sake. I can't—she's one of my officers. And now she's a Sibyl, too. The world's only living water Sibyl."

Jake kept his mouth shut as Freeman stared at the spot where Andy had been.

Freeman's voice turned almost reverent. "She could drown me if I piss her off."

"You might need to give that a little thought before you make her mad, then." Jake stood, waiting to be dismissed.

"Fuck you, Lowell," Freeman said, still looking lost and sort of miserable, too.

Dismissed. Yep. That was it.

Leaving Freeman to moon over his girlfriend-to-be-any-minute-now, Jake made his way out of the servants' cupboard, bypassed the entrance to the basement without looking directly at the door, and kept walking. Fast. He knew he had half an hour or so to burn before evening meeting, and he didn't want to spend it hanging around idle and getting stared at by curious OCU officers or Sibyls.

So, he poked around all over the townhouse and tried to find the Astaroths he was supposed to win over and control and all of that bullshit.

He wasn't sure, but he'd bet most of the money in Manhattan that the bastards were *hiding* from him.

Probably invisible. Probably staring at him and laughing each time he passed too close.

Maybe they wanted him to use his demon senses on purpose, extend himself into his demon mind-set. Maybe they wanted to see him change, just to prove that he could do it.

Not going to happen, he thought as he stalked back down the stairs toward the conference room.

The transient lodgers were as invisible to him as to everyone else. As far as they were concerned, Jake probably *was* everyone else. He didn't look exactly like them, and he sure as hell didn't act like them, winking out of existence and flitting around everywhere, claws and fangs hanging out.

Not going to happen—but for Sal Freeman, Jake knew he had to make it happen. Somehow.

Fuck.

Jaw clenched, fists clenched tighter, Jake reached the bottom step and strode down the freshly painted hallway toward the conference room on the townhouse's first level. He had to get to evening meeting. After a week with the OCU, he was more aware of how badly things were going in New York City. There was no time to waste—and the island had been going even crazier over the last few days. The OCU needed to hit the streets and stop whatever chaos the Legion had planned for tonight.

Focus. Concentrate.

Almost there.

Don't think of this as where you grew up. It's OCU Headquarters now—Head Case Quarters.

But no matter how Jake lied to Freeman earlier when his friend asked, the townhouse did indeed feel more like the steamy pits of hell than anything else.

Heavy bookcases, tables, and chairs seemed to press toward him. He remembered every piece of furniture, every book on every shelf. The dark wood and volumes of occult lore crowded the delicate Oriental rug where he walked, stealing all the space and air despite the gleaming, bright walls.

Yellow. My mother never would have tolerated such light colors.

She wouldn't have tolerated so many intruders, either.

Jake focused his attention on a small elderly woman scurrying past him in the hall, trying not to meet his eyes. Instantly, he recognized Delilah Moses.

Shock rattled through him, and he whirled and caught the diminutive woman by her elbow.

She jumped and let out a yelp. Terror etched itself across her wrinkled face as she tried to pull away from him, and Jake let go of her immediately. "I'm very sorry. I didn't mean to frighten you. I just wanted—you—you might not remember me specifically—there were so many of us. But two years ago, you saved my life."

Delilah held the elbow he had touched and blinked at him, clearly not grasping his meaning.

Jake wanted to drop to one knee to be eye to eye with her, put her on equal footing and perhaps help her relax, but instinct told him that would be over the top. "You put an end to the crazy bi—uh, ex-nun who had stolen my talisman. You freed me."

Now realization glimmered in Delilah's eyes and she nodded. "You were among the demons that nun had captured. The ones she was torturin'."

Jake faced his savior, feeling almost reverent. "Yes, and you killed her. I take it you've stayed friends with the Sibyls since then?"

"Yeah, I have." Delilah seemed to be growing more wary with each word. "But . . . you're a cop, aren't you?"

Jake nodded. "Yes, I am."

Definitely wary now. Almost outright suspicious. "I never heard of a demon cop."

"I'm the first demon cop ever hired on purpose." Jake smiled at her, hoping it would help her relax. "The NYPD's had a few before, but they were strictly off the record. I want you to know I owe you, okay? If you ever need anything, you come to me."

Delilah's face sharpened to that of a savvy old criminal so quickly Jake almost stepped back from her in surprise. "All right, Mr. Demon Cop," she said in a low, teasing voice that probably hooked and destroyed many a mark, back in her younger days. "That I'll be rememberin', and you might be hearin' from me. For now, though, I've got to get to the library."

She flashed him what could only be described as a wicked grin, then hurried off down the hall toward the steps.

Jake watched her go for a moment, wondering what in the living hell he had just gotten himself into.

Then he started back toward the conference room, turned the last corner—and there she was.

Not Delilah Moses.

His mother.

She lounged in one of the corridor's heavy oak chairs, her ash blond hair loose about her thin shoulders, shrouding her face as she read a book of spells and rituals.

Jake's gut lurched.

In life, Jake's mother had been a brilliant biosentient, always studying, always learning—and thanks to her elemental talent, capable of exploding cells, of murdering human life-forms with a single, focused thought.

He slowed down and pressed his fists against his jeans, closed his eyes, then opened them.

Now his mother's image shimmered beside him, dressed in a red silk dress like she had been the night . . .

The night I died.

The night she killed my human body and transformed me into an Astaroth.

Jake couldn't walk any farther. He stared more directly at her, at the ceremonial dagger now visible in her long, merciless fingers.

"Why?" he asked aloud, battling a childish urge to disarm her and throw the knife away before it could do its damage, like that would somehow turn back time and spare him his fate.

Of course, the phantasm beside him didn't answer. His mother's empty blue eyes gazed at his blue sleeveless T-shirt, at the spot right over his heart. The place where she jammed the dagger through tissue to complete his ritual slaying, scraping bone, piercing his heart, ending Jake's world.

The searing pain of that moment was etched through every molecule of his being.

Jake's biggest scar ached. He raised both hands to his torso and pressed against that wound—healed. It was healed now. And the other scars, too, reminders of where his mother had vented her wrath with belts and canes, and at times cut him open to harvest blood for some of her darker activities.

It was a wonder she had never turned the brunt of her biosentient talents on him. If she had, he'd be moldering in the family crypt instead of reliving the worst moment of his existence.

"Go away," he whispered, but his mother remained, dagger raised, gaze unfocused.

Jake realized his mother's memory had grown beyond his own consciousness until she had become a vestigial image. Through their collective recall and shared history, every Astaroth evermore would recognize this person, Jake's mother—or rather, the meaning of her presence. She represented the threat from within, the beloved betrayer, the traitor in the fold.

Why was she here, now? There were no traitorous, murdering bitches in the townhouse, not now that she was dead.

Not real. Not a portent. Just a personal memory.

"The snake in the gift box," Jake said aloud, wishing he could summon wind energy to blow away the ghostly figure.

"Excuse me?" asked a lightly accented woman's voice from behind him.

Jake startled so badly his fingers almost dug holes in his own sides. He bared his teeth, felt the punch of his fangs as they tried to form. His Astaroth body tried to rip itself out of his human shell. He'd fight this time. He'd tear off his mother's head if he had to—but his mother had vanished to nothing.

In her place stood Merilee Alexander.

The air Sibyl held up her dangerous, beautiful hands like *Down, boy.*

Jake shook his head and snarled, then tried to make himself breathe. Even half crazy, he could see that Merilee's pretty face was tense and worried, and he hated that, and despised himself for causing it. She didn't attack or even take a more aggressive posture. Instead, she let off a soft wind, and the warm breeze wrapped itself around Jake like a caress.

"Take it easy." She lowered her hands. "Just relax. I didn't mean to scare you."

"Sorry," he mumbled as the calm touch of her elemental energy put his demon instincts to rest. His fangs stopped trying to form. The push and tear of wings against his back—finished. His claws hadn't even grown—well, not over an inch, anyway.

Why couldn't he control these idiotic memories? He had learned all sorts of mental focusing techniques during his travels and at the Motherhouses, but they had failed him every day since he came back to New York. Now he had made an ass of himself in front of the one woman he would rather impress.

Merilee gradually took back her wind energy and studied Jake. Her light, sweet fragrance teased his nose. He focused on her blond hair, her blue eyes, nothing like his mother's. Brighter and more vibrant. So much more alive. Merilee's form-fitting jeans, the way her soft-looking tan shirt hugged the curve of her breasts—her presence engraved itself on his senses. The fantasy of her, that had been one thing.

Thc reality of her was quite another.

Jake felt the power of Merilee's personality and ventsentience—her elemental control over the wind and air—like a storm in his own soul. He was close enough to really see her. Close enough to touch her if he wanted to. His mind went completely and suddenly quiet, but the rest of him started to roar instead. Just the sight of her was enough to make his blood burn, make his chest tighten.

I want to taste you, his mind whispered to the beautiful woman he had once vowed never to touch. *I want to take my time with each slow, delicious bite.*

The roller coaster inside Jake made him physically sick and completely aroused all at the same time. He didn't need to be here in this place. He didn't need to be so close to Merilee—but what the fuck was he supposed to do? The war against the Legion was here, now, and she was part of it. He couldn't avoid her completely. And damn, he didn't want to, even though he knew he should.

"Where *were* you when I scared you?" she asked, her voice warm with concern.

Embarrassment made Jake stare at his feet.

"Hey, look, getting spooked in this creepy place is nothing to be ashamed of." Merilee brushed her fingers against his wrist, and Jake felt the contact like an electric buzz. "I was raised in a Motherhouse with a bunch of adepts who liked to tell horror stories about death spirits—and I still have nightmares about them."

Jake managed to raise his head in time to see Merilee's smile fade away. Her expression grew more serious, mixed with a dash of shame and regret. "What am I saying? It's not like I had any real trauma growing up. Not like—damn, Jake. Forgive me. I didn't mean to make a joke out of anything." Her fingers remained on his arm, holding him in place, rooting him where he stood, and he couldn't look away from her, even though he knew he needed to.

"It's got to be hard for you, being in this place," she said. "Do you remember it all? Your childhood and . . . what happened?"

Not sure he wanted to try speaking, Jake just nodded, feeling every last one of his scars throb.

"Shit," Merilee whispered. "The memories, all that pain, it must be suffocating. Why did you come back here?"

Jake tested his throat with a swallow before he gave the best response he could under the circumstances. "We have to fight. *I* have to fight."

Merilee's eyes flashed.

Was that approval? Understanding?

"You're . . . special, aren't you?" she murmured, her subtle Greek accent pleasing to his senses, her voice stroking him like her fingers. "I think I need to get to know you better."

Mesmerized, Jake stood staring at Merilee as she moved closer to him, only a few inches away, near enough that her presence blew through every inch of his body. His muscles ached from containing the urge to grab her and pull her closer, until he *could* taste her face, her ear, her neck. Maybe he'd unbutton that soft shirt and taste her nipples, too.

Footsteps and voices broke the mood and moment, but Merilee kept her gaze on Jake as Sibyls and other OCU officers approached, heading for evening meeting. When she slid her fingers lower and took his hand, the silky press of her palm against his skin made his cock ache so badly Jake was sure the damned thing would crack in two.

He could get lost in those eyes forever.

Maybe he would, right now. Or later tonight.

"Come on," she said, and her voice barely registered in his jumbled mind. "Only two minutes, thirty seconds left. We'll be late."

Jake blinked at her.

Even after hanging out at Motherhouse Greece, he had never gotten used to how exact their time sense was. All Sibyls could do that, keep time in their head, but air Sibyls were just . . . better at it.

Merilee led him forward, steering him toward the evening meeting. Through the door into the chaos of conversations and clattering chairs, all the way to the front row where her triad sisters waited, already seated.

Before her Sibyl family saw her holding Jake's hand, Merilee let him go and gestured to the chair at the head of the row. He took it without protest. She sat beside him as Sibyls and OCU officers filled the large conference room behind them. More folding metal chairs rattled against the wood floor. Dozens of different smells and colors and conversations assaulted his acute senses.

Growling softly to himself to fight the pain of so much stimulation, Jake shifted in his seat to steal another glance at Merilee. She had turned away from him, speaking in low, soothing tones to Riana and Cynda, her pregnant triad sisters. Andy, who called herself the triad's "extra," sat closest to Merilee, now wearing wet jeans and a water-streaked NYPD jacket over her damp blouse. Riana, the earth Sibyl next to Andy, had her dark hair pulled behind her head, giving her exotic face a sharp, determined look. Cynda, the fire Sibyl, was sitting closest to the wall. She seemed larger with child and more miserable than Riana. Sweat plastered her red hair to her head, and her black jeans gave off a steady stream of white smoke.

Jake concentrated on the musical sound of Merilee's voice, let it lift over the incessant babble and float through his very existence. Next, he isolated her tempting scent from the attack of so many others, and centered his focus on that delicious strand of white tea and honey. It kept him sane, seeing her, feeling her so close—but he knew he shouldn't let himself dwell on Merilee. No matter what Mother Anemone said about his light needing to shine, about him being a good enough man for this Sibyl, the truth remained firmly locked in Jake's unhappy mind.

He wouldn't ask any woman, especially one so beautiful and talented, to risk her future and her safety to be with a demon.

4

At the front of the room, a few feet away from Jake, Freeman moved behind a long metal table, scratching new shift assignments on the chalkboard covering the main wall. The veins in his neck stood out. Circles as dark as his hair ringed both eyes, and somehow he looked twice as tired as he did when Jake saw him, what, half an hour earlier?

The slate where Sal Freeman was writing had lots of cracks. From heat, no doubt. Jake's brothers, who had taken afternoon patrol, had told him that the room had once been furnished with wood and plastic, but fire Sibyls had made short work of all combustibles. Pyrosentients, or those with deep mental and emotional connection to fire, were notoriously unstable and poorly controlled. Now the whole place was decked out in elementally locked iron, fire-resistant cloth, and flameproof hardwood laminate.

Not exactly an aesthetic improvement, but functional.

Freeman turned and held up both hands, and the thunder of voices gave way to whispers, murmurs, and finally, to silence. Jake's ears ached from relief. Once more, he glanced at Merilee. Her blue eyes were fixed on Freeman. She had a pad and pencil now, ready to take notes, as all air Sibyls tended to do in almost any situation.

Damn, her hands were close to his.

Jake envisioned running his fingers over hers, holding her delicate wrists, lifting them to his mouth, and—

Concentrate, Lowell. Not *on her.*

"We've got serious shit happening," Freeman boomed in the now-quiet room.

Jake immediately caught Andy Myles's reaction to the captain. The way she sat forward when he spoke, the way her eyes brightened as they followed Freeman's every move. Freeman responded to her just as deeply, staring at her, then forcing his attention back to the room at large.

Trouble in the making, no shit. Jake's gaze shifted back to Merilee. *Like I've got any fucking room to talk.*

Freeman cleared his throat. "Our afternoon patrols just reported that paranormal groups in the city are pulling up stakes and running like hell." He paused to let that information sink in, and Jake frowned.

His arousal faded away as he considered what the captain had just told them.

Paranormals, fleeing New York.

What would cause that?

His attention automatically moved back to Merilee, who was taking notes. Shorthand. In ancient Greek. And coded, if he wasn't mistaken.

Impressive. He studied the side of her face, the way her cheek curved upward in a full, pink bloom, then jerked his attention back to the captain.

"Many known 'sensitives' and sentients aren't at their residences." Freeman recaptured Jake's attention by suggesting the disappearances were citywide. "Unknown entities we've been tracking, they've gone underground, too."

"Shit," Cynda murmured, and a spit of fire wrapped itself around the metal table leg. Jake sensed the wave of earth energy Riana used to snuff the flames, and appreciated the soft, fragrant breeze Merilee sent forward to blow away the smoke.

"Half the pagans left on flights to San Francisco this morning, and the rest are moving around the city, performing protective rituals," Freeman continued. "All the Vodoun mambos and houngans south of our position are already gone. The few still hanging around, they're buying bus tickets, renting cars, or just walking away, over the bridges and through the tunnels."

Merilee kept her eyes on her notes, jotting in the margins. Her expression had turned serious and worried.

Jake read the ancient Greek shorthand and mentally deciphered the code as fast as she produced it.

What do they know? Real info, sensation, instinct?

Check with Charlotte Heart, if still in town.

Stone Man?

Jake's brow furrowed.

The first musing was easy enough to understand, and Charlotte Heart must be an informant. But the Stone Man? Who—or what—was that?

Merilee never looked up as Freeman finished his speech with "Get out, get to your sources, and find out what the hell's going on—*right now.*"

Freeman rattled off patrol assignments, pairing Sibyl triads with OCU partners and available Astaroths.

Jake watched as the groups got up to leave and find their demon partners, and he registered that his brothers were opting to work a double shift.

Why hadn't his own name been called?

Was Freeman planning to stick him in the townhouse?

Shit. Jake tried to stay calm, but he wanted to stand and leave with everyone else. What the hell? He kept trying to catch Freeman's eye, but the SOB was ignoring him.

Pointedly keeping his eyes away from Jake, Freeman turned to the pregnant Sibyls. "Riana, Cynda, you've got townhouse guard duty with Jackson, Brent, and Hargrove—and figuring out next week's duty roster."

Jake relaxed a fraction.

Okay, not the townhouse—so . . . what?

Freeman offered Riana and Cynda a smile.

Both women glared at him.

Freeman sighed and let them glare. He kept ignoring Jake, and his next comment went to Andy. "We're joining up with Creed and Nick."

Andy's smile could have warmed the whole townhouse in the dead of winter. She started to get up, but Merilee caught her arm. "Andy can't work without a Sibyl to help her with her elemental control." Merilee didn't look angry or stubborn, but confident instead. Calm despite the newly re-forming storm of voices, chair clattering, and the door banging open, then closed, as assigned groups headed out of the conference room.

Jake liked her self-possession. At the same time, he wondered what it would be like to see Merilee crazy, gasping and moaning from his kisses, his touches.

His cock got hard in seconds.

Come on, *Freeman. Get me the hell out of here.*

Jake closed his eyes and imagined Mother Anemone in various naked poses to regain control. When that didn't work as well as he'd hoped, he envisioned the Russian Mothers, then the Irish Mothers—and that definitely did the trick.

When he opened his eyes, Andy had squared off with Merilee. Both women were standing beside him now.

Wind gathered around Merilee in tiny swirls. Jake figured only Sibyls could see the air energy moving. Well, Sibyls and demons.

"Our numbers suck right now," Andy said in the forceful, targeted voice of a longtime police officer. To Jake's surprise, no sprinkler heads blew off, and no water seeped through the walls in response to her frustration. "I go where I'm needed."

When Merilee started to argue again, Andy cut her off

with, "I was OCU before I knew any of you, Merilee. And that's what I am tonight—a cop, not a Sibyl—and right now, I'm more useful that way." Her eyes drifted to Freeman, and the tops of her cheeks colored. "Don't worry. I'll behave."

"Not taking the chance." Merilee gripped her pad so tightly her knuckles turned white. "I'm coming with you."

"Stuff it, all of you." Freeman's stern gaze moved to Merilee. "Last time I checked, I was still the captain, and *everyone* agreed to follow my lead."

Freeman leaned on the metal table in front of him and *finally* looked at Jake—with something like pity.

Unease stirred in Jake's gut as he got to his feet beside Merilee and Andy. He was missing something here, probably something he wasn't going to like.

Freeman gestured to Jake. "Merilee, you're with the new Lowell."

Merilee's shocked expression mirrored Jake's own.

A vibration traveled through his entire body as she tensed, chin forward, and glared at Freeman.

Damn, she's beautiful.

Shit, I can't work with her.

He hadn't told Freeman about his powerful attraction to Merilee. Kept it to himself. Mistake.

Stupid!

"Excuse me?" Merilee shouted over the room's noise. "No. I fight with Sibyls."

"Sorry, we don't have any Sibyls to spare," came Freeman's terse reply. "In case you haven't noticed."

Riana and Cynda started to argue Merilee's case, but Freeman silenced them both by banging his palm against the metal table and demanding order. Even Andy flinched at the sound.

Jake, however, was having trouble hearing and

processing anything. His insides pulled apart, then reconstituted.

Merilee.

He was paired with her.

Merilee.

Okay, fine. So he couldn't avoid her now. No problem. He'd watch after her while her triad was down, like he promised Mother Anemone. That was what he'd do. Watch after her. Take care of her.

Yeah, buddy. And how.

He scrubbed his fingers against his chin to keep himself visible.

Merilee was shouting again, and the wind in the room picked up to minor gale levels. "Don't I get a say in this?"

"No," came Freeman's answer. "I'm not crossing the Sibyl Mothers, and this little *request* came from them a few minutes ago. I'm to keep Jake with you until your triad can fight again—so if you don't like it, take it up with—what's her name? Aminome? Anomaly?"

Jake lowered his hand.

His eyes narrowed.

"Anemone," he said through his teeth.

"That's the one," Freeman said, both of his big fists still pressed against the metal table.

Rage surged in Jake's chest. He should have known. Of all the stubborn, willful, deceitful, manipulating—fuck! He was being played by a woman thousands of miles across the ocean, and he couldn't do a damned thing about it. Mother Anemone might as well have hold of his talisman again, jerking him around against his will.

No way. Not happening.

Mother Anemone should know better than to push him on this point. Besides, Merilee needed to work with other Sibyls, where she'd be comfortable and happy.

"Mother Anemone," Merilee echoed, still obviously stunned, but sounding resigned, too. "*She* wants this?"

Jake turned to tell Merilee never mind, that he'd take care of this stupidity, but when she looked at him, his anger dissolved so fast he felt dizzy.

Those eyes . . .

That face . . .

Everyone else in the room faded out of Jake's awareness, and he was standing just with Merilee now, her and only her. Warm air rose off her like sultry curtains, and he wanted to part that heat, step inside it, pull her against him, and press his lips against her hair. He wanted to breathe that white tea and honey up close, and taste her skin, and tell her . . . what?

I'll look after you.

Or, *I'll take care of you.*

Or maybe, *I think I'll fall in love with you . . . after I fly to Greece and stuff your favorite Mother upside down in the wine cellar.*

Merilee's eyes gleamed, sun on bright blue water, as the full impact of the situation seemed to roll across her. Her thunderous frustration faded, dissolved, and morphed into a sexy little smile.

"Okay," she said quietly, keeping up that smile until Jake's fevered mind imagined sliding his tongue between those full, perfect lips.

"Okay," Merilee repeated.

I'm dying here.

"I can do this," she said, still smiling. "I can more than do this."

Snickers and giggles reminded Jake that other people—like Andy and Freeman and Merilee's triad—were still in the room. His surroundings—conference room, Sibyls, cops, and all—came back to him with mind-jarring speed. Just as fast, he realized Merilee was completely aware of the thoughts and sensations battering his self-control.

That pissed him off enough to get a grip, at least for the moment.

With a curt nod to Freeman, Jake said, "Fine." Then to Merilee, to rattle her on purpose, "Are we going to see Charlotte Heart?"

Merilee's eyes widened.

Seemingly on reflex, she lifted her pad, and Jake saw her add up the fact that he knew shorthand, and ancient Greek, and that he had deciphered her code as fast as she wrote the words on her pad.

He expected that to wipe that teasing little smile off her face.

Unfortunately for his increasingly miserable cock, it didn't.

"Seriously." Merilee, who refused to wear her leather face mask because it was "too confining," blew Jake a kiss along with a gust of hot wind, then turned back to face the night-darkened neighborhood ahead of them. Her blond hair rippled like liquid gold in the breeze. "You can tell me you want me straight out. I don't mind. I'm a big girl."

Jake felt like his head might explode.

Heads, actually.

What was he supposed to say?

I don't want you?

He wasn't a liar.

Not to mention the fact it didn't take a shitload of vestigial memories to teach a man that telling a woman she wasn't attractive—well, that would be stupid, to say the least.

Merilee knew all of that. No question in Jake's mind, the way she was laughing.

Wind. The most relentless force on the planet. The next time I see Mother Anemone . . .

He and Merilee were moving north on foot, beside light traffic, four streets away from the townhouse and heading for the home of Charlotte Heart, coven priestess. Merilee had filled him in on Heart's info and history, in between teasing him until he was ready to throw her down on the sidewalk, take her in front of the entire city, and just have done with it.

Only the austere residential setting with its iron gates, swept sidewalks, porch lights, and potted plants dissuaded him. Some kid might see. That, and he was supposed to be concentrating on observation, details, and potential threats to New York, its citizens, law enforcement officers, his new "partner," and himself.

Not breasts crossed by a quiver's leather strap.

Not a leather-clad ass bouncing against the lower limb of an olivewood reflex bow, barely concealed by a silky black shawl.

Merilee dropped back to walk beside him, and her nearness made Jake's throat close.

This was too damned complicated.

She should be out with a triad, boosting their spirits with her never-waning sense of humor. He should be with a human police partner, or maybe his brothers, patrolling. Concentrating. Not drooling.

Keep moving. Don't look at her.

He studied the dozen or more political posters hawking this candidate or that candidate for president. They hung everywhere, on walls and fences, even staked in yards. But Merilee was right beside him, and it might ease the pounding in his body if he just took her hand. It would be so easy to walk with her like a friend, a lover, instead of a fellow officer and warrior. She made him comfortable like that.

And completely insane.

Her laughter once more tickled his senses. "Quit being so serious. If you aren't interested in me, why didn't you fight harder about us getting assigned together?"

"I wanted to." Jake's words burst out like a bark. "This shouldn't be happening."

Merilee's next glance was wounded, highlighted in the multicolored glows of streetlamps and traffic lights.

Fuck!

Jake took a breath, tried to get himself together again. "I didn't mean that in a bad way. Just . . . you're a Sibyl, and I know you'd be more comfortable with your own—but I did promise Mother Anemone I'd look after you until your triad could fight again."

Merilee slowed down. "Mother Anemone. Yeah." Her expression grew distant for a moment. "I wondered what she—"

She pursed her lips together and Jake waited, watching as she pressed her fingers against a small, faint white scar barely visible along her jaw.

"Sorry." She lowered her fingers and shook her head. "A while back, I got the impression Mother Anemone was up to something. Maybe this is it. You, I mean. You and me."

Jake felt his face get hot all over, and he had to rub the back of his neck to keep from staring at his feet. "Ah . . . yeah. That might be her plan."

Merilee snorted and folded her arms. "She never plans. She *arranges*. Just ask her."

Jake looked into her eyes—big mistake—and stood mesmerized for a moment before he got out, "Do you mind being arranged with me? For, um, work, I mean."

Merilee didn't break their gaze, and the corners of her mouth turned upward. She made him wait a second, then two, heart beating so damned fast she could probably see his chest twitching.

Then she said, "No. I don't mind at all."

He felt her smile somewhere in the center of his gut, not to mention a lot of other places.

Smile still at full blaze, she said, "Now tell the truth, Jake. Are you okay with being arranged with me?"

His gut and groin tightened so hard he almost groaned. "Fine with it."

Damn, he couldn't stop staring at her. "How did you get that little scar? The one on your jaw."

Her smile faltered a little, then turned into a wicked little grin. "Jumped off a roof when I was six. Did I mention the psychosis thing? Don't worry. It only hits me every now and then."

She started walking again and Jake trailed after her, shaking his head.

They turned another corner, and when Jake caught up, Merilee said, "I can't believe you've spent so much time hanging out with the Mothers."

Talking to her was hard when he wanted to touch that little scar. Maybe kiss it. "Guess that's not a typical choice for demons."

"Why did you do it?" she asked without looking at him this time, which spared him a tiny measure of discomfort.

"I'd rather not talk about it," he managed, wishing his lust would give him a break.

"But I want to know—that, and everything about you." She gazed at him briefly, and the sparkle in those blue eyes unraveled another section of Jake's resolve. "Like, why you don't turn invisible and fly the way Astaroths usually do."

Jake kept his mouth firmly closed.

"Come on," Merilee added with the little smile that drove him to the edge of his control. "I told you about jumping off a roof. You can tell me anything. Do you fly at all?"

"Not if I can avoid it." Jake was relieved that his answer didn't sound sharp or irritable. He could tell she wasn't just teasing about wanting to get to know him. She was trying to do just that. And she was putting out the invitation, telling him he could move forward with getting to know her, too—yet it didn't come across as overpowering or annoying. She didn't seem easy to offend, or insecure about her body, her sexuality, her allure.

She was bold. Aggressive.

Too desirable for words.

Fuck, fuck, fuck.

No, damn it, that's what you want *to do, not what you're* going *to do.*

He came back to earth enough to realize Merilee had stopped questioning him because she was pointing at a red townhouse on the right with a small, painted porch.

"It's . . . that one," she said, her voice unusually quiet and hesitant as she slid her bow from beneath her shawl and off her shoulder.

In a single instant, Jake's focus snapped back to the real world, to the streets of New York, and to the townhouse where Merilee expected to find Charlotte Heart. He scanned the house's dark windows, and his muscles tightened. His senses expanded—and he took in what had given Merilee pause.

The energy around this house was . . . off. Jake couldn't describe it, but the sensation poked at his gut like a burning stick. And the air smelled wrong.

Coppery. Strong.

He knew that stench.

Merilee nocked an arrow. "Somebody's dead in that house, Jake."

Jake ran forward, squeezing the button on his radio,

shouting for backup at the same time as he motioned for her to cover him—because his senses had told him the rest.

Yes, somebody was dead inside the red house.

But somebody was alive, too.

5

Merilee swept down the concrete walkway behind Jake, keeping up but giving enough ground to assess and guard, to have room to fire her arrows. Her breathing quickened. Her heart rate doubled. Despite her exhaustion from poor sleep, nightmares, and way too much work, she instinctively covered Jake just the way she would shadow Riana and Cynda as they charged into battle.

Please, great Hecate, don't let anybody shoot. Let Charlotte be okay.

As Jake reached the porch and drew his Glock, a blast of unfocused energy swept over Merilee. Bad energy. Dark, like something awful had . . . slithered . . . too near the walkway. She gripped her bow tighter, pushed back the energy with a spray of wind, and held focus on Jake as he skirted the door.

Seconds later, Jake smashed his shoulder into the wood. The red boards split into three pieces. Splinters and hinges banged to the porch.

Lights flared inside, and the glow spilled into the night.

Merilee tensed, ready to shoot, but no one fired through the open door, and nobody charged outside. Voices rose and fell, and she heard what sounded like sobbing.

Jake shouted, "Police! On the floor!" as he took his stance and gazed through the door.

Merilee approached on his left as he entered the townhouse. She bounded up the porch steps, keeping Jake in view and her bow and arrow at the ready.

As she ran through the door, the stench of the place struck her like a blow. Blood and salt and some horrible, terrible *wrongness*—like bubbling acid, burning as she inhaled. Then, just as fast, some other and even more incredible power mowed over her like a wide, whirring blade.

Merilee pulled up and stood just inside the entrance. Her eyes watered from the smell, the awful feel of the room, and the cutting punch of that power. She swayed on her feet and her vision fractured. Sights flew at her in kaleidoscopic images. Broken people. Colors. Prisms of light. Shapes crowded together. More sobbing battered her ears.

For a moment she caught sight of the Keres from her nightmares. Or maybe from that awful night, back when she threw herself off the roof of Motherhouse Greece to escape them. Feathers tumbled off their wings like black rain. Their fangs flashed as they hovered and shrieked loud enough for the hair-prickling sound to reach into her mind and make her want to leap off something, anything to get away from them again.

Did the creatures sound gleeful?

Or were they frightened?

A man walking . . .

The new image came clear, blotting out the Keres and everything else.

A statue man, the one I've dreamed . . .

"He *is* made of stone," Merilee mumbled as negative energy flowed over her like rogue wind, covering her no matter how hard she tried to shrug it off. The other power—the one with those biting, gnawing teeth—seemed to enter her, flow through her like new blood, giving her just enough strength to stay alive.

The Stone Man was huge and endless and lethal, and he was coming. Here. Now.

He's almost on top of us.

She had to go. Merilee knew she had to run, tried to turn back to the door, but her muscles wouldn't work. The world dimmed. She couldn't see a thing but the shadowy Stone Man striding forward, growing larger in her mind's eye. Couldn't hear a thing but the dreadful crunch of his footsteps on leaves and gravel. More wrongness pressed into her, crashed against her chest. Air wouldn't enter her lungs.

A wraithlike touch slid over her skin, cold and wet and absolutely unwelcome. The new, snarling power in her blood snapped at the disgusting sensation, pierced it with a thousand fangs, not with the force of her will, or even under her control.

The cold touch drew back.

Merilee thought she felt a dark, angry wave of surprise, followed by resignation.

The horrible touch dug into Merilee's being once more, fleeting, but scraping against the center of her existence. She tried to twist away from it, tried to cry out. Couldn't. Her hands shook. Her grip on the bow faltered. She couldn't breathe at all. Panic surged through her body even as the touch sucked away her energy, her essence. Her hands—where were her hands? Her feet?

Darkness.

I'm suffocating!

And the screaming of the Keres came back, this time definitely gleeful. Almost rabid. Starving.

"Merilee."

The new sound stabbed at the blackness around her. Familiar. Jake's voice. It was, wasn't it?

A sliver of hope arced through the fog of misery threatening to crush her to death.

The touch flickered and withdrew.

Images of the Stone Man faded as the dark energy moved away. Black to gray. Gray to white. The horrifying image blew into hazy fog, separated, and vanished.

With a wild pull on her air energy, Merilee reached for the sound of Jake's voice and managed to get a breath. Her awareness searched for Jake's presence, for reality.

His voice came again, more forceful. "Merilee. Open your eyes."

Were they closed?

Fuck. She didn't remember closing her eyes. Her teeth chattered, and she was so cold her fingers and toes ached. Damn, but she needed a long, hot shower to thaw out, cleanse herself, and figure out what the hell was happening.

When she opened her eyes, she realized she was standing in the entryway of Charlotte Heart's house, hands pressed against the sides of her head. Her bow and arrow lay useless on the wood floor in front of her. She was shaking all over and coughing. Jake had his gun holstered and his palm on her back, and he was speaking to her in low tones.

"Breathe. Again."

Merilee focused on the flow of his words and the warmth of his touch, and she did as he suggested, collecting a lungful of acidic, coppery air. Blood and . . . wormwood? Yes. Someone had burned a lot of it. Absinthe was for serious elemental protection, and only a few practitioners were strong enough to contain its energy and focus it for a purpose. It was probably responsible for that stubborn power Merilee had felt blending with her own to drive back—whatever that threat had been.

Remnants of her vision tugged at her consciousness, but the dark energy had evaporated with the image of the Stone Man from her nightmares.

What the hell *was* he?

And what did he have to do with Charlotte Heart and whatever happened in this house?

Merilee's heartbeat eased back to normal as the room

shifted into focus. A small space, lit by a single overhead fixture, crowded with silent people, staring at her and Jake. Twelve men and women. No, thirteen—the thirteenth was down. A woman with long, unruly red hair.

"Charlotte," Merilee whispered, but even as the name left her lips, she knew the pagan priestess was dead. Merilee's stomach tightened, and tears muddled her perceptions all over again. No air moved over Charlotte's body, and the priestess's normally pale skin was chalk white and streaked with blood from deep gashes running the length of both arms. From her body emanated a thick wave of elemental protection, touching everyone in the room, infusing them with the temporary power of Charlotte's lingering will and life force—the rest of the formidable protective power that had saved Merilee from the Stone Man. She recognized it and honored it immediately, though the cost of it seemed almost unbearable.

Charlotte's coven moved to surround her in a ring, heads down. Many of them started crying. Merilee remembered hearing sobs before, too—probably theirs—while she was confused.

No. Not confused. Under attack.

From somewhere in the distance, sirens droned.

Merilee shivered even though the icy chill from that unearthly psychic touch was pushing its way out of her body. She grabbed her bow and arrow and let Jake help her walk toward Charlotte's body and the grieving coven.

"Her people arrived at the same moment we did," he explained, his stormy blue eyes reflecting concern as he studied her. "Came in through the back and turned on the lights as we were coming through the front, but the priestess was already dead. Looks like suicide—but ritualistic. What do you think?"

The sirens drew closer.

Backup. Jake had radioed for backup before they entered. She remembered that much, at least.

Merilee noticed Jake didn't ask what had happened to her, or make a big deal over whether or not she was okay. He just got right back to business and treated her respectfully, professionally, which she appreciated—though she could tell from the questioning look on his handsome face that they would have to discuss her little "breakdown" later.

For now, there was work to do.

Jake's calmness washed over her, into her, and Merilee collected it like errant wind. She drew it into herself and battled back her grief over Charlotte's death, and regained another measure of her own focus.

Duty. Work. Yes.

It was time to clean up this mess.

Merilee gestured to the coven members, who moved back to allow her to study the protective design drawn on the floor around Charlotte's body. Sea salt mingled with human blood, definitely designed to repel anything evil or ill intentioned. Since Charlotte's coven had easily crossed the unbreakable elemental barrier she had established and sealed with her own blood and death, and since they were obviously receiving Charlotte's final gift of temporary powerful protections, Merilee had to assume they were clean, or at least not involved in whatever happened here.

She returned her arrow to its quiver and slung her bow over her shoulder. "This makes no sense, Jake." She told him about the pattern's meaning, but added, "Charlotte was one of the most positive, upbeat people I've ever known, and she had real talent, a deep sensitivity for all sorts of elemental energies. She would never do this to herself."

Yet, even as she made that pronouncement, Merilee

had a flash of the walking statue man, the creature that had . . . *touched* her . . . and turned her blood to frost.

Jake remained silent as Merilee gazed at the pattern surrounding Charlotte's body and took another deep breath of pungent absinthe.

Truth settled on her shoulders like a weight as she realized the Stone Man had been coming here, likely for Charlotte herself—but the pagan priestess's ritual and sacrifice had thwarted him, and offered her coven some fierce though transient protection as well.

And me, and Jake, too.

Had Charlotte known she was a target, that the man of stone was coming this night, for whatever purpose?

Is that why she chose death?

But what did the Stone Man want with Charlotte?

And what does he want with me?

The sirens grew unbearably loud, then abruptly shut off. Merilee heard tires squeal as cars stopped outside. Flashing lights blazed off and on, painting the faces of Charlotte's coven members eerie shades of red.

Merilee shivered again. "We need to question all of them and search the place for any journals or information Charlotte might have left behind. I need to know if she was having bad dreams."

Once more, Jake didn't question her. Instead, he greeted incoming OCU officers, made arrangements for the processing and removal of Charlotte's body, and requested that the descending crime scene techs clear at least one room where statements could be taken and interviews conducted immediately.

Grateful for the extra time to get over what had happened earlier and accept the reality of Charlotte's death, Merilee stood to the side and let him work. His efficiency impressed her, and she kept having to remind herself that Jake was a demon. Not a half-breed, either. A full-blooded Astaroth who just happened to be as calm and decisive as any Sibyl or police officer she knew.

Keeping her attention on Jake helped her heart, and kept her from crying over Charlotte. She didn't need to do that here, right now. That was for later, in private.

The perfect muscles in Jake's arms bunched and relaxed as he pointed and gestured, and Merilee couldn't help noticing his grace. Dressed in those tight jeans and that even tighter T-shirt with a blue overshirt unbuttoned, sleeves rolled up, Jake moved with the self-possession and balance of a seasoned dancer. He seemed completely comfortable inside his human form, earthy and grounded, and in charge.

Somewhere inside him, there's a storm, though. I can sense it when I'm close enough.

Like when he touched her and spoke to her to bring her back from that terrifying void. The warmth of his fingers snagged in her mind, along with the bass echo of his deep, encouraging whisper.

Breathe.

Yeah. That's what he had said.

She needed to do that now.

Especially when Jake broke away from the OCU officers and crime scene techs and came striding toward her. She took him in, from the short blond hair to the tanned biceps and those thick thighs bulging in his jeans as he walked.

"We can use the kitchen," Jake said, and the sound of his voice sent warm shivers all over Merilee.

"Okay" was all she could manage.

Merilee noted that Charlotte's green and yellow kitchen was smaller than most police interrogation rooms, and the little oak table only had four chairs. A single light fixture offered a meager yellow glow, and the room felt hot even though Merilee had opened a window and the back door.

She had been in here for several hours, sitting next to Jake, her leg pressed into his as they spoke to each of Charlotte's coven members. The sensation of his body against hers was distracting, but she had managed to keep her mind on the business at hand.

So far, through eleven interviews, the responses had been fairly uniform.

Yes, Charlotte had been upset lately, especially this last week.

No, they didn't know why.

No, Charlotte hadn't seemed despondent or suicidal.

Yes, they knew people with paranormal abilities were leaving New York, and they were thinking about going, too.

No, they couldn't say why. Just an instinct. A bad feeling.

Most of the people cried as they spoke, male and female alike, and Merilee didn't sense any deception. Only despair and desperation and loss.

As the twelfth subject, a petite, pale woman who looked to be in her early twenties, entered the little kitchen carrying a notebook, sadness emanated from her in hot waves. Merilee could barely breathe in the face of so much anguish. Beside her, Jake tensed, and she wondered if he felt it, too.

The young woman sat down across from them, put the notebook on the table, tucked her brown hair behind her delicate-looking ears, and began to cry. Hers weren't the noisy, jagged sobs they had encountered so far, but steady, silent tears that somehow dug even deeper into Merilee's soul.

"I'm Amy," the young woman whispered between rattling breaths. "I am—I was—Charlotte's apprentice."

Jake's leg pressed against Merilee's a little more firmly, and she realized he had straightened himself in the little kitchen chair. He glanced from Amy to Merilee, and his gray-blue eyes seemed a shade brighter, almost expectant.

Merilee immediately turned back to Amy and dispensed with some of the more basic questions they had asked the rest of the coven. "Can you tell us anything about the last week of Charlotte's life? I need to understand her state of mind, and anything that might have been troubling her."

"This will help." Amy slid the notebook a few inches toward Merilee with one shaking hand. "She told me some of it, but mostly, she sketched it. Charlotte always kept a picture journal. There are dozens of them in her closets, but this is the most recent. She gave it to me yesterday in case—"

The girl broke off, took a breath, then made herself finish. "In case something happened to her."

"So Charlotte felt like she was in danger?" Jake asked as Merilee picked up the spiral-bound sketchpad.

Merilee flipped to the first page, which was dated a week earlier, and went totally still, both mind and body.

The Stone Man, or rather the charcoal shadow of him, glared out at her from the stark white page. Malice radiated from his outline, from every blurred, indistinct feature. At first glance, he seemed stiffly human, statuesque—but the image shifted even as Merilee stared at it. He was birdlike now, with a giant maw. Wait, wait. No. He was too rounded, maybe scaly, like a reptile, only large. Even in two dimensions, he had a vastness about him, an endlessness she couldn't begin to describe.

"Charlotte *knew* she was in danger." Amy's voice penetrated Merilee's stunned haze.

Merilee looked up, surprised by the young woman's sudden surge of elemental energy. More powerful than Merilee would have expected given the girl's age and size—but then, Charlotte had picked Amy as an apprentice, obviously with good reason.

"Charlotte thought something was stalking her. Some creature too powerful for the coven to fight." Amy pointed toward the notebook. "It looks human, but it's not. That's all she knew, or all she told me. That, and she said he—it—was evil. Very, very old, very strong evil."

Even as her mind pushed against it, Merilee forced herself to look back at the changing charcoal image of the Stone Man.

That creeping, slithering cold gripped her again.

Stalking. Yes. He was stalking Charlotte. And now . . . he's stalking me.

"Do you know who he is, or what he is?" Amy asked from seemingly very far away as Merilee turned a page in the journal—and almost flinched back from it.

Familiar winged creatures glowered at her from the next page, standing atop a carpet of shed black feathers, leering grins revealing hooked fangs ready to gouge and slash.

Merilee almost pulled her fingers back from the likeness.

Charlotte dreamed about the Keres. Why? Was she already thinking about suicide when she drew these?

Sibyls or anyone else who knew about the Keres could go to them of their own free will, if they wished to take their own lives—but the death spirits couldn't come off Káto Ólimbos to claim victims anymore. That was part of the treaty.

Still, Merilee had never known of anyone but Sibyls—usually only air Sibyls—who saw visions of the Keres under any circumstances.

She tried to quiet her increasing unrest and confusion by turning the page.

The next drawing showed the sea at night, dark moonlit water, so peaceful, yet somehow ominous. The Stone Man came next, larger, more frightening, sketched in black pencil, though still lacking detail, and seeming to shift even as she tried to get a fix on his appearance.

And the Stone Man again. This time Charlotte had sketched so fiercely her pencil had ripped through the next and last page, which showed a tidal wave crashing into Manhattan, toppling buildings like toys.

"Why did this happen to Charlotte?" Amy asked, loud this time, but Merilee had no answers. All she could do was look from the picture of destroyed New York City to the young woman and shiver, and try very hard not to throw up.

"We don't know any more than you do," Jake said, his words rumbling out smoothly, almost hypnotically.

From the hallway near the kitchen, shouts broke out, and Amy squeezed her eyes closed. "They're arguing again. It's been happening all week."

One man was yelling about needing to get out of the city. A woman screeched back that their place was here, fighting if it came to a fight.

"How can we battle an enemy we can't even name?" the man hollered, and the wall rattled like he had punched it.

Jake's muscles bunched as if he might be getting ready to stand, but the next thing Merilee heard was a police officer encouraging everyone to settle down, no need for all this screaming.

The noise died away.

Jake relaxed a little, but Merilee didn't.

Neither did Amy. Her pretty features hardened, and

her lips trembled. "Charlotte always told me I could trust the Sibyls, especially you—but what am I going to do?" Her voice seemed too quiet now, and her tears were still flowing. She glanced at the notebook. "My coven does need to leave, I just know it. And I can't help them. I've been having those dreams, too. If that that *thing* comes for me—no way. I'll do what Charlotte did before I let him take me."

Merilee almost agreed with the young woman before she caught herself. "We can get you to safety," she said as she closed the notebook, and wished she could seal the evil being inside the harmless pages. "To one of our training facilities. No place on Earth is more protected than a Motherhouse."

"The Sibyls can help you escape New York," Jake confirmed. He gazed at the closed sketchbook like he could sense the horror of its contents and wanted to destroy it. "And my unit can arrange for your coven to have protection or leave the city, too."

This seemed to give Amy some comfort, but as Jake got to his feet, she stared into Merilee's eyes. "Running might work for now, but as long as this creature exists, he won't give up on what he wants—whatever it is. You know that, right?"

"I sense the same thing, yes." Merilee pushed herself up using the table for support. She was still way too cold, and her heart kept thumping away like it wanted to break through her rib cage. "For now, we'll have to take this one step at a time, and the first step is getting you out of New York. Come on. Other Sibyls should be here by now. We'll arrange for them to see to your transport, and put the word out about these . . . dreams."

Amy gave her a grateful, almost hopeful look.

Merilee escorted Amy out of the kitchen toward the worn-out-looking group of ranger Sibyls who had come to the scene, and she handed over the drawings for the fire Sibyl to send to the Motherhouses.

As Merilee explained what she needed the rangers to do with the drawings and Amy, she couldn't help noticing Jake yet again.

His intense, worried stare was hard to miss.

6

Dawn broke slowly over Central Park, leaving the ground, trees, and rocks coated with fresh-smelling dew. Merilee calculated the time at five forty-two A.M., give or take nine or ten seconds.

She kept pace beside Jake and took another slow breath, trying to clear her mind from the darkness and pungent absinthe of Charlotte's house. They had both decided to walk back to the townhouse, Merilee because exercise settled her spirits, and Jake because moving kept him focused, or so he said.

Even after plowing through the chaos of OCU officers, crime scene technicians, morgue personnel, and crime tape, Merilee still couldn't believe Charlotte was dead and lost to her, to that coven, to the world. Or that Merilee's own nightmares might be tied into what had happened to the priestess.

I knew they were bad, the visions I've been having—but bad enough to kill myself over?

She hugged herself as she walked, and shivered for the millionth time.

Yet if the Stone Man did come for her the way he threatened, what would she do?

Slay the bastard without any fucking mercy at all.

Definitely. That'd be her first plan. Fill him full of elementally locked arrows, then slit his throat with the sharpened tip of her olivewood bow.

If he was alive, then he could be dead, right? Anything truly living and of this plane of existence could be killed, and Merilee had a deep feeling the Stone Man did belong to this world, to this earthly plane. She just had to figure out what he was, and then how to take him out.

"Are you cold?" Jake asked, and Merilee realized he had stopped walking.

She hesitated on the paved path, then turned to where he stood only a few feet away from her. A deserted grassy field stretched out behind him, and if it weren't for the fog-shrouded high-rise buildings against the skyline, they might have been standing in the middle of some tree-lined country lane.

"Yeah, I'm a little chilly," she admitted, fighting off a new round of shivers.

Jake frowned and glanced at the sleeves of his overshirt. "I'm sorry I don't have a jacket. I can't take this off because of the holster."

Jeez. He honestly seems distressed because he can't give me a coat. "Uh, thanks." She couldn't hold back a smile, but she managed not to laugh outright. "I don't think a jacket would help that much. It's not that kind of cold."

He took a quick look in the direction of Charlotte's house, then at Merilee. "The drawings we had those Sibyls send to the Motherhouse upset you. Was it the black winged creatures—the Keres? I learned about the death spirits during my time at Motherhouse Greece. They're natural enemies to Sibyls. To every living thing."

Merilee raised her fingers to her scar. "I saw them once when I was just a kid. At least, I think I did." She traced the small, faint line on her jaw. "I wasn't joking before, when I said I jumped off a roof. It was to get away from them—or a vision of them."

Jake's gorgeous eyes blazed into hers as if committing every word to memory, writing it on some tablet in his head. "That must have been a painful experience—in a lot of ways."

She took her hand off the scar. "Yeah, well, I needed it. I was born to the Motherhouse, and I guess I was kind of spoiled, like all of us were—those of us bred for our power and raised by the whole community of Sibyls. I goofed off in lessons, but after that night, I knew I had to take being a warrior a lot more seriously. All business from then on—learning and training, and preparing for my duties as a broom."

Jake frowned. "You were only six."

"Right." She put her hands on her hips. "And how old were you when you learned life would kick the shit out of you if you didn't get tough in a hurry?"

Jake's face darkened, and he looked away from her.

"Point taken," he said in a thin, rough voice that kicked her right in the gut. "I guess neither of us had much of a childhood."

She cursed herself for being thoughtless about his past again, and she was about to apologize when Jake checked over his shoulder one more time, as if to be certain nothing was trailing them from the direction of Charlotte's house.

"The dark figure that kept shifting on the page," he said, sounding more normal, looking more normal when he faced her again, "I assume that was the Stone Man on the list you made at evening meeting?"

Merilee's mouth came open from shock before she remembered Jake was too damned smart for his own good, and that he had translated her notes in the conference room before they left to find Charlotte. She had written that phrase—*Stone Man*—in coded Greek, to remind herself to ask if Charlotte knew anything about him.

Artemis and arrows, but that seemed like two hundred years ago.

I miss my triad. I wish they were here beside me so I'd feel safe.

The cold permeating her body gave way to a bone-destroying fatigue that made her want to sit right down on the black pavement.

Jake moved toward her, and before she could react, he took hold of her arms and ran his hands from her elbows to her wrists and back to her elbows. His firm, warm grip sent pleasant thrills all over her, heating up the elemental air stored in every cell and crevice.

Merilee gazed up at him, into those dangerous gray-blue eyes, and didn't know what to say. A light breeze danced around them, stirring up the dew and tickling her face. "I've dreamed him, too. That figure. He . . . scares me as badly as the Keres. Maybe worse."

"Will this creature try to come after you like he came after Charlotte Heart?" Jake asked, his voice now so low it reverberated through her whole body.

"I think so." Merilee closed her eyes, then forced herself to open them again. "And soon."

Jake's expression turned so serious and severe that if he hadn't been holding her arms, Merilee would have stepped back. His essence seemed to flicker, grow taller, like she could see the outline of his demonic form against the brightening sky.

"The Stone Man will *never* lay a hand on you," he said, and each word sounded like a solemn vow.

She believed him, believed him so completely that she found herself sharing every ridiculous detail about what she saw at Motherhouse Greece when she was six. Air hitched in her lungs, and her heart started to beat hard and fast as her face flushed red-hot.

"Now in my dreams, they come for me, the Keres." She choked for a moment, then forced out the rest as he stroked her arms. "They drag me to Káto Ólimbos, even though I don't want to go—and he catches me there, the Stone Man, and . . . and eats me." Her breath caught as Jake pulled her against his firm, sculpted chest and held her, hands pressed against the small of her back. He was so warm, and he seemed oddly bright, like a light was shimmering from inside him to wrap her up and keep her safe from everything that terrified her.

She slipped her arms around his waist and held on, trying not to feel six years old all over again. "It's stupid," she whispered. "I know. I shouldn't be such a coward."

"It's never stupid to be afraid of shit that can kill you." Jake pressed his hands into her back, and that warm light coursed all over her. Her breath came easier, or maybe that was her imagination. "Didn't they teach you that in Motherhouse school?"

Merilee laughed despite her swirling emotions, the sound muffled against his T-shirt and part of his over-shirt. Damn, he smelled good. And it felt good, him holding her. Comforting her.

"I don't know what the Keres want from me, Jake, or if I'm really seeing them, and not some version of them the Stone Man wants me to see. Maybe they've joined him." She let herself push her face into the cotton of his shirt and take a deep breath of his fascinating, spicy scent. It eased her, like his warmth. "Maybe they're looking forward to all the devastation he'll bring. Keres like blood and battles, and supposedly, they really love it when somebody sticks it to a Sibyl."

Jake held her and listened, obviously without judging her. Just cataloging. When he pulled back and rubbed her arms again, she could tell from the look on his face that he was planning to research the details like the Mothers did, to see what he could find out about the Stone Man and the Keres, too.

"We'll work together to search the archives," he said. "There must be extensive information on these creatures, all of them. If we look every day, we'll come up with some bit or piece that'll help us understand the connections."

His tone was so certain it gave her hope—but she was incredibly tired and sad and confused. Maybe she just wanted to believe Jake could help her slay her old terrors, and her new ones, too. Probably just a fantasy. There was so much she didn't know about him, so much she needed to know before she could trust him.

In the pale dawn, her sharp Sibyl vision still registered every sculpted detail of his face, the thick muscle of his neck and shoulders, the way his nostrils flared as if he might be breathing in her scent and committing it to memory.

Did he have to be so handsome?

"If I could fly," she murmured, holding his gaze even though her stomach was churning like an F4 tornado, "I'd soar so far above New York and all the trouble and danger I'd never come down. Why don't you like to fly, Jake?"

He didn't let go of her arms or look away from her even though his eyes darkened to that stormy color that made her nervous and excited all at the same time. For a few sad moments, she thought he'd refuse to answer her, or give her some lame reason that would make it that much harder to understand him, to grasp who he was.

He sucked air through his teeth, seemed to consider his response, then said, "Flying makes me remember I'm not human." His grip on her arms lessened, and his voice got impossibly lower. "Flying makes it hard to come back to Earth. As long as I stay human, it's easy to *be* human. When I start shifting, control gets . . . more difficult."

He turned his head and closed his eyes. "I went to the Motherhouses to try—ah, hell. I asked the Mothers to make me human again."

Merilee drew a slow, slow breath, feeling the weight of Jake's words like weights settling on her own shoulders.

He let go of her arms and flicked the chain and ring hanging around his neck. "I asked them to free me from this damned thing, too."

Merilee almost reached for the talisman, but lowered her hand at the last second. "And they couldn't grant either request?"

Jake shook his head. "All the Mothers at all three houses tried, especially Mother Anemone and your people, but it was no good. I'm a demon. I'm just a fucking demon, and I'll never be anything else."

He stood with his arms at his sides, his head down, the talisman necklace and ring she now knew he despised glinting in the rising sun.

Merilee's heart ached for him.

If she hadn't been afraid she'd start sobbing and keep sobbing until the next day, she would have cried for him, and held him the way he had held her.

As it was, she reached out and rubbed his arms the way he had rubbed hers, then let her hands rest on his wrists. "I'm so sorry the Mothers couldn't give you what you wanted—but I think you're way more than you're giving yourself credit for."

He lifted his head and met her gaze again and consumed her with those gorgeous, unusual eyes. New ripples of hot wind crisscrossed her back and shoulders.

At that moment, Merilee wanted to kiss Jake so badly she could already taste his lips on hers, feel his tongue delving into the depths of her mouth. She wanted to drive away all the darkness and grief and fear of this night by running her palms over his muscled chest. She wanted to press herself against the steel of his hard flesh again, feel the air rising off his powerful body, breathe it into her, and never let it go. Her nipples got tight so fast they actually ached, and that response traveled the length of her being—that wanting, needing ache. Hecate's torch, she wanted him to touch her. Her fingers dug into his arms, and she knew her desire had to be obvious.

Jake moved like he just might lean down and grant her wish—but he held himself back, with some clear physical effort. His ardent expression faded to one of discomfort and uncertainty.

"We should get back to the townhouse," he muttered. "You need to get some sleep."

Merilee didn't know why he was resisting, but her instincts told her not to push. Not yet, anyway. She took her hands off his wrists, and it struck her that Jake wasn't at all the casual-sex type.

If we sleep together, it won't be just recreation for him.

That shook her up a little, but nowhere near as much as her next thought, which was way too serious for her liking.

And what would sex with Jake be for me?

Her pulse raced and she actually took a step back.

Her head felt fuzzy, and for a moment, she didn't know herself, didn't recognize herself. Merilee knew she had many strengths, but a solemn, mature outlook on relationships outside her Sibyl world just wasn't one of them. She preferred things light and disconnected. Fun.

Not—not whatever this was. Already.

She moved a little farther away from Jake.

He didn't stop her or even look offended or upset. Just relieved, and maybe resigned. He swept his arm in the general direction of the townhouse, then immediately scanned their surroundings as they started to walk down the paved path.

More cop than demon, definitely.

Merilee glanced at his rugged face, his set jaw, and

the way his body flexed with each step through Central Park.

Yeah.

Talisman or not, Jake Lowell was more *man* than anything else. That much she'd stake her life on. And maybe, just maybe, she already had.

7

The night's target had been lost—but this air Sibyl. What a perfect find!

Why had he even been considering settling for that human witch when this exquisite creature existed?

Bartholomew August let his essence blanket Central Park, soaked in moonlight, vibrating with excitement as he tracked the woman while she walked, traced her with his senses, all the while taking care to block her awareness of his presence.

Not easy, as powerful as she was.

The smallest slip in his control and she would know he was touching her at deeper levels than any human male could ever hope to accomplish.

Now that would be delicious.

He could let his shields waver on purpose. Brush his lips across the back of her neck. Reach inside her body and stroke those hollows and caverns known only to the most intimate of lovers. He could allow her to sense just enough of him to share his joy and fascination with her.

Merilee. Her name is Merilee.

But Merilee was still shrouded by the powerful elemental protections that cursed witch Charlotte had left behind, sealed by her own blood and her death by her own hand. August approached those death bindings guarding Merilee, but knew he could come no closer. No matter that her presence chased away his loneliness in a way few had ever done before, he couldn't approach her in any real way, at least not until those spells wore off.

Also, the *thing* that was walking beside her—August felt uncertain of that creature. It was not human at all, fully demon, Legion-created, yet more powerful than August expected. An unknown. August never dealt in unknowns or uncertainties.

He needed to find out more about Merilee the air Sibyl, and about her unusual companion, and August knew just who could tell him.

Seconds later, he rushed down from the night sky and coalesced beside a grave marker in the cemetery of Trinity Church. After a few moments of orienting himself to being on the ground, August drew his human form to him like a magnet attracts flecks of steel. First the veins and bones, then the skin, then form, substance, and clothing for finishing touches. City smells brushed his nose. The sick-sweet of automobile exhaust. Water. Dirt. Asphalt. The hint of garbage and sewage, faint but definite, flowing around the corners of tall, shadowy buildings.

When he finished assuming his earthbound shape, August glanced around the graveyard. He sensed he hadn't been observed by human eyes, but then, he knew that was unlikely. The streets of the Financial District were sparsely populated at this hour.

Barely able to contain the energy rushing through his now-human veins, August headed toward his luxury accommodations at West Street and Morris. In his elevated state, it didn't take him long to reach the stately historic structure where he lived, or to climb the stairs to the expansive penthouse condominium he had used some of his considerable stores of human currency to purchase. He had money from almost every country, deposited in every conceivable bank—the blessing and bane of such a long existence. Already, he was making new inroads, reaching into the business of Wall Street and New York and even Washington, D.C., planning his new political strategies in the absence of the human followers he had lost to the Sibyl assaults.

Everything was coming together quickly, as usual. Such was the benefit of higher intellect and abilities.

When August virtually exploded into the penthouse, the woman and the boy flinched away from his presence and cowered near the kitchen.

August ignored their subservient posture and strode to the woman. He grabbed both of her hands in his and jerked her up from her kneeling position. She gave a little squeal of pain at his tight grip on her wrists, but she didn't struggle.

Not wanting to waste even a moment, August poured images into her feeble brain, of the witch's suicide as he had approached the red townhouse to claim her, and of the Sibyl Merilee, and of the unusual creature who had been escorting Merilee throughout the night.

The woman's squeal gave way to moans of pure agony, punctuated by quiet snarls from the boy—who, to his credit, had fully learned compliance, and offered no challenge.

August knew it was nearly too much for the woman, receiving such a rush of power from his superior mind, but he kept it up without mercy until he finished, until he had forced her to see everything he intended. Then he shook her back to awareness, refusing to let her swoon from the onslaught. He pulled her against him and stared into her wrinkled face, her wide, wet eyes.

"Tell me more details about that particular Sibyl—and that demon beside her," he commanded—and mild surprise flickered in the depths of his mind as those wet eyes narrowed and turned shrewd on him.

The woman stopped shaking, studying August as he studied her. "That one may be out of your reach," she murmured. "She's too dangerous, even for you."

August let go of the woman, amused by her never-dying spirit and cheek. "You know better than that, my dear. What I want, I get."

And she told him then, many more specifics about the Sibyl's formidable triad, all the while regarding him with ferretlike bright eyes, as if she actually hoped he would try to take this Sibyl, and die for his efforts.

It's a wonder this one never went to human prison.

August had absolutely no doubt the woman would be loyal to him only so long as he had fear on his side. Fear and control of the boy. That combination was definitely all that kept her in line.

By the time his delightful little felon finished her tale, August had fixed the names in his mind, not just in a general sense as he had from her previous scouting reports on the townhouse—but definites, details, and specifics about the players who now seemed to matter most. Jake Lowell, the demon, and his half brothers Creed and Nick. Merilee's triad sisters, Riana and Cynda—who were pregnant, of all the delightful twists. Andy, a cop with newfound Sibyl abilities. Sal Freeman, the captain of New York's essentially useless Occult Crimes Unit.

"Freeman will have to be eliminated, of course, along with Jake and his brothers," August told the woman, who gave him no visible reaction. Neither did the boy, who had moved away to lurk in front of the main bedroom door. "The Sibyls Riana and Cynda, well, it seems they in particular owe me a bit of payback for all the damage they've caused my Legion followers."

The woman rubbed her bruising flesh and made a noise that sounded almost derisive. "You always said those who got defeated in fair battle weren't worth your time. Are you goin' back on that now?"

August found himself smiling at the disgusting hag. It really was a shame humans had to age to such unattractive, frail proportions. Inferior stock or not, this one always could make him laugh. In her prime, he would have taken her to the floor for her impudence and made her scream his name for hours.

He didn't answer her challenge, but instead admitted, "It's likely those women are high-quality stock, like Merilee herself."

He would hate to eliminate potential mothers for the return of his people, but if he had to, he would. More likely, Riana and Cynda would make good leverage to obtain Merilee's cooperation—especially given their . . . delicate conditions. Humans were sentimental in that respect.

August dismissed the old woman with a wave of his hand after ordering her to prepare him a meal, then return to the Sibyls when she finished. He did enjoy eating, though he didn't really require food to exist.

He turned his attention to the boy, who still hovered at the door to the condo's master bedroom.

"Stay close to your mother. Bring me all the information you can find on the townhouse where Merilee resides."

The boy cut his eyes toward the bedroom door, swallowed, then nodded and started to brush past August in the hallway.

August reached out, knowing he was moving faster than his son could perceive. He grabbed the boy's arm and forced him down to his knees, until the boy gazed up at him with desperate eyes.

"How is our captive?" August asked quietly, maintaining the pressure on his son's arm at a level just below what would be necessary to shatter the bone.

"F-fine." The boy spoke through his teeth, a valiant attempt to hold back a response to the pain August knew he was causing.

Good, good. That's progress.

August allowed himself a small flare of pride in the

boy's increasing fortitude. "I trust you've seen to her needs and comfort?"

The boy nodded, still maintaining a neutral expression though he was slowly going pale. August released him and watched as the boy managed to walk quickly away instead of running. Yes, definitely improving. A few more months and he might be worth something after all.

August then let his senses drift through the closed door into the bedroom, where last night's catch lay naked and gagged and bound to the four posts of his bed. The little mystic, a woman who made a living as a phony fortuneteller despite her immense elemental potential, was conscious, and to the boy's credit, clean and fresh and ready.

August touched her deep down inside, ignoring her sharp cry of terror and resistance.

He sighed.

Conscious, but not yet with child.

Ah, well.

His human male body surged with arousal at the stream of images already flowing through his consciousness.

He'd just have to try again.

8

Two weeks after the chaos at Charlotte Heart's house, Jake was pissed that his research into the Stone Man and the Keres hadn't turned up anything useful. He strode through the ceaseless gloom of the townhouse's hallway, intending to give a few new archive books a go—but a few steps away from the fourth-floor library door, he sensed them.

Damnit. Maybe this time . . .

Jake reached deep within himself, seeking silence, calmness, lightness as he entered the space. The heavy oak door stood open because Merilee allowed visitors and researchers during daylight hours, and kept her sleeping area and chaotic archiving section closed off with curtains strung between bookshelves.

Not that the curtains held back the mess. Papers peeked under the cloth—and behind those curtains . . . well. Managing the paper stacks was a major challenge. However, Jake had noticed a certain order to her seemingly explosive filing system. It was . . . kind of cute.

And so far, he hadn't had much trouble finding things, even when he was distracted by Merilee. Or hoping to see Merilee. Or hoping not to see Merilee. In general, torturing himself and finding nothing on his target subjects. Until now—only, it wasn't information he had discovered in the big windowed room.

It was demons.

Quiet, he told himself as he took a few more steps into the large paneled area with its shining, polished hardwood floors and fancy area rugs. He almost smiled and lost his concentration when he noticed how Merilee's paper stacks had begun to spill out on half the big tables in the library, but he caught himself and refocused as fast as he could. *Walk like you've got wings—not that it'll do any damned good.*

Every time he and Freeman went out for a bite or a beer, Jake's report was always the same. *Can't find them. And when I do, they won't talk to me.*

And Freeman's response was always the same. *Keep trying.*

Jake's fingers curled into fists.

Today would be different.

Today he'd finally make a little progress.

Tables and bookshelves and Merilee's . . . um, *mess,* filled up every inch of the space, but the terrace doors and six sets of tall windows stood open, mixing the scent of leather and old paper with city air and car exhaust.

Not exactly crisp and refreshing, but Jake inhaled it nonetheless, his mind stretching out at the sight of so much daylight surrounding him.

His intake of breath gave him away.

The three Astaroths standing in visible form near the back terrace doors winked into nothing.

Jake swore under his breath and almost kicked the nearest pile of file folders. Did the bastards fly away—*again*? He felt like a fucking cat after sneaky, sneaky birds.

"Darian," he said, hoping for an answer. "Jared? Quince? Come on, guys, cut me a friggin' break here. Captain Freeman *wants* me to talk to you. Work with you."

I sound like I'm begging.

Fuck.

Jake rubbed his hand across his short hair in frustration. If begging would help, maybe . . .

The air in front of him shifted.

A second later, the demon who called himself Darian returned to visible form, standing about six feet away from Jake. Close to the terrace doors, like any second he might change his mind and fly away. Jake wanted to snatch hold of him and anchor him to the floor, but at some deeper level, he recoiled from the idea of trapping another living creature. His gaze shifted from Darian to the soft, enticing light pouring through the terrace doors and the bluer-than-blue sky beyond. His heart beat faster and his blood surged. His essence and human form shuddered before he pulled himself back together.

Why does that keep happening?

Jake's gut tightened and he almost lost focus on the task at hand.

For two years, I have no problems staying human—then I come back to this damned townhouse and twinkle, twinkle like the goddamned little star. Shit!

Breathing high and tight in his chest, Jake forced himself to let go of his own concerns and study his quarry instead.

For a moment, Darian remained all Astaroth, fangs sharp and shining, clawed fingers curling as his two sets of wings extended. His talisman glittered against his pale flesh as he studied Jake with his clear golden eyes, then slowly, slowly, pulled himself into a vague semblance of human form. A sort of vampiric human with see-through white skin and almost white eyes, but close enough. Jake would take what he could get at this point.

"So you can shift," Darian said, his tone one of quiet surprise. "You almost did a moment ago. We've wondered if you could."

Jake sucked back a defensive comment and forced himself to keep a relaxed posture. "I can shift into demon form, yes. I choose not to."

Darian glanced from Jake to the open terrace doors. "Why?"

Okay, so much for relaxed. Jake's body went taut at all the joints, and he didn't try to hide it. "I have my reasons. For now, I'm an OCU officer and that's where I can do the most good in the fight against the Legion."

At the word *Legion,* Darian's eyes flashed golden and his lips pulled back around his fangs. Jake half expected the Astaroth to hiss.

"I would like very much to fight them," Darian said. "Every day."

Behind Darian, Jared and Quince materialized and assumed pseudo-human form. They didn't speak, but Jake could tell by their expressions they hated the Legion as much as Jake did. "How old were you when you were changed?" he asked Darian on impulse.

"I don't know." Darian's reply was open, not offended or angry. "We estimate two years of human age, perhaps three." He gestured to the other two Astaroths. "They were younger."

A dull ache bloomed deep in Jake's heart.

No wonder this bunch was so skittish.

To be so very young, to know nothing of the world in true human flesh. Their first memories would have been of pain and death and murder at the hands of those they trusted. The frustration he had built over the last fourteen days of chasing the elusive, uncooperative demons faded into concern and respect, and sorrow for the babies they once had been.

The three demons shimmered, as if perceiving his deep emotion, and Darian actually put a hand over his own heart.

"You . . . radiate," Darian said. "We have seen it before. It's disconcerting. Among other things."

Jake had no idea what the demon was talking about,

and he didn't really care. When he spoke, he made sure his tone was calm and even, and as friendly as he could make it. "Captain Freeman wants me to work with you so you can participate more in our patrols and operations—if you'd like that."

He paused, but Darian and the other two didn't say a word.

"I know you're excellent natural fighters," Jake added, "but I can teach you things. Techniques. Ways that humans think, ways they're likely to act. It'll make you more effective in combat with any human foe." He cleared his throat. "Again, if you're interested."

The Astaroths remained silent for what felt like a very long time. The afternoon sunlight kept playing havoc with Jake's thoughts, as if it could grab hold of his soul, yank out his wings, and propel him out that window to fly for hours, days, weeks—

No!

By the time he caught himself, he was halfway to translucent.

Shit. I never lose control like this. What the hell is happening to me?

Was it the Astaroths? Being so close to his own kind?

Pain stabbed at his temples, and he was actually glad for it. It pinned him to Earth, made his human form real and whole again. Jake breathed slowly, steadying himself as Darian nodded.

"We have desired to work with you, Leader, but we believed you did not truly wish to be near us."

Darian's expression remained nearly vacant, but Jake knew he had to look shocked as hell.

Leader?

What is that about?

"By your leave, we will work with you on mornings you're free, and any day it rains." Darian managed an expression that approximated a smile. "Afternoons like this," he lifted his hand toward the open doors as he reassumed his full Astaroth form, "weren't meant to be spent indoors or on the ground."

Voices drifted through the library, and Jake heard people enter the room behind him. For a moment, Darian, Jared, and Quince remained visible. Then Darian's eyes narrowed and his lips pulled back again. This time the demon did hiss—and all three Astaroths vanished.

Poof. Gone.

Air rushed past Jake's face.

"The Astaroths have left the building," he muttered as he turned to face Freeman, Merilee, Delilah Moses—and behind Delilah, the goddamned drifting, empty-eyed image of his mother. Wearing that goddamned red dress.

Jake's heart stuttered. He tried to swallow, but found his throat paper-dry and too tight to work properly.

He tore his eyes away from Delilah and the psychotic ghost-bitch, and his gaze landed directly on Merilee, who was standing beside them. She was dressed in a loose-fitting shirt and pants, and he figured she had been meditating or doing yoga in the basement gym.

Shit, but the thought of how she looked when she stretched, of her lithe, flexible body in various yogic poses, almost destroyed him on the spot. As it was, the way her flowing shirt draped against her breasts and the way those silky warm-ups hung at her hips absolutely pummeled Jake's rational thought process.

Her sea-blue eyes stole his ability to move. Run away. Fly into the sky like Darian and the others.

Why did I get up today?

Why the fuck did I ever *come here?*

Freeman was talking, and Jake wanted to slam his fists against the sides of his own head to knock sense back into his brain.

"Did you hear me?" Freeman sounded delighted as he

pointed to the open terrace doors. "I said great job. They were talking to you, weren't they? You got somewhere. I swear those three—they're weird. They're different from the other Astaroths we've dealt with, just like—"

He broke off, and streaks of red flared across his cheeks.

"Yeah," Jake said. "I know what you mean. It's okay."

Merilee's gaze was fixed on the open terrace doors. "They're like beautiful wild spirits that need to be tamed."

Her voice traveled all over Jake's body like warm fingers—but her words made him twitch.

Wild spirits and taming.

Does she like them?

Do they like her?

He had a sudden image of killing Darian in their first training session. Accidentally separating his long-haired head from his scrawny pale shoulders.

Leader, my ass.

Jake had to grind his teeth to bring himself back to reality, or as close to reality as he dared to get.

She's . . . my . . . partner for now. Partner. *No different from a fellow police officer.*

Merilee shifted her eyes to Jake and smiled, and he couldn't help feasting on the sight of her in those soft-looking workout clothes one more time.

Well, maybe not exactly a typical police officer.

Jake looked away from her—and once more came face-to-face with his mother's apparition, raising her—its—knife as if to stab Delilah Moses. The sight of it made Jake wish he could beat himself in the head without attracting unwanted attention.

Was the bitch attacking Delilah because she saved Jake once? Did his mother hate him that much?

He gazed at Delilah and his mother, relieved that

none of his mother's biosentient talents had transferred into the afterlife with her. No doubt his mother would be destroying Delilah's cells and vessels as he watched, collapsing the poor woman's body in on itself.

But you're dead, Mother. You have no power here.

With everything he could muster inside, Jake willed the ghost-image to disappear.

Slowly, slowly, it did, allowing Jake to breathe more normally.

"Delilah and I have a little research to do." Merilee gave Jake another mind-devastating smile. "I'll see you in six hours and fifteen minutes, at evening meeting."

All Jake could do was nod, try not to watch her ass as she walked away, and blow that little resolution all to hell.

After Merilee got a few steps past, Freeman got Jake's attention with a cough. He folded his big arms across his chest, and the sarcastic look on his face said it all.

Jake sighed. "Obvious?"

"She'd have to be pretty thick not to notice." Freeman grinned. "And I don't think she's thick."

Jake waved him off. "Fuck you. Twice."

Freeman snickered, then pointed toward the library door. "Come on down to my office. Let's go over some training ideas for your new friends." He cut his eyes toward the direction Merilee went and snickered again. "If you weren't about to go on patrol, I'd buy you a cold one. Sure as hell look like you could use it."

"You have no idea," Jake muttered as he followed Freeman out of the library, trying not to concentrate on the sound or smell of Merilee—or scan the surroundings for the homicidal apparition of his mother. "Two or three would be more like it."

Early that evening, Jake glanced at Merilee, who was strolling beside him on a crowded walkway in her leathers, armed as always with her bow hanging over one shoulder and her quiver slung over the other—this time concealed by a red shawl. Waning sunlight played off her blond hair, turning it to soft-looking spun gold.

As she paused in front of a store window full of high-definition television screens, people stared at her and he wondered if it was the weapons or her beauty.

Maybe both.

I'm pathetic.

It wasn't so much that he was wearing a Cynda-singed shirt, or that the right leg of his jeans was smeared with dirt from a little fit Riana threw before they left the townhouse. Pregnant Sibyls, in all their psychotic glory—he was getting used to that.

No, it was more that all of his plans to just do his job, stay professional, and remain detached were going to hell fast. It had taken Merilee less than three weeks to turn his mighty resolve into so much wind.

I'm supposed to be getting used to working with her. I'm supposed to keep myself under control, watching out for her, making sure that this nightmare creature, this Stone Man, never gets to her, especially now that the elemental protections from Charlotte Heart's sacrifice have worn off.

He had to have been insane, to think he could come to New York and blend in with the OCU and his brothers and just . . . ignore a woman like this.

But I have to. At least in that way.

If I can.

Damn.

Every time they worked together, she impressed him. He didn't know what he liked more, her body or her brain.

Merilee was still staring through the store window at several flashing television screens. On the screens, head-shots of political candidates scrolled by. The evening news caption spoke of "dark horses" and new-to-the-scene politicians who might make a stir in the current race. Merilee pointed to one of them, a man who looked to be about fifty. Tall and fit and muscular, with dark hair. "Does that guy look familiar to you, Jake?"

He moved behind her, almost close enough to touch her, definitely close enough to feel the soft, warm breeze flowing off her perfect skin. Her scent filled his awareness as he studied the snapshot and let the image sink through his consciousness. At first, nothing resonated, but the troubled expression on Merilee's face drove him to try harder. The caption identified the man as Bartholomew August, international evangelist and leader of the Peace Warriors, a man who had only recently begun allowing himself to be in the public eye.

The name wasn't familiar to Jake, though he did remember something about the Peace Warriors. Sort of a new-age Peace Corps, building homes and community centers and opening food-and-clothing charities in more developed countries, to help the "working poor." *Teach a man to fish—and give him his first pole.* That was one of their slogans.

"I'm sorry, no." Jake eased a step away from Merilee, folded his arms to be sure he kept his hands to himself, and stared at the screen. "I don't think I've seen him before."

Even as the words left his mouth, something stirred in his gut. An unease, a vague discomfort, like he *should* know the man.

But why?

And from where?

Jake frowned at the television image, which was already flickering through some other story about a small riot in the Garment District, and about how street violence seemed to be on the rise this month. The extensive files of information he had stored in his brain—was there some obscure detail in one of them that involved this Bartholomew August? He'd have to think about that during some quiet time away from Merilee, when he could focus.

"Maybe I'm just edgy," she said as her gaze traveled from the storefront to two elderly men shaking fists and canes at each other across the street. "Everything seems so upside down right now. So . . . I don't know. Melancholy. Like there's some agitation in the air itself, and the water and the earth."

She looked so troubled and sad Jake wanted to touch her all over again, this time to take her in his arms and hold her, offer her comfort. If he could shield her from any unhappiness, he would do so without hesitation.

Would she allow that?

She faced him and his eyes met hers and locked into place.

The air around Jake stirred against his skin, and his pulse beat in his ears. Even on this crowded sidewalk with a few feet of concrete separating them, he felt connected to her. She could make his body respond with a frown or a smile, with a twitch of those red, full lips—and she responded to him, too. He didn't miss the tightening of her muscles, the ways she straightened and shivered and leaned toward him.

He didn't take a breath, because if he smelled her arousal, he would lose his mind.

Merilee broke the spell by looking away, then reached out and brushed her hand against his before she started walking. Jake followed, trying not to get more distracted by the warm spot where she had touched him, or thoughts about where he'd like her fingers to go next.

"With so many people with paranormal ability leaving so suddenly," he said, his voice low and husky, "and your friend Charlotte's death last week—it's bound to have some effect on the city's energy."

Jake offered his theory with some confidence despite his drunken thought process, because it made intuitive and scientific sense. New York City was enduring a sort of psychic displacement, leaving a vacuum that had to be filled with something—like the melancholy agitation plaguing Merilee. Jake felt it, too, but he figured not as acutely as she did. Demon senses tended to resonate to underlying designs and patterns to events, not so much fluctuations in energy or sensory phenomena.

"A lot of the paranormal groups tried to do positive elemental work." Merilee kept her gaze straight ahead, leaving Jake to study the exquisite lines of her profile. "They poured good into the city. Without them, it's darker here, I guess. I wish we could figure out why they left—and what's happening to those who stayed."

For a time, they walked in silence, flowing past people on the crowded sidewalks. Jake reviewed what they did know, which was next to nothing. Interviews conducted by Sibyls in other cities had turned up information from a few New York refugees, but all they could say was the city's energy felt "wrong" or "very bad." That they had a vague but definite sense of danger, and fled on reflex rather than confronting the problem, whatever it was. A few practitioners with strong paranormal abilities had stayed behind, as the OCU was learning, but many of them were beginning to drop out of sight.

Taken?

Murdered?

Suicides, like Charlotte Heart?

As yet, they had no idea.

And even after reviewing dozens of texts on spirits, essences, and paranormal manifestations, Jake and Merilee had not been able to find any creature that resembled the Stone Man in her nightmares—though the legends of the Keres were clear enough. Vicious air spirits of death, motivated by the chaos and gore of battle. Sibyl archival documents held accounts of the Keres trying to trick air Sibyls to their doom, enticing them to Káto Ólimbos as suicides, but that was rare and mostly in ancient times.

The Mothers were concerned about the dreams, and the likelihood that Charlotte Heart had died to protect herself and her coven from this bizarre manifestation, but equally at a loss as to what the Stone Man might be. They also didn't dare approach the Keres to obtain more information, because that would violate the ancient protective treaty with the creatures and place Motherhouse Greece at direct risk of attack. The Mothers shared Merilee's opinion that she might not be seeing the actual Keres, but rather the Stone Man's interpretation of them as he sought an image that would frighten Merilee.

Bastard. Jake's insides went rigid as he thought about the Stone Man attempting to find his way into Merilee's head and weaken her with her own fears. *I don't care what he is, or what he thinks he's doing, he's not getting near her, now or ever.*

(9)

Car engines revved and buses and cabs barreled past. The entire city seemed to be getting off work at the same moment, but the crowd didn't faze Jake or his errant thoughts. He kept glancing at Merilee and thinking about protecting her, then about kissing her. She had as much as invited him to touch her several times, but so far, he'd been able to resist.

Would it hurt to make love to her just once?

Would that make things easier—or twice as miserable?

Shit, he had to stop letting himself get lost in thoughts like that. Small talk. Conversation. Anything would be better.

"So, uh, was it easy when you got chosen for your triad?" He swallowed, hoping he didn't sound too lame. "I mean, did Riana know you were her broom right away?"

Merilee kept a brisk pace and didn't seem put off by his nosing around. "She spent days with my class of adepts, talking to all of us and watching us fight. There were twenty-three of us ready for assignment, but she kept coming back to me, and I was glad. I felt a connection with Riana right away. Now, Cynda—whoa."

Merilee laughed, and the sound flowed all over Jake just like her wind. "Cynda was another story. When Riana brought me to New York and I met Cynda, I wondered what I had done to offend Olympus. First day, she cooked part of my wardrobe and two of my books. The whole first month was kind of rough, but after I saved her ass from six Asmodai in a hand-fight near Strawberry Fields, it got better."

That made sense to Jake. Fire Sibyls might be in charge of communication, but at base, they were all about the fighting. "The two of you seem very close now."

"Absolutely. She's my triad sister, my sister of the heart." Merilee pressed one hand against her chest, then lowered it. "Before she got married, we used to go to the gym together all the time and pick up hot—"

Merilee slowed down and made a little choking noise. Turned purple-red. "We had a lot of fun together."

Okay, this is not working.

They kept walking, only now in silence.

Jake opened and closed his fists and did his ever-loving best not to imagine Merilee at a gym cruising men. Or worse yet, men cruising her. It made him want to kill things. Or take her straight back to the townhouse and make love to her, right now. Please her so intensely and completely she'd never think about any bastard from the gym again.

Sibyls aren't nuns. What did you expect? Shit, Mother Anemone showed me their course schedule. They have classes *in sexual techniques, for God's sake. To prepare them for a healthy, active adult life once they leave the Motherhouse.*

Merilee . . . has had . . . classes *. . . in sexual techniques.*

Fuck.

He should just find a damned bridge and jump off it. That was the only way he'd get any relief.

Jake tried to will himself back to here, now, the real world. This wasn't happening, no matter how much he toyed with the idea.

He was what he was, and no amount of wanting a human woman would change that. He had to keep reminding himself of that maddening reality, or he'd cross the lines he had drawn. He'd go back on his word to himself, and he'd complicate Merilee's life and his own beyond all feasible limits.

As they turned onto West Fifty-seventh, he felt glad that she didn't like to be cooped inside vehicles any more than he did. He didn't think he could handle being in a small, closed space with her. Too easy to reach over and stroke her cheek, or her shoulder, or slide his hand lower—

"Here it is. One of the oldest large apartment buildings in New York City." Merilee's silky voice slid against his senses as she brought them to a stop, fueling his fantasies instead of settling them into stasis. "It was built in 1881, I think—before the Gramercy, even. I used to think nobody lived here, but we came here to break up a paranormal fight a couple of years back."

She gestured to the building in front of them.

Jake barely registered the run-down brick façade, but his law enforcement mind finally took over, cataloguing details and specifics. About seven stories, old-style architecture, lots of boarded-up windows, some with fire department markings to let firefighters know which path was safe to take in case of a fire. He leafed through information in his head, bits and facts he had gathered scanning Merilee's archives and roaming across the Internet. Yeah, he remembered this place. The Windermere. Designated a landmark in 2005, recently slapped with code violations and improper removals of fire escapes during early-stage renovation. So if they got in, it might be tricky getting out in a pinch.

"Only a few people live here now, right?" He looked at Merilee for confirmation.

She nodded. "Some who refused to move years ago, when building owners tried to force them out. Tenants were beaten and threatened and strong-armed out of here, but Phila Gruyere's family endured. They stayed."

She pressed her lips together, and her expression told Jake she still didn't want to believe that the Vodoun mambo, one of the most popular voodoo priestesses in the area, had just vanished or left like so many other paranormal practitioners. Especially not after standing fast with her family and refusing to be driven from her home.

But that apparently was the case.

A concerned friend had called the police to check on the small apartment after Phila didn't show up to complete her usual duties at a Vodoun celebration. Then OCU had been asked to come to the apartment to assume custody of an archive of magical texts and writings, and "objects typical to the practice of the occult."

Translation: We sure as hell don't want to touch this creepy shit. YOU take it.

He and Merilee had been dispatched to see what it would take to safely pack and store what might be some seriously dangerous materials.

"Was Phila your friend like Charlotte?" Jake asked quietly, hoping Merilee wouldn't be handed another burden to bear on top of her friend's death, the insanity in the city, and her triad's incapacity.

Her pretty blue eyes seemed clear as she said, "Not really, no, but I hope nothing's happened to her. At this point, we could use her strength, if she could be persuaded to be reasonable."

That was a relief, at least—Phila wasn't someone close to Merilee. In the moment of silence that followed, Jake barely managed to avoid locking eyes with her again.

Merilee opened the main door of the antique apartment building and swept her hand toward the darkened entryway. "After you."

Jake entered, alert, arms relaxed but ready for action.

Even though his pulse picked up, nothing seemed unusual. Just a poorly kept entrance, and badly maintained walls and windowframes, most of which were boarded shut. His keen vision allowed him to sort through each shadow and bit of floor debris, despite the low lighting.

Typical derelict building.

Well, almost.

He took a slow, deep breath of mildew and dust, and the tang of transformed elemental power lingered in his nose, on his tongue.

There's power here, or there was.

But no immediate threat that he could discern.

"Clear," he called to Merilee, who entered and came to stand beside him.

"Do you feel it?" she murmured, her fingertips fluttering against Jake's knuckles, sending shocks of pleasure up his arm. "Those remnants of elemental workings? Phila's abilities are *so* strong. A couple of years back, we had to break up a fight between her and one of her cousins. They were trying to sacrifice the same pig to feed Bosou Koblamin, a three-horned war god—well, god of protection. Phila almost got the better of Cynda before we got the situation defused. Sent Cynda home covered in pork blood."

Jake glanced down at the burned fringe of his shirt and remembered the sudden inferno during evening meeting a few hours ago. Anyone who could control fire elements enough to give Cynda a run for her money had his respect, no discussion needed.

Merilee showed him the stairs, and they climbed to the fourth floor, located the police-taped entrance, and greeted the officer on duty who had been guarding the possible crime scene. He opened the door for them, but didn't seem at all interested in going inside.

"Watch your six," the officer muttered to Jake as he passed. "Wouldn't catch me dead in that fucktrap."

Jake nodded at the officer, understanding why he was bugged. Even a non-sensitive would be rattled by the random flickers of elemental power bouncing around this place. Still, they had work to do, so Jake led Merilee into the small two-bedroom where Phila Gruyere had lived and practiced. He looked left and right, hands flexing, half convinced he'd have to draw and shoot *something*.

The air smelled wrong. The whole atmosphere felt wrong, and yet nothing seemed too freaky on the surface.

Jake immediately took note of the spotless, colorful kitchen and living area. Yellow walls. Bright blue highlights and fixtures. Red and green and white flags, strings of shells, painted coconuts—the place could have doubled as a full-page travel ad for Jamaica or one of the other Caribbean islands. A few markers and tabs let him know that the apartment had already been processed by crime scene technicians.

In the back of the apartment were two bedrooms, one an actual sleeping space with the bed, and the other—

Jake whistled.

The other room was the source of the raw bursts of power. He drew his Glock and started for the tiled space on the back right.

Merilee stopped Jake with a hand on his free arm. "I need to go first. Wait here."

"Not happening." Jake edged forward, but she pulled hard at his elbow, and he stopped again—not because he wanted to.

A wind kicked up in front of his face, well controlled and circumscribed, enveloping him and only him like a personally designed hurricane. His cheeks pressed inward, his ears popped, and his bones jarred from sudden low air pressure and whistling gale-force currents—but the rest of the apartment remained completely still and unmoving.

Merilee let go of his elbow. Jake barely kept hold of his Glock. His eyes watered from the wind. His shoulders bunched against the force and his fingers tightened around the grip of the gun.

Damnit, he couldn't get loose.

He'd have to shift to his full demon form to battle against Merilee's wind-field

No way.

He wouldn't resort to that, no matter how much she pissed him off.

Her voice rose above the roar, magnified by her affinity with the air currents trying to smash him into a long, tall Jake popsicle stick. "Don't make me shoot you in the nuts with an arrow, you stubborn asshole. That room's full of free elemental energy. If you walk through that door before I contain it, it'll cook you or rattle out your eyeballs, or maybe blow you to bits."

Jake squinted through the curtains of wind to see that she was standing right beside him, shawl off, bow in hand, arrow ready.

He eyed the polished olivewood.

Would she really shoot me with that thing?

"I'm not a stubborn asshole," he said, forcing the words into the dancing air.

The wind relented a little.

"Really?" Merilee sounded amused, and when he checked, she was smiling that sexy little smile that made him want to forget police work for the next, oh, three hours or so. Maybe four. Or five. Hell, a week or a month. "What kind of asshole are you then? Arrogant—or maybe just macho?"

"Stop the wind," he said as steadily as he could manage with his lips plastered to his teeth. "Now."

Merilee drew her air energy back to herself, stepped in front of him, and tapped his chest with her bow. "We need an understanding. You, Tarzan. Okay, fine—but me *Sibyl.*"

He blinked at her, not comprehending, leafing through his mental files on old jungle movies and Rudyard Kipling tales as quickly as he could, but coming up with nothing but character names like Cheetah and Jane and Boy and—

Merilee shouldered her bow, stood on her tiptoes, and kissed his cheek.

The shock of her warm, moist lips touching his body removed all capacity for logical speech.

Her palms rested on his chest.

Jake stood still, inches from her, seeing her naked in his mind, spread beneath him, lids heavy and half-closed, cheeks flushed, arms and legs open, ready, waiting to take him deep in her hot, wet depths. His cock went from zero to rigid in .03 seconds, and he lost all track of where they were and what they were supposed to be doing.

She was talking.

How the hell was he supposed to comprehend words right now?

But she was using syllable after syllable, gazing at him with a serious expression, using an earnest "You've got to understand this" tone.

"You're honorable and strong and very, very sweet. I honestly believe all this guy-protectiveness bullshit comes from a sincere place inside you."

Jake got *guy, bullshit*—and did she say *sincere*?

He loved the sound of her voice. He gazed at her hands on his chest and imagined them stroking his cock and thanked all the gods he had no elemental energy to burn anything down around them or cause an earthquake or spawn a tornado.

"But I'm a Sibyl," Merilee continued. "What I mean is, you're a cop and a demon, even if you don't use the demon part too much. You've got your strengths and I've got mine. So I'll handle diffusing elemental protections and energy, and you cover me, watch my back, and do the heavy lifting when I ask you to. Is that a deal?"

"Watch your back," Jake echoed.

Yeah, he could definitely do that.

His brain swam a little closer to reality again, but before he could recover, Merilee left him standing like an idiot and headed into the tiled room on the back right, skirting the intricate pattern painted on the floor in what looked like blood and the bits of melted candle strewn all over the place.

The sight of her walking into danger sobered him instantly, and he regained control of his faculties in a matter of seconds. He lunged toward the room's doorway, but didn't enter. He did what Merilee asked, examining the space for potential threats, backing her up as best he could.

Merilee had positioned herself in front of the design on the floor. Her arms were out, and Jake sensed the elemental energy radiating from her hands, her fingers, her entire body. Wind rushed through the space, totally controlled and directed. Merilee's bow and quiver trembled against her back from the force of the air she was moving, and the roiling power Jake had been feeling since they entered the building began to calm almost immediately.

Jake noted statues filling the corners of the small area, towers of books leaned against the walls, and shelves stacked on shelves full of jars of different colored liquids and powder, pickled animal body parts, and, if he wasn't much mistaken, a few human body parts, too. Nothing moved. Everything seemed . . . under control.

"You can come in," Merilee said as she lowered her arms, "but stay out of the vévé."

Yeah, no kidding.

Jake edged into the room. He studied the pattern on the floor, which he knew was used in the ritual practice of voodoo, and his sensitive vision and sense of smell told him the drawing had been created with chicken blood. Raw elemental energy radiated from each blackish-red line, malignant and waiting, like a carnivorous plant hoping to snap up a helpless fly.

In the center of the vévé lay a single open volume, which looked like an encyclopedia of ancient gods and goddesses. Jake's gaze traveled from that book to the jar on the shelf beside his shoulder.

A lidless human eye floated in a murky solution, staring balefully at his nose.

"I wouldn't touch anything either," Merilee said as she moved her hand a few inches above the nearest stack of books. "Not until I've checked it and released whatever protections I find. Phila might have put some nasty elemental traps on her tools."

Jake considered the eyeball. "No worries."

The officer in the hallway had been right. This was one freaky fucktrap of a place. Merilee had been right earlier, too, when she blocked him with that maelstrom.

This was definitely her area of expertise, not his.

Jake thought about shifting to demon form and retracting his arms at the elbows to be *sure* he didn't touch anything, but discarded the idea. Instead, he turned his attention to Merilee, to the books she was cleansing, to anything but the eye beside him. Like the bowl of chicken feet near Merilee's left ankle.

Okay . . .

"Jake, this doesn't look deliberate to me, like Phila staged a scene, then left." Merilee handed him an armload of books. "Stack these in the living room. They're clear."

He obliged and Merilee continued to talk as she worked. "I think Phila was performing a serious protection ritual and got interrupted."

Jake settled the books near the living room's white wicker couch. "Maybe she got eaten by whatever horned war god she was trying to feed to gain its favor?"

"Funny. And eminently possible with voodoo—but, no. Not Phila." Merilee sounded definite as she picked up the rest of the first stack of books. "Once we've cleaned the room, I'll risk getting into that vévé for a closer look at that book at the center—but that's always tricky."

Jake grimaced as he relieved her of the next load of books. He didn't like the sound of *tricky*. Too risky for her, as far he was concerned. "You deal with the protections. I'll retrieve the book at the center, or do whatever's necessary to break the pattern."

Merilee blew out a sigh as she turned away from him to the shelf with the eyeball, and the air in the room stirred from the touch of her elemental power. "You're acting like a Lowell again."

Jake studied her supple shoulders and the way her leather jumpsuit hugged her curves. "Thanks," he muttered, then wondered if that might have been an insult.

She didn't say she didn't need his protection, though.

Maybe they did have a new understanding, to work to their strengths. Merilee could handle the, er, eyeballs, and Jake would watch her ass.

He coughed.

Figuratively. He meant that figuratively.

Sure.

About an hour later, as evening began to dim the ambient light seeping through the windows, the room's contents save for the book anchoring the vévé had all been cleansed, removed, and stacked in the living room for packing and storage. Jake had called Freeman and told him what cartons and boxes would be needed and what size truck to bring. Now he and Merilee were taking a much-deserved break at Phila Gruyere's small kitchen table before delving into the chicken-blood design and what it contained.

Merilee sat back in the metal chair, clearly tired and worried. Her voice was distant as she said, "I wonder how many practitioners have left and how many might have disappeared like Phila. Do you think—do you think maybe *he* took her?"

"You're talking about the Stone Man from your dreams." Jake clasped his hands together on the table, wishing he could crush everything that frightened Merilee in his two fists and dispose of it forever.

She looked at the floor between their chairs. "I think he's real, Jake. I know he's real. I haven't had any nightmares for about three days, but the protections from Charlotte's death just dissolved."

"He might be collecting practitioners with powerful abilities in hopes he can compel them to complete rituals." Jake made an effort to relax, but his fingers kept trying to curl into fists. "That would make sense, and the Legion has tried things like that before—though without much success. It's very difficult to make someone perform spells and energy transfers against their will."

"I don't think that's it." Merilee glanced toward the back room and the intricate blood design still awaiting their attention. "He'd have to know if he turned Phila loose in some ritual, she'd set a flock of zombies on him or draw down some pissed-off god to kick his stone face to dust."

Jake reached for his talisman before he realized what he was doing, then lowered his hand, frowning. "Maybe he has some way to force her to cooperate."

"Possible." Merilee's gaze lingered on Jake's talisman. "But not likely."

The longer her eyes stayed on the cursed thing, the more Jake wanted to rip it off or turn away from her and never turn back again, never allow her to see that awful part of him, that glaring weakness. The chain and ring felt heavy and hot around his neck, like the gold was digging into his essence and leaving a fresh, thick new scar.

"Freeman will be here in half an hour with the packers and the truck." His voice was too loud, but he couldn't help it.

Jake stood so suddenly he shoved the table away from himself without meaning to. The metal legs scrubbed against the floor and he missed catching the edge of the table. It slammed into the kitchen wall so hard the corner punched into the drywall.

Merilee sat for a second, her attention riveted to the spot where the table now dug into the wall.

Then she got to her feet.

Heat rose through Jake's body, something like rage or humiliation, but he couldn't sort it out. He expected her to lecture him or yell, or convey her disapproval in a gesture or expression.

Merilee didn't say a word.

She also didn't give him a strange look or seem upset by his behavior, which somehow made him feel worse. She just slipped around him, left the kitchen, went back into the tiled room, and stood at the edge of the vévé.

Jake moved into the room behind her.

I'm a shithead.

He needed to apologize for his loss of control, right now, but Merilee was already working, eyes closed, hands at her sides this time. Wind energy stirred against her hair and face, and spread out through the room. Slower this time, more deliberate, but no less intense in force and focus.

It wouldn't be good to distract her, not when he already felt her elemental power flowing to meet the pulsing energy in the design.

Merilee would do whatever it took to get the job done in any situation. As she had reminded him, she was a Sibyl. The broom of her triad. This was a woman—a warrior—used to cleaning up big messes, and Jake better not forget that ever again. He owed her more respect than that. So he kept still, and he kept his mouth shut.

Seconds went by, then a few minutes.

One branch and limb at a time, Merilee tackled and subdued the elemental workings of the blood-etched pattern, and Jake sensed its untamed elemental power dying away. She wasn't so much breaking it as wrapping it in wind, redirecting it, calming it into nothingness.

It amazed him, how Merilee could stir up wild energy so quickly when she wanted to, yet just as quickly recapture it, absorb it, and soothe it completely away.

Earlier, she really would *have shot me with that arrow.*

He was pretty sure he was falling for her. How could anyone not fall for a woman like Merilee?

As he watched her work the vévé so completely and methodically, he had no doubt—about the arrow or about falling for her.

Another few minutes passed.

Merilee opened her eyes, glanced around the room, and took a breath.

"I think that's got it," she said. When she shifted her attention to Jake, her expression was steel mixed with the sure confidence and forcefulness Jake had grown accustomed to seeing in the Sibyl Mothers. "I'll get the book."

Jake tensed, but didn't challenge her decision.

Merilee's face softened a fraction, and she smiled at

him, obviously pleased he had grasped what she said earlier about being a Sibyl—even if he still hadn't figured out the Tarzan part of it. That might take more study.

She eased forward, skirting through the points of the vévé, until she reached the design's center. There, she hesitated, and Jake realized she was checking the book for additional protections. After a few seconds, Merilee bent down and retrieved the leather-bound volume.

She held it up, studying the pages. "It's open to an entry on the Egyptian god Thoth."

Jake called up facts and details about Thoth much more easily than he could about Tarzan. Thoth had been considered the tongue and heart of the sun god Ra, ruler of sky, earth, and underworld—the physical embodiment of a god's mind. Thoth was usually portrayed with a man's body, but the head of an ibis.

Merilee glanced at the entry again. Then she looked toward the ceiling, obviously confused. "Do you—do you hear anything, Jake?"

Jake tensed. He reached out with all his senses, but detected nothing beyond normal city noises and activity. "No. Nothing unusual."

Merilee shook her head. "The Keres—the death spirits from my dreams. I thought I heard them screaming just now."

Jake glanced at the ceiling, then back to the book in Merilee's hands. "Maybe you should put that down."

"Okay, but there's one more thing." She touched the passage to read him something—and the moment her finger pressed against the page, the room started to shake.

She looked up, wide-eyed. "Oh, shit."

Adrenaline poured through Jake's body, lighting up his senses, his nerves, his muscles.

Hands trembling, Merilee dropped the book.

Before the binding struck the floor, Jake shed his human form.

Wings unfurled, arms outstretched, he shot blindly forward, praying he'd get to her in time—and the walls and floor exploded.

10

The world around Merilee blew into bits of tile and wood and plaster.

Air punched from her lungs.

A bestial, vicious power crashed into her body and hurled her backward.

Merilee's mind spun with her body as she sailed out of the Windermere building.

Energy grabbed at her, gripped her, held her in the air.

Not an elemental trap. Shit. No!

A god.

The Vodoun Loa that Phila Gruyere had been summoning when she vanished or got taken.

Merilee sensed something huge and elemental with a lot of horns and teeth.

Something very, very, *very* pissed.

I'm so dead.

The energy holding her flung her toward the ground.

Merilee's heart caved against her ribs as her body tumbled into dark oblivion. Pain thundered through her joints, her bones. The god was smashing her as she fell. She felt like it was pulverizing her with its massive elemental energy.

Merilee screamed but heard nothing. She couldn't see anything but sky and stars and streaks of light.

Down.

Her pulse shot up even as her body jetted downward. Faster now. Hurtling toward the sidewalk and street below.

No!

Mouth open, chest on fire as she fought for air, Merilee pushed against the ground with her wind. And pushed. And pushed even harder.

Not strong enough.

She felt stretched. Pressed. Too weak, too flat.

If she kept using her power to push upward, the god's power would crush her—but if she stopped, she'd smash against the sidewalk in less than two seconds.

Images of Riana and Cynda flashed through her mind. This was it. She'd never see them again, or meet their babies, or find out what it was like to make love to Jake Lowell.

Jake . . .

He'd probably died when the apartment exploded. She had gotten him killed.

Hecate save him!

Something heavy slammed into her so hard she felt her ribs crunch. Pain fired through her whole body, making her teeth snap together.

She was flying again, only not downward. Sideways.

Strong arms cradled her and held her so, so tight. And that smell, that delicious, arousing, strangely comforting Caribbean mix . . .

"Jake," she whispered, sliding her arms around his neck despite the agony in her belly and sides. She held on with all her remaining strength.

Jake in his Astaroth form.

The chain of his talisman necklace pressed into her skin, and warmth coursed through her. Relief. Gratitude. Even after all he'd said about despising his demon nature, about intentionally keeping his human form, he had shifted to save her.

"Jake," she said again.

He didn't answer. He just flew.

Something about the tension in his muscles let her know he was in significant pain. That, she could relate to. Her body throbbed as she pressed herself into the hard curves of Jake's bare chest. His translucent pearly skin glowed in the moonlight and the radiance of the streetlamps. His huge wings, four of them, pumped against the dark sky, taking her away from the Windermere, then up toward the glittering stars.

Merilee did a mental check to be sure she was in one piece, noted the sharp, tearing pains emanating from her ribs, and sent what healing energy she could spare to soothe them. A flood of relief washed over her when she sensed her bow and quiver still intact, though pressed tight against her back by Jake's unrelenting grip. Her leathers had a few tears and holes, and there was a mother of a splinter lodged in her left shin, but all in all, save for the cracked ribs, she was doing well for somebody who just got exploded out of a building by a pissed-off god, then rescued out of midair by a big, silent demon.

From somewhere in the distance, she heard a soft shrieking, as if the Keres were trying to call to her again, directly from the forbidden slopes of Káto Ólimbos. The sound made her shake for a moment before she got hold of herself and lifted her head to peek over Jake's powerful shoulder.

Something red and glowing and snarling fired toward them across the New York City skyline.

Merilee went stiff.

Fucking wonderful.

She dug her fingers into Jake's neck. "I think the mad horned voodoo god is chasing us." Talking hurt, but she could stand it with a little force of will, and she hoped he could hear her over the increasing rush of wind.

"Let it come." Jake's normally calm, low voice was nothing but a resonant growl as he carried them out over open water. The Narrows, best she could tell, between

Staten Island and Brooklyn. The dark expanse looked endless and menacing, like a pit of nothingness stretched between lighted shores.

"That thing doesn't need to be loose in Manhattan," Jake added, still more growling than talking.

"Good point." Merilee eased her fingertips out of his flesh, then squeezed her arms against his neck even though the movement sent bolts of pain across her sore ribs.

Yeah, good point, great point, but insane.

There was no way they could kill the god. They'd have to try to wound it badly enough that it would retreat back to its own plane of existence. About as likely as bringing down King Kong with one kick to the shins.

When the god caught them, it would no doubt eat them. The thing had to be hungry after being trapped in book pages for who knows how long, waiting for Phila to complete its release.

Cool wind whipped across Merilee's cheeks as she raised her head again and glanced over Jake's shoulder. The roiling cloud expanded and barreled closer. "The mad horned voodoo god is gaining on us, Jake."

The only answer she received was a rumbling, carnivorous snarl.

Before she could use her air energy to stir the wind and propel them faster, Jake cradled her closer to his chest and plunged out of the sky.

Merilee's heart rate rocketed to full speed. She bit back a scream and dug her nails into the rippling muscles of Jake's Astaroth-pale shoulders. Cold wind rushed past her, chilling her right through her leathers, and it was all she could do not to let loose a burst of elemental air to stop them cold.

The stench of rot met her senses, mingled with sour water, dirt, and chemicals she couldn't quite sort out. Her nose seemed to go numb and quit smelling as she blinked at the expanse below them. Jake touched down abruptly yet gracefully, and he set her on her feet so gently that the vibration didn't make her double over from pain.

A quick examination told Merilee they were standing on an unusually high swell of ground and debris, and she realized where they were.

The Fresh Kills landfill on Staten Island.

Four square miles of New York City garbage, which were slowly being reclaimed and converted into a park.

Above them, the boiling red cloud came to a stop and churned in place, as if gathering menace and strength.

Okay. We're at Fresh Kills. Plenty of legroom to do battle with a god and get cannibalized. And nobody knows where we are, so our remains—if there are *any—won't even be found. No problem. Fresh Kills. That's just what we'll be.*

Her attention shifted to Jake as she got ready to tell him they were toast, but the lethal look on his face froze her words in her throat. Jake's eyes looked like flat golden plates reflecting the crescent moon. His lips pulled back to show large, pointed fangs, top and bottom, and a mouthful of sharp teeth.

Teeth made for ripping and tearing.

Equally fearsome claws jutted from his long fingers as he curled his hands into fists.

He was an Astaroth, but bigger and fiercer than any Merilee had ever encountered. A fiery glow seemed to burn through his skin, lighting him from the inside like some terrifying alien creature.

"Stay back," he commanded in a spine-digging rasp. "Let me handle this."

Merilee thought about arguing with him, but instinct kept her mouth tightly closed. Her breath kept catching and jerking, and she had to force herself not to look away from him. This Jake she didn't know. Not at all.

Uncertainty rattled her down inside, and her muscles alternated between shocky slackness and painful tightening. Maybe she should be more afraid of the demon eating her than the slowly descending god.

Jake gnashed his scary teeth, then turned and strode away from her, leathery wings flexing with each step he took. His arms were stiff and rigid by his sides, and a dark, dangerous energy radiated from his presence.

Murder. Devastation. Challenge.

Violence hung around him in the night like a prickly ebony cloud.

Merilee's hands shook as she took her bow from her shoulder and worked harder than usual to nock an arrow. Each action felt like knives ramming into both of her sides, but she ignored the pain and stared at demon-Jake.

How stable is he in Astaroth form?

Will he take out the god, then come back to kill me?

She couldn't go there.

Not now.

Right now she was a broom, even if she had no triad. Jake would fight, and she'd keep her vantage point and help. If necessary she'd clean up the mess. That was her job, right?

Merilee gathered her air energy and focused it around her arrow. Her eyes narrowed, tracking Jake, and she held her breath as the Vodoun Loa reached the ground.

The red cloud coalesced rapidly into what looked like a ten-foot crimson man with a bovine head and three horns. The air took on a new smell, the stinging rotten-egg odor of sulfur. The god screamed as it assumed its full form, and that scream sounded like the wounded, enraged cry of a baited bull.

Merilee's chest squeezed, making her shout with pain.

"Bosou Koblamin," she muttered, gasping, coughing from the sulfur stench and fighting back the misery of her ribs.

As she called its name, the strongest of the fiery Loas in the Petro Vodoun tradition lowered its horned head and charged across Fresh Kills, straight at Jake.

"Shit!" Pain made Merilee's grip waver, and her bow twitched up and down as she cursed again and tried to steady herself. Her mouth went dry as the pulsing red god closed in on Jake, who hadn't slowed at all. Demon and god barreled straight for each other.

She had to do something. Now. If that thing got its hands on Jake . . .

Merilee sucked in a rib-stabbing breath, let her Sibyl instincts claim her awareness, and loosed her arrow. With every ounce of elemental strength she possessed, she drove the shaft forward, aiming for one of the god's bull-faced eyes.

At the same moment, Jake launched himself off the ground, pumped his wings, and shot forward.

Merilee's arrow landed on target, lodging in the beast's right eye.

It let out a satanic bellow. One huge hand grabbed for the arrow. The other flailed and knocked Jake aside like a big white fly.

Merilee's gut twisted as Jake slammed into the landfill, sending up a spray of dirt, water, and trash.

She was at least three hundred yards away. No way she could reach Jake.

New tears blurred her vision. Her ribs screamed in protest, but Merilee ground her teeth, drew another arrow, fired, and powered the shaft toward the lumbering, roaring god.

This time, her shot went slightly wide and bounced off the thing's thick bull skull.

It wheeled to face her full-on, right eye bleeding and

obviously out of commission. Behind it, the Brooklyn coastline glittered, and to its left, the Manhattan skyline etched itself into Merilee's consciousness.

Her city. The people she was supposed to protect.

But Jake . . .

He still hadn't moved.

Even with her intense Sibyl vision, Merilee couldn't pick out his fallen form from the jumble of debris around him. And she didn't have time to keep looking.

The god's intact left eye swiveled down to glare at her. She fumbled with the arrow she had drawn, sweat coating her skin under her leathers as she tried to focus despite her jagged breathing and the hot-poker sensations lancing her ribs each time she shifted her weight. Artemis and arrows, she was going to puke from the pain and from worrying about Jake and from not wanting to die at the hands of a ten-foot bull god in the middle of a stinking landfill.

The god let out a grating howl and stormed toward her, covering ground so fast Merilee barely had time to fire.

The arrow left her bowstring, screaming forward, pushed by all the wind she could hurl without killing herself outright.

The god's gigantic head snapped backward as the arrow took out its remaining eye. It pawed at the bleeding hole in its bull-head—but it kept coming, blind and hard and fast.

As the god reached her and swept out its deadly hand to grab her or squash her, Merilee threw herself sideways. She struck the ground with brutal force and momentum, rolling through the trash-studded dirt. Her bow and quiver tore from her shoulder. Pain lanced her ribs. Her mind almost went blank from the torture and she wailed louder than the blinded god. She couldn't help it. The sound would draw the beast down on top of her, but Hecate help her, she couldn't stop crying out with each jam and jar and bounce.

The ground shook beneath her as the god stomped after her, no doubt tracking the noise she was making. Merilee couldn't breathe at all anymore. Debris and foul mud rammed into her eyes and nose. Her body felt like it was splitting apart at her rib cage.

I'm tearing in half.

And if she didn't, the god would crush her to bits in a matter of seconds.

She rolled to a stop, wheezing, her breath actually bubbling up her throat, liquid-filled and hot. Barely understanding, barely perceiving, she dug filth out of her eyes and watched the bull-faced god lower its horned head and bear down on the spot where she lay, absolutely unable to get out of its way.

A flash of silver-white caught her attention.

The flash streaked into the god, slamming it so hard and fast the big creature toppled sideways. It struggled to rise as the silver streak lashed at it again and again. Bloody streaks appeared all over the god's powerful body.

Familiar but deeply disturbing snarls filled the night as Jake pummeled his blind, shrieking rival. Gashes opened on the god's face and neck. As it managed to get to its feet, black liquid spurted onto the landfill dirt, sulfurous and sizzling through whatever it struck. Merilee coated herself with wind to be sure none of the acidic, poisonous blood fell on her.

Her vision swam and flickered, but she saw plainly enough that Bosou Koblamin's essence was beginning to fade.

Jake didn't seem to know he couldn't kill a god.

Didn't seem to care.

He sailed in and out almost too fast for Merilee to see. Darting, striking with his claws, ripping with his fangs. Then he simply attached himself to the god's back and seemed to be trying to tear off the ten-foot creature's head.

The god's essence rippled.

It let out a brain-rattling bellow and vanished.

The entire earth seemed to shake and buckle as the god fled back to its own plane of existence in one massive elemental surge.

Jake shot past the space where the creature had been, wings pounding, claws raking into empty air. Merilee heard his inhuman shout of triumph and shivered at the sound.

Then she wrapped her arms around her ribs and groaned and coughed up some blood of her own. Her vision swam again, and this time she almost faded out of awareness.

Clawed hands cupped her face, but didn't scratch her at all. The touch was gentle, concerned. Probing, yet very cautious.

This time, Jake's snarl sounded more distressed than anything.

Merilee's eyelids fell shut, and she couldn't open them.

Pain gripped her again, blotting out everything as Jake's strong arms lifted her off the filthy landfill ground. She almost didn't have time to hope he didn't drop her before her mind shifted into complete nothingness.

(11)

The Keres. I hear them shrieking.

Black feathers brushing my face, falling loose . . .

Why are they so loud?

What in the name of all the goddesses do those bloody fanged monsters want with me?

I can't—oh.

Oh, Hecate save me. He's *here.*

The Stone Man is with me.

Merilee screamed.

Her fists closed around black feathers and she held them as she ran even though her body was cleaving into fiery halves, stumbling across a vast landscape of trash and twisted metal. Seconds later, she was scrambling up the side of a familiar mountain. Bone-icing cold grabbed at her, and a chilled, heavy fog coated her in suffocating moisture.

Broken ribs . . . Cynda's voice drifted across her awareness, from somewhere very far away.

Punctured lung. That was Riana, louder, seemingly closer.

Andy came next with, *What the fuck?*

But Merilee was still on the mountain—was it Káto Ólimbos?—and the Stone Man was still coming.

He scrabbled up the sheer rock below her, chewing up the distance between them until she was sure she could feel him breathing down her neck. Hot breath. Flames. His presence burned her like he had changed into a fiery, murderous Vodoun god.

Then she wasn't burning.

Just . . . warming.

The mountain began to lose form, turn softer.

She heard the Stone Man's enraged roar. He grabbed her ankle.

She jabbed a fistful of black feathers at his eyes and he dodged. His fingers dug into her flesh, bruising and tearing.

Merilee.

Jake's voice, reaching for her, guiding her to him. She searched for him, saw nothing—but wait. A light. There beside her, and it was getting brighter.

The warmth in Merilee's body grew stronger.

Yellow-white light blazed in her mind. She felt it deep inside her, like a huge anchor weighing into her soul, diving into her mind, her blood, her cells, binding her together, at first holding her down, then drawing her inexorably forward. Toward the brightness. Toward the heat.

Merilee.

Jake's call and that light shielded her from all the horror around her. She focused on it, drew the resonance into her body, and drifted toward the sound, her wind energy building as she flew.

The Stone Man tried to yank her back, but he couldn't hold her, not with the strength of Jake's power dragging her in the other direction.

She slipped out of the Stone Man's grip and fell—no, no, not falling.

Waking.

Naked. Cleaned off. Under silky covers, in a soft, soft bed.

Her bed, in the library of the Upper East Side townhouse. She inhaled the smell of old books and aged paper and wood polish, felt the brush of her satin sheets against her bare skin. For a long moment, she waited for the nightmare to snatch her back—or to be hit with a brutal blast of pain from her injuries—but neither came.

Merilee almost sobbed from relief.

She opened her hands to be sure she wasn't holding on to any black feathers, and she was so glad to find them both empty.

Riana stood on one side of her bed, wedged between two piles of documents on ancient demons. Cynda and Andy stood on the other side, crammed against piles of notebooks holding details and facts Merilee had amassed over the last few years. Behind them, huge bookcases towered toward the ceiling, crammed with more notebooks and cups full of pencils. Merilee wasn't sure she had ever seen such comforting, beautiful things—her triad, Andy, and her books and papers.

Her triad and Andy leaned over her, all wild-haired, wild-eyed, and dressed in nightgowns. Cynda's gown was smoking, and Andy's, of course, was dripping. They had their hands outstretched, healing elemental energy flowing from their fingers directly into her needy, aching bones. Merilee could taste Riana's earthy contribution. She breathed in the heat of Cynda's power combined with the cooling, wonderful trickle of Andy's water ability.

Merilee realized she felt more healed than she should be, even with all of their efforts. It must be the water energy pushing things along at a faster pace. Merilee had no other explanation for why she felt so much better than she expected.

Even while Riana, Cynda, and Andy filled her with so much positive energy, their expressions were tense and worried.

Merilee's eyes moved to the foot of her bed where Jake stood, shimmering between human and demon form. One second he was all man, dressed in jeans and a sleeveless black T-shirt. The next, he was naked and translucent, winged and fanged and clawed, golden eyes flashing a mix of rage and worry.

Merilee.

He called to her in his Astaroth shape, and his voice reverberated so loud in her skull that she shouted, "What, Tarzan? I'm right here!"

Jake snapped back to man-form instantly. He stood, mouth open, beautiful blue eyes glaring at her so intensely she almost yelled at him again—this time for making her heart stop.

Athena's teeth, every inch of her hurt, but she was alive thanks to Jake, and she could tell that her healing had begun in earnest, thanks to her triad.

Cynda, Riana, and Andy eased back from their nervous stances, and turned loose the elemental energy they had been directing into Merilee's broken body.

Merilee tested her breathing, and everything seemed to work. Somebody had washed the crusty gunk off her face and hands, and when she glanced at her knuckles, she didn't see a hint of dirt smears or blood.

Riana rested one hand on her own swollen belly. With the other, she stroked the side of Merilee's head gently. "You scared the *shit* out of us."

Cynda underscored that point with a brief burst of flame from both of her elbows, melting the corner of Merilee's sheet.

Andy flicked her wrist upward and doused the fire with a spurt of water from the sprinkler overhead. "Damn, Cynda. There's like fifty trees' worth of paper within eight inches of your butt. Ease up."

Water droplets sprayed into Merilee's face, and she used the crumbly, burned sheet to wipe her eyes. "Sorry I scared you," she said, scraping a bit of mess from beneath her thumbnail. "It *was* a god, you know. Not exactly as easy as fighting stupid-asshole everyday demons." Her gaze flicked to Jake, who was keeping up his intense glare. "Other demons," she amended quickly. "Bad demons, I mean. You know. Asmodai and stuff."

At that, Jake's expression mellowed a fraction. His lips twitched, like he might be considering a smile. Merilee marveled at the fact that he was clean, too. He wasn't bruised, and he didn't have a scratch that she could see. Amazing. After all, she did sort of cause him to get smashed by the god's fist. Which she'd probably hear about in great detail later, when they were alone.

The silence in the room made her realize that Riana, Cynda, and Andy were staring at her. Or rather, from her to Jake and back again. "Listen," Andy said as she shoved a wad of damp red curls behind one ear, "if you're not about to die or anything, I could use some sleep, and all these piles of papers and notebooks make me feel claustrophobic."

Merilee flushed and did her best to look away from Jake. "I'm okay, really, but you don't have to—"

"Leave." Riana was still rubbing her own belly with one hand. "Actually, yes, that's a good idea. You need to rest, Merilee. At least a few days without patrol. No stress, no anything but good food and recreation." She squeezed her eyes shut, then opened them, her lightly tanned skin coloring red along the lines of her jaw. "I mean, relaxation."

"Yeah, right." Cynda's grumble was unmistakable. She held both of her hands under her stomach, as if to support the weight of her soon-to-arrive baby. "Look, blondie," she said to Jake, eyeing him like she might cook a part of his body any second now, "you're leaving with us, okay?"

"Cynda—" Riana started, but Cynda cut her off.

"Jake. Is. Leaving. With. Us." Her green eyes blazed at him, as if daring him to argue.

Without comment, Jake shifted into Astaroth form and glared right back at her. Merilee caught her breath, which hurt like hell, afraid he was actually planning to fight with Cynda. A day ago, she would have put all her money on her triad sister, but after what she witnessed tonight, the thought of Jake angry with *anyone* gave her a deep case of the shivers.

Jake made no move against Cynda. He also didn't flinch when fire broke out on the floor beside him. Instead, as Riana used her earth energy to smother the flames, Jake turned, strode to the balcony doors, and pushed open the big beveled panes of glass.

Merilee drew an involuntary breath as fresh wind rushed into the room and settled across her head and shoulders. She thought about calling out to him, asking him to stay, but she couldn't find the right words.

Jake paused, as if absorbing strength from that same moving air—or maybe waiting for Merilee to say something. When she remained silent, he didn't look back at her. He simply raised his arms and took off into the still-dark sky, wings pushing more wind behind him.

Andy stared at the space where he had taken flight. "Good going, Cynda. I think you really pissed him off."

Cynda sent a jet of fire through the open balcony doors. "I don't give a fuck. I piss everybody off—and he needs to leave her alone for now."

Merilee levered herself upward on her elbows, hoping her ribs didn't crack all over again. "He took out a horned voodoo god, Cynda. And what if I don't *want* to be left alone?"

When Cynda stared down at her, her green eyes were full of worry and anger. "Okay, great, yeah, I'm glad he fought well at Fresh Kills, but he's a demon, Merilee. Full-blooded. Not a mix—and he tried to kill me when we first met him."

"But he didn't kill you, even though he was being compelled to do so," Riana reminded Cynda, looking ever more weary with each word. "He saved Merilee's life tonight, and he's an Astaroth beloved by and *approved* by the Mothers."

Cynda's jaw worked for a few seconds before she spoke. "The Mothers didn't see him when he lost it with me a few years back—or when he brought Merilee home. He looked rabid. Like an animal. Like he could have—"

She stopped and looked away, but Merilee finished the sentence in her mind.

Like he could have ripped out my throat.

She remembered the sound of Jake's shout back at Fresh Kills, when the god vanished.

He saved me.

She remembered how he had slashed and torn at the creature, refusing to surrender for even a second, determined to kill what could never be killed.

But he saved me.

Still, Cynda was right. Jake Lowell was a dangerous man. Demon. Whatever.

So why don't I care?

Why didn't he scare her?

Merilee's eyes traveled to the open balcony doors, her insides aching in a new way, wishing he would reappear.

Meanwhile, Andy was busily guiding Cynda and Riana away from the bed, urging them out of the library. "For your own good, and especially Merilee's, let's get the hell out of here and give her some peace and space."

"We'll be back in a few hours," Riana called. "With breakfast."

"Delilah's still here," Cynda added. "She'll make you something Irish."

The door banged shut, leaving Merilee alone in the library's low, peaceful lighting.

The spot by the open doors was dark except for the moonlight, and no matter how hard she willed Jake to appear, he didn't.

She sat up without much discomfort and sighed, and the sound echoed in the room's expanding silence.

All of a sudden, she wanted to talk to him so badly the desire hurt worse than her rapidly healing ribs. She rubbed the sore spots, grateful for superior Sibyl healing capacity. By tomorrow, next day at the latest, she'd be good as new again, even though her own jagged rib bones had been sitting in her lung tissue less than an hour ago.

If Jake were here, she'd thank him for saving her ass at Phila's apartment, and again at Fresh Kills. She'd ask him what he thought about the book in the diagram that summoned Bosou Koblamin, and why Phila had it open to the image of that Egyptian god Thoth. She'd work with him to form a plan to search the city for Phila. She'd tell him she'd never met an Astaroth as powerful as he was. She'd ask him why he was so different from other demons of his kind.

Merilee hugged herself and rocked, eyes closed.

Then she'd probably kiss him. Lead him to her bed, and let him stroke and kiss and lick away every ounce of tension, every gram of doubt and pain and worry.

That light inside him was *so* bright. If any man, demon or not, could please her, satisfy her, truly make the world go away and leave her alone, capture her completely—it would be Jake.

Merilee turned loose another sigh, this one hurting her ribs enough to bring her back to reality. Even though somebody had cleaned her up pretty good, she still felt filthy, like she needed to wash any lingering traces of the landfill off one more time, for good measure. And change the sheets, too.

Slowly, carefully testing herself with each motion, she

slipped out of her covers, grabbed one of her notebooks, and recorded quick details of the fight at Fresh Kills, as well as her most recent dreams. Then she put the notebook and pencil on the floor by the bed and did a few standing stretches to ease her tightness and discomfort.

After she was sure all the movement wouldn't kill her, she gathered the bedclothes and pulled them into a pile, then dropped them on the floor beside a bookshelf. She'd get fresh ones from the closet—after a long, hot shower.

With one last glance at the balcony, she padded across the library toward the door.

Jake landed so quietly Merilee almost didn't hear him, but the soft thump made her turn around.

He stood holding the beveled glass doors, perfect skin shimmering a bright silvery-pearl. His wings folded to resting position as his golden eyes fixed on her, swept from her face to her bare breasts and below, all the way to her toes and back up again. His lips parted, and moonlight glinted off his formidable fangs.

I still feel so filthy. But her nipples tightened and heat rushed between her legs. A soft, insistent wind stirred off her skin, ruffling her hair before reaching out and wrapping itself around Jake.

Damn, but she hoped that wind didn't stink like the landfill, yet if it did, Jake didn't seem to care. Merilee trembled under his appreciative scrutiny, and she couldn't make herself move, not for anything, not with his eyes on her, touching her everywhere she wanted his hands and mouth.

He stepped out of the window to the floor, shifting as he moved toward her. No wings now. More solid. Darker-skinned. Scars flecked the perfection of his bare chest and muscled arms. He didn't re-create his shirt, but jeans formed over his tapered hips. Then he was standing in front of her, right in front of her, inhaling like he could smell the musk of her desire.

Merilee wondered if Jake could hear her heartbeat grow louder, faster—or her breathing, the way she couldn't get a full gulp of air. He could definitely hear the whistle of the growing wind as it circled them and pressed them closer.

Jake's blue eyes burned with hunger as he reached out and brushed a finger against the scar on her jaw, then gripped her bare forearms and pulled her against his hard, smooth chest. Her sensitive nipples rubbed against the ridge of his muscles, sending blazes of heat from her chest to the throbbing spot between her legs.

His obvious erection pushed into her belly, and Merilee almost moaned. The wind she created did moan, and a few books rattled on nearby shelves.

The man hadn't even kissed her yet, and already she could feel that steel-hard cock inside her, pumping into her depths, and oh, sweet Aphrodite, she wanted him right here, right now on the floor, even if it shattered all of her barely knit bones.

Jake bent his face toward hers.

Merilee closed her eyes and moved against him, electrified by the feel of him, the sense and smell of him, so hot and spicy and perfect, just what she needed, just what she wanted, now, damnit, *now*. Her lips tingled, waiting for his.

But nothing happened.

She tensed, and her air energy ebbed, quelling the wind.

Merilee opened her eyes, confused and disappointed.

Jake was studying her, his expression flat, unreadable, except for his eyes, which flickered and stormed and brooded all at the same time.

He let her go, pushing her gently away from him.

"I'm sorry," he said, his voice husky with what had to be desire.

Merilee gaped at him, then more or less hurled her naked body back against his and wrapped her arms around his neck. "Are you kidding?" she murmured, then kissed him with the full force of her arousal.

Jake groaned against her lips, then kissed her back, pushing her head down with his barely controlled strength. She felt his embrace, swift and rough and hard, squeezing her, setting off the agony in her chest and belly and ribs, but she didn't give a damn, not at all, because he was kissing her.

Yes, yes, yes. He was really kissing her.

His tongue delved into her mouth, twining with hers, and she started to sweat and ache in better ways, deeper ways. His hands traveled to her hips and stroked the curves, then gripped her ass, pulling her bare sex against his rough jeans and that tempting, hot, and growing bulge.

Merilee arched into him, rubbing herself against the zipper, reaching for the snap with both hands as once more, her wind whispered around the library—and once more, Jake's lips broke apart from hers. So sharp this time, so firmly and abruptly that she felt it like a blow in the center of her being. All air in the room stopped moving.

For perhaps the first time in her life, Merilee didn't find any quick retort, any sudden humor. No asinine joke lunged into her mind to spare her from the moment's intensity, and she didn't see anything at all to laugh about. She just wanted to cry. Maybe even beg.

Jake stepped away from her and she instantly shivered and ached and almost sobbed to have him back again.

Had she ever wanted a man this much?

A demon . . .

But she didn't *care* what he was.

She had to have him.

Except he had turned from her now, and he was flickering between human and demon so quickly it reminded her of an old-style broken film hopping from image to image until it snapped and left nothing but a glaring white screen.

"I'm sorry," Jake said again as he reached the open balcony doors once more, finally settling in his Astaroth form.

He glanced back at Merilee, who was deciding if she could grab him and hold on to him tight enough to keep him from flying away. Only her aching ribs gave her pause—that and the look of pain on Jake's face.

Once more, he moved his eyes, now a bright, glittering gold, over her naked body, nearly setting her completely on fire.

"I want—" he started. Stopped. Looked away from her, out into the night.

Merilee held her breath and thought about grabbing Jake again.

"This can't happen," he said quietly. "It wouldn't be right. It wouldn't be fair."

And then, with one flap of his leathery wings, he lifted himself through the window and vanished into the stars.

It was almost a full minute before Merilee got control of herself enough to march to the open doors, look out at the moon, and yell, "Right and fair? What the *hell* are you talking about?"

She got no answer, of course.

And she still didn't feel like joking or laughing or even making a weak, pathetic wisecrack.

She stewed about Jake's words all during her shower—which was miserable, and she had to admit, a little dose of reality with respect to her sore muscles. As she soaped her arms and legs, her muscles groaned and protested, and she realized that if she and Jake had proceeded to sex, she probably would have needed morphine before sunrise. Not that the realization made her any less pissed off or frustrated and overall, completely miserable, as she climbed out of the shower and toweled herself dry.

The ass.

Right and fair.

Was he a head case?

What wouldn't be fair? Why wouldn't it be right?

Was he secretly married or something? A monk in disguise?

To quote Andy, *What the fuck?*

"Seriously," Merilee said out loud as she stalked—stiffly and a little gingerly—back into the library and slammed the door behind her. "What the fuck? Men. Demons. I swear to every goddess on Olympus."

She shed her towel and slid under the covers, muttering to herself and stewing even more fervently until she realized that she hadn't brought sheets out of the hall and made the bed.

A little burst of her startled air energy shoved the nearest bookcase back a good half inch.

Merilee sat up and gripped the perfectly tucked and arranged fresh bedclothes, glancing around the room.

The dirty sheets were gone, too. Her bow and quiver and arrows had been retrieved from the landfill and propped against a bookcase, the notebook and pencil she had used to record the fight and her dream rested neatly atop the stack of papers closest to her bed—and all the stacks seemed neater. Nothing moved that she could tell. Absolutely nothing rearranged. The papers had just been carefully compacted and patted into more stable towers.

And the balcony doors were closed.

While she showered, somebody had come in and—no, not somebody. Jake. It had to be. She was sure of it.

And it struck her that Astaroths *could* be invisible, couldn't they?

"You jerk," she whispered, not really meaning it. "Are you in here with me?"

She quieted her breathing, turned loose her Sibyl instincts and listened and watched. Strained, even, to catch the slightest motion, the smallest sound.

But . . . nothing.

Merilee sank back in the bed, refusing to cry or laugh. She didn't know whether to be relieved or disappointed.

A few minutes later, as she drifted between waking dreams and deeper sleep, she couldn't shake the sense that she wasn't alone. That Jake was there in the library guarding her, watching over her, protecting her from anything that might menace her—even himself.

12

Bartholomew August seethed over his latest failure to make inroads with the air Sibyl Merilee.

Only a few days earlier, he had attempted to reach out to her mind, as he had done with all of his victims—and something repelled him yet again.

Earlier this day, he had circled near her place of residence, only to meet a solid wall of raw elemental power he couldn't penetrate. As strong as steel. As strong as—his own.

How was that possible?

The dead witch's protections should have been well dispersed.

So, what new energy shielded Merilee from him now?

Grinding his teeth from the building rage, August led Klaus—not his real name, of course—off the street and into the building August had prepared. With a few deep, slow breaths, he managed to let go of his frustration for the moment and pay attention to the surroundings.

It was a magnificent old warehouse, turn-of-the-century architecture, now fully restored and cleansed of all life energy that was less than desirable. Inside the warehouse, the cool, pitch-black air smelled of bleach, cleansers, and the sage August had instructed his Legion servants to burn to rid the warehouse of the residual signatures of whatever pathetic creatures had once labored in this facility.

"Don't you worry?" Klaus asked, his normally resonant voice tight and nervous as they moved into the cavernous space. "Traveling like this, without body-guards, without weapons?"

"The Sibyls have more than enough to keep them busy." August offered that platitude, knowing it would suffice. He suppressed a fresh wave of rage at his new protégé's foolish question and walked a few more steps into the main room, the soles of his crocodile driving shoes making the faintest whispering sound on the hardwood floor. August needed no bodyguards, no base henchmen with weapons, to see to his safety. Klaus should realize that by now, but the politician seemed to have difficulty accepting realities outside of his limited understanding of the tangible world.

"I would never travel unescorted without offering the witches of Greece, Ireland, and Russia an appetizer, a taste of what we have planned for them in the very near future," August added, knowing Klaus would enjoy it.

As for the New York Sibyls and Merilee Alexander, the Sibyl he most wanted, August almost had sufficient information about them at present—thanks to his many sources, especially the woman and their wretched off-spring. Head count, rough number of Astaroth demons and OCU officers assisting them, and good schematics on their current headquarters. Soon, he'd have even more, and probably enough to act.

And he *had* offered them a few scant diversions this night, enough to keep them away from his traveling route and destination, just outside of Harlem. Let them think the Legion was in trouble. Oh, yes. Let them think the Legion was disappearing because the numbers were low. He had suffered heavy losses in the attack on Motherhouse Ireland two years ago, but he had also gained a few converts, and learned valuable lessons about Sibyl powers and fighting strategies.

Perhaps enough to claim Merilee and any others who caught his fancy, and eliminate the warriors who wouldn't be useful or attractive to him. Enough to finally remove this last obstacle between him and the righteous cleansing of the world's filth.

August had to swallow a snarl as he sensed Klaus strolling up behind him.

It was time for those of strong mind, of higher intellect, to take back the positions due to them, in government, society, and life. It was time to seize power, worldwide. To initiate not just the right to act, but the *moral imperative*.

Still, he had to admit, Klaus's anxiety was not unreasonable. Those tattooed women of the Dark Crescent Sisterhood, they were worthy adversaries. Which was more than he could say for most who had fought his Legion—and his other organizations—across history. Alone but for a handful of deluded law enforcement officers, the Sibyls had held him off for nearly a century.

No, he wouldn't be sorry to sway a few like Merilee to his cause. It would be a much better use of her talents and intelligence.

August let Klaus get close, but not too close, then walked a few more steps, confident his employees had left not a scintilla of dust in the five-story structure. Nothing would soil the light sand shades of his three-piece pinstriped suit. Italian silk. The best humans had to offer.

"Lights," he commanded, and the voice-activated system responded, pouring an impressive amount of wattage into what would become Klaus's public face to New York—and thus, the world.

The huge space glittered in the bright glow of hundreds of lamps. Rows of desks. Phones. Posters. Stacks of flyers. All prepared. All ready to receive more than two hundred workers.

Klaus's mouth dropped open.

The effect was much as August had hoped.

Keep lesser men, albeit key men, awed and indebted. August had lived by that principle for years now.

As for Klaus, the man couldn't help his unfortunate inferiority. He was handsome, articulate, and for his intellectual level, quick-witted—but he was a pawn. To Bartholomew August, a man who had known too many years to speak of in polite company, most people served that role. His genius was that so few people ever knew it.

"What—how can we possibly pass this off?" Klaus asked, obviously stressed near to his meager capacity. "We don't have the funds for something on this scale."

"The paper trail is neat, and all perfectly legal." August did his best to sound sure of himself, comforting. The slightest bit obsequious. "We've had a number of recent donations which make us more than competitive in this race, I assure you. And this place—this place will keep the money rolling in, to support your cause."

August let his voice rise slightly at the end of his sentence, conveying a touch of anxiety, as if he wanted Klaus's approval. Klaus needed the illusion of control. August was a generous man. He could offer that, and sustain it.

Until the moment arrived for Klaus to die.

Klaus examined the expansive, luxuriously remodeled warehouse, and August knew he was imagining it filled with busy campaign workers (with a few beautiful hot young things mixed in, no doubt). The man already could see his banners, posters, and buttons stacked against the walls. He already could imagine the interviews, the press coverage of the grand opening of his new national headquarters.

The door clicked, and Klaus jumped so hard his teeth clamped together.

August didn't react to the door, or to the almost unbearably loud sound of Klaus's shock. Sometimes, it was all August could do to keep his acute senses in check, but he managed.

One day, I will live in a world where the only life-forms are calm . . . and quiet.

As he expected, two more men entered the building, cued to approach by the flaring of the warehouse lights. These specimens, in their caps and jeans and nondescript dark jackets, were far below what August considered human. Even Klaus knew enough to react to them. He recognized these Neanderthals, of course, from their previous uses.

The candidate looked briefly stricken, then recovered himself.

That's my boy. August smiled. *Everyone gets their hands dirty. Only, I can wash mine, can't I? By setting up this exchange here, I've ensured you can't walk away clean.*

From his pocket, August withdrew a single folded page and handed it to the troglodyte in front. "I need this man at the *other* headquarters tonight, in the private room we constructed in the basement. Alive. No mistakes, or I'll take your hides in payment."

The man glanced at the paper, a group photo from the Fordham University catalog, with a single face circled. He nodded, then handed the paper to his companion.

August gestured to a bag he had placed in the corner of the big main room, before he had brought Klaus for this little visit. "You'll find everything you need there—and below, in the basement."

At this, the Neanderthals gave him matching heavy-browed frowns.

They eyed the bag, no doubt realizing what it contained. Bits of cloth. Simple talismans for simple, yet deadly creatures.

The two thugs didn't have much taste for the supernatural, but August knew they would comply. Awed and indebted, like all good pawns.

These two would do anything for proper payment, and the false "status" he had given them by allowing them to sport the Legion's crest on their forearms like true inductees. He had sold them his Legion bill of goods, and they were nothing if not perfect, starry-eyed converts.

August glanced at his signet ring, a coiled serpent. It gleamed in the bright lighting, as if giving shine to the greatest of August's many fronts and hoaxes.

The Legion itself.

A vehicle. A means to a glorious and well-deserved endgame with this shabby, deteriorated world.

As the men collected the bag and headed for the basement door, August smiled at Klaus once more, this time showing a few teeth.

Klaus had gone very, very pale.

Yes, he knew what was in the basement, too, and he had no taste for the brutish but highly effective Asmodai demons.

"Perhaps we should be going." August gestured to the door and allowed the perfect measure of tension and concern to lace his tone. "*Before* they return with our demon friends."

With no further prompting, Klaus all but ran back out to the waiting streets.

13

Black mist draped the mountaintop like a burial shroud.

In the moonlit night, nothing looked real or right or normal, yet everything seemed familiar.

Merilee's heart thundered as she let herself down from the brief lift of her air funnel. Wind stroked her skin, then abandoned her. Her feet touched rock and dirt, and she knew, knew *she had been to this cliffside before.*

And it hadn't been pleasant.

Káto Ólimbos.

No!

I'm not supposed to be here. It's a transgression. It's forbidden.

On instinct, she reached for her bow—and found it missing

Shit. I'm not even wearing clothes.

She sucked in a breath and the copper stench of carnage filled her senses. Cold seeped through her skin, chilling her deep inside. Death itself seemed to ooze around her, drifting in that black fog, obvious even though she could see only a few feet in each direction.

Everything inside Merilee rebelled against standing on the bleak, rotting mountain.

This was a mistake. Time to go.

She had to get away from here right now.

Too late, *her mind whispered in a rough, harsh voice that didn't even sound like her own, as three or four black feathers drifted out of the mist to land at her feet.*

They're coming.

My life is forfeit now. I came here of my own free will. I'm just a suicide, as far as they're concerned.

Mouth dry, chest tight, Merilee reached for her wind. Her elemental power grabbed so harshly at her own insides that her gut ached—but nothing happened.

"Damn it!" she yelled out loud, but the sound fell flat against the fog.

She could barely force in her next breath.

A shadow emerged from the unnatural mountain mists. Another, and another. Five, ten, too many to count, too fast to distinguish.

Confused, disoriented, Merilee assumed a defensive stance, circling as the dark shapes clotted into a solid wall around her. She felt like a novice. Her hands shook in ready position, and her muscles went weak from the primal terror coursing through her body.

The shadows began to take shape. Tall and lean, almost gaunt. Limbs, then torn, feathery wings. Heads with long, wild black hair. Red robes spattered with blood and filth. Hooked fangs, stained with Athena only knew what, curled from the creatures' mouths, and gore-coated claws pressed into their palms.

The Keres gazed at her with eyes blacker than space itself, moonlight glinting off the white patches of their fangs. Despite their horrific appearance and the grave-stench rising from them like a putrid miasma, the creatures struck Merilee as distinctly . . . female.

But nowhere near human. Not even demon.

The circle of black winged monsters tightened and moved toward her.

Merilee tried to react, but fear froze her in place.

This is where I die.

The Keres grabbed at her arms.

Claws tore into her bare skin.

Blood rushed across her neck and shoulders. Bolts of pain blasted from her head to her fingers.

Merilee screamed, but the sound got lost in a whir of wings.

Her feet left the ground.

Wind shrieked past her as if it didn't recognize her as an air Sibyl at all.

What'shappeningwhat'shappeningGreatHerawhat—

Blood from the claw gouges streamed across Merilee's eyes. She struggled. Her arms wouldn't move. Her skin burned everywhere the creatures gripped her.

She screamed again. Kicked harder. More rough, clawed hands snatched at her legs. Agony! She hurt. She hurt everywhere, and she couldn't move even a damned inch!

Her brain lurched as they shot forward, flying so fast Merilee's skin pressed in against her bones.

Higher. Higher.

Through a fog of misery, Merilee wondered if the Keres planned to hurl her off the mountain. She almost hoped they would.

So much pain . . .

Abruptly, the pressure eased—but not the wrenching throb in her hundreds of cuts and stab wounds.

Merilee felt herself move downward and hang in place, as if suspended in the talons of a giant eagle.

She was staring at the Earth, closer, closer, until she could make out towns and cities—flattened. Floodwaters lapping at neighborhoods. Buildings burned and ruined. Great holes in the countryside.

What the hell? Did somebody set off a bomb?

With a twist, the creatures turned her north. In seconds, she was gazing at New York.

Lower. Closer.

Streets littered with dead Sibyls.

A few triads were still standing, still fighting—but they couldn't last much longer.

Revulsion and disbelief surged through Merilee. Her

breath came so short she got dizzy. She wanted to scream again, but when she opened her mouth, no sound came. She couldn't hear or smell, or feel anything but frigid cold and the terrible, tearing pains in her neck, shoulders, and arms. All she could do was hang there and stare, and see, and refuse to accept the absurdity her eyes registered.

Elemental powers and human hands and weapons tore apart houses and buildings . . . and suddenly, she knew he *was there. She felt his presence as brutally as the dig of talons in her skin.*

He *was in the middle of it all. Behind it all. The man carved from cold gray stone.*

Merilee forced herself to squint at the heinous scene below her.

He *was standing a few hundred yards away, on the shore of what looked like Ellis Island, in front of the Statue of Liberty, arms folded, thin, raptorlike face sharpened by a vicious, bloodthirsty expression barely visible underneath locks of black hair.*

"Take me lower," Merilee urged the Keres, ignoring the blistering ache in her arms. She had to see the Stone Man better. She had to find out more.

The creatures let her go.

Just . . . dropped her.

"No!" Merilee plummeted down, down toward the Stone Man.

She tried to call the wind howling around her—nothing.

Reached for the air, for her power—nothing!

The Stone Man unhinged his jaw and opened his terrible beak of a mouth.

Silvery moonlight glared off huge, sharp teeth—

Jake sat up and threw his sheets onto the floor, sweat coating every inch of his flesh. His room—*not* the room he had known in childhood—was empty except for a bed and two dressers. The space around him lay dark and undisturbed, but inside him, the world crashed down in murderous chunks.

Merilee.

Tortured by the Keres.

Then eaten by him. *The Stone Man.*

That Stone Man bastard looked damned familiar, almost like an ibis, the symbol for that Egyptian god Phila Gruyere had been focused on when she summoned her Vodoun god.

Whoever—whatever—he was, if he so much as snapped one fingernail off Merilee's hand . . .

Jake hurled himself out of bed, grabbed his jeans, and stepped into them as he shouldered open his bedroom door. He had trained the Astaroths for hours over the last two days, but at night he had been checking on Merilee constantly, even sitting outside the library door. Tonight was the first night he left her alone, and now this.

He lunged up the steps from his third-floor bedroom to the fourth floor. His wings punched against the skin of his back, almost emerging in response to his alarm for Merilee. Jake ground his teeth and held the wings back as he ran down the hall and pulled up short in front of the library's locked double doors.

Behind him, groups of wind chimes suspended from the ceiling jerked and clattered.

"Merilee?" He pounded on the solid wood. He'd yank the doors off their hinges if he had to. "Merilee!"

His voice echoed through the townhouse, drowning out the erratic twitch of the chimes.

From inside the library came a loud thud, followed by what might have been a dictionary recitation of every swearword known to humanity.

Merilee's voice.

Relief rushed through Jake. He stopped banging on the library doors and rubbed his throbbing knuckles.

Was she okay?

He glanced from his knuckles to the doors.

If she was okay—what the hell had he just seen?

Voices rumbled from the floors below. Doors opened. The ground gave an ominous shake-and-rattle, and footsteps sounded in the townhouse halls.

Jake ignored the commotion. In OCU headquarters, there was always *something* going on somewhere. Whatever it was, it wasn't important to him, not at the moment.

He focused on the library doors, willing them to open and show him Merilee in one piece, no wounds, no bruises or missing legs.

The library doors slammed against the outer walls, powered by a terrific gust of wind that ripped one set of chimes free from its moorings. The little copper pipes clanged together as the set crashed to the top step and bounced down to the landing.

Merilee stood staring at him, mouth open, blue eyes wide, her blond hair scattered and dancing across her forehead like soft wisps of down. She was wearing a sheer blue tank top that reached to her thighs, apparently put on hastily and backward.

The outline of her figure was clearly visible against the thin, rippling fabric.

Jake blinked in the increasing wind, and his mind scrambled and rang like the frantic chimes.

She sleeps naked.

His cock bucked against his jeans as he remembered what it felt like to hold her body against his own, to feel her hard nipples pressed into his chest, the muscles of her ass pliable beneath his hands as she arched from pleasure at his touch.

He squeezed his aching knuckles to focus, and gazed

from her angry face to her neck and the smooth olive skin of her nearly bare shoulders. No vile cuts. No streaks of blood.

Thank God.

Before Jake could ask about what he saw in his dreams, Merilee's blue eyes flashed. She stomped out of the library, came straight up to him, stood on her toes, stuck her face in his, and shouted, "What the *fuck* did you do that for?"

She punched his chest with both fists.

Not gently.

Jake coughed as air swirled and whistled around them in one great dust-stirring funnel. Even without the small tornado, her nearness unsettled him in ways no woman had done—and in his two years of traveling, he'd made it his business to know as many females as possible. Research. Learning. Understanding. And hell, catching up to his body, his age, his life *now*.

This woman, though . . .

He fought a desire to take Merilee in his arms, close his eyes, and breathe in her gentle scent of white tea and honey.

She would probably beat him to death with wind-devils if he tried.

"You kiss me and then you vanish for two friggin' days," she was saying. "I don't care if you *were* training demons down in the basement. I don't care if you *are* so goddamned handsome you could be a billboard model. You could have stopped in. Said hello. Spent a few minutes? I'm not some toy you can pick up and play with and then toss in the corner. I don't—"

With what little self-control Jake yet possessed, he raised his voice over the low roar of the wind and said, "You were dreaming about the Keres again, and dead Sibyls. About the Stone Man. Only tonight, he was a carnivorous statue that looked like an ibis."

Merilee's fury and resistance changed to abject shock. The tornado stopped abruptly, and the air on the fourth floor went completely still. Chimes tinkled to a rapid halt, and the sudden silence pressed against Jake's ears.

Merilee rocked back off her toes, arms hanging loose at her sides.

"Was it a prophecy?" Jake took her hands in his, worry mounting as he saw the truth in her face. "I know air Sibyls sometimes see the future in their dreams."

She didn't pull away from him. "How do you know—you saw my dream?" Her voice came out quiet and low, like a child whispering a secret. "As in, dreamed it with me?"

Jake nodded, still battling a fierce urge to wrap his arms around this woman, *his woman*, touch her, check each joint and curve to make sure she was real and safe.

Merilee swallowed as people clattered up the stairs behind them. "Shit, Jake. That's weird. We need to talk to the Mothers about that."

Jake lifted Merilee's wrists toward his lips. He wanted to kiss her fingers and soothe her, but pain flickered across his consciousness.

He dropped Merilee's hands and looked down.

The waist of his jeans was on fire.

He pressed out the flames with his palms and turned to find himself facing his brothers, Riana, Cynda, and Andy, along with Sal Freeman, who looked asleep on his feet. The men and Andy all had on boxer shorts or briefs. Andy's boxers and T-shirt were wet. Everyone else was dry.

"You're leaking, Andy," Merilee said, her voice still too quiet. She sent a burst of warm air toward her friend, drying the wood floor beneath Andy's feet.

"Sorry." Andy scrubbed a hand through her long red curls, and kept dripping water from her elbows.

Freeman reacted to the sound of Andy's voice, eyes coming open and his cheeks flushing. He moved closer to her and put his arm around her back, and Andy leaned into Freeman's touch.

Jake shook his head.

Finally. Shit.

He was about to say that out loud when he realized Cynda had a sword raised in front of her large gown-covered belly. Flames danced off the menacing blade as Jake's brother Nick said, "Steady, firebird."

Cynda's green eyes narrowed, and smoke rose from holes in her gown. "Jake, I thought we had an understanding about you staying the fuck away from Merilee while she healed. Explanation, please?"

Jake didn't respond. He glanced at his other brother, Creed.

Creed gave him a look like, *On your own, buddy,* and draped his arm around his very pregnant wife, Riana—who had on a gown, too. Silver, to match the daggers in both of her hands. Riana's dark hair hung in glossy waves at her shoulders. Elegant, almost stately—for a woman who could sink a city with a burst of her elemental earth power.

They don't trust me yet, Jake realized. Merilee's triad. Her fellow warriors of the Dark Crescent Sisterhood. Despite everything he did at Windermere and Fresh Kills to save her—or maybe *because* of that—they thought he was a threat to her.

Freeman's apologetic look told Jake he had seen the problem, too, and that he regretted it.

After Jake's behavior two years ago, he couldn't blame the women for how they felt, but the realization still dug at Jake's gut. All of that seemed so long ago to him, so far away.

Can't they see what Freeman sees, what I've made of myself? That I'm—I'm almost human now?

"I had a bad dream—" Merilee began, but Jake raised a hand to silence her and took over, wanting to shoulder responsibility for his own actions.

"She had a bad dream," he repeated to the armed women and the dripping water Sibyl. "I'm the one who made all the noise, banging on the door to wake her."

Riana lowered her daggers, looking surprised.

Cynda lowered her sword, too, though her expression said she'd really rather behead Jake. The fire Sibyl's green eyes traveled from Jake to Merilee. "How did he know?"

Merilee hugged herself and shivered. "I think he had the nightmare with me. At the same time, I mean. He dreamed the same dream."

Shock registered on Riana's regal face. "What?"

"I need to speak to the Mothers about this," Merilee said as she came to stand in front of Jake. "All of them. Tonight."

As if to punctuate her statement, the still-intact chimes in the hall began to ring in a rhythmic pattern Jake recognized as an incoming message.

Cynda stared up at the dancing metal tubes. "Calling the Mothers will have to wait." Her expression turned tense to match Riana's, and Jake guessed that both women were frustrated at their inability to respond to the emergency. "Asmodai spotted on Sixty-first, near Fordham University. They're headed straight for the dorms."

Blood surged through Jake's veins.

Demons menacing a college.

This he had trained for. At least in this situation, he knew exactly what to do.

Merilee groaned, and Jake heard the weight of her fatigue at having to pick up all the slack for the North Manhattan triad. "The Young Democrats are camped out at Fordham for a rally."

Andy wiped a stream of water off her forehead, put her hand on Freeman's arm, and beckoned to Merilee. "Come on. You're still low in the energy department, so we need to stick together on this one."

Riana and Cynda stood aside, still looking resentful and irritated at their own incapacity to fight. No doubt if they were in top form, they would have insisted Merilee stay behind and continue to rest for another couple of days, but as it was, they didn't have that luxury.

Nick and Creed kissed their wives, then jogged toward the steps.

Despite his lack of invitation or orders, Jake waited the two minutes it took Merilee to pull on her leather bodysuit and grab her bow and quiver, then walked beside her down the hallway.

She didn't object.

Neither did Cynda or Riana, though Jake was more than aware of their gazes burning into his back as he followed Merilee down the stairs.

14

Bow tight in her hand, polycarbonate goggles in place, Merilee jogged through the glowing New York night, across the stretch of grass in front of the Fordham University amphitheater. With her were Andy, Sal Freeman, and ten OCU officers in full riot gear who had disembarked from the tactical van left at the curb at the front of the college.

Merilee felt the absences of Riana and Cynda so acutely she kept shivering, even though it wasn't cold.

Of course, she wasn't wearing her leather face mask. She never did, if she could get by without it. And Riana wasn't here to bitch about it, was she?

Wind whipped around Merilee's shoulders, and she held to the element, drew it toward her, around her, taking the scant comfort it offered. Above her, the waning crescent moon hung like a baleful frown in the dark sky. She totally understood that her triad sisters couldn't fight, not at this point in their pregnancies—but the world still seemed canted, completely wrong, without them.

Merilee squinted through the specially treated polycarbonate lenses of her goggles, designed to pick up telltale sulfurous traces left by Asmodai, the dangerous foot-soldier demons used most often by the Legion. Asmodai had to be created from an element such as fire or air, with a liberal helping of dirt to give it shape. It took a long ritual and a lot of space, and they were only good for a few hours, with a range of a few miles at most—but the fuckers could do a ton of damage.

So far, nothing showed in the goggles even though

the response team was already running down Amsterdam Avenue. Lights blazed from buildings and streetlamps, and from a slight distance came the ever-present whirr and thrum of traffic.

"You okay?" Andy murmured, adjusting her new weapon, an HKP-11 underwater dart pistol from the Special Boat Service frogmen. It was waterproof (since she drowned three standard firearms in the first month she manifested her talents with water), with five darts, good for short distances even on dry land—but a total bitch to reload. Andy's shots had to count, big-time.

The night air seemed to shimmer with a breeze and the winking lights of nearby cars, buses, and cabs.

Merilee nodded in spite of her massive unease, and gripped her bow even tighter. "I'm fine."

She forced her focus back to the pounding of boots on grass as the OCU assault team rushed toward Fordham. Andy flanked her on her left, while Sal Freeman held a position on her right, Glock drawn, black NYPD raid jacket flapping in the air stirred by Merilee's elemental energy. The police officers all wore Kevlar body armor, and sported a full complement of elementally locked bullets—specially treated metal that would take down any demon, no matter what substance had been used to create it.

Jake kept pace directly behind Merilee. She felt his presence deep inside, sensed him as a tangible force, like a solid, moving wall. After Fresh Kills, she knew he would be worth his weight in demon kills. Knowing he was there made her feel better, which in turn freaked her out another notch.

I hate this. I fucking hate not having my triad.

Not that anyone's fighting with a whole group. Not anymore.

The remnants of the South Bronx triad—Bela Argos and her young air Sibyl, Devin Allard, would be forking down from their usual territory to meet them. Serlena and Tavis, the young earth and air Sibyls from the South Manhattan triad, had sounded the alarm.

Merilee tightened her jaw to control her trembling.

Those girls were out there somewhere in the dark, defending students and rally-goers. Facing Asmodai. Hoping help would come in time.

Her heart thumped, and her breath came shorter and shorter with each running step the team took. At least she wasn't cooped up in the raid van. This close to target, they didn't bother loading up—they just booked it on foot. Faster anyway, in Manhattan.

As they swept onto Fordham's campus, abandoned political banners and signs hung from buildings and trees. No students or campaigners still out from the rally, though. The plaza seemed deserted. Thank the goddesses for small favors.

But Serlena and Tavis—so young! Little more than adepts. The seasoned fire Sibyl in their triad had been murdered two years back, and still no replacement was available.

We've been maimed. We're holding this city by a thread.

Merilee tried to breathe normally.

Her senses told her that Astaroths—three of them—were flying above, invisible and deadly.

So they did have additional backup.

Assuming the surfer boys stayed on task and on target. Jake had only had a few days of working with them while she was recuperating. Would that little bit of combat training make a difference?

Merilee's fingers curled tight around her bow.

They approached the brightly lit buildings of the campus, brushing past staked campaign signs hawking this candidate or the other. Bartholomew August and his Peace Warriors, Alvin Carter and the Strength Now group, Martin Jensen and his New Deal–New Day—it made no difference to Merilee. She just wished the damned election would come and go, and the crowds and rallies would stop, cutting off at least some of the opportunities for the Legion to kill or make chaos.

As she moved past a small grove of trees, spurts of dark crimson flared across her lenses. She pulled up short, gasping more from nerves than exertion.

"There." She pointed at the dormitory with her bow tip. "And there. And there!"

Andy and Freeman, also wearing goggles, saw the traces at the same time she did, and they were already gesturing, deploying OCU officers in different directions, fanning out between the residential buildings on the campus.

"Hearts or heads!" the officers yelled in unison as they split up and thundered forward.

Merilee's muscles bunched.

Hearts or heads. Use the weak points and bring the demons down.

Her mind buzzed. Everything looked so strange from the front of the assault line. Air Sibyls usually fought from vantage points in trees and high places—rarely from the ground—and she desperately missed the comfort of Riana's earthy energy and the searing power of Cynda's fire.

"With me," Freeman barked to Jake as Merilee and Andy peeled left and away from him, hammering toward the side of the large dormitory literally covered with demon trace. The other Astaroths would shadow the rest of the OCU and help as much as possible. That was always the plan, yeah, but the minute Jake got some distance from her, Merilee's gut spasmed. She wanted to call him back, keep him next to her.

I'm losing it.

But his energy—steady, like Riana's, and forceful,

like Cynda's. And he had already saved her twice. She had a feeling he'd do it again, if she needed him.

But why the hell did he stay completely away these last few days?

Roars and gunshots exploded in the direction Jake, Sal Freeman, and the OCU had gone.

Droplets of rain—Andy's barely tamed water energy—splattered Merilee's cheeks. Andy drew water from the moist air, the ground, and unfortunately, from water mains, sewers, toilets, the ocean—whatever was handy. At least this water smelled fresh as it seeped through the scent of city exhaust, trees, dirt, and the unmistakable sulfur of Asmodai.

A high, piercing scream cut the night in front of them, followed by the unearthly bellow of a Legion demon.

Merilee drew an arrow and nocked it without breaking stride. Andy steadied her HKP-11. Rain fell harder, and started to spread. A jet of water ripped up from the ground nearby. One more water main shot to hell.

"Control yourself!" Merilee shouted to Andy as they plunged into the semidarkness at the dormitory's edge, burst into a small grassy courtyard surrounded by trees and benches—and came face-to-face with five towering, glowing Asmodai. The evil Legion demons almost filled the small gardenlike space about a hundred yards in front of them.

Shit! Too many.

But they had to stand, fight. The dorm—the students—and it sounded like OCU had its hands full over at the law school.

The few lampposts still shining shorted out from the rush of elemental energies colliding over the grass and bushes, and the courtyard went dark.

An Asmodai exploded into bits of earth and dust, thanks to a well-placed dagger hurled by Bela Argos.

The South Bronx earth Sibyl stood on one of the benches and yelled, more a furious wail—as she guarded what looked like a body on the ground below her. Merilee's Sibyl vision picked out every detail of Bela's appearance, from her exotic, slanted eyes to the dark hair pulled back in a tight bun, making her look twice as dangerous. All around the courtyard, the ground shook with her rage.

Merilee looked at the body below Bela, and her whole being lurched.

Great Hecate. That's Devin on the ground.

The darkness next to the dorm seemed to get darker, but Merilee's sharp eyes tracked Bela as the earth Sibyl aimed a dagger at one of two demons nearest her. The demon waved a fist, and a blast of air knocked the blade to the ground.

Air Asmodai.

Merilee steadied herself on the shaking earth, aimed at one of the beasts—but the other two lumbered around to face her and Andy.

Normal-looking men one second, and the next moment, too tall, and the following moment, too short. Human, yet not human. One had on a NEW DEAL–NEW DAY T-shirt. Slack, vacant faces, and those horrible eyes, just empty, burning sockets. They bashed fists against tree trunks and the side of the dormitory, leaving trails of black flame wherever they touched.

These are made of fire.

Andy raised her dart pistol and squeezed the trigger. A massive blast of water lifted from the ground in front of her, first a geyser, then a streaming jet, following the dart, forcing it forward, deadly and blinding-fast. The wave and projectile struck the first demon directly between its flaming eyes. The beast exploded into spits of flame, charring the grass in a wide circle even as Andy's wave crested against the dormitory wall and shattered five windows.

From inside the building, people screamed.

"Damnit." Merilee squinted at the windows, hoping, praying no students had been injured.

No time. Can't go there.

"Stay put!" she yelled to Andy, and ran forward again as Bela's rumbling earth energy poured over her. "Cover me, but try not to use your water."

Merilee dropped to one knee for balance. She loosed her arrow at the second fire Asmodai and coated the shaft with a blast of wind for speed as it flew, guiding it, guiding it—yes!

The elementally locked steel tip buried itself in the demon's heart, and the thing blew up with a sulfurous *whump,* rattling tree limbs and sending sticks spinning in all directions.

This was easy pickings.

Almost too easy.

The thought made Merilee shiver.

She drew another arrow from her quiver just as Bela took a hit of Asmodai wind in her face. Bela stumbled off the bench and fell flat over Devin's body.

The ground stopped shaking.

Both air Asmodai blasted forward, feet hardly touching earth, and leaped for the fallen Sibyl.

Merilee jerked out of her stance. No shot.

"Goddamnit!" Adrenaline slammed through her system. She jumped to her feet and charged toward Bela. "Take the left one," she yelled back to Andy. "And be careful!"

She'd pull the fuckers off the Sibyl and bash their brains to a pulp if that was her only option—or let Andy tear up half the mains in the city and drown the bastards.

They couldn't lose another warrior. For the sake of all the goddesses, they couldn't lose Bela.

Something wet and cold slammed into Merilee's back with the force of a speeding van.

All the breath smashed out of her lungs and she flew forward, tumbling, her bow flying out of her flailing hands.

"Shit!" Andy screamed, seemingly from two hundred miles away. "I'm sorry! I'm sorry!"

Water jammed itself into Merilee's ears, eyes, mouth. She pushed against the wave, forced a shield of air into a bubble around her, and crashed herself straight out of the moving water-wall, slamming hard into the ground about fifty feet from Bela and the Asmodai. Her goggles shattered from the impact and fell off her face.

She sucked air as pain tattooed every square inch of her body. Her chest seemed to tear in half from the pressure of reinflating, and water squirted out of her nose. Her fingers dug into wet dirt and grass.

Air howled around her, almost a funnel. She bit her own lip, pulling her wind energy to a manageable level.

Where the hell is my bow?

The quiver? Arrows probably broken . . .

Everything smelled like water and dirt.

"I'm sorry!" Andy was still yelling and the wave, oh, shit, the wave!

The water, easily two stories high, plowed over the grass and broke over Bela, Devin, and both air Asmodai.

Bodies flew.

"I'm sorry!" moaned Andy.

"Shut up and shoot something!" Merilee yelled back. She staggered to her feet, groping for her weapons.

Nowhere. Nothing.

The Asmodai were up. Bela and Devin weren't.

Merilee threw herself between the demons and the fallen Sibyls, facing the beasts and the brick face of the dorm.

Merilee coughed out another lungful of water and readied herself to take on the Asmodai with her fists and feet. She could barely get a full breath, but she snarled as her heart pounded against what felt like a broken rib.

Air burst around her in powerful eddies as the demons approached, and she did her best to keep it off Bela and Devin, and channel the air into punishing funnels.

The demons might get her, but by the strength of Artemis, she'd take a piece of them with her.

Demon-wind screamed in Merilee's ears, trying to batter her. She met it, grabbed it, controlled it as both demons charged her, and fed it into her funnels.

Why wasn't Andy shooting that frigging dart gun?

Because she's freaking out. She's not trained as a Sibyl, not enough. Fuck, fuck, fuck!

This was insane.

So much for easy pickings.

Both Asmodai blasted through her shield-funnels and reached her at the same time.

Merilee screamed as loud as she could, battle rage bursting out of her in wide swirls of wind even as one bleak thought drilled itself through her consciousness.

Game over.

15

Asmodai roars filled Merilee's senses.

Her wet leather bodysuit strained against the force of the air the demons pushed at her. She stumbled, then flew backward, slamming into earth and rock and something metal.

Park bench. The one next to Bela and Devin.

Her shoulders burned. Her lungs felt like fists had punched holes through her entire chest.

Gotta get up now. They'll tear me in half.

She forced herself forward, rocking like a sprinter about to take off, and jumped to her feet, wheezing.

The demons came at her again, shoving air like battering rams. Merilee steadied herself, rode the wind, let it lift her. Ignoring the pain in her back and the squeeze in her chest, she got off a perfect roundhouse kick.

Her foot struck the left-hand demon in the head so hard the beast spun in a circle, staggered, and fell. The second one grabbed her by the throat and pulled her to the ground.

Her air choked off. She looked into the swirls of black wind where the thing's eyes ought to have been. It opened its mouth, spewing more black, rotten wind into her face.

She thrust both fists between its arms, smashed outward, and broke its hold.

The other Asmodai was getting to its feet.

The demon closest to her reached for her again—but its head turned sideways and suddenly tore right off its body.

Merilee coughed and grabbed her throat with both hands as the Asmodai exploded into a fetid swirl of wind and mud and shredded grass.

The night cleared to reveal Jake standing quietly, arms up, hands extended, where the demon had been. His expression was blank yet stern, but his normally blue eyes blazed with gold-white fire. He was fully visible, fully human, yet Merilee saw the shimmer of wings, the hint of fangs and claws, almost like an afterimage surrounding the man.

Behind him stood his three Astaroth trainees, Darian, Quince, and Jared, lips pulled back, massive fangs wet and gleaming. They gazed at Jake with blazing golden eyes, approval and respect obvious on their pale white faces, and made no attempt to interfere in the battle.

Jake brushed off his palms to clear them of dirt, turned to face the remaining demon, let it grab for him—and calmly reached forward and tore its head off, too.

The demon exploded into fits of sour-smelling air.

Oh. Sweet. Holy. Shit.

The strength that took!

As the three Astaroths growled at the destruction of their foe, Merilee coughed again and shivered.

She scanned the courtyard—no more Asmodai. No demons at all . . . except for Jake and his Astaroth trainees.

She had never seen anything like what Jake had done in her entire life.

Wasn't sure she wanted to, ever again.

When Jake turned to face her, she had to fight every instinct she possessed not to back up a step and give the man *plenty* of room. The golden blaze in his eyes faded until she saw blue again, and she managed to think enough to rasp, "Uh, thank you."

"Are you injured?" His deep voice came out low and even. Determined and controlled, yet clearly concerned.

"No," Merilee said, fingers still massaging the skin of her neck, and heard her own voice shake. "Just bruised. It'll heal fast."

Jake touched her neck, and Merilee felt a slight shock. A burst of heat. She jerked back in surprise.

With a frown, Jake looked at his own fingers, then lowered his arm and didn't try to touch her again. His stance relaxed a fraction, but that didn't calm Merilee one bit. Damn, she was shaking all over. And wet. And getting cold.

"Freeman has Andy," Jake reported in his bass, matter-of-fact tone, never taking his unsettling gaze from hers. "She's not hurt. Two OCU officers wounded, one dead, ambulances on the way." He paused, then glanced back toward the three waiting Astaroths. Shadows seemed to flicker across his handsome, frightening face. "You can go now, and thanks. All the Asmodai have been handled."

Handled. Gods and goddesses and all the earth's demons. Handled. *No kidding?*

"The fight seemed too easy," he said as the Astaroths vanished, as if he might be discussing some research paper or theoretical battle simulation. "Do you agree?"

Merilee swallowed hard, actually welcoming the pain of her sore throat muscles to keep her grounded—not too sore, though. Not as sore as they were a minute ago.

She raised her fingers to her throat, which didn't feel so puffy or painful, and kept staring at Jake.

In the two years she had been fighting alongside Astaroth demons, she was used to the surfer boys functioning like Harrier jets, swooping in, slashing with claws, or picking up enemies, throwing them—never anything like what Jake did.

He ripped off their heads.

With . . . his . . . hands.

Jake looked away from her, then moved to her right, and reality came whistling back to Merilee's numb brain.

Bela.

Devin!

She hurried to follow Jake, who had knelt beside the young blond air Sibyl. He touched Devin's throat, held his fingers still, then closed his eyes and shook his head.

As he stood, Merilee reached Bela, who was, thank the goddesses, moving and moaning on the ground.

And sobbing.

Tears streamed from Merilee's eyes in response. She sat right down on the grass and pulled the dignified, powerful earth Sibyl's head against her chest and cradled her, rocking Bela gently, in case she had broken bones or injuries other than the horrible, horrible wound to her heart.

Another triad sister gone.

Another young one, dead.

We're running out of trained fighters. What the hell are we going to do? What's Bela going to do?

Bela was alone now. The legendary mortar of the South Bronx triad had no pestle, no broom. Nothing and no one but herself, and the woman's empty, torn sobs ripped at Merilee's insides.

She kissed the top of Bela's head. No words came to her.

Words wouldn't help, anyway.

Somebody started swearing, and Merilee vaguely realized it was Sal Freeman.

"Is Bela hurt? Do we need another ambulance?" Freeman's voice was thick with frustration as he gestured toward Merilee and Bela. Behind him, six OCU officers limped along, clutching weapons. They clogged the entrance to the courtyard.

"Bela isn't wounded," Jake said to the captain, and Merilee wondered how Jake could be so certain—yet she was certain, too, wasn't she? With tear-blurred eyes, she shifted her gaze from the dormitory wall with its shattered windows, to the trees, to the dark street-lamps, then back to Jake, Sal Freeman, and the OCU. She stroked Bela's head with one hand, and her Sibyl instincts told her again, more certainly, that Bela's physical injuries were like her own, minor and manageable.

What kind of instincts did Jake have, anyway?

Jake was saying again that the fight had been too easy.

Merilee's grip on Bela tightened.

Devin was dead.

What was easy about that, damn it?

But Freeman was agreeing. "It was a diversion." He gestured over the heads of his officers, back toward the main campus. "While we were busy over here, the bastards smashed into a laboratory and snatched a professor. A grad assistant told us the doc's name was Holston. Derek Holston."

Merilee's eyes widened, and her heart beat even faster. Holston. Holston. That name was familiar. She tried to make her thoughts function, to do her job as an air Sibyl and remember. Damn it, remember! Where had she heard—

"Derek Holston was married to an air Sibyl from the North Staten Island triad," Jake supplied before Merilee could even begin to retrieve the information from the archives stored in her brain. "She was killed two years ago, in the Battle of Motherhouse Ireland."

Jake then proceeded to give the Sibyl's age, years of service outside the Motherhouse, the name of the Mother who trained her, the manner of her death in the final charge against invading Legion enemies, and the date of her interment back in Greece.

One of the shorted-out lamps flickered and came on,

bathing Jake in a soft yellow glow. In his black NYPD jacket and jeans, he looked so . . . so normal.

For someone so completely *not* normal.

A second of silence passed before Merilee realized her mouth was hanging open.

Bela Argos had gone still in Merilee's arms.

Merilee looked at the earth Sibyl, who sat up slowly, wiped her teary eyes, and stared at Jake, obviously dumbfounded, too.

Sirens wailed, coming closer by the second.

The OCU officers scattered to meet the paramedics.

Meanwhile, Freeman seemed to take Jake's human-computer routine in stride. He must have learned to expect that from Jake, maybe even counted on it. Freeman was already outlining search vectors to hunt for the professor, but Jake held up a hand to stop him. He turned away from Freeman and strode over to Merilee and Bela, then knelt in front of them, the lines of his body tight, both fists doubled.

His first glance was for Merilee, and it was soft, and kind, and so gentle she sucked in a fresh breath and held it to keep from crying all over again.

Jake turned his attention to Bela. Sincerity radiated from his blue eyes as he said, "I'm sorry for your loss."

An odd light seemed to flow out of Jake, just a tendril, linking his heart to Bela's. Merilee blinked at the image and it was gone.

Did I imagine that?

Bela didn't speak—or do anything to hurt Jake.

Completely out of character, especially given that Bela Argos had a long history of being suspicious of any and all demons, even those fighting together with the OCU.

"New York's few fire Sibyls will be busy with the search for Derek Holston." Jake's eyes shifted to his tight, large fists and back to them. He opened his hands as if making a deliberate effort to relax, but his next words seemed to hurt him. "With your permission, I'll take Devin home."

Bela stared at Jake.

Merilee did, too, gradually processing his meaning, and the truth of his words.

Fire Sibyls handled communication. It would have to be a fire Sibyl who used projective mirrors to open ancient channels to Motherhouse Greece. Probably more than one fire Sibyl—in order to transport Devin's body back to the City of Gods for a proper ceremony and burial on the Motherhouse grounds, as befitted any fallen warrior. Transporting an object as big as a human being took a lot of elemental energy. Cynda couldn't even do it alone, since she was so far along in her pregnancy. That kind of effort might bring on early labor.

So unless there was some other solution, Devin's body would have to wait for burial, which would be beyond painful for Bela. For all the Sibyls.

But Jake was offering a solution, wasn't he?

Astaroths had wings, and they could fly faster than most fighter jets.

"You'll take her to Mother Anemone?" Bela asked, her voice catching between each word.

Jake held Bela's gaze. "Directly, and to no one else."

Bela studied him with her dark, fierce eyes. "You aren't afraid to go to the Mothers?"

Jake's answer was simple and immediate. "No."

Merilee imagined she could hear the creak of the Earth on its axis as Bela hesitated. She knew Bela couldn't believe Jake was so willing to expose himself to the dangerous, powerful Sibyl Mothers. Even with all she knew about Jake's history, Merilee still couldn't quite believe it, either, since the Mothers were only marginally receptive to nonhumans.

And a nonhuman carrying a dead Sibyl . . . well, that could get dicey.

Bela let out a breath, then nodded her agreement.

Jake gave Merilee one more brief, heart-squeezing look, then stood and walked over to Devin.

Merilee coughed to cover her sharp intake of breath, but she couldn't do much to stop the little burst of wind that followed Jake and stirred his short blond hair.

Freeman folded his arms, and Merilee could tell he wasn't planning to stop Jake. In fact, Freeman looked serious and respectful, like he was impressed with Jake's decision. Jake quietly asked Freeman to see to Merilee's safety until he returned, which made her consider planting an arrow in Jake's perfect, squeezable ass.

When he looked at her, though, the genuine concern in his blue eyes held her in check.

Tarzan, damn it. No, wait, Batman. Batman's a lot sexier than the King of the Jungle, but still just a total complete male.

With his back to Merilee and Bela, Batman-Jake took off his NYPD jacket, his body armor and his weapon—Astaroths could shift simple clothing, but nothing too complex, and nothing metallic—and placed them on the ground at Freeman's feet. In the light of the single lamppost, he stepped clear of the captain, and the muscles around his shoulders rippled and shifted.

A sound escaped Jake, like he might be in terrible pain.

Merilee tensed.

She had seen Astaroth demons shift in and out of human form before, and they hadn't ever seemed to be as uncomfortable as Jake was.

Not like this.

And it never took this much time.

Was something wrong? Only two days ago, she had seen him shift easily, without so much effort.

Jake's muscles rippled again. He held out both arms like he was pleading with the stars and moon to help him, and he shouted so loud and long that chills broke out along Merilee's neck.

Just when she was sure he couldn't keep standing, two sets of wings burst out of Jake's back and unfurled, and his body sagged.

Bela caught Merilee's hand and squeezed it, and Merilee had never been so glad for human contact in her life. She was terrified Jake would collapse on the ground, that the transition had cost him something vital and he'd die right there in front of them—but he seemed to collect himself and marshal his strength.

Unlike other Astaroths, Jake didn't become invisible, or even completely translucent with his wings present. In fact, he stayed fully human in form this time, except for those wings. As soon as he seemed able, he bent forward and lifted Devin from the ground, and cradled her to his chest.

In that brief second before he took off into the dark night sky, as he stood there so tenderly holding the fallen air Sibyl, he looked just like a Christian painting of an angel, preparing to take a faithful servant straight up to heaven.

An archangel of mercy . . .

The image transfixed Merilee.

Even as she grabbed for something silly to say to herself to beat back the pain of yet another death—not to mention her deep emotion at seeing the way Jake tapped into the demon self he so hated to make sure Devin got the honor she deserved—that endless vein of humor inside Merilee ran dry. Gravity glued her to the earth more firmly than she remembered experiencing in the past. Jake looked lighter, but she felt heavier, as if she herself carried the weight of her fallen comrade and his sacrifice, too.

Then Jake was gone, and Bela was staring at her, and Freeman was striding toward them saying, "What can I do to help, Bela?" And then to Merilee, his expression softer, with a lot more worry. "Andy's in my car. She's pretty upset. Public Works is raising hell about hydrants blowing up all over the damned place. Can you help before she floods Central Park?"

16

A few days after the assault on Fordham University, August sat in the secret room's wooden chair. Behind him, back pressed against the impeccably soundproofed wall, stood the woman, holding a pair of gloves and a bag of stolen tools.

She had her head down, but she made no move to interfere.

August paid her little heed, instead studying the sobbing man chained to the room's only other chair, this one a stark, dull metal. The man's skin bore dozens of cuts, stabs, and other wounds. His eyes, when open, rolled and widened, streaked with red like his skin and the floor beneath his feet. His ribs pressed harshly against his skin, as if they might burst forth and put an end to his suffering.

But not yet.

August knew the man wouldn't last much longer, a day at the most, possibly two. He felt a measure of pity and regret. His prisoner was not a fool, not the typical piece of societal flotsam August eliminated for his own gain. He wasn't even a pawn in August's ever-widening American political machinations. No, this man was a scientist, an intellectual, and taken for August's purely personal pursuits. The man had been bound to a warrior of the Dark Goddess. As such, his intellect and bravery were, at the least, admirable, if insufficient.

"Have you told me all you know, Professor Holston?" August worked to keep his voice neutral. "All the weaknesses of the air Sibyls?"

Holston answered him by turning his face to the wall in shame, and weeping yet more openly.

This brought a sniff and cough from the woman, who was overly prone to feeling sorry for August's human prey. He clenched his fists, but managed not to hit her or the prisoner for their weaknesses. After all, he owed Holston now, for his valuable information.

August had been frustrated in his psychic pursuit of Merilee Alexander. Contrary to his experience with all his other targets, Sibyl or otherwise, he hadn't been able to dissolve her defenses to reduce her resistance, her willingness to fight, and make her ready for capture. This one kept eluding him. He would get close, reach into her thoughts—but something always threw him back before he could weaken her resolve enough for him to make a physical approach and take what he had claimed for his own. He needed to understand the situation better—hence his capture of the good professor. Who better to advise him than the consort of one of the air Sibyls?

"Come now, Professor." August wasn't above offering some comfort, extending the tiniest bit of false hope for mercy, to get what he needed. "Your wife is long dead. You showed her no disloyalty by disclosing a few of her secrets under duress."

"You'll never get to Merilee," Holston rasped, keeping his face turned to the wall. "The old woman there, she's been telling you the truth. Merilee *is* as strong as any Mother. One day, she'll *be* a Mother. Her whole triad has that kind of power."

August studied the broken man before him and mused over that bit of information.

Was that part of the problem?

Excess elemental energy?

"Merilee's triad sisters are incapacitated by late-stage pregnancy," August said, delighting in the fresh out-surge of misery from Holston. "Certainly, they're weak links, like the untrained water Sibyl and the human police officers comprising the OCU."

Holston gave him no answer, confirming that suspicion, and opening new potential avenues of attack against Merilee's formidable power and resolve. Thanks to Holston's earlier confession, August already had a better handle on at least two of the Lowell brothers, who were apparently Curson demon halflings created by the late and great Senator Davin Latch and his unstable but useful biosentient wife, Raven. The brothers had mastery of their talismans and would not be easily compromised, so August left them out of this final discussion.

Derek Holston groaned, and his breathing grew more shallow. August soaked up the outflow of the man's life energy, took in Holston's misery like elixir, letting it strengthen his muscles, his mind as he pondered what he did—and didn't—know.

The final Lowell brother, the youngest, was Jake, an Astaroth. Definitely a wild card, an unknown, and unfortunately mostly a mystery to Holston.

"Let's return to Jake Lowell," August said, determined to glean something useful about this one potential catch in his plans for Merilee.

"Please, just let me die." Holston's voice was only a whisper, drawing a growl from low in August's throat. A warning. A hint and a promise, that Holston's pain could be increased, no matter the cost.

The woman shifted against the soundproofed wall, her movements so soft and slight few would have detected them. August sucked in the flow of her unhappiness and discomfort. So satisfying.

"Professor," August began, but he didn't need to continue.

Another groan issued from Holston, then an almost

imperceptible nod. Perfect. August smiled. The professor had traveled far beyond any measure of resistance, which would save them valuable time for a few more inquiries.

August leaned forward and clasped his hands, gazing at his fading prisoner. "You're certain Jake Lowell issued from Latch stock, the same 'parents' as Creed and Nick."

The professor let out a slow breath, then managed, "The Latches murdered their youngest son, Jacob, to create him, yes."

Trying to offer some humanlike encouragement, August nodded. "Relate what you know of his history again, please."

The professor complied, going over Jacob's politically explosive "murder," and how Senator Latch brokered his child's ritualistic death into political capital, all the while using the new Jacob, the Astaroth demon, for his own personal gain as well. Professor Holton then covered how Jake had fallen under the control of a half-crazed nun with a grudge against fire Sibyls, and nearly eliminated Cynda.

"That's the fascinating part," August said, almost conversational in his thoughtfulness. "That he managed to resist commands placed on his talisman, that he had power enough to push back against that which tried to enslave him. And how he ultimately rallied many of his fellow demons to assist in the downfall of our Legion attack on Motherhouse Ireland."

Holston made no response, but the woman muttered to herself, growing ever more restless as she waited for August to have a use for her. August ignored the minor distraction, and once more prided himself on not getting physical with the ancient bitch. She was so frail, too likely to break—and too well conditioned to dispense with as yet.

"Powerful indeed, this Jake," August continued, studying Holston's closed eyes and agonized grimace. "Unusual for his breed. What could have given a created demon that kind of strength? Surely the Sibyls have some theories. Did Raven Latch make some critical error in her ritual—or was it something inside the boy she murdered? Something about that poor, unfortunate child?"

Of course, Holston had no answer for that, or he would have provided it.

Had the Sibyls spent time and effort on that question, or was that another potential chink in their powerful elemental armor?

August stood, moving quickly and silently, to pay his debt to Derek Holston by bringing him to a swift, painless end. It took little to no strength to twist the professor's weak neck until it snapped.

The woman let out a strangled little grunt as the man died, but she didn't move until August beckoned for the gloves. She brought them to him and stood quietly as he pulled on the thick leather and made sure it was secure.

Then he took the bag of tools from her and completed Derek Holston's final role—that of victim of a heinous and perverted sexual assault and murder.

This usage of the good professor, it was very *much* tied to August's broader political ambitions.

Just for kicks, and for an extra infusion of misery and discomfort, August forced the woman to watch.

When he finished, and after he milked every bit of horror and disgust he could from her, he took the gore-spattered tools and her quaking, blubbering wreck of a body out through the secret exit and used his own command of the elements to seal it well enough that no human could tell it had once been a door. Dragging the woman behind him, August covered the tunnel's length in a handful of strides, sealing it behind him as he went.

Of course, he left a little gift behind.

August smiled as he hauled the woman out of the tunnel mouth, through a hole in the ground floor of a neighboring building.

"Thank you, Professor, for your valuable information," he said, and smacked the woman on the backside to get her moving toward the door. "Thank you very much."

17

Jake's muscles bunched as he slammed his wings up and down, barely keeping himself aloft in the night sky. Winds swirled off the dark Atlantic below him, fighting his efforts, driving him first right, then left as he ground his teeth and tried to hold course. Salt air and spray stung his eyes, and he knew he was flying weak. Flying low.

Too damned bad.

He didn't care.

He hated flying and all that it represented—but Mother Anemone's worried face swam through his thoughts.

Thank you, agapitos, she had said when he arrived in Greece with the body of the air Sibyl Devin Allard, to present the poor woman for burial at her Motherhouse.

But after the ceremony, Mother Anemone had lectured him for choosing to stay in solid, human form for such long stretches that his Astaroth "advantages" were beginning to fade.

Even now, as he sped toward New York City, Jake felt the pain of that stubborn decision to remain day in and day out in human form, and the bodily stress of so many recent sudden shifts.

His wings seemed clumsy and unnatural. His body felt like a stone in the air. He found it hard to remember the sensation of lightness, of insubstantial existence.

Could he even become invisible if he wanted to?

A few days ago, it had been easy, driven by so much pure emotion to make certain Merilee was safe and comfortable.

But now, after claiming his human form again, his Astaroth abilities were definitely not cooperating, as if he had ignored them, then overused them and maybe burned them out.

Good.

Yet . . .

Show me, Mother Anemone had demanded. *Agapitos, my dear, my favorite, you must use your demon essence consistently, frequently, or risk losing it and never being whole again.*

Jake had refused to try. *You can't make me human, so I'm doing it my way.*

A partial existence is no existence. Mother Anemone's green eyes had studied him like one of her archival record books as she gestured to the damnable bit of jewelry around his neck. *Even if you cannot transform into Astaroth form, you won't be freed from your talisman.*

Jake drove himself forward in the bright moonlight. The sooner he reached land, the sooner he could ditch the wings—and maybe leave them ditched, forever. Besides, four days was a long time to stay gone from his responsibilities with the OCU.

And Merilee.

Knock it off. She's a fantasy. Just a dream you've let yourself play with far longer than you should.

Merilee was a fellow warrior in the fight against the Legion. She needed extra help he could provide while her triad sisters waited to give birth. It couldn't be more than that between them, because he wouldn't let it be more. No one had a clue what would happen if an Astaroth and a human mated beyond transient sex. He would *not* limit anyone's life as his own had been limited, or risk someday being trapped by his talisman, perhaps ordered to kill the woman—or the family—he loved.

Despite arguing over *that* decision, too, Jake and Mother Anemone had parted on civil, even warm, terms. But Jake had made himself clear to the Mother, despite his infinite respect for her.

Don't push me.

As he sped through the night, he gained strength. Staying in his demon form, even partially, lent him power. A sensation like being freshened, or renewed. Which galled him.

The glow of the United States's eastern coast competed with stars on the horizon, and the ocean's brine took on a stronger smell. Traces of oil and garbage. Dead fish. Civilization.

Another few minutes of this torture, and his flying would be finished. Maybe forever. No matter what the circumstances, he didn't want to let loose his wings again.

I'm human, damn it. He closed one fist around his talisman as he flew. *Controlled by this fucking piece of gold—but human.*

Was Merilee out tonight, patrolling, on guard for Legion activity?

He didn't like the thought of her vulnerable, without him or her triad. Though Andy, Freeman, his brothers, and the entire OCU offered powerful backup—when Andy controlled herself reasonably well.

Instinctively, Jake reached out with his mind, searching the coastline for Merilee's powerful energy signature. As an Astaroth, with his attention fully focused, he could find anyone if he knew how they felt in the grand scheme, the brightness of their particular inner light.

Merilee's signature had always been so intense. It

fascinated Jake, how such a strong woman could subjugate herself to any leader. Not that Riana Dumain was a poor mortar to her triad. Quite the opposite. To bat cleanup for heavy hitters like Riana and Cynda—no easy task, he was certain. He supposed Sibyl triad hierarchy, with earth Sibyls always choosing and leading the triad members, was much like police command. Necessary organization, to prevent chaos and move the team forward.

Jake homed in on the life signs of New York City, street by street, passing up the small handful of people with paranormal abilities, even Sibyls he sensed weren't Merilee.

As his thoughts swept over Central Park, her signature flared like a torch.

Too bright, even for her.

Jake's teeth clenched.

She was fighting. Maybe in trouble.

Blood pounded in his ears and he soared high, all four wings beating the salt air. Miles passed in fractions of a second. Ocean spray coated him, followed by the water of New York Harbor.

Jake blasted past the Statue of Liberty, sped back into his city, hooked around the Chrysler Building, and sailed toward mid-park, near Seventy-ninth. Taillights stained the edges of his vision a brilliant neon red, and the heat and stench of automobile exhaust clogged his senses.

He had fangs now, and claws. Jake could feel them extending, along with that lightness of body he had struggled to achieve for hours and miles.

Goddamnit, not now!

He tried to pull back on his demon essence, grab hold of his human form and regain some control.

But . . . no uniform. No gun. He had left his gear with Captain Freeman, the night he left with Devin Allard's body.

Shit.

Shifting between demon and human forms, Jake spied the dark granite structure towering atop Vista Rock. Belvedere Castle. That's where they were.

He folded his wings and shot toward the shadowy, unlit loggia where Merilee's energy signature blazed like lightning.

As he soared toward one of the four archways in the open-air stone corridor, Jake counted eleven other life-forms, seven on Merilee's side and four at the other end of the long covered walkway.

We've got numbers, at least.

Gunshots cracked through the New York night.

Jake burst through the castle archway, hit the stone floor of the corridor as a human in jeans, and ran toward Merilee, who was about fifty yards from him. Andy had her right flank, with two OCU officers charging forward on her left.

Several prone figures lay another fifty yards in front of them, and Freeman and Creed stood between Jake and the Sibyls.

Merilee shimmered like a beacon in the darkness, outshining everyone else, casting a golden glow on the Gothic stone structure around her. For a moment, Jake felt like they were back in time a thousand years, on a covered stone bridge, suspended in the middle of nowhere.

His vision dimmed back toward human, but still he could see her in her form-fitting leather bodysuit, bow firm in her delicate, deadly hands. She had an arrow nocked, string taut and ready. The air hummed with her elemental energy, and wind rushed past Jake's ears.

As he reached Freeman and Creed, Jake finished processing the scene before him and pulled up. The wind in the loggia died to a simple breeze, then stopped, leaving the cool April air oddly motionless. Jake's demon senses receded another notch, and the night grew darker.

"Hey, bro." Creed holstered his SIG. "About time you got back from vacation."

Jake shot Creed a quick glare, understanding that this battle was over.

The OCU officers were checking pulses on the prone forms and shaking their heads. The four bodies on the ground—all of which appeared to be human—twitched a bit, but Jake knew they were already dead. The bitter, nutty scent of poison hung in the darkness.

"We gave two of these bastards leg wounds," one of the OCU officers examining the bodies called. "Nothing fatal from our weapons—I think they took themselves out with cyanide pellets."

Freeman tapped the mike on his shoulder and backed away from the Sibyls. Jake knew when he got far enough from the elemental energy Merilee and Andy created, he would call for the medical examiner.

"They were trying to create Asmodai," Creed explained as he swiped a wet shock of black hair out of his face, pulled out his flashlight, and clicked it on for the benefit of the OCU officers. Being half demon, Creed didn't need the light any more than the Sibyls or Jake did. "One of the Sibyl rangers was close by and sensed the energy surge. These freaks had all the materials—and I think they were about halfway through the ritual. Probably planned to send them into the Republican rally after-parties. Too bad we couldn't take one alive to question about Professor Holston's disappearance."

Blood still hammering through his veins, Jake glanced at Andy, who stood in a growing slick of water. Little tongues of water licked up from cracks in the stone around her, splattering against her raid jacket.

"That's another set of water pipes shot to hell," Captain Freeman muttered as he returned, but he didn't sound too angry. In fact, he was smiling at Andy. His hands twitched like he wanted to touch her.

Andy flushed. "Hey, I knocked one of those assholes off his feet so you didn't have to shoot him. Don't bitch at me."

Freeman didn't answer outright, but the look on his face was only an inch shy of adoring.

Andy grinned and looked away from him.

Merilee still had her back to Jake. When the officers finished checking the dead cult members, she eased off on her bowstring, pulled her unfired arrow free, and slid it into her quiver. Before Jake could speak to her, three Astaroths materialized around her, coalescing into long-haired men dressed in jeans and white sleeveless T-shirts.

The tallest of the three, Darian, and the smallest, Jared, each put a hand on her shoulders and spoke to her in low tones.

Jake's attention zeroed on the contact points between Merilee and the two Astaroths like he was sighting a target.

To blow it to bits.

He moved before he had time to think. In three steps, he reached Merilee just in time to hear her laugh at something one of the demons said.

Rage frothed inside Jake. He grabbed Jared. "Move," he said, hearing the gravel in his own tone.

Merilee jumped and turned toward Jake as Jared raised one blond eyebrow and gave way, easing toward one of the stone archways and vanishing into nothing.

Jake threw the force of his sudden fury into the look he gave the other two Astaroths.

Darian took his hand off Merilee and vanished along with Quince, leaving Jake face-to-face with Merilee, barely an arm's length from her tempting curves.

Obviously surprised, Merilee stared at him with her

Mediterranean eyes. Her expression conveyed amusement mingled with remnants of energy from the battle.

Beautiful. And teasing. And maddening.

He wanted to kiss that adorable little scar on her cheek.

A warm breeze wrapped itself around Jake, rather like a sultry feminine caress.

In fact, exactly like a caress.

In the few seconds that followed, Jake got a devastating taste of what it might be like to have Merilee's fingers rushing across his bare chest, across his entire body.

Which reacted way out of his control, just like his temper.

Merilee's gaze traveled over his shoulders and chest, and lower, to the extreme bulge in his jeans.

Jake's essence flickered, and that only pissed him off more.

What the fuck were you doing?

Those assholes touched *you.*

I'll kill all three of them. Then we'll talk.

All of these greetings flashed through Jake's rapidly melting mind.

Fists tight, arms straight, he opened his mouth.

Hesitated.

Forgot how to talk. Remembered and growled, "Hello."

Loudly.

From somewhere close by, Creed snickered, and Jake considered beheading his sibling and feeding his guts to the pigeons.

Must . . . get . . . a grip . . . here . . .

He made himself breathe and turn loose some of the tension in his muscles. Merilee moved toward him until she was only inches from brushing his chest with her leather-clad breasts. The hot air enveloping Jake got hotter, exploring every inch of him.

All the tension came rushing back and concentrated in his cock.

Jake tried to get hold of himself. Couldn't do it. Thought about sprouting wings and flying back to Greece. Squashed that idea, and came up with, "Let me take you home. It's late."

Merilee's eyes brightened. "Can we fly?"

Jake's mouth came open.

He clamped it shut and collected his wits before countering with, "I just flew ten thousand miles in less than four days. I'd rather walk."

A whistle from Creed, and now Andy was laughing. *I'll feed them both to the sewer rats.*

The warm breeze rubbing all over Jake slowly faded away.

When he saw the disappointment on Merilee's lovely face, felt it in the flagging of her elemental energy, he cursed himself for not realizing how much she would have enjoyed the open sky.

His eyes moved to her right forearm, where he knew the mark of the Dark Goddess was concealed by her sleeve. She was an air Sibyl, after all.

And he was a demon who didn't want to have wings. Who didn't even want to be a demon, even if that meant losing abilities this special, enticing woman might enjoy.

No doubt Darian and company would fly her if she asked.

He wondered if they *had* flown with her—in any way—and his gut churned with fast-building fury all over again. When he looked at her, he hoped she couldn't see the insanity blotting out his caution and better judgment.

"Okay, then, I'll walk with you." Merilee's sweet voice drifted beneath the discussion of the officers waiting for the M.E., and Freeman telling Andy that her cute little ass and her underwater dart pistol better get lost before the regular uniforms showed up.

As for Creed, the son of a bitch was whistling a tune Jake recognized as Elvis Presley's "It's Now or Never."

Before he could say or do anything else to look like an idiot, Jake took Merilee's soft, warm hand in his and led her out of Belvedere Castle.

18

By the time they got out of the castle, Merilee had adjourned the worried jury in her mind. The one urging caution, reminding her she was walking with a creature who tried to kill gods and twisted heads off necks with his bare hands. She also dismissed her lingering anger over his previous rejection and his weird comments about fairness and rightness.

The verdict was in, swift and definite.

She was taking this man—demon—whatever the hell he was—back to the townhouse and screwing his brains out, fair or right or not.

From the moment she saw him in the loggia—hell, from the minute she saw his naked ass getting out of her shower, no sense denying that—she had been blown away by wanting him. Physical attraction, yes, of course it was. Who wouldn't want the hunk of the century? But it was more than that, too. It was that serious, totally unlaughing feeling he gave her. That deep emotion, so warm and intense it threatened to melt her insides to so much goo.

She even got a total kick out of his oh-so-obvious protectiveness, and that silly, irrational jealousy that almost made him eat two of his fellow Astaroths just for talking to her. Plus, the little-boy way he reacted to her drove her half insane.

She needed to take him to bed, maybe every night for, say, the next month or two at least. Later, they could worry about realities like fighting the Legion.

Assholes. How's a girl supposed to have hot sex

when insane cults keep sending out Asmodai to disrupt political rallies?

Jake held her hand gently, and she noticed he wasn't in a huge hurry as he guided her down a paved path around the center of the park. The others would probably get home well ahead of them, assuming formalities with the NYPD regulars didn't take too long.

Wind rustled through trees, her wind, flowing from the rush of tension building in her belly. Her skin hummed with air as it moved beneath her damp leathers, stroking her like she wanted Jake to do. With each step, her bow and quiver offered soft pats against her back, barely keeping her focused enough to put one foot in front of the other. The night smelled like fresh grass, leaves, and damp earth. The park's dark ambience and Jake's spicy, exotic scent pushed away typical city smells—secret Caribbean islands, ripe with coconut and baked cinnamon and that unusual splash of pepper, or something hotter. Merilee couldn't help imagining crystal blue waters and breaking surf, and straddling Jake's muscled body on some deserted beach.

She was about to ask him if the flight home was pleasant when he said, "Mother Anemone sends her greetings and well wishes."

Merilee's eyebrow arched at Jake's tone, like he knew the Mother, and knew her well. Merilee glanced at his profile. *So handsome. I want to run my fingers through all that soft, blond hair.* "Uh, thanks. Do you—have you spent a lot of time with Mother Anemone?"

Jake's expression, what she could see of it, didn't change. "I spent a lot of time with her, yes. More than any other Mother."

This time, both of Merilee's eyebrows flew up, and she almost stumbled. "Why?"

"Because she gave me more hope than the rest." Jake kept his eyes forward as they made a turn on the path, heading north toward the townhouse. "Russia and Ireland gave up on me almost immediately. At least Mother Anemone and Motherhouse Greece tried to help me."

Okay, fine. Merilee concentrated on keeping her wind at a reasonable level. Branches swayed as they passed, and dust eddies stirred along either side of the path, making brownish-white streaks in the darkness. *Brave son of a bitch, isn't he? Or crazy.*

"What did you do back then, when you were just . . . hanging out at Motherhouse Greece?" She couldn't help asking. It was so unusual for anyone outside of Sibyls to do this, much less be allowed to do it. "I mean, I know you didn't just sit in your room and wait."

He shrugged without letting go of her hand, giving her arm a little tug. "I needed training to understand my vestigial memories. Some . . . assistance catching up in life, and finding direction."

Catching up in life.

Merilee struggled with that phrase a moment, remembering that a few years ago, Jake had been a normal human boy. His own parents had subjected him to an unthinkable evil, stripping him of his body, his life essence, and converting him into an Astaroth for their own purposes.

Now, though, the child-Jake was long gone.

Once more, she let her eyes wander over the handsome, shirtless creature escorting her slowly through Central Park. This one was all man, grown and mature in every sense of the word. She had no doubts or questions about that, but a lot of scientific curiosity.

The rest of what he said settled in her mind as they walked. "Vestigial memories. Of course. I read about that possibility when I was studying you—er, Astaroths. You're the first of your kind I've known with that ability."

Jake shook his head. "All Astaroths have vestigial

memories. The others might not discuss it, or might keep the flashes of knowledge blocked away as much as possible."

The implication was clear. The shared memories of the Astaroth species must be burdensome or distressing, or at the least uncomfortable, or maybe overwhelming.

Her chest tightened as she wondered if Jake's training had hurt him, physically or emotionally. She hoped not, and her eyes moved to the scars flecking his powerful pecs and biceps. For the sake of all the goddesses, the man really had endured his share of suffering. She squeezed Jake's hand. "Are your memories painful when you have them? Intense?"

Jake seemed to consider this. He didn't sound threatened or offended at her prying when he answered, "More like a library I can access when I need information. After the training—but it's kind of hard to get to sometimes."

Merilee got lost in imagining the luxury of a vast computer archive in her head—a computer not affected by Sibyl energy—crammed with information and wisdom gathered by all Sibyls, everywhere, since the beginning of time. Painful or not, she would have to learn to use it, like Jake did. Even if taming the ability meant risking asking for help from three different sets of Sibyl Mothers, as Jake had done.

Merilee cut Jake another sidelong glance. Her nipples tightened, rubbing hard against her leather bodysuit. *A hunk* and *a genius. Like . . . Spock on steroids? No, wait. Aragorn from* Lord of the Rings*—with a Ph.D. in physics. Sweet Aphrodite, I think I'll just come now and get it over with.*

Where was that damned townhouse?

She glanced around, grateful to realize they were only a few blocks away. Soon, they'd leave the park and hit sidewalks and streetlamps. Then home. And to her room, to sort out this unbelievable attraction in the best, most efficient way possible.

Merilee gripped Jake's hand and licked her lips.

If anything even thought about stopping them, she'd shoot it full of arrows.

"Did you discuss your nightmares with the Mothers again?" he asked, sending a cold chill through the hot breeze of her desire.

The question caught her sideways, but she managed to answer cleanly with, "They told me to keep recording what I see, so I've been doing that. They didn't seem too concerned that you saw what I was dreaming about." Her face and body heated as she realized he didn't ask if she'd had more nightmares. He asked if she had told the Mothers. So he probably knew she'd been running from the Stone Man in her sleep. And . . .

Merilee suppressed a massive, self-conscious twitch and barely kept walking. "Have you—um—seen any more of my dreams since you left?"

Like the ones where I'm riding you like a bucking mustang?

Jake said nothing, but the corner of his mouth twitched, and he held her arm closer to his body as they headed toward the boundary of the park.

Oh, shit.

In one quick second, Merilee's sense of control over her own destiny slipped away from her, and jets of wind escaped to tease nearby trees and grass. They actually whistled as they went, damnit. And the surface temperature of her skin rose to at least five hundred degrees.

Were her hands starting to sweat? That would probably gross Jake out, if she did the slick-palm thing before she ever got him between the sheets. Merilee kept the air moving so no matter what, she'd stay passably dry. Outside the bodysuit, anyway. The thought of his viewing her intimate dreams, her fantasies about him, freaked her right out—and made her ache between her legs—in the exact spot she wanted his mouth, his hands, that impressive cock she had glimpsed under her bathroom towel.

Maintain . . . maintain . . .

At the edge of the park, at the point where a few more steps would take them back to the reality of cars and buses and cabs, Merilee got too dizzy to keep moving.

She paused and tugged Jake to a stop with her.

He let go of her hand and faced her, his expression a mixture of confusion, concern, and unmistakable raw male desire.

On either side of them, bushes swayed in the cool April darkness. Budding leaves dotted branches above, clearly visible in the silvery light of the crescent moon. Grass stretched toward empty, sloping rocks on either side of them, while the path they had taken from Belvedere Castle remained deserted.

Every detail etched itself into Merilee's reeling mind, along with the definition of every muscle in his upper body.

The world seemed very, very distant.

Trying to keep her wits, Merilee fixed her keen Sibyl vision on his unusual gray-blue eyes. Tonight, they were as dark and velvety as the sky above them, with a full complement of glittering stars. "*Have* you seen my dreams?" she asked, her voice coming out a whisper against the steady breeze.

Jake glanced at the ground, then met her stare as his short blond hair stirred in the fits of wind Merilee couldn't begin to hold back. "A few. The ones that were more . . . intense."

Was he blushing?

Actually blushing?

Goddamn, she was going to fall in love with this demon bastard before she ever got to sleep with him.

Am I already in love with him?

Is that what this too-serious thing is all about?

Shit.

She cleared her throat. "I'm not sure how I feel about you dreaming my dreams."

Jake's storm-cloud eyes, bright in the moonlight, held her tighter than any embrace. "It's not my . . . intention to invade"—the color in Jake's cheeks deepened until Merilee's heart fluttered—"ah, your privacy."

Despite her flustered state, she didn't miss the first hesitation in his statement, and she was sure he had been about to say *choice*. That it wasn't his choice to dream her dreams. But he had changed direction because that wouldn't have been true.

As it was, the truth of his desire filled the space between them. It was evident in the crackle of his gaze, the tight lines of his powerful body.

He wants to see my fantasies about him.

He wants me.

Why did they have to wait for the townhouse? There was a nice big bush right behind him.

Merilee moved forward and pressed both hands against his smooth, tanned rock of a chest. He stood still, staring at her as she brushed her palms across each taut strip of muscle, moving up to his shoulders, then down, over his hard, cut abs.

She couldn't breathe, but wind rumbled around both of them in a wide circle, shutting out anyone who might dare to come too close.

Jake didn't move until Merilee's hands reached the waist of his jeans. That's when she felt his fast, firm grip on her elbows. So much power. He could pick her up and fling her halfway to Greece, she was sure of it.

Instead, he jerked her to him at the same time her air

energy forced them closer. Into a tight sleeve of moving, whispering wind and hot skin and leather, and his wonderful, unusual scent, and then he was kissing her, but not just kissing her, dear goddesses, no, taking her with his mouth, his tongue, wrapping his heavy arms around her, forcing his body against hers. Sweet and rough. He tasted as spicy as he smelled. Her lips tingled. *All* of her tingled. Jake's stiff cock pressed into her belly, and Merilee imagined she could hear his blood rushing in the same rhythm as hers.

She fell completely into the kiss, into the sensations she had been craving since that night in the library, when she had first gotten a good sample of Jake Lowell. This time, by Athena's teeth, he *wasn't* getting away from her.

Merilee clung to his neck, letting him hold her on her feet as she rubbed her leathers over his chest and jeans. She wished she were naked. Wished he was already inside her now, right now. Damn, she ached for him. She wanted him on top of her, driving hard inside her as the wind beat leaves and branches all over New York City.

When he bit her lower lip, Merilee moaned from the stinging, throbbing pleasure of it.

His strong hands gripped her ass, squeezed, and he made her moan again as he moved into her, showing her, giving her hints of how good he'd be.

Jake broke the kiss, but Merilee grabbed the sides of his face and reclaimed his mouth. She couldn't let him go, not with just one, or two, or even three or four. He stroked her back, her shoulders as he kissed her, more tender each time. She felt like she was standing in the deceptive, silent eye of a hurricane, surrounded by walls of wind reaching toward the stars.

Her heart beat so fast, so hard she didn't think she could speak, especially not when he pulled his lips away from hers and whispered, "I still don't think this is a good idea."

She found her voice fast enough, though. "Okay, yeah, all that fair and right bullshit the other night. What the fuck were you talking about?"

The question sounded like a gasp.

Pathetic. But I so don't care.

Her face was only inches from his. His arms still held her tight. Yes. And that cock. Sweet Aphrodite. All she wanted was that, inside her. Her mouth on his again, his teeth on her nipples, his hands inside her leathers finding every hot, wet spot she wanted him to touch.

But Jake let her go just as he did in the library, and he carefully pushed her back a step.

Her insides screamed to throw her body against his all over again. It felt wrong to be away from him. And she was so worked up, she might just explode into one big windstorm if he didn't want to see this through.

"If you frustrate me again, I think I'll just kill you. At least if you're dead, I might get my sanity back."

"I can't pretend I don't want you." He studied her with those eerie eyes, his voice husky, barely controlled, which only made the air encasing them rush all the faster. "But I'm damaged goods, Merilee."

He glanced down at his chest, and she knew he was talking about the scars under his shirt. "My mother cut me to pieces using me for her damned rituals—and then she murdered me and turned me into a demon. Not half demon. Not part demon. I'm an Astaroth. Full-fledged. Do you get that?" His voice cracked, and Merilee almost cried for him then and there. Would have, if she hadn't known it would shut him down totally and completely.

"I would never be able to give you a normal woman's life," he whispered, once more meeting her eyes. "And on top of that, my talisman, or the risk somebody could swipe it and override my will, that makes me dangerous."

Merilee gazed back at Jake and swallowed despite the tightness in her throat. "No normal life. A dangerous lover. Got it. And I don't care."

Before he could argue, she grabbed hold of his neck again, and found his lips, and he didn't push her away. Not that kiss, or the next, or the next.

When she finally did let him—and herself—breathe, she said, "Don't ever make decisions for me again, Jake Lowell. That's disrespectful. Share the information, tell me your concerns, but I make up my own mind about what risks I choose to take."

Jake's expression went from heavy-eyed to stunned to understanding mingled with surprise. His arms tightened around her. "I'm . . . sorry. I hadn't thought about it that way."

He's adorable. Merilee kissed him again, then whispered in his ear, "Yeah, well, I'll give you a pass, but only this once."

As Jake bit her neck, she eased the zipper of her jumpsuit low enough for his roaming hands to move inside. Immediately, he cupped one breast and squeezed as his mouth moved to her ear, her cheek. Electric pleasure flowed straight to the center of her being.

Had she ever been so wet? So ready for anything?

Jake's palm rubbed her nipple, rougher than her leathers, and then his fingers found the taut nub and pinched as he kissed her until Merilee was sure she'd have an orgasm just from that. Her body shook in his firm grip, and she couldn't control it, didn't want to control it even for a moment.

"I want you inside me," she said as he switched hands, and breasts, and threatened her sanity with another tight pinch. "Bushes? Right here on the ground? I don't care, Jake."

Wordless, he gazed at her, massaging her nipple until he moved the jumpsuit zipper so high he had to let her go and remove his hand. "Townhouse," he growled. "I want to take my time."

Her knees nearly buckled.

Oh, hell *yes.*

Merilee hoped she could walk that far . . . without ripping off his jeans.

Only they didn't exactly stroll, which was just fine with her.

Hands tightly clasped, both breathing heavy and ragged, they walked so fast they might have won an Olympic race-walking trial. Bolted right out of the park and up the street.

Not too much farther and we'll be there, Merilee's mind kept telling her as she wished he'd turn loose his wings, fly straight up, and take her in the sky over Manhattan.

19

Jake led Merilee into the townhouse, ignoring the presence of his brothers in the hallway as he and the most beautiful Sibyl in the universe headed for the steps. He was vaguely aware of unusual powers running through the place, very strong elemental energies, but he really didn't give a damn.

His mind, his body was consumed with Merilee. His thoughts kept firing back to Central Park, to the moment he realized he had been making Merilee's choices for her, disrespecting her needs, her instincts, her ability to decide for herself as a grown woman and a warrior of the Dark Goddess.

And now that he understood, truly understood in his depths, that she grasped the implications and potential consequences of sleeping with him, he had to have her. Not in a day or an hour, but now.

"Jake," Creed called as they reached the first stair. "Merilee. Hold up. We need to talk."

Merilee braked so suddenly she blocked Jake, or he wouldn't have stopped.

"What?" Jake snarled, wheeling around to face Creed and Nick, too.

"The Mothers are here," Nick said, sounding more grim than apologetic. "One from each Motherhouse—the really old ones—"

Jake interrupted Nick by turning back to Merilee.

He didn't care if every Mother on the planet had showed up in Manhattan. They could wait. Everything could wait.

Merilee turned her face upward to gaze at him, and the exhaustion he had seen earlier fell away. Her eyes, so deep and bright, moved over his face, then the rest of him.

"If the Mothers needed us, they'd be out here," she whispered. "Do you want to talk to your brothers, or do you want to go upstairs?"

"Go on," he said, hardly able to get the words out through his teeth. "I'll meet you. A minute. Maybe two."

Merilee leaned a fraction closer, electrifying every inch of Jake and tripling his physical misery. "Don't disappoint me."

Jake couldn't speak, or he knew he'd make improper use of the first-floor landing. It was nice and flat. If he threw Merilee down on the polished wood, his brothers would get the point soon enough—if they hadn't already.

After flashing him a devastating smile, Merilee bade Creed and Nick good night and headed up the stairs. Slowly. Letting her leather-clad hips sway until Jake almost groaned aloud from his need to touch her. At the first-floor landing, she paused and gave him a look that nearly made him come unglued.

With every bit of iron resolve he possessed, he nodded to her and tried to let his expression communicate his meaning.

Paybacks are a bitch, Merilee—and I will *get my due.*

She winked and wiggled up more steps.

Only Creed's firm grip on Jake's arm made him turn around.

"The Mothers are here," Creed repeated, his eyes flicking from Merilee to Jake and back again. "And they're threatening to stay to work with Andy."

"We need a plan to survive this," Nick said, coming to a stop on Jake's other side. "Freeman wants—"

"Cowards." Jake pulled away from Creed, toward that first step. "Quit spooking every time the Mothers come around. If they want to train Andy, then we'll have to deal with it. *I'll* deal with it tomorrow."

Nick started to say something, but Jake stopped him with a look. He felt like a pent-up storm ready to thunder all over Manhattan. Muscles beyond tight, he left his brothers and took the stairs two at a time, up toward the sky, toward Merilee, toward a measure of relief for his body's torment.

She's mine now.

His thoughts wouldn't focus past that point, and what he was going to do to her when he got to that library.

Only, he never got that far.

As he reached the fourth floor, Merilee stepped out of the hall bathroom she claimed as her own.

Naked.

Wet.

So beautiful Jake didn't think he'd ever breathe properly again.

Steam billowed through the open door behind her, caught in her wind energy, caressing her, blowing in wild, streaming puffs toward Jake. He blinked as the warm, moist air struck the cool dampness of his face and skin.

Droplets of water traveled slowly down Merilee's cheeks, following the path Jake intended to kiss, reaching toward the hollows of her neck, her shoulders, all the places he planned to explore with his tongue. Her breasts made his hands and mouth ache to squeeze, to taste, and the velvety skin of her damp belly looked so damned soft he knew he'd never get enough of her. The blond hair between her legs glistened along with her athletic thighs, and Jake wanted to move now, needed to move, but couldn't. All he could do was stare and wonder if his cock really could rip through his water-soaked jeans.

Merilee crooked her finger, telling him to follow, ordering him to hurry with her eyes, then turned and vanished into the foggy recess of the bathroom.

Damn.

Oh, yeah. Damn!

Jake finally moved.

Fast.

Into the bathroom, into the steam.

He barely sensed the door slamming behind him, driven into place by the force of her directed wind as Merilee wrapped her arms around his neck. Her body pressed the length of his own, warm everywhere he was chilled, and she shivered, and gooseflesh broke out across her chest, her neck, and her arms as she rubbed against him.

"Condom," Jake managed to say before he totally lost himself.

Merilee shook her head. "Sibyls don't need birth control or disease shields. We can do that for ourselves."

Then she rubbed against him again, robbing him of the ability to speak.

Jake ran his hands up and down her unbearably soft sides, drunk on her boldness and fragility. He gazed into her blue eyes, even more crystalline and endless in the smoky, hazy light of the bathroom. Her blond curls lay against her face, begging to be kissed aside. The shower was running, a soft whisper against the flow of elemental air through steam and the ragged pull of Jake's breathing as he bent down and pressed his lips to the scar on her cheek, running his tongue along the thin, short line of it.

Merilee sighed and closed her eyes, rubbing herself harder against him as he let the water from her face trickle across his chin. He ran his mouth over her forehead, her hair, her cheeks, both of her eyelids, her nose, and she held him, arms firm around his neck, leaning back as he nipped her ears, her neck, every dent and cleft, then moved to her lips.

Gods, but she tasted perfect, fresh and female and so, so sweet as he kissed her, wishing he could bind her to him forever with that simple, hungry act. As his tongue found hers, Jake felt the pounding of Merilee's heart, and new, hotter desire pummeled through his every muscle. His essence shifted even though that was the last thing he wanted, but Merilee didn't seem to notice or care that the tone and color of his skin kept swapping erratically between demon and human.

His flesh and scars sizzled everywhere her skin touched him, and the air currents in the bathroom doubled. The steam became a swirling wash of heat and droplets, wrapping them both like a damp, teasing blanket. Jake refused to release Merilee's mouth even as her embrace grew tighter, more desperate. His cock throbbed as she rocked against him, slow and sensual and demanding.

He gripped her ass, kneading the tight muscle, pulling her closer, closer. His body screamed for him to act, now, instantly, to throw her down on the tile floor and take her hard, hard, hard, with no pause, no reprieve, no mercy.

She wouldn't stop him. She'd take everything he had and then some, and that thought almost finished the process of converting Jake's mind to complete bubbling soup. His emotions stormed inside him, crashing and roaring louder than thunder. He was past drunk with desire now.

Her palms slid down from his neck, across his chest, lingering first on his talisman, then on the rough flesh of his scars before dropping lower.

Jake brought his hands up to press the sides of her head, allowing her a second's breath, then kissing her again, keeping her, putting his mark on her as much as any man could dare with a woman like this.

With sure, agile fingers, Merilee found the snap of his jeans and pulled it loose. He felt the zipper moving down, tugging, then sweet release as his cock found freedom. Merilee moaned into his mouth as she gripped him, palm firm against his erection, and stroked him once from base to tip.

He damn near came from the electric shock of her touch, the exquisite pressure of her fingers on the sensitive, pulsing head.

She pulled back from his kiss to murmur, "Demon or not, I knew you were all man."

And then she was moving, sliding down his body even as she held his cock with one hand and pushed his jeans down over his hips with the other. Jake stepped out of them without moving away from her, unable to even think of her letting go of him. Too good. Too right. He ground his teeth to hold himself back, to have a single prayer of lasting more than two minutes with this kind of attention.

Merilee knelt on the tile floor at his feet, keeping a firm grip on him, holding him right where she wanted him. Mist swirled around her, the moisture highlighting her body as she leaned forward and flicked her tongue over the head of his cock.

Jake's hips bucked.

He forced himself to be gentle as he slid his fingers into her hair and groaned as her mouth moved down his aching shaft, taking him deep, deeper, so hot and wet, and dear sweet gods, she was looking at him still, those sea-blue eyes fixed on his.

Up and down.

Again.

Any second, and he would die where he stood. Or combust. Or melt.

Merilee kept her gaze on his as she slid her mouth along his cock, holding the base tight in one hand, using the other to cup his balls and softly, softly tease the skin, touching, squeezing gently.

"I can't last much longer," he growled.

His fingers tightened reflexively, pulling her hair, making her moan against his cock. Tremors of pleasure rolled through his entire being.

"Not much longer," he repeated.

She seemed to take his words as a challenge, gazing at him, moaning again against his shaft even as she stroked him with her lips and tongue and fingers.

Jake's groin tightened so fast he couldn't have warned her if he tried. He went straight from misery to volatile orgasm, shouting with the strength of it, exploding more than coming.

Merilee didn't stop. She didn't even slow down, stroking and swallowing until Jake had to grab her by both shoulders and force his still-pulsing cock from between her lips.

She kept right on looking at him, claiming him, melting him inside and out.

Jake knew he was still shifting, man to demon, demon to man, and he didn't care. He pulled Merilee to her feet, picked her up, and carried her straight into the square tiled shower. She felt like silk and wet heat as he pushed her against the wall, stretched her arms above her head with one hand, gripped her waist with the other, and watched the water spill down her tight, naked body.

He knew his expression had to be feral. Frightening.

That's how he felt as he moved toward her, intending to please her like she had never been pleased before.

20

Merilee gasped as Jake pressed her back against the shower wall.

The salt of his seed still teased her mouth as water tumbled down her face, her nipples, coursing between her legs as her heart pounded so hard she felt dizzy.

He's shifting.

Demon. Now man. Sweet Aphrodite, what will it feel like when he's inside me?

Keeping her wrists firmly above her head, Jake kissed her like she had never even imagined being kissed. His strength tipped her face into the water, then scrubbed her shoulders along the firm, steamy tiles as he fit himself to her, lips to lips, chest to chest, already-swelling cock rubbing her aching sex.

His grip. His lips. Yes. *Yes.* Soft and hard at the same time, so hot, so strong, insisting, commanding, showing her exactly what he wanted, exactly what he planned to do. Merilee trusted him completely, let him support her as his tongue thrust into her mouth, as he used his entire body to deliver wave after wave of sensation and pleasure. She could barely stand how good he felt. How good this felt. Being close to him, being naked under his touch, vulnerable, ready.

No way she had ever felt like this.

She had never even come close to allowing a man to be this much in control of her body, her sensations.

His tongue filled her mouth even as he seemed to touch her everywhere at the same time, all the while keeping her captive against the tiles. He held her helpless, molded to the steel of his muscles, as he rubbed her nipples with his chest, his cock doubling the hot, hot misery between her legs.

She flooded even more, water and juices coating her thighs until she was sure she could smell her own desire blending with Jake's unusual, stimulating musk, and still he kissed her, still he held her, swallowing each moan, answering with low, untamed growls.

He freed her wrists and Merilee instantly slid her fingers into his hair, tangling the short strands in her fists. Seconds later, she was pretty sure she was close to ripping it out of his head, but he didn't let her go, didn't stop kissing her or running his hands from her breasts to her hips, his palms sliding across her water-splashed skin like so much heated, hard silk.

Jake demanded trust and surrender with each thrust of his tongue, his hips, and Merilee knew she would never be able to resist him. She wanted him so badly, and she didn't think the desire screaming and bellowing inside her would ever be satisfied.

When he moved his hands to her heavy breasts, Merilee shuddered at the contact and almost came from just his touch. His lips moved from her lips to her chin to her neck, then quickly to her ear, where he nipped the lobe gently.

"You're beautiful," he said, his tone jagged and barely controlled. His mouth moved across her ear, sending a rush of breath inside the curves, driving her nuts as he squeezed her breasts.

Merilee pulled at the short strands of his hair, enjoying the wet, soft sensation. "I want you," she said, surprised she could talk. "You feel like the wind, Jake. I need you like air."

Teeth nibbled her earlobe again, then her throat. Jake bit her on the other side of her neck, and she felt the sharp press of fangs. Fear mingled with her pleasure, making her even more dizzy as he tasted and sucked, bracing his hands beside her now, moving his mouth down, down, until he sucked a nipple into his mouth and bit it softly.

Merilee heard herself cry out.

Artemis and arrows, that felt so good. Too good. His teeth scraped and bumped the pebbled nub and he held the tender flesh in place, flicking his tongue against the tip over and over until Merilee cried out again.

Damn, but it ached and burned and throbbed. Too good. Too, too good. She really had to be ripping out his hair. She knew she was. Her orgasm curled inside her, mounted, threatening, waiting to howl outward like a hurricane and swirl away every rational thought.

One more bite.

That's all it would take.

Jake seemed to sense her level of madness. He moved slower then, even more gently, sliding his mouth to her other nipple and teasing it with his stubble, then his lips. Merilee's body shook, suspended between satisfaction and complete madness.

"Like silk," he murmured. "How is it possible for something to be so soft?"

Merilee twisted and groaned, tugging his hair as he tenderly licked her nipple only, his tongue so soft, barely there, sweet mother of all the goddesses he was going to turn her into a cyclone and let her blow away to nothing.

"Do you want more?" he asked, his voice vibrating against her tender nipple.

"Yes!" She pulled his hair harder.

"Can you hold back?"

The question was taunting and warm and she arched into him, pressing her breast into his mouth. Finally, finally, he let his teeth do the work, relieving the throb, giving her what her body demanded. Merilee shouted from the relief, then immediately cursed him when he stopped.

He took her mouth with his, and Merilee knew she belonged to him now, whatever he wanted, however he wanted to take her. As she went completely limp in his arms, Jake broke away from the mind-altering kiss and stared at her with those stormy gray-blue eyes she absolutely couldn't look away from. They flickered to gold, then back to gray-blue, making her heart stutter. His lips pulled back and his skin shimmered from tanned to pearl as his fangs flashed in and out of existence.

"Do you really want me?" he asked, his voice so low, so ominous that delicious chills charged all over her skin. "If you say yes, I won't stop."

Jake's eyes flashed golden. Merilee's breath caught painfully in her chest, but she absolutely could not deny the raging want, the *need,* that filled her.

"Yes," she whispered, wrapped in the blaze of his eyes, the glow of his skin, the hot pounding and steam of the shower. Just the feel of his arms excited her so badly she thought she might melt, or simply become the drum of the pulse pounding in her body. Wind energy escaped her in big, hot gusts, damped but barely controlled by the shower.

For a moment, Jake didn't move. His eyes went from blue to gold all over again, and the pearly glow of his skin deepened. He seemed to be considering something, struggling with himself.

Merilee almost stopped breathing. "You bastard. If you walk away from me again and leave me like this, I'll kill you. Slowly and painfully. Two or three times." She yanked at his hair. "I'll burn your body and blow your ashes all over that stinking friggin' Fresh Kills landfill."

Jake let her go.

With a swift, fluid motion, he slid off his talisman necklace and slipped it over her head.

The heavy chain settled against her chest. The ring dangled between her breasts, its heated metal vibrating into her skin. Merilee stared first at the talisman, then at Jake, unable to believe the trust he had just given her. Tears jumped to her eyes.

Did she deserve that kind of trust?

Does anyone?

Jake didn't waver. "It's the only way. I keep almost shifting—can't . . . can't completely control it. If I get out of hand, use that. Protect yourself."

"All the merciful gods and goddesses of Greece and Rome and the whole damned world, please get out of hand. Right now."

Jake's eyes, somehow a beautiful mix of gray-blue and glowing gold, traveled from the talisman to her face. He cupped both of her cheeks with his hands, pressing into her again, his strength and weight acting like some crazy aphrodisiac, exciting each nerve ending and skin cell until Merilee thought she'd scream from the intense sensation.

"Are you sure?" he asked again in that low, sexy voice.

Her own voice low, barely able to form the words at all, Merilee said, "Oh, yeah. I'm yours."

Jake's lips pulled back and Merilee saw his fangs become more visible just as he grabbed her hips, rocked against her, then lifted her until she was eye to eye with him, breasts rubbing his firm chest. She gripped his neck with all her strength, wanting, needing, half-dying to feel him inside her.

His muscles rippled as he positioned her over his cock, teasing her folds, stealing her breath, taking her heart, stirring a heat within her she had never felt before. His talisman bounced between her breasts, then crushed into her skin as he moved her closer, up, then down, down, sliding his cock deep, stretching her, pushing hard, forcing a moan of pure ecstasy directly from the windy depths of her soul.

He felt like hot ivory, hard and smooth, and so, so thick.

Merilee reveled in the joining, in the way he felt, in the squeezing throb of her body as her inner walls gripped him, drew him deeper.

"Better than I imagined," she said aloud. "Better than I dreamed."

She groaned and moved her hips as his powerful arms slid her up and down, up and down, rubbing her back against the wet tile as he thrust up into her, hard, then harder, pushing her higher, toward an edge like Merilee had never known. "Like that. Just like that."

Her lids closed from the absolute pleasure, but Jake whispered, "Look at me," and his voice sounded only the barest part human.

Merilee's eyes flew open.

His face seemed impossibly handsome then, almost beautiful, as his features mixed between demon and human. "Angel," she whispered, then moaned as his cock drove toward her core. She felt like she was floating in his steady grip, drifting atop strong wind, making love in a warm rainstorm.

Her gaze locked with his as she lost herself in the rhythm of his thrusts, in the pound and slap of his cock sliding into her, seemingly straight through her, in and out, in and out until she knew she couldn't stand another second. Her hands shook as she gripped his neck.

Was that the universe blazing at her through those unearthly eyes?

"Don't stop," she repeated. "Don't stop. More. Yes. *More.*"

Jake's movements got faster. More powerful. His lips

pressed into hers, his fangs nipping at her as his hips rocked her again and again, his cock pushing deeper, unbelievably deeper. He seemed to be changing inside her, hotter, longer, even more powerful as his skin glowed a brilliant white.

She felt wings nudging her fingers.

She felt wings in her mind.

Merilee didn't want to come. She didn't ever want to come and make this end, no, please, no, no, she wanted the sensation to last forever.

"I want to fly," she shouted, leaning back hard against the tile so he could go deeper still. "You're making me fly!"

Her mind took off then, a split second before her body, hurling her awareness upward, high, higher, straight into the sky.

Steam swirled through her being, through her elemental essence, and her wind answered with a long, roaring howl. She felt blown apart even as her thoughts swirled into the sun. Lightning shocks seemed to fill her whole body, shooting from the spot where she joined with Jake. Her inner walls closed tight around his cock, throbbing and pulsing as she came.

Merilee moaned from the incredible force of her orgasm, and she held on to Jake's neck with every bit of her fast-ebbing strength.

His wild growl filled her ears as his seed roared into her.

Crazy, thrashing from the almost painful pleasure of an orgasm that wouldn't stop, didn't seem even close to stopping, she bit Jake's shoulder, then his neck and ear, buried her face in his hair, pressed her mouth against his head, and screamed.

Wind burst from every inch of her.

If Jake had been human, that much elemental energy would have sent him slamming out of the shower, probably all the way down four flights of stairs—but Jake held her just as tight, still moving, still thrusting until she starting begging him to stop and finally screamed again.

"Stop, Jake!" Her fingers touched the talisman at her neck. "Stop!"

She felt his jaw clench, his neck muscles bunch. He slowed as if fighting her command, snarling softly as he eased her down from that high, soaring place he had sent her. Her whole body ached and throbbed as he finally held her still and slid his spent cock from the depths of her body.

He didn't put her down, and somehow, she found the strength to wrap her legs around him.

Almost as fast, panic flickered through her.

She was wearing Jake's talisman—and she had ordered him to stop.

Was that wrong?

Had she crossed a line?

Massive emotion, so close to the surface from her soul-jarring orgasm, flowed to the surface, and Merilee sobbed. She pulled her face back and looked at Jake, into his mostly golden eyes. "I'm sorry. I'm sorry. I didn't mean—"

He stopped her with a kiss, holding her tight against him.

A few kisses later, her tears left as quickly as they came. Her mind started to soar again from the sweet, probing contact of his tongue and the way his strong hands gripped her ass.

"You *are* a demon," she muttered when he let her breathe. "I think you're possessing me."

That made him laugh, and the sound lingered in her ears and heart.

Jake's eyes were almost completely human again when she gazed into them this time. No sign of pearl skin or fangs or wings—not that she would have minded. Those things seemed like a part of him, a natural aspect, easy for her to accept even if he couldn't. Not yet.

"Can I give you another command?" she asked, unable to stop herself from smiling.

Jake held her with one hand, and with the other, he shut off the shower, sending a new rush of steam all around them. "Absolutely," he said, and Merilee noted the complete lack of hesitation in his answer.

She shifted in his grip and bit his bottom lip, making him growl again, and loving the sound.

"I order you to take me to bed and kiss me everywhere. Kiss me all night. Kiss me forever, until I tell you to stop."

Instantly, Jake's muscles corded, and she realized he was resisting, choosing how to comply, and how much, and the thought gave her shivers everywhere.

After a few moments of thinking, Jake carried her out of the shower, set her on her wobbly legs, and dried her off, kissing every place the towel moved.

Then he did exactly as she had instructed, carrying her naked, hair still dripping, straight down the hallway to the library, and on to her bed.

Far, far too soon, she drowsed and whispered her permission for him to stop, remembering his kisses even as she tumbled into a perfect, dreamless sleep.

21

"Uh, you can cover up now."

Jake opened his eyes at the sound of Cynda's voice, followed by Merilee's quiet, "Oh, shit. Hi, Cynda."

As Jake came fully awake, he saw Cynda standing in the library at the foot of Merilee's bed. She was dressed in jeans and a short-sleeved T-shirt that looked like it belonged to his brother Nick. Her mouth was open, and she was staring straight at Jake's exposed cock.

On reflex, he grabbed a blanket they had tossed on the floor and pulled it over his waist, but Cynda's expression didn't change. She shifted her attention to Merilee, who was as naked as Jake and busily tugging a sheet under her chin.

Merilee flushed a brilliant scarlet.

In a totally calm, matter-of-fact tone, Cynda said, "Okay, I surrender. I *totally* understand the attraction now."

Merilee grinned and let go of the sheet, revealing Jake's talisman lying against the smooth olive skin of her chest. "You have *no* idea."

Jake found himself getting hot around the neck and face, and he didn't enjoy the sensation. He was, however, pleasantly surprised that Cynda hadn't cooked him to well done the instant she arrived in the library.

Women. Especially Sibyls.

No doubt he could learn volumes about their biological and psychological composition—and still not understand them at all.

Cynda looked apologetic as she spoke to Merilee. "I

know you've only had a couple of days to get better, but the NYPD liaison called. They got an anonymous tip and checked it out, and now we've got serious shit happening at one of the political headquarters." She put her hands under her belly as if the weight of it might actually be hurting her. "They found Derek Holston's body. He was murdered, but maybe not by the Asmodai who kidnapped him."

Merilee frowned and sat up, letting the sheet fall away. "Was it ritualistic?"

Despite the seriousness of the conversation, Jake's eyes locked on Merilee's pale pink nipples, and he could almost taste the sensitive, rough flesh in his mouth and hear her moans as he sucked it between his teeth. His talisman dangled between her bare breasts, where it had remained for all the hours they had been together.

She was so delicious.

Murder and chaos or no, Jake wanted her again. He wanted her now.

Blood rushed to his cock, and he had to swing his legs over the edge of the bed and grab his jeans to hide his erection. The feel of the cool cotton gave him back a little of his concentration and allowed him to process Cynda's next words.

"The murder's not ritualistic in the supernatural sense. More like a well-crafted imitation of a serial killer." She made a stabbing motion with her right hand that Jake recognized as a parody of Norman Bates from the Hitchcock movie *Psycho*. "A sexual sadist—but when the responding officers checked the scene with polycarbonate lenses, they found a lot of sulfur trace, too powerful for Asmodai."

Jake's brain kicked in a little more directly as he fastened his jeans. "Was the room sealed? Airtight?"

Cynda glanced at him as Merilee got up and padded toward the stack of boxes where she kept her clothing in her library bedroom. "Not airtight, so that's another weird thing. The sulfur traces should have broken down by now, but they're not only still visible, they're *strong,* according to Bela."

Already, Jake was flipping through the pages of information stored in his mind, trying to identify creatures that might leave such intense sulfur residue. He didn't come up with anything right away, and knew he'd have to think more deeply on the possibilities later.

Merilee stepped into one of her leather jumpsuits and zipped it. "Some new kind of demon?"

Cynda shrugged. "No idea. The residue leads to a wall, then vanishes, as if whatever killed Holston faded through steel and bricks, then several feet of solid earth to escape."

Jake dressed quickly, as did Merilee.

They were just about to leave when the three Astaroths, Darian, Quince, and Jared, materialized in the library just inside the terrace doors.

Jake swore as he realized it was time for their training session, then quickly gave the demons instructions on which books of human warfare to read until he returned. The three Astaroths nodded and immediately went to the bookshelves he indicated, which drew a look of surprise and approval from Cynda.

"Are they coming along?" she asked, pausing near the library door. "In their training, I mean."

"Absolutely," Merilee said before Jake could answer. "I snuck a look in the gym when I was recovering from my Fresh Kills wounds—when he was putting them through their paces. They learn *so* fast. I pity any asshole who takes a shot at them. I know he's taught them evasive moves, defensive moves—even a little close-quarters combat."

Cynda gave the demons a quick glance. "You don't need them on this outing. The damage is already done—besides, they'd make one hell of a stir at the scene."

As the three of them left the library, Cynda continued, "See, the kicker is, the body's underneath Alvin Carter's political headquarters—in a secret, soundproof basement."

"The 'Strength Now' guy?" Merilee sounded stunned as she led the way down the townhouse steps. "Wasn't he in the lead to take his party's nomination for the presidency?"

"He *was*." Cynda struggled, waddling to the first landing. Instinctively, Jake took her elbow to assist her, and he was pleased Merilee's triad sister accepted his help and didn't try to singe him.

Merilee shook her head, already at the next landing. "When this gets out to the news, Carter will be history."

"Toast," Cynda agreed as Jake guided her to Merilee, then on to the first floor. "But, uh, we've got a more immediate problem to handle before you hit the streets."

Merilee started to ask about the problem, but they had reached the conference room—and the problem was apparent.

Freeman, Creed, Nick, Riana, and Andy were waiting, along with five OCU officers and Bela Argos—and three elderly women with very large weapons.

Everyone looked uncomfortable except the stooped, wrinkled visitors.

Mother Anemone from Greece, Mother Yana from Russia, and Mother Keara from Ireland nodded at Jake as he entered.

Fuck. I forgot about the whole Mother thing. And Andy—

Yep.

Andy was definitely a problem.

She looked very pissed off.

Jake could smell water in the air, as if Andy might be

drawing every droplet in New York closer and closer to the townhouse. He slowed to a stop a reasonable distance from the furious redhead, but the sprinkler over his head tore off.

Cold water poured across his face and shoulders as Andy marched forward and squared off with Merilee—about two inches from Merilee's cute little nose.

"Tell them to leave!" Andy shrieked, fists doubled, red hair dripping and plastered to the sides of her head. "I'm a cop, not a Mother. Tell them I don't have time for this shit."

Water drizzled down the walls at the head of the room, making dark streaks down the chalkboard and ruining one of the OCU's well-designed raid plans. Probably a ruptured pipe. Freeman cleared his throat and headed out to turn off the main to the townhouse, but with water standing in the feeders, that wouldn't offer immediate relief.

We need an emergency shutoff for the whole line.

Not that the rest of the block would appreciate that.

"I won't ask them to leave, Andy," Merilee said in an amazingly calm, powerful voice. "Whether or not you ever become a Mother, you're the world's only water Sibyl, and you need more training than I can give you."

Damn, Merilee's sexy when she's firm like that.

Jake stood very still, letting the sprinkler's offering soak him. He could use a cold shower anyway. Merilee was several feet away from him, but her sweet smell of white tea and honey almost erased all other scents from his mind.

"That's what Riana and Cynda said," Andy grumbled as Sal Freeman came back into the conference room. His sleeves were wet, and as he rolled them up to his elbows, Jake noticed Andy's underwater dart pistol wedged awkwardly into Sal's gun belt.

Andy glanced at Sal, and Jake's cold shower waned, then stopped altogether.

"This is how it must be," Mother Yana said in her thick Russian accent, her hands reflexively gripping the Russian hunting daggers sheathed at her waist. "Ve vill help you and teach you at a higher level. Ve could have even more problem, because vere there is a Motherhouse, the talent begins to show itself nearby."

Andy's face went slack. "What . . . are you saying?"

"It's as if the universe knows where Sibyls are," Mother Keara explained. Jake eyed the Irish hand-and-a-half blade belted at her waist and at her shoulder, the hilt of what had to be a five-foot Chinese great sword strapped to her back. A little puff of smoke drifted into the waning sprinkler drizzle, as if to punctuate her statements. "Others with water talent—even children and infants—may come here or be presented for training. They will be drawn to your energy."

The golden, claw-shaped hilts of Mother Anemone's *falcata* swords glittered as she spoke, her voice lifting over Jake like a wave of warm air. "We should have given this more consideration, dear girl. For that, we're sorry."

"You're . . . sorry." Andy's laugh could have frozen all the water in the room. She wiped water from both eyes, and the glare she directed over her shoulder made Jake glad Freeman had taken her HKP-11 away from her. "You're telling me other water Sibyls, kids and *babies* could just . . . what, pop through the front door any second now? And that I'd be responsible for them?"

"The townhouse is a Motherhouse now," Riana murmured too quietly for Andy to hear her. "Goddess help us all."

Mother Keara spoke louder with, "We may be fortunate and some older children and young women may turn up. Perhaps even some adults. There are accounts of such in the archives. After this crisis is over, we can build a new Motherhouse for all of you."

"But for now," Mother Yana said to Andy, "Keara, Anemone, and I, ve vill help until you are completely competent vith your new abilities and potential responsibilities. Ve vill stay here as long as it takes."

"Goddess help us *all,*" Nick and Creed said at the same time.

Freeman's jaw seemed to come unhinged.

Elemental energy surged outward and scorched, shook, and blew Jake all at once. He saw the other men react to the chastising, too. They all closed their mouths tightly.

Jake wasn't sure he grasped all the details, but he did understand that Motherhouse New York had apparently opened for business.

Here.

Now.

Others could come. Adults, girls, even infants.

And . . . the Mothers would be staying, and that would probably kill both of his brothers and drive Freeman to lunacy, and who knew what effect it would have on the Sibyls, the OCU—the city?

Jake watched Freeman as Freeman watched Andy, and he wondered if the presence of the Mothers would keep the big dumb-ass from breaking down and telling Andy how much he cared about her. Jake also wondered when Andy would lose it over the Mothers and their demands and start making the same *Psycho* motions Cynda mimicked earlier—only not in jest.

If *she* didn't, his brothers might.

Jake spent the next few seconds studying his siblings and their miserable expressions and negative reactions to the presence of the older, more powerful Sibyl leaders. Nick and Creed hadn't exactly hit it off perfectly with the Mothers. Okay, so Creed had almost been eaten by Mother Yana's wolves and Nick almost had his head cut off by Mother Keara's freaky Oriental sword—but the Mothers tolerated both men fairly well now. No significant amount of blood had been shed.

Still, his brothers didn't seem very interested in spending time with their unusual guests. Neither did the five OCU officers, who were on the other end of the conference room, sitting as far from the Mothers as they could get.

Their loss.

Jake couldn't understand people who feared power greater than their own. Why not seek information? Why not learn from anyone who could teach?

Jake moved to Merilee's side, all too aware of Mother Anemone gazing at him. Her lips twitched into a smile that threatened to explode across her face.

Andy backed off and stood next to Sal, sulking quietly. Apparently, the possibility that other water Sibyls could arrive at the townhouse, raw and untrained and maybe even still in diapers, had taken the fight out of her.

The Mothers demonstrated impeccable judgment by leaving her alone for the moment and letting her return to her role as an OCU officer. Tentative conversations broke out between Merilee's triad and Jake's brothers. Bela Argos gestured to the hesitant OCU officers, who came to join in the planning for how to handle the Derek Holston situation.

Mother Anemone kept smiling at Jake, and Merilee seemed to become aware of Mother Anemone's attention. Her hand drifted to the bulge of Jake's talisman, partially concealed beneath her jumpsuit.

As her fingers brushed against the few exposed gold links, Jake experienced a combination of physical shock and incredible arousal.

His body shuddered and he almost groaned. On instinct, he caught hold of her arm and pulled her hand away from the jewelry before she drove him to complete madness here, in front of everyone.

Merilee looked startled, then contrite. She started to take the chain and ring off to return it to him, but Jake's instincts surged, and he made a split-second decision.

"Keep it," he said so that only she could hear, shocking himself as much as Merilee. "That way you can always reach me if you get in trouble."

Her expression and the way her lips parted, the soft sound of her happy sigh, sent all of Jake's blood southward again, and Jake let go of her arm and had to look away from her.

Fortunately, Captain Freeman was asking for everyone's attention and starting to discuss courses of action and assignments.

Freeman eyed Jake and Merilee. "Lowell and Alexander, I need you at Carter's headquarters gathering information with Bela. You three are my detail people." Freeman shifted his gaze to Bela, then back to Jake and finally to Merilee. His expression turned to one of genuine concern. "If you're up for it, Alexander. If you're not, tell me now. I know you've had a helluva last couple of weeks."

"I can handle it," Merilee said, despite Riana's sniff of disapproval.

Jake's gut twisted, but Mother Anemone's expression remained placid. Surely if Merilee was too tired to perform her duties, the head of Motherhouse Greece would step in to suggest she remain at the townhouse.

Merilee took Jake's hand openly, obviously not caring who knew she was now involved with Jake, which pleased him and made him uncomfortable at the same time. He noticed the frowns on the faces of the OCU officers, men and women he had barely forged a working relationship with, who didn't trust him much anyway because of what he was.

Now that he was clearly involved with a Sibyl, would those relationships get even more tenuous?

He hadn't thought about that.

And even as he did now, he knew Merilee was worth that, and far, far more. He squeezed her fingers with his, and she smiled at him.

They started out of the conference room.

"Be careful of the press," Freeman called after them. "If reporters show up, get the hell out of Dodge—fast."

22

Jake's blood hummed as he led the way into the basement of Alvin Carter's Strength Now headquarters, instinctively keeping Merilee behind him as he sampled the air, the energy.

No active threat. Nothing immediate, but something harmful, something evil had been here, not long ago. He gazed around the basement, which was roughly the same size as the townhouse conference room. The space seemed smaller with Bela Argos and a small army of crime scene technicians—both regular and OCU-affiliated—revolving around Derek Holston's mutilated body. If Jake wasn't much mistaken, the techs seemed a little . . . surly. All tense and frowning.

Did the two groups not like working together?

He motioned for Merilee and she started forward. At the entrance, she stopped and gripped both sides of the steel doorframe with her gloved hands. Her leather-covered chest heaved, and her sudden pallor made Jake's gut lurch.

"What is it?" he asked as quietly as he could, his gaze moving from one of her hands to the other, acutely aware that she might be disrupting trace evidence.

Merilee let her arms fall to her sides and shook her head, making the bow and quiver slung over her shoulders twitch back and forth. "I—I don't really know. I'm sorry." She glanced at the spots on the door where she had touched the steel. "Shit. At least I have on gloves. Maybe I didn't do too much damage?"

A small gust of wind stirred around her face, sending

the sweat on her forehead toward her eyes. She wiped her brow with her leather-clad knuckles before it could drip.

"Probably no damage." Jake almost reached for her, but thought better of it. Not here. Not at work.

They both had to concentrate, and he had to allow Merilee to have her normal Sibyl reactions. Her instincts and Bela's were as important as any trace they gathered. Jake trusted Merilee would sort out her impressions later and relay them to him, and until then—well, until then, he could worry like hell and watch her very, very closely.

Merilee strapped on her polycarbonate-lens goggles and they moved into the basement together. Regular technicians followed instructions from the OCU techs, collecting evidence all around them but avoiding any areas where the OCU techs dropped little orange evidence cones. Both sets of techs skirted the already-marked sulfur trails.

The red ribbons of lingering sulfur were obvious to Jake's sensitive vision. Almost too bright to look at directly. They were so powerful Jake could actually *smell* them over the sweat of the technicians and the coppery, putrid scent of Holston's blood and end-of-life waste.

Bela Argos, dressed in battle leathers and fully armed like Merilee, met them beside the chair containing Holston's remains. She pulled up her polycarbonate goggles. "Poor bastard was mutilated before he died." She glanced at his body and grimaced. "And after."

"Since he got swiped by Asmodai, we've got to assume the Legion is behind this." Merilee was still papery-pale as she adjusted her goggles. "Did they want information about Sibyls—or about what he was doing at the university?"

Bela folded her arms. "Nothing exciting there. Derek studied biopolymer degradation."

Before Jake could retrieve the definition, Merilee said, "Eyeball stuff? You're right. I can't see any state secrets or national intrigue in collagen distortion and dystrophic corneas."

Bela's serious expression darkened. "Then this was about Sibyls." She gestured to the sulfur traces. "And whatever did this, it's some freaky new monster the Legion's come up with."

"Derek was married to an air Sibyl, so maybe they needed specific info on us." Merilee studied the body. "But what information could he offer that the Legion doesn't already know?"

Bela had no answer, and neither did Jake. However, he didn't like the possibility that someone in the Legion wanted specific intel on air Sibyls. The last time the Legion targeted a specific group of Sibyls, Motherhouse Ireland almost got destroyed. "Perhaps they needed something subtle, some minor personal information that wouldn't seem too important." He spoke quietly for Bela and Merilee's benefit alone, below the range of the nearby technicians. "Something that might help the Legion with a specific plan or cause? Another attack on a Motherhouse, this time Greece?"

"Maybe," Bela said, moving to where she didn't have to look at the gruesome sight of Holston's body. Jake couldn't blame her for that at all.

"So why did whoever—or whatever—did this," she continued, "go to the trouble of making this look like a sadistic sexual killing? And why do it here, of all places?"

Merilee let out a weak-sounding breath. "Sure does make a shitload of problems for Carter and his Strength Now campaign, doesn't it?"

"Psychotic demons with political agendas." Bela offered a stream of colorful expletives about that combination while crime scene technicians stared at her and Jake's thoughts shifted to the Stone Man.

If the Stone Man was real, and he was pretty sure it was, could it be Legion-affiliated? It would be just like the Legion to monkey with elections, to put their people in power. They had a long history of doing just that—his parents had been part of it.

Or was this some step in its plan to come after Merilee, and maybe other Sibyls?

Like the practitioners who keep disappearing. All people with very strong elemental talents.

Maybe both aims had been in play.

As theories went, it hung together, but it was very speculative. They didn't have any way of tying Charlotte's suicide or the disappearances to this murder. Hell, they couldn't even prove Phila and the rest *had* disappeared. Not yet, anyway.

Pain knifed through his temples, and he realized he was clenching his jaw.

Clusterfuck.

That was one of Nick's words, but Jake liked it.

Yep, bro. This is a clusterfuck.

Beside Jake, Merilee gazed through her goggles at the traces on the basement floor. "I've never seen anything like this," she said in a shaky voice.

Jake wasn't certain if she meant the traces or Holston's remains. Either way, he hadn't expected her to have such a powerful reaction. The sharp pain in his temples flared again, and he made himself loosen his jaw. Merilee sounded so uncharacteristic, like something was dragging her down. Something beyond the obvious factor of this brutal murder scene. Her tired, listless sound dug at him down deep, along with the fact that he couldn't do a damned thing about it.

"I'm picking up weird things," Merilee admitted, speaking louder to make herself heard over the rising conversations of the techs. "Smells. Images on the air, flashes of scenes . . . like under the ocean? And these traces, the sulfur's so strong it's reminding me of volcanic residue."

Bela stepped around a pair of kneeling techs and agreed immediately, but she clarified with, "It's not rock, though. Not real rock, anyway, but yeah, the sulfur's just as strong."

From the tight line of Merilee's mouth and the way she kept avoiding his gaze, Jake figured there was something she wasn't saying, or maybe wasn't ready to say yet in front of Bela. He left it alone for the moment, but his jaw got tighter by the second.

Should I take her out of here, or would I be getting in her way? Disrespecting her as a professional? Fuck, this is complicated.

"Sulfur traces like this absolutely can't be from Asmodai." Bela smoothed her dark hair tighter against her head. "Curson either." Her eyes flicked toward Jake, then away. "Even Astaroths don't leave behind that kind of trail."

"Could it be some sort of god?" Merilee scowled as she knelt near the widest and strongest of the traces, leading from Holston's left ankle to the spot on the basement's stone wall where the bright pulse of crimson seemed to evaporate. "Maybe something related to volcanoes? We dealt with a Vodoun god a couple of days ago. A Petro Loa—a fire being."

"I heard. And there's still no sign of Phila Gruyere." Bela's face darkened as her tone grew more stressed and disgusted. "Rumor says a new-age guru went missing the same night you had your showdown with Bosou Koblamin at Fresh Kills. That, and all of *this* mess—what the hell is going on, Merilee?"

A couple of crime scene technicians started to squabble in the far corner of the room, and Jake gave them a glare that stopped the confrontation. He noticed both techs were perspiring, much as Merilee had done when she first entered the basement. As she was still doing.

Jake sniffed the air. Did his best to resample the energy in the room, let it flow into him, through him—but he didn't sense anything off or wrong beyond the sulfur stench and the lingering smells and sights of Derek's violent death.

"I've got no idea what's up in this city," Merilee muttered as she inched along the big sulfur trail, holding her hand above it without letting her glove touch the shimmering red. "Wish I had a clue."

Jake was seized with the impression that Merilee damn well did have a clue, but she was keeping it to herself. The whiter her skin got, the more her hands shook, the more certain he was that whatever had happened in this basement was related to the Stone Man. That was the one thing he had seen Merilee get upset about, and the more she got upset, the more he thought about yanking her the hell out of the basement. Maybe carrying her all the way back to the townhouse and locking her in the library. It was getting hard to keep his mind on the scene and gather those details Freeman expected him to bring back to the townhouse for discussion.

He followed her to the stone wall, facing away from the bulk of the evidence techs, who continued combing through the larger part of the room with sour expressions and jerky, frenetic motions. Merilee focused on the spot on the stone wall where the sulfur trace vanished, and Jake felt her outflow of elemental wind.

Watching her work made his blood surge with worry. It wouldn't be good to interrupt her when she was this deep into a task, but damn it, he didn't want her using up any more vital energy. Bela Argos obviously noticed her fellow Sibyl's unusual reaction, maybe even Merilee's growing weakness, and Bela came to stand beside Jake, right behind Merilee. "Air Sibyls are more sensitive than the rest of us," she told Jake, as if he might not know that. "Maybe she's feeling something we're too dense to notice."

Jake didn't correct Bela about his level of sensitivity, or his awareness of Sibyl strengths and weaknesses. Better to appreciate her friendly tone, and the way she seemed to be trying to include him in her thoughts. From what he understood, Bela had never been an open, amicable Sibyl at the best of moments. He wondered what might have swayed her toward being nice to him, then remembered that it was her triad sister he had taken to Greece for burial.

Loyalty, then. Jake glanced at Bela's stern, straightforward expression, and noticed the way she stood ready to grab Merilee and offer her physical support if necessary.

He decided he liked Bela.

Loyalty.

Yes. Loyalty was good.

Damn gorgeous woman, too, a lot like Riana, and scary-strong inside and out like so many of the earth Sibyls. It would take one hell of a man to tame Bela Argos. If Sal Freeman weren't so totally wrapped up with Andy, Jake might have dared him to ask Bela out for dinner.

Merilee's gloved hand drifted toward the wall and traced an invisible line in the stone. "Bela, can you sense the earth on the other side of this spot?"

Bela's earth energy surged outward, catching Jake in the elbow as it moved. He stumbled sideways, but righted himself, then watched as the woman used her terrasentient abilities to explore the earth behind the wall.

"It's . . . disturbed," Bela said quietly. "Freshly turned—and for quite some distance. One or two hundred yards, possibly three. A tunnel, maybe? Entrance and exit for the killer, unobserved by people in the Carter headquarters?"

Merilee nodded. "My air energy moves too freely around these lines." She traced without touching the stone again, this time indicating a rectangular shape wide enough and tall enough to have been a doorway. "I think the stone was recently sealed. Elemental energy—but, hasty. Not perfect."

"We need to open this up." Bela stretched out her arms, and Jake felt her earth energy pushing against the shabby elemental seal on the stones. "I'm going to move the dirt and see where this goes. Maybe we'll pick up the strong sulfur trace as we go."

One of the stones shifted, and a spray of dirt burst through the opening to land between Merilee and Bela.

Merilee swayed.

Jake caught her immediately, pulling her into his arms. She was so warm—almost too warm.

Feverish?

Failing?

Shit!

Enough. She was leaving.

"I need to get you back to the townhouse," he said, but Merilee pulled out of his grip.

"I'm fine," she said in a shaky voice, giving him a wicked, intense frown. "We've got work to do."

Bela lowered her hands and gave Merilee a nervous glance. "Okay, honey, you better tell us what's wrong with you, right now."

Merilee stood on her own power, but Jake kept his hands on her hips, not trusting her strength or her balance. "Sorry. Just—my head keeps swimming. Something's off here, but I just can't put my finger on it."

Jake's gaze shifted from the back of Merilee's head to the furious red sulfur trace clinging to the dirt on the basement floor near her feet.

To their right, one of the OCU technicians screamed at a standard tech.

"Hey!" Bela wheeled on the arguing pair. "Knock that shit off. We're trying to move air and earth over here."

From the corner of his eye, Jake saw a standard tech pick up one of those little orange plastic cones and pound her rival in the head with it.

"What the hell?" He started to pull Merilee closer to shield her, but she evaded him, gazing up at the ceiling like she was hearing the Keres again.

Another couple of techs swung at each other, shouting about clumsy evidence handling.

Bela let off a tiny wave of earth energy to knock the warring techs apart. All three of them were facing the techs in the greater part of the basement now, but Jake heard the creak of stone behind him. A second stone shifted in the wall, and more sulfur-coated dirt spilled into the basement at his feet.

The moment the debris hit the floor, Merilee fainted.

Jake's heart pumped. He caught her and swept her into his arms before she got near the floor. "Bela. Bela!"

Bela shook her head and staggered, almost falling and using the crumbling wall to hold herself upright.

Behind them in the basement, all hell broke loose as roaring, screaming, flailing techs threw down their supplies and instruments. Fists pounded heads. People yelled. Metal clattered and glass smashed against stone and dirt. The stench of rotten eggs flooded the entire space, which didn't help the battle calm down at all.

Every synapse in Jake's body fired at the same moment. He lifted Merilee's unconscious form against his chest with one arm, grabbed Bela with the other, and plowed up the basement steps, through the line of five regular officers guarding the basement entrance, and into the main campaign headquarters.

Their appearance caused quite a stir among the three dozen or so campaign workers manning the desks and phones, but he couldn't worry about that now.

As soon as she reached the fresh air upstairs, Bela seemed less woozy. She helped Jake settle Merilee on the floor, then glanced over her shoulder toward the door to the basement. With a tense expression, she looked at Jake again.

He took her meaning.

It tore at his gut to leave Merilee, but he knew he had to go downstairs and try to get the techs out before they killed one another.

"Stay out," he instructed the officers at the basement door, who were turning to go intervene. "Something's bad down there. Poison or worse."

As he ran back toward the chaos, he tried to shift to demon form, figuring he could move faster, better, take more people out at once.

He couldn't reach that essence inside him.

With each lunging step toward the noise and fighting, Jake tried to tap his full Astaroth abilities, strained for them, demanded them—but nothing happened. As he plunged into the room full of warring techs, Mother Anemone's words echoed through his mind.

You must use your demon essence consistently, frequently, or risk losing it and never being whole again. . . .

"Shit!" Jake yelled as he waded into the fray, still trying to shift yet still staying human.

Not knowing what else to do, he started grabbing snarling, kicking, howling people and punching their lights out. Man, woman, it didn't matter. He just wanted them down. Unconscious.

How many were there? Eight? Ten?

Felt like a goddamned ten dozen by the time he

punched the last two—and some of them had already hurt one another pretty bad.

"Call for ambulances," he said to the guarding officers as he got the first two unconscious women up the stairs. "We've got nine down. And call Hazmat. And OCU headquarters—and the medical examiner's office. We need a full team here, in a big fucking hurry. Tell them to bring masks and suits."

He glanced to his left and saw Merilee pale, but sitting up. A measure of relief nudged against the fury and frustration almost shorting out his mind. To Bela, he said, "Get her out of here. Get all these people to the street, Bela."

The earth Sibyl reacted immediately, pulling Merilee to her feet and shouting orders at the campaign workers, who grabbed their bags and coats and ran like hell.

Jake turned and headed back to the basement. Stubbornly he dug inside himself, trying to force out his fangs, his wings. Trying to claim that more feral—and much stronger—part of him.

What the hell?

He had shifted so easily, almost out of control, when he had been with Merilee.

Was that some sort of flame-out? A final burst of my demon self? Fuck!

Some damned aspect of his demon essence must still be functioning, because he hadn't been affected by whatever got hold of Merilee and Bela, and whatever drove all the techs nuts.

Jake reached the basement, started to pick up the closest two female techs—and stopped.

Their sightless eyes gazed back at him like a mute accusation.

Too late, Jake.

Too late, demon-man.

Cursing, Jake reached for the next-closest tech, but

the man was as dead as the first two. Increasingly numb, Jake checked the last four.

Dead. All dead.

Did I kill them? Fuck, I didn't hit them that hard! I couldn't, not in my human form. Not all of them. Could I?

Instinct told him it had to be something else, some other cause. Something unnatural.

Jake turned a slow circle in the dark room, until he was facing Derek Holston's brutalized corpse. The red traces all around the body, the trails leading to the sealed stones in the wall, and the coating on the spilled dirt were slowly fading away now, as if they had discharged whatever malice they had been holding.

An image formed in his mind then, of the picture of Thoth from Phila Gruyere's book. It shifted to an ibis. Then, less definite in shape but more definite in presence, Merilee's Stone Man.

Jake's lips pulled back to give his fangs room, even if they didn't descend.

He didn't give a shit if he didn't have the evidence to tie this asshole to Charlotte Heart's suicide. He knew it connected to the disappearance of Phila Gruyere and the other strong practitioners. And Holston's murder and the death of these techs laced into everything, too. Jake knew the Stone Man was responsible, and more than that, an active danger to Merilee, to the Sibyls, to everyone in New York City. Maybe the world.

If his claws had emerged, he would have used them to dig straight through the sealed wall, through all the dirt, following that ribbon of red before it left his vision completely.

"You fucker," he whispered to the arrogant, murdering son of a bitch, wherever he might be. "I don't care what you are. Now it's going to be me, coming after *you*."

23

Merilee planted her feet firmly on the floor, leaned forward, and pressed her palms into the table. Her knees shook, and she had to tense her whole body to control her spinning head as she glared at Sal Freeman across the long table in the townhouse conference room. Andy was, for the moment, out of harm's way with another Sibyl, sending messages to the Motherhouses. Good thing, because Merilee was plotting to blow the captain of the OCU to some other planet.

Without opening the windows.

Mother Keara in her green robes and Mother Anemone in blue stood behind Freeman as if to shield him from Merilee's fury, but her triad and Creed and Nick stood with her at the opposite end of the table. Jake sat in a chair at the table's center with his Glock on the table in front of him, hands folded beside the gun, eyes focused on a point somewhere in the back of the room.

Wind surged through Merilee's still-weak body and she barely held back disaster as she snarled, "You *can't* suspend Jake."

Freeman's dark eyes blazed. "I have—" he began, but Jake finished for him.

"He has to do it. Seven people died this morning under suspicious circumstances—after I knocked them out." Jake kept his gaze straight ahead on nothing at all. He didn't move. The sleeves of his jacket didn't so much as twitch. Even at an angle, Merilee could tell his expression was as flat as his voice. "It'll be a while before the M.E. gives us anything definite."

In her thick-headed, confused state, she couldn't stop focusing on him or his talisman, which still rested between her breasts, beneath her leather jumpsuit. Her fingers itched to touch it, rub it, force him to respond to her in some real, emotional way. But no. She wouldn't let herself do it, couldn't allow herself to override his will, but *damn*it she wanted him to fight this.

"It's my fault," Jake added in that terrible toneless voice. "The techs are dead because of me."

"That's not true," Mother Anemone argued before Merilee could sputter out the words. "Some terrible, wicked power killed those unfortunate technicians, and when Yana returns from conducting her investigation, she'll tell us what it was."

"I'll still have to suspend Jake until our own internal investigation is completed." Freeman looked genuinely sorry, miserable actually, but Merilee still wanted to kill him. "It's policy—and with Alvin Carter and the presidential race involved, and the existence of the OCU spilling into the open—damn. The media is swallowing this whole. The entire city is losing its mind, panicking about supernatural activity and potential paranormal threats."

"Policy sucks," Cynda snapped from behind Merilee as a tendril of smoke snaked across the table. "The media sucks! They don't know what Jake is, and they haven't found out about the Sibyls yet."

"Careful," Nick said, and Merilee knew he was trying to calm Cynda's fire energy. "I agree with you, but take it easy with flames."

Powered by Cynda's unexpected but very welcome support, Merilee let loose with more of her frustration. "Who gives a shit about a bunch of reporters or some half-assed political candidate instantly pulling out of the presidential race because Derek got murdered in the candidate's secret basement? Bela told you if Jake hadn't smacked those people in the head, they would have torn out one another's throats."

"My brother did what he had to do." Creed's voice had the steady quality of an earth Sibyl, but Merilee caught the edge of frustration in his tone. "He's no murderer."

Another tendril of smoke curled past Merilee's face, and she wished Cynda would just torch Freeman and have done with this goddess-awful nightmare. She'd fan the flames herself.

Freeman released a long breath and lowered his gaze. "I respect that. I believe that, and I believe in Jake. But—"

Riana's calm but angry voice overrode Freeman's lame explanations. "Jake saved Merilee's life. *Again.* And Bela's, too—and a couple of those insane evidence techs. Doesn't he get credit for that?"

"Damn straight." Merilee's woozy head pounded as her wind fought to jump across the room. She imagined Freeman caught in a whirlwind, spinning off to Antarctica. If Riana's steadying hand hadn't rested on her shoulder at that very second, it would have happened. "You can't do this, Sal. You're supposed to be his friend, for the sake of all the goddesses. You know Jake's a fine officer and good man."

"I'm not a man, Merilee." Jake turned his head just enough to face Merilee, and the pain devastating his handsome face completely twisted her insides. "I'm an Astaroth demon, for all the fucking good it did me or anyone else today. Freeman risked his career when he advocated for my training, and again when he hired me. He *is* my friend, and he's doing the right thing now. Leave it alone."

It was the words he didn't say that hurt her worse.

Not out loud, no, but in his posture, in the dull darkness of his normally bright eyes.

Leave me *alone.*

"Your phrasing concerns me, *agapitos.*" Mother Anemone's voice was as sharp as her gaze, piercing Merilee's dizzy consciousness even as her words seemed to pierce Jake's soul. "For all the good it did you . . . what do you mean by that? Did something go wrong with your demon essence today?"

Jake turned away from Merilee to stare at nothing again—and he didn't answer Mother Anemone's question.

The shock of that reality finally brought Merilee all the way back from whatever happened to her in that accursed basement.

"Jake?" She willed him to look at her, and it took every scintilla of her self-control not to press her palm against his talisman and force the issue. "What is she talking about?"

Freeman's face turned an unpleasant shade of red. He put his hands on the conference table and leaned toward Jake. "What aren't you telling me, Jake? Every borough is on the brink of rioting over this, and our ass is hanging in the wind. By God, you *better* not be holding anything back at this point."

Creed and Nick walked past Riana, Cynda, and Merilee, and they went to stand closer to Jake, partially blocking Merilee's view of him. "Whatever it is, you can tell us," Creed said. "Nick and I have been through some serious shit with our Curson demon aspects."

Jake stood, shoving his chair back with the same explosion of temper Merilee remembered from his outburst in Phila Gruyere's apartment. The metal and plastic seat slammed against the wall behind him, cracked the unit blackboard up the middle, and broke into two pieces.

"It's not the same." Jake's voice shook with an emotion Merilee couldn't identify. She started toward him, but Riana and Cynda each grabbed one of her arms, and Mother Anemone held up a hand, sending a steady wave of air energy directly into Merilee's chest to hold her where she stood.

Jake crammed his fingers in his pocket and pulled out his shield, gripping it so tightly that Merilee was sure the metal would bend. "You change when you choose to change," Jake said to his brothers. "It's never been the same for me. It's not that simple. I have to be one or the other, Astaroth or human."

"We have discussed this." Mother Anemone lowered her arm and freed Merilee from the restraint of her directed wind. "The answer is to release the light inside you, to be all of what you are, both demon and human in equal measure. It may not be too late, *agapitos*."

"When I spend any time at all in demon form, I get less human, and I can't tolerate that." Jake slammed his shield on the conference table beside his Glock. "Now I've stayed in human form, and I can't use the demon powers when I need them. That much, you're right about, Mother." He looked at her then, and Mother Anemone stepped back, clearly shocked by the force of Jake's rage. "The rest, though, you're wrong about the rest. I can't be two things at once."

He glanced back at the shield he had more or less crushed into the tabletop. "And I suck at both."

He stormed around the table then, past Freeman and the two Sibyl Mothers, and straight toward the conference room door. Merilee struggled with Cynda and Riana, who wouldn't let her go. If her triad sisters hadn't been so pregnant, Merilee would have forced the issue, but as it was, she bit her lip and tears of frustration streamed down her cheeks.

"Want I should stop him?" Mother Keara murmured to Mother Anemone.

Mother Anemone shook her head with a sad look on her regal face. She pushed a strand of her ash blond hair behind her ear. "I think it's essential that he sort this out for himself." Her gaze traveled to Merilee. "Jake has much to reconcile. Many decisions to make."

As if rendering his opinion on the subject, Jake slammed the conference room door so hard the walls shook.

Almost at the same moment, three Astaroths materialized at the back of the conference room—Darian, Quince, and Jared, the demons Jake had been training.

They glared at the closed door, then at the conference table—and specifically at Freeman and Merilee.

Shit.

Freeman echoed her thoughts aloud with another, "Shit."

Merilee stared at them, at their confused, angry expressions, and realized the Astaroths believed Jake had been betrayed.

"Look," Freeman was saying. "It's not as simple as you're thinking. Not as clear-cut. If you'll wait a minute, we'll try to explain."

Betrayed. Merilee closed her eyes. That was right, yet wrong, too, yet—*shit, shit! We can't afford to lose these Astaroths now.*

The demons vanished.

The door opened, then slammed again.

"Too late," Merilee said aloud, and she wanted to scream.

Cynda and Riana kept hold of Merilee's forearms as

Creed and Nick both turned to Freeman and said at the same time, "Jake didn't kill anybody."

"Goddamnit, I know that." Freeman rubbed the side of his face like his jaw was hurting. "Demon or no, he's—he's my friend, and he's *not* a killer. Ah, for Chrissake."

Freeman rubbed his jaw again, the look on his face growing more miserable by the second. "Look, I've got to stay here and wait for Mother Yana to get back. Whatever she can find for us, it's Jake's best and fastest shot at being cleared."

He locked eyes with Nick, then Creed. "Go after him. Make him tell you what did happen with his demon powers. I've got to put something in my report, and for fuck's sake, it'll probably make the national news—but I want to shield him if I can, so I've got to know the truth of it."

Nick and Creed nodded.

"Oh, and get those Astaroths back, too," Freeman added. "I mean, the *other* Astaroths, if you can, okay?"

Creed led the way as he and Nick went after their younger brother and his disappeared demon friends. Merilee watched the men go and wished she could make them move faster, or get hold of their talismans and force them to bring Jake straight back to her so she could reason with him. Comfort him. Hold him. Do *something*.

"Let me go," she told Riana and Cynda.

They turned her arms loose as Mother Anemone said, "I believe I can shed some light on what Jake meant about not being good at being both Astaroth and human."

Everyone stared at Mother Anemone, even Mother Keara, and waited.

Mother Anemone gazed at each of them in turn, until her eyes rested on Merilee. "It's very simple, and something I warned him of many times. He has remained so long in human form that he couldn't shift to his full demon essence when he chose to do so."

"He shifted easily enough when he was with me." The words were out before Merilee could censor herself. She felt her face flush. "I mean, well, yeah. He could shift. During sex."

Nobody seemed greatly surprised about the sex part, least of all Mother Anemone. "But was he in control? Did he *wish* to shift?"

Merilee thought about it, remembered the wild blaze of Jake's eyes as they mixed from gold to gray blue and back again. She balled one fist as her body remembered the rest. "I—I don't know. Maybe not?"

Mother Anemone gave her a sad look. "Likely not. If he has shifted recently, it would have been in moments of great emotional excitement or duress, a last gasp, if you will, of his ability to control himself."

Merilee thought about the times Jake had shifted. At the Windermere apartments, when they almost died, and during the battle with the god. Then again, when he took Devin Allard home to Greece for burial—but that was only partial, wasn't it? When he made love to Merilee, he shifted a lot, but no, he absolutely hadn't been in control of it.

That's why he gave me the talisman.

She raised her fingers to touch the necklace, checked herself, then lowered her hand again.

"He is very stubborn, your Jake." Mother Anemone's smile seemed kind even as Mother Keara laughed in her agreement with that statement.

"Oh, really," Merilee muttered as Cynda choked out a laugh, then covered her mouth and smoked with embarrassment. "Jake, stubborn. You think?"

"He *is* a Lowell." Riana patted Cynda's shoulder, then waved away more smoke.

"Jake may be able to heal from his foolhardy disregard of his true nature, but it will be a difficult process." Mother Anemone's expression grew grave. "There is . . . more, I fear."

"Okay, I don't like the sound of that," Merilee said, feeling her voice choke off at the last word. She definitely didn't enjoy the worried look on Mother Anemone's face, either.

"It is possible that if Jake does manage to shift to his Astaroth form," Mother Anemone said slowly, carefully, as if to be sure every word was understood, "he might never be able to take human shape again."

Merilee fumbled for the nearest chair and sat down hard, not quite able to accept what she had just heard. She was too stunned to scream or cry, though both responses seemed reasonable, completely logical, and absolutely appropriate for the gut-stabbing despair that attacked her. She stared down at the table, rubbing her throat to ease a sudden choking sensation.

"Shit," Cynda said, giving voice to a fraction of Merilee's shock as Riana leaned down, put her arm around Merilee's shoulders, and gave her a brief hug before standing beside her like a guard, arms folded.

"Are you serious?" Freeman sounded uncertain and upset. "Somebody better warn him about that, don't you think?"

The sound of Freeman's voice startled Merilee into looking up, and she realized she had been ignoring him completely, willing him into nonexistence. Like Jake and most men, and it seemed fate itself, the bastard wouldn't cooperate with her wishes at all.

"Very good idea, Captain Freeman." Mother Keara's usually rough voice flowed as smooth and hot as Irish whiskey. She gestured toward the door as a fine sheen of smoke rose from her skin. "Why don't you go use your phones or radios to reach Nick and Creed, and have them do just that?"

Freeman frowned at her. "But Mother Yana will be back any minute. I need to hear what she has to say."

Mother Anemone turned her most winning smile in the captain's direction, along with enough wind to blow his thick black hair into his face. "After *we* hear it, of course. Could you find Andrea Myles—sorry, I mean your Andy—and send her to us?"

Freeman, Merilee realized, might be as stubborn as Jake, but the man was certainly not a fool. He could read the invisible sign in the air flashing *Sibyl business, Sibyl business*. Freeman pushed his hair out of his eyes, mumbled a few more apologies, then made his way straight out of the conference room without looking back.

Merilee hoped he would spend a few minutes alone with Andy before he sent her to the conference room. The two of them needed a little time, more than ever now. They seemed to steady each other.

As soon as he was gone, Mother Anemone came to the other end of the table and knelt in front of Merilee. She gripped both of Merilee's wrists, lifted her hands, and kissed them gently. "Do not lose hope, my dear. We *will* find our way through this. We'll find a way to help Jake."

24

We'll find a way to help Jake.

Merilee replayed the words in her mind two or three times as she studied Mother Anemone's open, sincere face. With all her heart, Merilee wanted to believe the Mother who raised her, who trained her, wasn't offering empty comfort.

"We could lose him, Mother. You said that."

Mother Anemone's gaze moved to Merilee's neck, to the bit of gold chain visible through the open part of her jumpsuit's zipper. "You're wearing his talisman, aren't you?"

Merilee nodded, still not able to swallow properly or think in a straight line.

"Good, good." Mother Anemone let go of Merilee's wrists and patted the backs of her hands. "Protect it with your life and do *not* use it. Do not force him, under any circumstances, or we could lose him to his demon essence forever."

"I would never force Jake to do anything he didn't want to do." Merilee sat up straighter and tried to ignore the pangs of guilt over how many times she had already considered using the damned thing for just that purpose.

She wouldn't do that again. She wouldn't even *think* it again.

Hecate's torch, he might change to demon form and never be human again. . . .

"You understand that Jake is special." Mother Anemone stood and smoothed her blue robes. "We think he might be key in the coming fight against the Legion."

"So there is a big battle brewing," Riana said, distress lacing her overcontrolled tone. "Merilee's been having dreams about that."

"We're almost certain of it," Mother Anemone confirmed. "Many air Sibyls have been having vague, unpleasant premonitions—though most have not seen the detail Merilee has reported, and none have seen that menacing figure."

Menacing figure. A hot rush of anger shoved the vestiges of her recent dizziness out of Merilee's consciousness. Her teeth slammed together at the thought of the Stone Man.

This was proof, then. Absolute. Incontrovertible evidence that he was real and here in New York.

And sooner or later, coming for me.

Her hand burned to touch Jake's talisman, and she hated herself for the urge.

What about the Keres? Are they coming for me, too? Damn. Damn! I can't think about that right now.

Mother Keara picked up Mother Anemone's thread as the two once more stood together on the opposite side of the table from Merilee. "We think this might be . . . a final battle. The last battle with the Legion, win or lose—though we don't understand the details, the specifics. It's as if the instigator's plan isn't yet fully formed."

The door opened, and Andy escorted Mother Yana into the conference room, holding the older woman's elbow for support. Mother Yana had left her walking stick propped in the corner of the conference room so she would attract less attention when the OCU and the NYPD regular units snuck her into the basement at Alvin Carter's headquarters. For that same reason, the elderly Russian paragon had her usual riot of white hair pulled back in an austere bun, and she was dressed in casual American street clothes.

An unarmed Mother wearing blue jeans and a short-sleeved white blouse was about the strangest, most unnatural thing Merilee had ever seen. Even stranger was red-haired, ultramodern Andy wearing the canary yellow robes that identified her as a water Sibyl.

Merilee would have laughed just to blow off a little steam if Mother Yana's face weren't so tense. Hectic red spots marred both of her cheeks, and her breath came shallowly with each jerky step she took under Andy's guidance. When Mother Yana saw Merilee sitting at the conference table, unmistakable relief shone from her wrinkled face. "Good, good, oh, thank the Goddess. I feared for you, child. There vas poison in that room, poison meant for air Sibyls above all others."

Merilee sat up straighter, along with everyone else.

Andy helped Mother Yana get seated across from Merilee, and then Andy pulled up a chair for herself and sat by the Mother. Beside them were Mother Keara and Mother Anemone, and Riana and Cynda took chairs on either side of Merilee.

"It must not have vanted you dead," Mother Yana continued, her wolflike eyes bright with concern and certainty. "If it vished to kill you, you vould not be here. Hydrogen sulfide gas, mixed with a powerful, powerful bit of elemental containment and other energies I could not analyze. Very tricky. Very . . . elegant. Keyed to release in small measure vhen you vere present, then flow in earnest once there vas no air Sibyl present."

Merilee thought about the unnaturally bright and strong traces of sulfur. An unusual elementally locked trap, one *she* had sprung just by showing up? "So, when I arrived, my presence released the poison?"

"A bit. A tiny bit—but vith it being gas, vith it being borne by the air, you vere more vulnerable."

"Sibyls are exquisitely sensitive to poisons carried in their element," Mother Anemone explained to Andy, who looked extremely confused. "We'll succumb to a very small amount, much too tiny to cause a reaction in most humans."

"Until there's a shitload," Merilee said, thinking about the thickly coated dirt that had spilled into the basement. "Bela reacted, too, but only after a lot more gas entered the room."

Mother Yana nodded. "And after your Jake removed you and my Bela, the snare tightened." She raised a gnarled hand and curled her fingers, making Merilee shudder. "Only Jake could survive in the poisoned air, since at base, he is not human."

"Jake didn't kill those techs," Merilee mumbled. "I did. In a way."

"A monster killed them." Mother Yana spoke like an elementary school teacher, albeit with a heavy accent. "A true monster, I fear. My initial tests suggest this creature may have unusual energy. The capacity to stir unrest and discord vherever it goes. It may *feed* on human misery and distress, like vhat is happening in your streets of New York City as ve speak. Riots. Beatings. Panic." She turned her gaze on her fellow Mothers. "Keara. Anemone. I cannot be certain, but ve must entertain the possibility, ve must face the probability that ve are dealing with an Old Vone."

The shock on Mother Keara's face was unmistakable, as was the horror conveyed by Mother Anemone's expression.

"There can't be an Old One in New York City," Mother Anemone said so quietly Merilee barely heard the words. "Here. Now. In the modern age. You must be mistaken."

Mother Yana shook her head. "The traces vere very strong, and I do not believe any other creature could have vorked the elemental snare. It vas too complex, even for the best of Sibyls. The energy I sensed—it vas ancient. More ancient, by far, than our Sibyl orders."

At the same time, Cynda and Riana both asked, "What's an Old One?"

Andy, who was uncharacteristically dry, kept quiet, but she went back to looking confused.

Merilee was confused, too. "One of the original paranormal entities on Earth," she said. "A natural demon, not created, but present before the first human life appeared on this planet." She couldn't understand how that was possible. "Our records say all the natural demons were wiped out before recorded history began."

Mother Yana opened her wizened hands. "All things considered, this vone vas not."

"There are mentions of natural demons roaming the Earth in recorded history, actually," Merilee said, fighting back a resurgence of her earlier light-headedness. "Many ancient texts, like the Bible and the Kabbalah."

"Many Sibyls believe we ourselves are the descendants of the Kabbalah's Lilith and her unions with natural demons," Mother Anemone said, looking thoughtful.

Mother Keara grunted and banged the table with her small fist. "Too much theory. Always with the theories, you air Sibyls. If we're to go dealing with an Old One, what are we going to *do*?"

Mother Yana frowned at her. "Vat ve alvays do. Analyze. Plan. Implement. Ve vill discover the nature of this monster, kill it, and have done vith this chaos."

Her confidence flowed around the table like elixir, briefly raising Merilee's spirits until she thought about her nightmares of a destroyed New York, of Sibyl fighting Sibyl, of herself being consumed by a giant, man-eating ibis. Then she thought about Jake, somewhere out in the city, miserable and without his badge, the only thing that had defined him other than his talisman since he came to awareness as an Astaroth.

Does he know I care about him?

She squeezed her hands together to remove all temptation to let them get anywhere near the talisman around her neck.

Please don't let him shift and be lost to me forever.

As she sat straining to master her own impulses, something occurred to her about her dreams and the terrifying ibis. As succinctly as she could, Merilee shared what she and Jake had discovered at Phila Gruyere's apartment.

"Yes," Mother Anemone said, her eyes growing brighter after Merilee gave the details of the fight with the god. "We have to assume that all the strange happenings in this city are related to the presence of this Old One."

"Like the exodus of the paranormal practitioners." Riana leaned back in her chair, folding her hands over her rounded belly. "That makes a lot more sense now."

"And the disappearances," Merilee agreed. "Especially Phila's. Maybe she was summoning that protective fire Loa to send it after what she thought this monster was. That Egyptian god Thoth, the one in the book she placed at the center of her vévé. Could we be looking for Thoth?"

"It is possible—but most of those older gods were simply representations," Mother Anemone said. "Bits of the true essence of natural demons the culture encountered or remembered."

Mother Yana's wolf eyes grew wide now, probably calculating a hundred possible avenues of attack against this creature. "Yes. Old Vones did not have determined form. They could change at vill, except in the element that spawned them."

Andy tugged at the neckline of her yellow robe, her expression definitely more law enforcement now than Sibyl Mother—which Merilee actually found comforting. "So Thoth," Andy said, "might be only part of this—this *true* demon's persona?"

"Yes, exactly." Mother Anemone reached over and gripped Andy's hand. "Very good."

"And we might be looking for a creature that can shift his appearance any time it chooses." Cynda massaged her temples and let off a new round of smoke. "Shit."

"There's more." Merilee shifted uncomfortably in her chair, trusting her instincts but still feeling a shade idiotic, putting her thoughts about this into words. "I think it's trying to breed."

Everyone at the table stared at her, openmouthed.

She ignored the agitation building in her chest and plunged ahead. "That's the only thing that makes sense. The stuff in my nightmares all points in that direction. The practitioners who have disappeared, they're all very powerful—like Phila. And all female. Like it's handpicking stock to produce its next generation."

Mother Anemone's clear blue gaze fell on her, and Merilee saw the light come on in the Mother's face. "Your dreams. This creature—he has his sights fixed on you as well?"

"Well, that's not happening," Riana said immediately, punctuated by Cynda's "Oh, *fuck* no."

Water trickled from the sprinkler above Andy's head. "I'll drown the son of a bitch if he gets anywhere near you."

"I'm certain he tortured Derek Holston to learn about our weaknesses. Air Sibyls, I mean." Merilee stared at the table in front of her. "I think he used that weakness to get my attention. That he's trying to scare me. Wear me down, so maybe he can grab me when my defenses are low."

"No, no, no, no." Riana's voice was firm, like her quick grip on Merilee's shoulder. "I don't care what he—it—thinks, or what it's trying to do. Screw that, Merilee. And I don't care how pregnant Cynda and I are. We'll be right beside you."

This time when Merilee lifted her hand to touch the talisman, she stopped her fingers just inches away from the leather-shielded ring hanging between her breasts. "How many more people will die if it doesn't get what it wants?"

The conference room door burst open.

Freeman strode in, his expression more thunderous than usual. "We've got an emergency. The Jamaica Bay ranger triad was on its way here with everyone else, to figure out how we're going to deal with this media exposure, but we lost contact with them around Hell's Kitchen."

"Lost . . . contact?" Andy's voice sounded as weary and shaky as Merilee felt.

"They didn't check in, and they're not responding to that wind chime–tattoo communication you guys do." He pointed to the inside of his right forearm, then frowned.

Bela Argos came into the room, looking more upset than Merilee thought possible for the normally stone-faced earth Sibyl. "We've checked everywhere," she said, panic edging through every word as she stared at them with wide, fierce eyes. "They're missing."

(25)

Bartholomew August couldn't help smiling as he stood on his balcony and gazed at the increasing tumult in New York City.

Sunset.

The perfect time for a riot.

He took long, slow breaths, drinking in the fear, soaking up the unrest, which was growing stronger by the moment. As he took in the delicious energy of conflict, he released it back to the universe in stronger, more targeted waves, striking every human energy form he could find.

Let the chaos come.

Let anarchy and commotion build now and grow until he chose to calm it—for his own purposes.

He imagined even the Sibyls were agitated by now, since they would have heard about their missing warriors.

Thus far, his plans were working out to perfection. Soon he'd have New York, and as a bonus, all the Sibyls he had chosen—especially Merilee. Oh, especially her.

He turned from the balcony to find the woman and the boy waiting. Just standing and waiting for his commands.

"Go back to the Sibyls," he said to the woman, but she shook her head.

"The streets aren't safe." She kept her eyes on the floor in front of her, but her voice had that harsh carny's edge again. "I won't make it, and you'll be losing your spy."

"I trust you to be resourceful, my dear." August tried to sound patient despite the sudden burst of rage pounding through his human form. "I require additional assistance with the air Sibyl since I can't reach her myself."

The woman finally raised her head, and when she did, August was amused by the defiance and resolve marking her withered features. "I don't want to go there anymore. I've betrayed the only friends I've ever known—the only ones to be kind to me. So you can kill me now and have done with it. That's all I'm worth, after what I've done."

August reached her in one stride and struck her with enough force to drive her to her knees, but he held back on breaking her jaw. If he damaged her, she couldn't perform her duties, and as of late, her observations and reports had proved beyond useful.

The boy let out a croak, but he didn't try to defend his mother. Not this time.

"Get up," August instructed, but the woman didn't comply. He grabbed her shoulders and yanked her to her feet. She stayed limp in his grasp, and even with her face turned, he could see the purplish mark rising along her right cheekbone.

His next instruction came out more calmly, the way he preferred. "Look at me. Now."

The woman complied this time, but defiance still registered on her bruised face.

"You have no friends," he murmured, bringing her close, so that his breath had to be tickling the skin of her forehead. "You've never allowed anyone that close to you. Not even me." He embraced her, for an instant remembering how it had been when she was young. The way they fought, then made amends. Such a brief moment in his long life, but spicy nonetheless. "Especially not me."

She didn't relax at his reminiscing, because she was smart, because she knew him too well. "You delude yourself if you think you matter at all to the Dark Crescent Sisterhood. You're disposable to them like any other servant."

At this, he thought he caught a flicker of unhappiness, and that pleased him. "Refuse me if you wish, my dear. Always your prerogative—but remember, I won't kill *you*." He let her go, then pushed her back from him and pointed to the boy. "I'll kill him. Slowly."

She cursed him then. She called him ancient names he had taught her years ago, names most humans didn't remember, much less understand, but in the end, she agreed.

As August had known she would.

It was part of their game. It was all they had left, this push and shove, this resistance and dominance.

If the woman had been eternal, he would have enjoyed keeping her for occasional pleasures. What a pity most humans were so frail, so completely temporary.

After the woman left to do his bidding, August returned to the balcony and once more enjoyed the misery below. Though he would never tell her, nor indeed admit it to anyone, he did make a path for the woman, to be certain she reached her destination. He told himself that such attention to her needs was expedient, and ensured that his own would be met. In truth, though, it would have pissed him off if someone else killed her.

When the time came, he would kill the woman. His hands and his hands alone. No one else would touch her. No one else would stare into her eyes as life's breath left her forever.

A rattling sound behind August caught his attention, and seconds later, the boy came out to join him. As usual, the boy kept his head down and his eyes averted.

A surge of goodwill flooded through August at the sight of his offspring, as well as anticipation for the full night of activities he had planned. August wished the boy would have the balls to meet his gaze, but at the same time, he appreciated the respect and deference. "Are my new captives secure in their elementally locked chains?"

The boy nodded again.

"You're quite certain?" August put a hand on the boy's shoulder, then let his fingers slide to the back of the thin neck he could so easily snap. "If one of them escapes, I'll take your life for payment."

The boy said nothing and didn't move at all except for a quick, sharp swallow that sounded way too loud to August's sensitive ears. August couldn't help the way his lips pulled back across his teeth. He let out a low snarl.

I could do it right now, kill the boy.

So many different ways. Crushing. Pulverizing. Tearing his weak flesh with teeth and claws sharp enough to serve as surgical blades. August knew he could rip the boy's pounding heart right out of his fragile rib cage.

He stroked his son's neck, let his palm travel upward to the base of the boy's delicate skull. Power built inside August, wild and heady as he drew energy from the increasing madness in the streets below—but he hesitated.

Even as he almost gave in to his murderous impulse, the loneliness that had plagued him so many long nights, so many endless years, came growling, snarling back to chew at his insides.

August snarled again.

Gripped the boy's neck.

And stopped.

He let go and shoved the boy away from him. No death tonight. He needed this one to get to the air Sibyl, and the boy was far from ready for his role in that plan.

"Go inside and get the gun with the elementally locked bullets," August said. "You have a lot of practicing to do."

The boy bolted away from him.

August watched him go, half-relieved, half-furious. For a moment, he hated himself with a fierceness he had never before known.

That boy is *mine.*

Disappointing, pathetic—but mine.

His children, no matter how much failure they represented, meant something to him. He had never been able to kill any of them or their mothers, though he had never quite understood why.

It had to be the loneliness, or rather, the small respite from it that his "family" offered. Until he could resurrect his own, he had so little real company. The women, his hostages, they didn't count. His interactions with them brought him no real pleasure beyond purc carnal satisfaction and the hope of repopulating his race.

Yet when his kind was reborn from this better stock, when they once more took dominion over the earth, he would have to dispose of inferior little toys like the boy and the woman. Probably all of his lesser children across the globe. There would be no place for them in a superior world order.

An unfamiliar sensation twisted at his guts, and Bartholomew August put his hands on his belly.

Was he ill?

Had he actually contracted some sort of human virus?

Was that even possible?

He didn't think so, yet some creeping germ cell had to be responsible for the uncomfortable pains he was experiencing. There could be no other explanation.

"I have no time for this," August said aloud, but talking to himself only doubled the sense of loneliness crawling through his consciousness.

With great force of will, August turned his attention back to fanning the flames of discord and fear in the streets. He'd get to kill later, anyway—and with his own hands.

Moreover, unlike crushing the boy for sport, the murder August had planned would accomplish something. It would help him get closer to what he truly needed.

So for now, he would focus and ensure the necessary riot, then work with the boy and the gun until he was certain the boy knew what he was doing.

After that, he would service the newly captured Sibyls and the other females who weren't yet pregnant. Then it would be time to head out on his other missions.

The discomfort in his gut faded.

August smiled.

He was looking forward to his little excursion and the blood he'd spill, the pain he'd inflict. Nothing like a little misery to set everything inside him completely right again.

(26)

Sirens pounded the night air as Jake elbowed through clumps of people who were gesturing and shouting and crying. Half the city seemed to be fighting or rioting, and the other half clogged the sidewalks. All of the anxious crowds chattered or screamed about witches and vampires and zombies and the Occult Crimes Unit, mixed with murder and Carter's rapid withdrawal from the presidential race. Dozens of men and women wearing bright orange shirts reading PEACE WARRIORS held out their hands and spoke in soothing tones, obviously trying to settle everyone down.

It was just so much noise to Jake as he forced his way back toward the site of the worst disaster in his life—save for his own murder, which he had been too young to do anything about. He jammed his hands into his jacket pockets and his nostrils flared, taking in the tang of sweat and fear and panic. Jake knew what it felt like to die. To have his life ripped away from him as he screamed and ached and pleaded for mercy that never came. He couldn't believe he let that happen to so many other people.

The deaths of all those crime scene technicians—he could have saved them if he had been smarter and faster.

If I had changed into my demon form.

Jake strained with all his muscles as he walked, willing his body to shift, reaching for the sensation of his wings and fangs, for the lighter bones and clawed hands of his Astaroth form. He didn't care if he popped into a pure white flapping demon in front of the multitudes, but nothing happened.

Snarling in absolute frustration, he imagined the last time he managed a full shift.

With Merilee.

While he was making love to her, sinking his cock deep inside her warm depths as steam rolled through her shower.

The memory made his body burn, but still Jake didn't shift. He just kept walking down the streets of New York City headed for his target, remaining completely human—and without his talisman. Merilee still had it, so he couldn't even hand the jewelry to somebody and force them to give him a command to change.

Would that work?

He wanted to pound his fists against his skull.

Damn Mother Anemone for being right. Damn me *for not listening to her.*

Everything seemed clear to him now. No, he couldn't be both human and demon—but to do the most good, he needed the power his demon form offered him.

He needed to be an Astaroth. That would have to be his choice. In the end, he could help far more people with his increased strength and speed, with his Astaroth qualities.

As for Merilee—shit, but thinking about her made his gut ache.

Would she keep seeing him if he spent most of his time in demon form?

Should *he* keep seeing her?

Jake was pretty sure he knew the answer to that, but he didn't want to face it.

Still, no matter how angry or emotional he got, he couldn't shift.

"It doesn't matter," he muttered through his teeth as

he came to a halt in front of Carter's headquarters, or as close as he could get to it with all the pandemonium.

It was too late for heroics now, anyway, wasn't it?

Nothing would ever make up for the deaths at this place.

Orange-shirted Peace Warriors roved in every direction here, too, using tiny orange flashlights to light their way and gesture to the crowds.

Jake didn't think they were doing much good.

The *whump-whump* of helicopters and the silvery sweep of search beams filled the evening, as well as yammering from dozens of news crews with bright, round lights. Jake scanned the sky, picking out police helicopters and news choppers, too.

As many of the crowd gazed upward or just stood around openmouthed, obviously in shock over the media revelations about verified paranormal activity in the city, another helicopter joined the swarm. Jake figured it for New York State Police or maybe FBI, but it was angled away so that he couldn't see its letters. A dull ache started in his head, and he realized he was clenching his jaw again.

It was time to get to work, to do what he came here to do. That was the only thing that might help, the only thing that mattered now, and the best way to help Merilee and see to her safety.

Shit, Lowell, does everything come back to her?

Jake massaged his tight jaw and had to acknowledge that, fuck, yeah, just about everything came back to Merilee.

Hadn't that been the case since he first laid eyes on her two years ago? It damn sure had been true since he came to New York and met her face-to-face.

And kissed her . . .

And touched her . . .

He shook his head and refocused his attention on the Carter headquarters, then tried to calm his mind. He thought about the sealed tunnel in the basement and everything Bela had told them about the displaced dirt before all the fighting and dying.

One or two hundred yards, maybe three . . .

Jake scanned nearby buildings, estimating distance and potential. The tunnel could empty into the sewers or even the subway system, or maybe even rise through the ground in some green space or park corner—but Jake doubted that. The Stone Man would have wanted absolute security and privacy. If Jake didn't miss his guess, the bastard had located his escape hatch somewhere indoors, probably the ground floor of a deserted or derelict structure.

He noted four likely candidate buildings and set out toward the first and closest. A voice of reality nudged at the back of his mind, reminding him that he had no badge to gain admission and no gun to force any issues or defend himself. That same voice whispered that he couldn't shift to Astaroth form and become invisible.

He didn't give a damn.

One way or the other, he was getting a look in those buildings.

As it turned out, the first building wasn't much of a problem. Apartments with a doorman who was wrapped up in hollering at somebody else—and a completely intact ground floor, well tiled from what Jake could determine.

Jake's second target was a business, and once more, he didn't see any sign of disruption in the floor. He also didn't think the Stone Man would choose an inhabited space, so he moved on quickly.

The third building—now this one had promise.

Twilight gripped the city as Jake stood outside what

looked to be a four-story tenement, boarded tight, with renovation permits hammered to the wooden front doors.

Which were locked when he rattled them.

He glanced over his shoulder, back toward the clamor around the Carter headquarters a little over a block away. The street around him was mostly deserted, no onlookers paying attention to him, so he lowered his right shoulder and slammed it against the tenement doors.

The doors rattled, but didn't give.

Jake rubbed his shoulder. The pain from his failed strike helped him focus. He checked the street behind him again, made sure no one was watching, and hit the doors again. And again. Hurting worse each time. Grimacing by the fourth blow, wondering if his shoulder might be pulverized.

On his fifth assault, one of the doors groaned and cracked. It opened enough for him to force his hands between them and break into the dusty foyer, where he stood for a long moment, realizing he at least had his demon senses intact. He could still see in the dark fairly well and make out the fresh dirt strewn on the floor of the room adjacent to the foyer. And the mound where the tunnel entrance had been. And the dark splotches of poisonous red sulfur clinging to the mound.

Jake sniffed in the darkness, and caught a definite trace of rotten eggs, just like he had noticed in the basement of the Carter headquarters. His pulse picked up and he let his awareness spread outward into the room.

Nothing else alive in the space, not that he could sense.

Like that meant anything.

Some freaky-ass monster could explode from that dirt mound any second now. His recent experience with the trapped Vodoun Loa had been more than enough to teach him *that* lesson.

Jake's hand automatically moved to his holster, but his Glock was back at the townhouse, on the conference room table with his badge.

Shit.

He tried to keep his arms and body loose, ready for anything, as he slowly edged into the murky room, heading toward the dirt and sulfur traces. The air was cool and still, but thick with dust and the faint, rotted leavings of strong sulfur.

Training and instinct drove him to study the floor in all directions, and in a few seconds, he picked up a trail of footsteps, laced with that same strong but slowly degrading red sulfur trace. Jake moved to the glowing footsteps, crouched to study them, and immediately saw the size differential. One pair of large men's shoes made the main trail. The other trail, marked only lightly with sulfur, had been made by very small feet. Sneaker-clad. Probably female, or universe forbid, a child.

His fists tightened.

The desire to get hold of this Stone Man, to choke the life right out of him, nearly overwhelmed Jake. Deep inside him, somewhere in the center of his gut, he felt the first stirrings of his true Astaroth energy, and fed it with his rage as he followed the prints through the darkened building.

Here and there, the woman or child wearing the sneakers had been dragged.

Son of a bitch.

Who do you have captive now?

What's your endgame?

The angrier Jake got, the more clearly he imagined confronting the Stone Man in person, the more his gut churned and those demon instincts stirred.

Here, he caught a trace of energy.

Definitely female. Older. So not a child, then. An elderly woman. *What kind of sick bastard drags a grandmother to a sadistic sexual murder?*

The old woman's energy felt . . . overshadowed, somehow. As if she were being eclipsed by a much stronger source. Maybe forced to comply with its wishes.

Jake narrowed his eyes, tracking the prints through a small kitchen, to a back door. He put his hand on the frame—and a blast of energy surged through his fingers, his arm.

He staggered backward.

Ancient energy.

He *touched that place, that exact place on the doorframe.*

Jake's skin was on fire. His bones were melting!

The ancient energy hammered through him. Dozens of images flew through Jake's consciousness as he clutched his arm and fought not to puke or fall down.

Con men, ministers, prophets, priests, and finally gods showed themselves in Jake's mind, each older than the one before. Back through time, to seemingly *before* time. Blood rituals. So much blood. So much death to keep him—it—alive.

How could something so monstrous, so evil, be permitted to breathe air on this Earth?

Primal fury racked Jake as his demon essence recognized an archetypal enemy too old to be true, too powerful to be real. His lips pulled back to make room for fangs trying to emerge. His claws pricked at the ends of his fingers, and his back tingled where his wings wanted to burst out.

More images flowed through his brain, this time of women. Charlotte Heart. Several females Jake didn't recognize. Phila Gruyere. Three women dressed in Sibyl battle leathers.

And last, strongest, a flaming out as the contact with the ancient energy finally passed out of his body like a rotten puff of grave-stench, one more picture, clear as the sun in a cloudless sky.

Merilee.

Jake roared and threw himself toward the back entrance. As fast as he could, he forced his muscles to cooperate enough to remove his jacket. He used the thin material to cover his hand, give him a little shield from that energy, and yanked the door open.

The trail of prints led down the back steps, to the sidewalk—and then dissipated to nothing a yard or so later.

Jake put his jacket back on and stood in the back door rubbing his numb but otherwise undamaged arm. He glared at the spot where the prints vanished.

They were headed south, maybe a little southwest.

Central Park? The Financial District? Farther?

He wants Merilee. He wants her more than all the rest. He'll try to take her soon. Maybe right now.

Out in the foyer, the doors rattled.

Jake wheeled before he thought about moving. He charged back through the kitchen and into the dark room with the sealed tunnel exit. His wings, fangs, and claws were halfway out now, almost free, almost there.

Yeah, motherfucker. He stormed toward the foyer, fists primed for punching the Stone Man, legs flexed and ready to spring. He'd claw off the asshole's face, then bite straight through his neck. *Come right on inside.*

As the tips of Jake's claws poked into his palms, his brother Creed strode into the main room, followed closely by Nick. Both were dressed in black NYPD jackets and jeans, and both looked worried.

"Don't," Nick said as he grabbed Jake's shoulders and broke his charge. "Calm it down. Don't let the change proceed."

"Are you fucking nuts?" Jake heard the Astaroth-resonance in his voice. "I've been trying to do this since—"

Creed joined Nick as Nick shoved Jake back a step, his frown just as deep. "If you change, you might never be able to take human form again, Jake. We've been tracking you since you left the townhouse, trying to catch you to warn you. The Mothers sent us."

Jake felt like some essential part of his brain was shorting out, unable to connect truth and sensation and what his brother just told him.

"Human," he mumbled.

"Yeah. It sucks." Nick took hold of Jake's arm and gave him a firm squeeze, as if to hold him in his partially changed state.

Creed grabbed Jake's other arm and squeezed harder. "Knock it off, piss-brain, or you'll be winged and pale for the rest of your existence."

For a few seconds, Jake stood suspended between his twin brothers, feet on the floor, but barely. Wings almost completely out. Tips of fangs bumping his lips. Another few moments, and he'd be an Astaroth. Strong again, faster, ready for anything, Glock or no Glock.

The pull was unimaginable, almost irresistible. He had to change. He wanted to change. This was what he had decided, to be a demon again.

But forever?

Merilee's image filled his awareness.

As an Astaroth, he wouldn't be able to give her any type of real relationship, man to woman. Yet he could keep her safe, make certain no harm ever came to her.

But I'd never touch her again. Never hold her or kiss her or make love to her.

Nick shook Jake's arm. "I'll take off my talisman and kick your ass until you aren't conscious anymore."

Creed was already glowing golden, showing the

larger, more powerful outline of his Curson demon form. "I don't need to take off a talisman to shift," he snarled, his voice echoing with demon force. "You need to make a careful decision before you throw away the life you've chosen."

Nick let go of Jake's arm. "Being a cop. Working with us—your family."

"Merilee," Creed said, more demon than human now. His fingers crushed into Jake's arm, and the pain almost jerked Jake's focus away from his own shifting process. "Don't forget Merilee."

Jake managed to yank his arm free from Creed's powerful grip. "Like I *ever* forget her. I have to keep her safe. The Stone Man. You don't know what's—"

While Jake was looking at Creed, Nick's fist caught Jake off-guard.

Knuckles smashed into his jaw.

Sparks exploded in Jake's mind.

He toppled backward and lost all grip on his Astaroth form as he crashed to the floor, sending up a brown cloud of dust and dirt.

"Sorry, bro," he heard Nick say as his consciousness ebbed.

Jake thought Nick didn't sound sorry, not one fucking bit.

He wasn't able to think anything else.

(27)

Merilee tried to focus as she dabbed blood off an earth Sibyl's forehead in the townhouse entrance hall.

This was insane.

The city was crazy. It felt like the world—her world—was falling apart and she couldn't do one friggin' thing to stop it.

She pressed her cloth against the Sibyl's wound and tried to speed the healing, but her mind kept wandering to Jake. Then to the talisman hanging around her neck, concealed beneath her leathers.

Where is he?

She absolutely could not use the necklace and ring to summon him, to force him to return to the townhouse. But, Athena's teeth, did she want to. The stupid talisman was torturing her, almost whispering to her that she had the power, if only she'd use it. Fucking nightmare of a thing.

I won't do it. I will not.

But . . . is he still human?

Or a demon forever?

Her chest clutched. If she didn't stop dwelling on Jake, she'd cry or get pissed, and she couldn't afford either reaction at the moment. Her healing energies, which were stronger than most, were in high demand. That was the only reason she wasn't out hunting Jake herself.

When his brothers tracked down his stupid stubborn demon ass, she and Jake would search for the missing Sibyls and help the NYPD and the OCU handle riots and street brawls.

For right now, though, the greater good was served by her presence at the townhouse–turned–field hospital.

Damn it.

The streets of Manhattan were turning into a battleground of frightened people, angry religious nuts demanding that the media admit the paranormal headlines were all lies, and story-thirsty local, national, and international newshounds competing for leads. Helicopters thumped back and forth overhead, and the wail of fire and police sirens rose and fell over and over again.

"It is the Old Vone," Mother Yana said from behind Merilee as Delilah Moses brought her a batch of fresh clean towels. "The creature's chaos energy must be stirring this unrest—though thank the Goddess it does not affect Sibyls. If people vould go home, get off the streets, it vould die avay. Or he might choose to stop the mayhem after a point, depending on his goals."

Merilee glanced back at Delilah Moses and the Mothers, who were tending three OCU officers and two Sibyls. "If my dreams are accurate, he—it—may not be planning to calm things down at all. I think he wants the city destroyed."

Delilah, who looked exceptionally pale tonight, slipped to the back of the entrance hall and headed toward the kitchen and laundry area carrying soiled towels. Merilee lifted her hand, almost touched Jake's talisman—and thought she saw something following Delilah.

No, wait.

Merilee squinted at the air behind the old woman.

More like . . . hovering along behind her.

A ghostly shape—vaguely woman-formed.

Am I imagining this?

She realized she was about to touch the talisman and jerked her hand back to her side.

Whatever was following Delilah, if there had ever been anything, vanished.

I'm losing my shit. Completely.

Delilah hurried onward and Merilee watched her go. What kind of hell had Delilah faced as she struggled to reach the townhouse to take shelter with the Sibyls? Merilee kind of liked the old woman. Tonight, though, she was missing some of her usual fire. Unlike Cynda and Mother Keara.

Mother Keara blew air through her nose. "We must find this ancient menace and kill him—it—outright." She cut her gaze toward Mother Yana, then Mother Anemone. "Analyze, plan, implement. Now that would be implementing." She snorted again and her shoulders smoked.

The sprinkler over Mother Keara's head started leaking water in big, sloppy drops. If Andy hadn't damaged most of the sprinklers in the townhouse, it probably would have exploded into a fountain due to the heat rising off the little Irish woman.

Mother Keara glared upward and blasted the little faucet with a jet of fire so hot the metal turned red, then blue and melted shut as the ceiling all around it scorched a flaky, dark black.

Mother Yana sighed.

Merilee shook her head as Mother Anemone chastised Mother Keara for damaging the surroundings. A few bursts of wind energy later, and the Mothers settled down again. It would have been nice to have Andy around to occupy them, but as second in command of the OCU, Andy was leading a contingent of officers and techs to the Carter headquarters to make another attempt at evidence collection, and to find out where that tunnel went. They'd be gone all night and probably some of the morning, too. Freeman had also gone out with Bela Argos, leading all the Sibyls who had reached the townhouse on a hunt for the three missing warriors.

Cynda and Riana were helping Merilee patch up a young ranger triad from New Jersey. The Sibyls had been jumped by a bunch of teenagers, and they hadn't wanted to draw weapons on children.

Like Merilee, her triad sisters kept looking at the main door and flinching each time it banged open.

"Where are they?" Cynda muttered, rubbing her hand over her belly as she smoked even harder than Mother Keara had done, and sparked, too. The shoulders of her maternity top and the legs of her maternity jeans smoldered in several places, and little scorch marks appeared in the fabric. The distress in Cynda's voice was so palpable Merilee wanted to hug her, reassure her, but Merilee didn't relish the thought of being melted like the sprinkler. She settled for letting some of her air energy flow around Cynda to join with Riana's gift of subtle earth power.

As her triad's support engulfed her, Cynda's smoke eased to a few random puffs. Her hands moved from her belly to her back, massaging the muscles strained from bending, stooping, and working in the final days of her pregnancy. Her face relaxed a fraction, and Merilee and Riana made eye contact, sharing a look of relief.

"They'll get here soon," Riana said to Cynda, but she was just as worried. Merilee could see it in Riana's misty green eyes. "Any second now."

But seconds kept going by.

With each one that passed, Riana looked more fragile herself, and a little more desperate to know that Creed was safe.

Merilee's hand wandered toward the talisman a dozen or more times as OCU officers and Sibyls flowed in and out, sharing information, bringing in wounded, and keeping a sharp lookout for any hint of a media assault. As far as anyone knew, Head Case Quarters hadn't been compromised. This assumption was reinforced by the fact that OCU's official location, an inconspicuous police annex on West Thirtieth in the old Fourteenth Precinct building, which housed the Traffic Task Force, had been overrun by reporters and curious citizens.

If anyone knew about the townhouse, they'd get swamped, Merilee had no doubt. It could happen any second.

"All the boroughs are this insane," said the next Sibyl that Merilee bandaged up. The young woman had been injured in a fight with placard-wielding God-is-coming fanatics near Trinity Church. "People think it's the end of time or something."

Merilee ground her teeth as she sent healing wind through the redheaded fire Sibyl's wound to cleanse it.

So that's what the Stone Man wanted people to think, then. That all was lost, that everything was hopeless.

We've got to find that asshole and take him out. But how? Who the hell is he?

The redhead touched the clean gash on her forehead. "Thanks. That feels a lot better." She stood and picked up her sword, obviously ready to rejoin the search for the missing rangers. "That guy Bartholomew August, the candidate, he stopped a riot near the Carter headquarters, or we wouldn't have made it here. His Peace Warriors are out trying to calm everybody down, but some of them are getting in fights, too."

"I don't care who gets elected," Riana said as she helped an air Sibyl to her feet and handed the young woman her weapons—tiny throwing knives. "I just want all the campaigns and rallies over. Fewer gatherings, fewer people in the streets. And August is an idiot if he's putting himself in the middle of this fray."

"An idiot or a hero," the redhead said as her triad sister joined her. They nodded to Cynda, Riana, Merilee, and the Mothers, then headed out the door, leaving the triage area in the entrance hall blissfully patient-free for the moment.

Merilee stared at the spot where the young Sibyls had been. Her fingers curled as she thought about what the young woman said.

"An idiot or a hero," she repeated.

"Hmm?" Cynda asked as she settled her pregnant bulk in a nearby chair.

"Do we have a television set in this place that works?" Merilee asked, something agitating her thoughts. Something she couldn't quite grasp. She wanted to get another look at Bartholomew August. Hadn't he seemed familiar to her before?

The dark horse candidate . . . maybe about to become a front-runner? Maybe secretly a horny ancient demon who doubles as a ravenous ibis in people's dreams. . . . Oh, now, wouldn't that be fucking perfect?

"Television." Riana shook her head. "Uh, no, sorry. I don't think so. Way too much Sibyl energy for electronics lately. The last one blew a couple of days back, right after your latest computer."

Mother Keara gave yet another snort. Merilee knew most of the Mothers in Greece and Ireland thought modern technology was pointless and unreliable—and in the presence of so much elemental energy, yeah, *unreliable* would fit. Motherhouse Russia embraced technology more, but had their own, far advanced from anything available in the everyday world. Better shielding, better elemental balance, so it didn't go on the fritz as often. Problem was, it didn't work so well outside that Motherhouse.

Where the *hell* was Jake?

Damn it.

Merilee caught her right hand with her left and pulled her own wrist away from the talisman. When Jake got back, after she kicked the shit out of him for leaving like that and scaring her half to death, they'd have to make a run to the nearest sports bar or coffee shop to get a look at the news reports, or figure out where August was and get a look at him in person.

Tears snuck up on Merilee, flowing before she could stop them.

Jake. Please. Show up.

Had she ever cried over a man before?

And show up human.

I'm not calling you. No matter what, I won't compel you—but you better come home to me.

Riana and Cynda were both resting now, and the Mothers were offering them a bit of healing energy and pain relief for their backs and feet. Merilee turned away from them so they wouldn't see she was upset.

Could I love him if he stays an Astaroth all the time?

Oh, shit. Do I love *him?*

She wiped her eyes and stared at the door, willing it to open.

And it did.

So hard the hinges rattled.

Merilee jumped and readied herself for another disappointment—and a new influx of beat-up Sibyls or officers.

At first, her brain could barely accept what her eyes were seeing, or wouldn't believe it, not until a rush of earth energy rattled the townhouse and Riana said, "Creed!"

It was Creed.

And behind Creed came Nick, with a limp, unconscious Jake slung over his shoulder.

Cynda let out a dragon-sigh, all hot air and fire, leaned back in her chair, and covered her face with relief.

Heart pounding so hard she could barely breathe, Merilee threw herself toward Jake, slammed into Creed, blew him sideways in Riana's general direction, and reached Nick.

Nick held up his free hand and grumbled, "No fucking tornados. The trip here was enough fun for one night." He shifted Jake on his shoulder. "It's calming down, though. One of those presidential candidates is on television asking everybody to be peaceful and go home. I swear you can feel the calmness spreading like a wave. Guy's pretty charismatic. Bet he wins."

Merilee ignored Nick, keeping her back to Creed, her triad, the Mothers, the whole entire townhouse. Not caring who saw or what anybody thought, she touched Jake's arms and ran her palm against his short blond hair. He was still warm and breathing. Still alive. And human. With one hell of a bruise on what she could see of his jaw.

The sight of it made Merilee wince. "What did you do? Try to kill him?"

She loosed a burst of wind that smacked against Nick so hard he had to shift his legs to glowing gold Curson-demon form and burn off his jeans to keep standing.

"Well, shit." Nick shifted back to human, now naked from the waist down. "Guess I'm taking loverboy here to your library, then getting myself some new pants."

Merilee spun to follow him, but froze when she caught sight of Cynda covering her mouth to hide a laugh even as tears coated her cheeks.

Hormones, or love?

Merilee touched the still-damp tears on her own face

and gazed at Riana. Riana had her arms around Creed's neck, and he was speaking softly to her, one arm around her waist and his other hand resting against her round stomach.

The sight filled Merilee with a rush of warm air, followed by a round of queasy nervousness.

Her duty was here helping the injured, or out in the streets searching for the missing rangers. But Jake—

She looked up to see Jake and Nick's naked ass disappearing up the stairs.

All three Mothers looked from Cynda to Riana to Merilee, and then toward the steps. Mother Anemone smiled. "Things do seem to be slowing for the moment. See to Jake's healing and get him back in shape so you two can join the hunt as soon as possible."

Merilee took off like an arrow fired from her own bow.

Her feet barely touched the stairs as she climbed, her heart beating faster with each movement. Her rational mind knew Jake was okay, that Creed and Nick had done what they had to do to keep him safe from himself, probably from his own stubbornness—but damn it, he was injured. He wasn't conscious.

What if he didn't wake up?

She tried to smother her anxiety and let the energy inside her build so she could help him heal, but all she wanted to do was get to the library and see him and touch him again, see him open those stormy eyes and gaze up at her.

When she hit the first step on her landing, Merilee was running so hard she almost ricocheted off half-dressed Nick coming downstairs, but he dodged her, mumbling about friggin' unstable air elementals. It was all she could do not to blow him down the steps, but he did bring Jake home. For that, she'd let him live.

Merilee hurried into the library and closed and bolted the door behind her.

Nick had put Jake on her bed in the middle of a bunch of papers, chip wrappers, and soda cans.

He lay very, very still, his head on her pillow, his arms draped across his T-shirt and unzipped jacket.

She walked toward him, past her bow and quiver leaning against the edge of a bookcase, and she watched the rise and fall of his chest as she quickly cleaned all the junk off her bed to give him more room. She also checked his fingertips for claws, making sure she saw no signs of fangs creeping from his mouth.

But . . . if she did see those things, if Jake were lying on her bed with wings and pearl-pale skin and long, dangerous claws, would she be less worried about him?

Would she be less eager to touch him and heal him and wake him and talk to him?

"No," she whispered.

The frenetic pound of her heart slowed to something steadier, something deeper. Merilee breathed in rhythm with Jake as she eased herself onto the bed beside him and rested her palms against the cotton covering the hard muscle of his chest.

She wasn't sure how they could relate if he assumed his demon form and kept it, but she would find a way. *They* would find a way. By all three faces of Hecate, she wouldn't give him any choice about that.

Merilee closed her eyes and let her air energy flow out of her and into him, lending him all the strength she could spare, and then some. His pulse seemed fine, and his respiration. Nothing inside him sounded or felt wounded, other than his jaw. Merilee focused her healing on the bruise, hoping that when Jake did wake, he'd experience less pain for her efforts.

"Thank you." Jake's low, quiet voice rushed through her like wind.

At the same moment, Merilee felt his hands cover hers and press her fingers into his chest. The shock and thrill of his touch registered everywhere at once, as if he had found some way to stroke her entire body at the same time.

When she opened her eyes and gazed at him, she couldn't read his expression, but his gray-blue eyes seemed to swallow her whole. The battles, the city, the worries, the anger at him for storming off and scaring her—every bit of it faded.

Merilee curled her nails into his T-shirt. "If you worry me like that again, I'll blow you into a thousand pieces. Nobody will ever find all of you, Jake Lowell. Do you understand me?"

Jake answered her by sliding his hands up her arms, pulling her down, and kissing her.

Merilee surrendered immediately, no thought of resisting. She needed this. It felt like protection, like healing, like air magic fused directly into her soul. She moaned into Jake's mouth and stretched herself along his length, her legs on his, her arms around his neck. His fingers traveled through her hair as their lips moved together, their tongues touching and twining.

She loved his spicy taste. So unusual. So Jake.

He broke their kiss and found her ear with his teeth, nipping her once and giving her sweet chills before he murmured, "It all comes back to you."

"What comes back to me?" She rose up enough to look directly into his gorgeous eyes.

"Everything." He kissed her again, still toying with her hair, but also sliding down the zipper of her jumpsuit.

For the first time in her life, Merilee wished she were a fire Sibyl so she could burn off the leathers and his clothes and feel him naked right now, no waiting.

Jake gripped her ass and sat up, turning her over and

sliding her beneath him so smoothly, so gently she barely noticed. Now she was looking up at him. Once more giving him complete control of her body and mind.

Her heart?

My heart . . .

He slipped his hand inside her jumpsuit and caressed her breasts, kissing her again and again, touching her like it was the first time all over again and he wanted to explore every curve and angle. Each time he pinched her hard nipples, she gasped as hot shocks traveled directly to her wet, throbbing center.

When Jake began to push her jumpsuit off her shoulders, Merilee almost ripped the damned thing in half shrugging out of it, getting rid of all the barriers to touching him, feeling him, being with him.

His lips captured hers again, and she groaned as his jeans chafed bare legs and sex. His shoulders felt strong beneath her palms as she pressed and kneaded, then held on as he rocked her body against his, trying to drive her insane.

"Are you safe?" she whispered as she reached down to unfasten his jeans. "Will this make you change?"

"We'll have to find out." Jake's voice was low and tight, and his blue-gray eyes flared as he gazed into hers. Gracefully, he rolled off her, pulling away from her fingers and sitting up before she could work the snap and zipper.

She started to protest, but he lowered his head, took her sensitive, tight nipple in his mouth, and worked it with his probing tongue.

All the air hissed out of Merilee's lungs. She arched backward into the bed, pressing her breast against the stubble of his cheeks, then against his hand as it slid up her belly to squeeze and fondle her other nipple. Her hips moved of their own accord, rising up and down.

Her whole body wanted him, ached for him. Wind slid across her belly, pulling Jake toward her, holding him, binding him like he bound her.

His rumble of pleasure made her nipple vibrate.

This time, her head slammed into the pillows.

She managed to look at him, even though she couldn't focus. "You make me hurt, I want you so much."

Jake shifted positions ever so slightly, and his hand slid from her breast down across her belly, then into her lower curls. She felt the motion like a burning trail along her damp skin.

He moved his lips from her nipple to her mouth, covering her breast with his free hand and pressing the tingling flesh against his palm as he kissed her. Deeper and sweeter with each passing second.

His tongue slipped into her mouth at the same moment his fingers parted her moist folds and found her swollen center. Merilee cried out from the heated pleasure, unable to think of anything past the way he circled and pressed, direct, then indirect, back and forth, oh perfect, beyond perfect, she was going to lose her mind now.

"Jake" was all she could choke out, but he was moving again, sliding down her body, his cotton T-shirt tickling and teasing everywhere it touched. When he snuggled between her thighs, Merilee moaned out of control, then cried out as his powerful hands took hold of her ass and his mouth replaced his circling fingers.

He groaned as he tasted her, the sound thrumming through her body, driving her even more wild. She thrashed beneath his tender kisses and the strokes of his tongue.

Gently, slowly, Jake teased her with absolutely no mercy at all. He sucked and kissed, tugged and released, sometimes stopping long enough to run his tongue the length of her sex, sampling her flowing juices.

Merilee's breath jerked in her throat. She grabbed his hair and tugged at it, wanting to pull him closer and shove him away at the same time. So good. Hecate's torch, how could she stand another second? But she wanted minutes. Hours. She tried to hold back, tried to make it last forever and forever again, but Jake pushed his whole face against her, kissing, sucking harder—then with a deft tilt, he thrust his tongue inside her.

Merilee's whole body seemed to burst at the center, shaking from her orgasm as she let out an endless moan and clamped her legs against the sides of his head.

His tongue alternated between invading her pulsing channel and sliding higher, higher, each movement creating new tremors of pleasure until Merilee was certain, absolutely positive she would come apart and release all her wind straight back to the universe.

Her orgasm wouldn't stop. She couldn't stop it, even though she knew so much emotion and feeling would take her sanity. Any moment now. Her brain would melt. Her body would turn to liquid and trickle away across the library floor.

Jake pulled his face away from her and she sucked air like a dying woman. Her vision blurred, making his handsome face swim in her gaze. She tried to find words, say anything to tell him how he made her feel, but he was moving again.

He shifted once more until he rested above her, his jeans unzipped now, his cock free and hard and pushing at her swollen, oversensitive sex.

She moaned. Her body twitched and jumped outside her control.

When he braced both arms beside her head, Merilee screamed and thought she'd die.

Her heart skipped from the overload of sensations.

"Stop," she panted. "I can't take it. You've got to stop!"

Jake's eyes flashed gold, and Merilee thought she saw fangs instead of teeth when he grinned.

All he said was, "No."

Then he drove his cock inside her, deep and sweet and hard and so perfect, and Merilee screamed as her soul-dissolving orgasm started all over again.

28

Jake clenched his jaw so hard he thought bone might snap.

Can't shift. Can't change. Have to stay human.

Goddamn, it was hard. Impossible.

He fought back claws and wings and fangs, focusing on Merilee.

So beautiful.

Her eyelids fluttered and her red lips parted as she moaned and moved beneath him, lifting her hips to meet every stroke.

This woman was hotter than any fire, sweeter than any treat he could imagine. Her wet walls gripped his cock as he plunged into her again and again and again. Each motion forced a sharp gasp from Merilee, then more moans. Her intoxicating scent drifted around him. White tea. Honey. He could taste it. He could taste her musk on his lips, in his mouth. Each breath, each gulp of her stole away his control.

Jake pushed as deep as he could.

Gods, but she fit him so completely. Her wet channel expanded and released, expanded and released, and he hoped she was coming over and over again. So many orgasms she'd forget her own name.

Damn.

Yes.

Only his name.

That's what he wanted to hear from her.

"Jake," Merilee moaned, like she was reading his mind. She gripped his neck and pushed back, raising her ass to let him move deeper. Her muscles quivered along with his.

In and out, in and out went his cock, harder, faster, opening her even more, taking her for his own. Her swollen nipples rubbed against his chest as perspiration rolled between her breasts.

"So sexy," he murmured, pushing with as much strength as he dared. She squeezed against his thrusts, and when she groaned again, he felt the sound in his arms, his shoulders, his chest, his heart.

Jake loved the feel of her wet silk all around his cock. So right. So warm.

He was close.

Gods, he couldn't hold back. He felt the explosion building deep in his gut. Knew he'd blow like a wild volcano. She made him crazy.

Jake forced himself to slow down, speed up, slow down again, then go faster, trying to draw it out for her, double her pleasure. Her entire body was flushing a soft, edible pink, and now she was saying his name like a chant each time he drove into those delicious depths.

Heated wind rose off her skin and rushed around Jake, blasted around him, warming him to a level he could barely stand.

"With me." He slammed deeper into her, pushing her as wide as he thought she could go, gaze fixed on her beautiful face. "With me."

Merilee screamed like her wind, need and pleasure and desperation swirling together. He picked up speed once more, pumping, pumping, pushing himself toward the finish, but holding back as much as he could.

Merilee's arms went limp and dropped to the bed, but her hips still moved, thrusting to meet him, grip him, take whatever he gave her.

"Now," he said through his teeth as he came, gale

force, blowing himself into her like a howling wind. "Right now!"

Her cry rose from somewhere in her center, flowing over him in a rush of air and energy like nothing he had ever experienced.

It took all his strength to weather that storm, hold himself in place and keep pleasing her, keep pleasing himself, bring them both over the top together.

Her channel gripped him as spasms shook them both, and still he kept going, made himself keep going, fight for every inch, every second inside her, every bit of moaning, screaming pleasure he could offer her.

Until he was spent.

Until she was spent.

Until her wind energy shoved him down so forcefully he couldn't keep himself braced above her another second.

Jake collapsed and rolled to his side, pulling her with him, leaving his now-limp cock in her pulsing channel.

Then he held her, unable to speak, and she didn't say a word either. Merilee lay in his embrace with her arms wrapped around his neck, absolutely still and quiet. So open and vulnerable. So completely soft and exhausted.

Jake didn't think he could ever let her go again. Wouldn't think about it.

"I'll make you happy every minute of every day," he said, pressing his lips against her ear. "I'll find a way."

Her arms tightened. "Jake," she whispered, and for a time, nothing else.

That was fine.

That was all he wanted to hear.

She was his now, all his. He relished the sensation of her breath brushing his face, her chest rising and falling against his own. He'd never be able to stay away from her. Couldn't completely remember why he tried.

"If I do shift and can't get back to human form, I'll probably hang right beside you, invisible, always there like some pathetic demon stalker."

Merilee laughed. She leaned back, and her sea-blue eyes sparkled as she stroked the stubble on his cheek with her palm. "You belong to me, Jake Lowell. I belong to you. You capture me completely."

He kissed her forehead. "As much as any man can catch the wind."

She laughed again, and the sound made his heart smile.

"I'm falling in love with you, Merilee." He kissed her forehead another time and another, but kept his eyes closed, almost afraid to see her face.

Her breath caught, then started back, and Jake felt her lips move across his cheek, his nose, until she kissed his mouth. Gentle. Like the softest breeze.

"I . . . don't do serious," she said. "I mean, I've never done serious, but now—now I'm falling in love with you, too."

Words went away and he held her and he kissed her until she fell asleep, her soft breathing like elixir, flowing in and out of his mind, giving him strength and hope.

Jake promised himself to take care of her ten thousand different ways, in a million different situations.

It all came back to her. Everything. And yeah, it always had.

It had only been a few hours, but Jake knew that was all they could have.

Not wanting to, trying to think of excuses not to do it and coming up with none, he woke Merilee with a kiss.

Morning light touched each of her features, from her pretty blond curls to her lips, still swollen from his kisses. When she opened her blue eyes and gazed at him all soft and sleepy, his chest tightened. Another second and his cock would get in on the action. No time to waste.

Jake brushed her cheek with his knuckles. "We have to get dressed. Go to work—if Freeman will unsuspend me. Even if he doesn't, we need to hit the streets and look for the missing triad and the Astaroths, too. If I can talk to them, I think I can explain all this and get them to come back and fight for us."

Merilee yawned and nodded and kissed his cheek, the heat of her breath tickling him in every way possible.

Less than half an hour later, they were both showered, back in the library, and getting dressed—Jake slower than Merilee, because he couldn't help appreciating her wiggling ass as she pulled up her leather jumpsuit.

To distract himself, he told her everything he had found in the building with the tunnel entrance, especially all the images he had seen when he encountered the Stone Man's energy.

She explained to him about what Mother Yana discovered in her investigation, and Jake barely could wrap his mind around the concept.

"A true demon." He fastened his jeans and pulled on his T-shirt. "One no human created?"

"Old Ones were like gods in their own way." Merilee picked up her bow and quiver. "This one may be some sort of chaos demon, or at least spreading unrest and misery might be one of his skills."

Jake grabbed his jacket and threw it over his arm. "Do we know which one, specifically, he might be? Do we have a name?"

Merilee shook her head as she smoothed her curls with her fingers. "Every adept at every Motherhouse is working on that one, trust me."

"Should we look?" Jake gestured to the room around

them. "It's not like we don't have our own resources, and the two of us are pretty fast with research."

Merilee cast a longing gaze at the books lining the library shelves. "If we get time. For now, I think we're more brawn than brain in this fighting machine."

Jake conceded with a nod. "Do now, think later."

"That's about it." Merilee smiled at him, and Jake felt the warmth of the breeze she shared with him before turning for the door.

He stared at the way her hips filled out her leathers. She was something else. Grinning, he followed her until she reached the door and stopped short.

Her head came up and tilted, and Jake's gut twisted.

She was hearing them again.

The Keres.

By now, he knew the signs.

And every time Merilee heard the death spirits screaming, shit happened.

Bad shit.

Jake moved faster than he thought possible in human form, reached her in one big lunge, and pulled her against him.

"The Keres," she said, clearly afraid. "Something's coming. Something's about to happen." Her arms tensed. "Already happened. Damn! Is he close?"

She struggled against his grip, still distracted.

Jake knew she wanted to reach her weapons, but he couldn't make himself let her go. His mind raced with his pulse as he shielded her with his arms, his head, his body.

Where the hell was the threat this time?

Where would it come from?

The other side of the door?

Jake moved her back from the door, then turned her loose so she could ready her weapons. Confusion radiated from her face as she grabbed for the olivewood bow. "Sorry. I heard—"

"I know." He turned away from her and held out his arms to keep her behind him, make himself a bigger target. His training took over and he automatically assessed every threat. The library was so fucking big—and it had so many windows, and doors leading out to a balcony, too.

The windows seemed the most likely spot for trouble to enter, so Jake put himself between Merilee and all that glass, facing the rest of the large library. If he had to, he'd defend her from every direction at the same time.

Jake didn't have time to take another breath.

The balcony doors burst open, and a blast of wind rushed through the library, knocking over pile after pile of Merilee's papers.

Jake's heart slammed against his ribs. He instinctively tried to draw the Glock he didn't have.

Merilee had an arrow nocked before he got his fists raised, and she was standing beside him ready to shoot.

Three Astaroths in jeans and white T-shirts materialized in front of them, staring straight at Jake.

Darian, Quince, and Jared. Lips parted. Fangs bared. Snarling.

Talismans. Jake counted three of them. Glittering around three pale necks.

Not captives on a murder mission.

So why the hell did they come bursting into the library?

Blood pounded through his body. His answering snarl was instinctive. The push of wings against the skin of his back, just as natural. He fought it, refused the change, but fangs poked at his tongue.

"Jake," Merilee said, quiet, steady—and that sound helped Jake stay present in human form.

Barely.

The three demons lifted their hands as if in surrender.

Jake didn't lower his fists at this gesture, and Merilee didn't lower her arrow. Jake heard the rasp of her quick breathing. Then, from outside on the streets, the sound of car engines and buses and voices rose like a familiar refrain, making the moment twice as surreal.

"What the hell?" Merilee said aloud, her voice too quiet. Still ready for a fight.

Leader, said Darian, mind-to-mind, his golden eyes wide and sad and worried as he appraised Jake. *We must leave. Find your wings and take us away from this place before it's too late.*

"I'm not going anywhere," Jake said, confused. "Speak out loud. Merilee needs to hear you."

Three pairs of golden eyes gazed from Jake to Merilee and back again. Quince spoke next, his voice a whisper. "The city is no longer safe. There is monstrous evil here. We *must* go."

From the corner of his eye, Jake saw Merilee's frown. She let the tip of her arrow point toward the library's hardwood floor instead of the demons. "What's happened? What changed?"

"Tell us, Leader," said Jared, ignoring her questions. His tone was remarkably young and childlike, and the sound tore at Jake's insides. "Where should we go?"

Jake shook his head and finally lowered his fists. "Why are you asking me? I mean, I know you call me Leader, but I'm just helping you train. You're under Sal Freeman's command just like every other lawfully aligned demon staying in New York City. Where did he tell you to be?"

The three demons gazed at him with obvious surprise.

Darian said, "Captain Freeman's instructions died with him. We assumed you were his second, that command of us would fall to you, Leader."

Jake's entire world seemed to stop, and a buzzing, vibrating pain descended on his mind.

Freeman's . . . instructions . . . died with him. . . .

Died *with him?*

"Freeman . . ." Jake felt dizzy, unable to accept what his ears heard, what his brain was telling him. Everything inside him seem to sink, then fly up again and rebel.

His entire being started to burn and ache, and he looked at Merilee, desperate for her to give him some other interpretation, some other reality.

Her mouth was open. A look of absolute horror slowly claimed her face, making everything terrible and wrong—and real.

"No." She glared at the Astaroths. "Sorry. I'm not believing that."

The three demons stood still, clearly distressed, their lack of guile radiating outward like a soft silver light.

Merilee blinked.

Then she started crying and moving all at the same time.

"No, no, no!" she yelled as she ran to the library door, shoved back the bolt, and took off down the hall toward the stairs.

"Stay here," Jake told the Astaroths, his throat tightening, each word harder than the last. "Wait for my instructions."

Darian, Quince, and Jared nodded as Jake turned away from them and charged after Merilee.

Awareness gradually spread through his mind, his body, making him sick, then turning him numb.

Freeman. Dead.

"No. Fucking. Way." His heart punched his chest with every word.

Captain Freeman's instructions died with him. . . .

Not Freeman. Not *him*.

Jake caught Merilee at the third-floor landing and they ran together, straight down into the long entry hall.

The Mothers were near the foot of the stairs, kneeling around the prone form of a woman, hands outstretched, obviously doing serious healing.

When Jake got closer, he could see it was Bela Argos, and he remembered she had been out on patrol with Freeman.

Energy rolled around the healing circle in visible waves, almost obscuring Riana and Cynda, holding each other and sobbing.

Instinctively, Jake shifted his attention down the hall, toward the conference room door. Nick and Creed stood in the hallway, faces drawn and pale. Their arms were folded, and their posture suggested they intended to guard whatever was inside that room.

Merilee glanced once at Bela and the Mothers, once at her triad sisters, then headed straight for Nick and Creed.

As Jake reached them, Nick caught hold of both of Merilee's arms. "No," he said, his voice as rough as a dry engine. "You don't want to see him."

"Fuck you!" Merilee's hot blast of wind knocked Nick sideways as she tore free of his grasp, only to be captured by Creed.

"It's bad, Merilee. He's gone. There's nothing anybody can—"

Jake's thoughts cracked in half. His demon essence almost ripped right out of his human skin as he shoved past his brothers. He didn't feel bad when he heard Creed hit the floor behind him, another victim of Merilee's wind.

"Don't try to shelter her," Jake growled as he grabbed the handle and yanked open the conference room door. "She's a Sibyl. She makes her own decisions."

He stepped inside.

Merilee was beside him a second later, closing the door behind them.

She took Jake's hand as all his air left him in a rush.

It took everything he had to stay human as grief slammed him in the gut like a baseball bat.

"Oh, fuck. No." Jake shook his head as Merilee squeezed his fingers. "I'm not—that can't be—"

But he knew it was.

There was a body on the conference room table, covered by a blood-soaked sheet. About Freeman's height. About Freeman's size—but misshapen. Oddly wide in the middle.

Jake's legs felt too heavy to move as he forced himself forward, made himself approach the table.

Not Freeman.

This isn't Freeman.

This isn't my friend. The guy who risked everything for me.

No matter how Jake tried to lie to himself, with each step he took, Freeman's black hair became a little more obvious. Thick, thick black strands, coated with drying blood.

Holding Merilee's hand like a lifeline, Jake stopped at the edge of the table. Before he could bullshit himself one more time, he lifted the sheet enough to see Freeman's pale, bloody cheeks. His blue lips. The closed eyes that would never open again in this world.

The sight of his friend's motionless, dead face punched Jake in the gut again so hard he turned away from the body and doubled over, hands on his knees.

Fuck he wanted to puke.

Then he wanted to kill something with his bare hands.

Merilee came to stand beside him, but she seemed to understand not to touch him. "Hecate take him and bear him home," she said in a sob. "Light his way and slay his enemies."

Her words sounded like a prayer.

Jake stood up fast, the urge to kill something doubling and tripling. He didn't want to think about prayers, or gods or goddesses or any other bastard of a deity that saw fit to look away while Freeman died. He just wanted to find the bastard who did this and rip off his fucking head.

After a few seconds of getting his shit together, Jake made himself turn back to Freeman's body. He gripped the sheet with shaking hands and pulled it up for a better view, then lowered it quickly as Merilee choked.

Or was that me?

Maybe both of them.

"Something tore him apart," Merilee whispered, her voice so quiet Jake barely heard the words.

Freeman's body—

Mangled.

Like a prehistoric bear had grabbed the man and ripped him open at the rib cage.

Or maybe a natural demon. An "Old One."

Jake's head swam as he grabbed Merilee's arm, eyes still fixed on the bloody sheet covering his friend. He felt gut-sick. Torn. Like he might tear open at the center himself and bleed out on the conference room floor.

"It was *him*, Merilee. It had to be."

"I know," she said, the rage in her voice matching his own. "I sense him, too."

Jake couldn't keep standing there staring at Sal's corpse. He had to do something. Right now. He had to find the motherfucker who spilled Freeman's guts like the man didn't mean anything at all.

He wheeled around and kicked the nearest desk aside as he stormed back toward the conference room door.

"Jake," Merilee called from behind him. "Wait a second. We need to figure out what—"

Her voice cut off as he jerked open the door and

lunged into the hallway, already halfway to Astaroth and roaring.

A wall of elemental earth energy smashed into him so hard it knocked him forward against the far wall. Pain blasted through Jake's bones and joints as he jerked against the wood and stone and found he couldn't move at all.

Jake tried to bellow, but nothing happened. He pulled at his demon energy as he glared at Mother Yana, but couldn't complete his shift.

The ancient woman stood not three feet from him, arms outstretched, eyes blazing with the force of the power she wielded.

Behind her, the other two Mothers watched, along with Nick, Creed, Cynda, and Bela Argos, who was leaning against Riana, still pale, her face streaked with blood.

"Hold him, Yana," Mother Anemone instructed. "I'm sorry, *agapitos,* but you must get control of yourself. You must not shift until you've had ample time to consider the consequences."

Fuck you! Jake wanted to shout, but he knew he couldn't make a sound. He couldn't even make his lips twitch.

And . . . he didn't really want to speak to Mother Anemone in such a disrespectful fashion, not even when it felt as though his heart had been ripped and shredded like Freeman's. The pain inside Jake was so goddamned intense he would have dropped to his knees if he wasn't being held prisoner against the wall.

Merilee came out of the conference room, and her appearance made Jake stop fighting his earthly bonds. Her mouth opened as she stared at him, at his half-transitioned skin and fangs, at the partially formed wings flat against the wall behind his arms. The tears in her blue eyes made him want to tear out his heart.

Shit. I'm so sorry.

He hoped she could sense the truth of that emotion, since he couldn't move a goddamned muscle.

But he had almost changed.

He had almost left her forever without so much as a kiss-my-ass or goodbye.

What kind of raving asshole does a thing like that?

But, Freeman . . .

He had to avenge his friend. Just—not as an Astaroth. As a human. As a cop. It's what Freeman would have wanted, and what Jake would do.

As if sensing his concession, Mother Yana relaxed her earth energy enough that Jake began to reassume his full human form.

As his skin grew more solid, Merilee sagged against the doorframe and wiped her eyes. A few seconds later, she seemed to recover herself, but when she straightened up, she didn't look at Jake.

He set his jaw at the sting in his chest, but figured she had a right to her anger. Hell, she had a right to land a kick to his groin if that's what she wanted to do. He deserved it.

"You must see this." Mother Anemone held up a folded piece of paper for Jake and Merilee to see. "We found it in Sal Freeman's pocket, though Bela cannot shed light on how it came to be there."

"It's a miracle Bela made it back here, all the way from Central Park," Nick said, his voice gruff, his eyes averted from Jake and the conference room, too. "I can't believe she got Sal home like—like he was."

Merilee took a shaky breath. "What happened to Sal?" she demanded, her eyes sweeping past Jake, then zipping back to him. "What . . . happened?"

Mother Anemone handed her the paper.

Merilee unfolded it and took a good look.

Jake saw pure revulsion spread across her face. Her

lips pulled back like she wanted to bite something, and her fingers twitched against the paper.

"Aloud," Mother Anemone prompted, her voice grim.

Merilee swallowed hard. Her words spilled out in a hot rush of fury, her voice growing louder as she read.

"You're a difficult woman to reach, Ms. Alexander. I'd like to meet with you and discuss how our organizations might assist each other in our mutual pursuit of peace." She paused and held her hand to her stomach as it heaved, like she wanted to throw up.

"How about tomorrow," she continued, every word punctuated with anger. "I'll be free following my mid-day press conference at Martin Jensen's headquarters. Sincerely, Bartholomew August."

Mother Yana eased the barrier around Jake again, though not enough to free him. His breathing was still too fast. His face was hot, but he was thinking now. About whether or not that note meant what he thought it did.

From Merilee's reaction, from her aversion to even touching the paper, much less reading its words, Jake was pretty certain the Stone Man now had a human name, at least, even if they still didn't know what kind of demon he was.

The son of a bitch was smart, too. No way to tie that generic, friendly note to the killing, other than the circumstantial issue of its presence in Freeman's pocket—but that would never hold up in court, or even for a warrant. August could have passed that note to Bela or Freeman at any time in the last few days, even mailed it for all anyone could prove.

Still, Jake knew August had killed Sal to send a message, more to Merilee than anyone else.

He wasn't coming for her.

He expected her to come to him.

Creed and Nick were checking their weapons as Merilee crumpled the paper in her hands and let loose a blast of air that blew the thing all the way back to the door. Bela Argos hobbled toward her sword. Even Cynda and Riana were heading for the steps, fists tight, expressions furious, as if to dress for battle.

"Bartholomew August." Jake forced out the words against the earth energy still binding him to the wall. "Are we beheading this cocksucker now, or five minutes from now?"

Mother Yana freed Jake with a flick of her wrist.

"Guess that's now," he growled, and wondered where Freeman had stashed his badge and gun.

Shit, Freeman.

I'll get that motherfucker if it's the last thing I do.

29

I can't believe Sal's dead. And I almost lost Jake, too. That fast. That completely.

Merilee's heart thundered as Jake shook off Mother Yana's earth energy and turned toward Freeman's office. She knew Jake wanted his Glock, probably his badge, too, though the mayhem and death blazing from his blue eyes had nothing to do with traditional law enforcement.

The burn in her chest matched the burn in Jake's gaze. Sal's murderer—they were going to tear the fucker limb from limb, *like now.* But Jake needed to keep his cool. They all needed to keep their cool. It wasn't going to do any of them a damned bit of good if they charged into a trap

Jake hesitated when he saw Merilee watching him, and he seemed to sober, gain another measure of control. His wounded eyes widened, then darkened, and he mouthed, *Sorry.*

His expression showed how much he regretted his outburst and the fact he got hotheaded and nearly turned demon forever. Almost against her own will, she nodded, letting him off the hook.

Why the fuck did I do that? Guilt might have kept him in line a lot better—but no. That's not the point right now. Sal's the only point.

Jake gazed at her for another brief moment before his fists doubled, his jaw clenched, and he stormed off down the hall, and Merilee felt like a dozen knives had just pierced her chest.

What if he lost control while he was searching?

What if he walked out of that office as an Astaroth, never to be fully human—or hers—again?

Her hand lifted toward the talisman she wore. If she just grabbed it once and ordered him not to change . . .

Jake headed into Freeman's office and disappeared from her view.

For a moment, time seemed to shift and Merilee imagined that Sal would be in that crowded little room, waiting to bark orders at Jake, then stomp out to give assignments.

But the OCU captain was gone.

Merilee glanced at the conference room and forced herself to remember the torn body under the bloody sheet. Tears burned at her eyes. Gone—and the bastard who did it was going to pay.

Merilee clenched her fist before even one finger touched Jake's gold necklace. He'd keep his shit together for Freeman. No way Jake would go demon before he brought down his friend's murderer.

She spun and faced the entry hall, which was rapidly filling with Sibyls and OCU officers called in for reorganization in light of Freeman's death. Delilah Moses was there, too, making her way toward the stairs, probably heading for the library.

With the horror of Sal's death, his body ripped open like someone had scooped out his insides—something as mundane and ordinary as Delilah continuing her service to the Sibyls almost seemed odd. Maybe it was how she dealt with tragedy.

Merilee swallowed and turned her attention to the rapidly gathering crowd.

Good thing the damned hallway was so huge—and even so, it was still starting to feel cramped in a major way.

Mother Yana, Mother Keara, and Mother Anemone emerged from the crowd and came toward Merilee.

"No one can reach the water Sibyl to tell her to return here," Mother Keara said. "She doesn't answer her radio—probably elemental interference. There's a possibility she'll find out about your captain's death with no support. No control."

"Ve must inform the Motherhouses and seek help *now,*" Mother Yana said, her wrinkled face drawn tight with worry. "The city might not vithstand her distress."

New dismay wrapped itself around Merilee, and her wind escaped her in little bursts, rattling chimes and furniture up and down the increasingly crowded hallway.

Andy.

She wasn't back yet from collecting evidence at the Carter headquarters.

Was she on her way?

Would she find out about Freeman all alone, walking down some impersonal city sidewalk?

Hecate keep her. Hecate keep us all.

"I understand," Merilee said numbly, reeling back her air energy as best she could. "We'll send some people to find her and bring her back here."

Andy's control over her elemental talent had improved in the two years since it manifested, but no way would she keep herself together when she realized Freeman was dead. Andy and Sal's attraction had been growing, especially these last couple of months. When Andy learned he was dead—oh, no. No, no, no. The burst of emotions she released would be enough to harm any nearby living creature with water talent. She might even agitate the rivers, the harbor, the bay—the ocean.

Destroy all of Manhattan with a tsunami.

"We haven't yet determined how to kill this Old One." Mother Anemone clutched Merilee's arm briefly, then turned her loose. "His death could have tremendous elemental consequences—explosions in earth, wind, fire, and water—we just don't know. We have to conference with the other Mothers on this point as well."

True to form, Mother Keara simplified the situation. "So for now, capture the bastard and contain him—but don't slit his throat until we know how to manage the fallout."

"Understood." Merilee heard the note of confidence and calmness in her voice. Total fraud. Total lie. Freeman was dead, and Merilee couldn't fight with her own triad to bring down his killer. Andy was about to get her heart ripped apart. Jake was at risk. Merilee would rather blow down the townhouse than hold herself together at this moment, but what choice did she have?

Capture the bastard. Contain him. Sure. No problem. It's just an unknown creature as powerful as that Vodoun god that almost ate me. She would have laughed, but that might have started her screaming over all the wrong, terrible things in her world, so she held it back.

About a minute later, the Mothers had collected enough fire Sibyls to handle communications and transportation, and they rushed upstairs to return to their Motherhouses. As she watched them go, Merilee's mind flashed to the picture Charlotte Heart had drawn before her suicide, of a tidal wave crashing into Manhattan. Water surging through the streets. Buildings toppling in every direction.

Merilee's own dreams came next, of flattened towns and floodwaters. New York's streets littered with dead Sibyls.

Was this how it would begin?

Tonight? Right now?

Would Andy kick off the destruction of the world as they knew it?

Think. She rubbed the sides of her head. *I've got to think!*

Where would Andy go? What should she do next? The situation seemed too huge to handle. Merilee felt completely alone, cut adrift in a windstorm like she'd never known before. Her thoughts reeled and fragmented as she tried to decide the next best step, the first action she should take.

Jake hadn't come out of Freeman's office, but Creed and Nick had pulled on their body armor, and they were zipping their raid jackets.

More OCU officers and Sibyls filed through the front entrance. Merilee checked each face, half-dreading, half-hopeful, but Andy wasn't among them. The incoming forces lined up on either side of the hallway, and soon they were shouting at one another about tactics and strategies and who was in charge.

Riana and Cynda pushed past Merilee, crammed into their maternity leathers, weapons sheathed in belts that barely fit around their pregnant bellies.

The sight of her triad sisters acting like they were about to hit the streets jarred Merilee into action and offered her a sudden, very clear perspective on what course to follow.

"Oh, no way." She grabbed Riana's elbow before Riana took another step. "You absolutely *cannot* be serious."

When Riana didn't answer or even look apologetic or repentant, Merilee's heart crawled into her throat at the mere idea of two more people she loved so much putting themselves at such risk. "For the sake of all the goddesses, you two can't even zip your jumpsuits all the way up."

"Whatever," said Cynda, smoking more than usual as she grabbed Riana's other arm and pulled against Merilee. "Andy's going to be beyond crushed. Somebody's got to go get her and be with her when she hears the news about Sal."

Merilee blew out a breath and kept hold of Riana. "Well it's sure as fuck not going to be you."

"We can do it," Riana said. "We won't fight—we'll just go to the Carter headquarters and pick up Andy and bring her home."

With her free hand, Merilee gestured to the hallway full of Sibyls and officers. She made sure her voice was as loud as possible, hoping her words would carry over the din and attract Creed and Nick's attention. "There are plenty of people to go after Andy. We don't need to have to come rescue you after you drop babies on the sidewalk!"

As Merilee had hoped, Creed and Nick stared in their direction.

Both men gaped.

Matching furious expressions spread across their faces at the sight of Riana and Cynda dressed for battle, and they started to glow gold as their Curson demon halves surged forward in a protective rage.

"Shit," Cynda grumbled as Nick started for her at the same moment Creed started for Riana. "You fucking tattletale. Merilee. Riana and I need to do *something*."

"Yeah. Keep your pregnant ass right here in case Andy shows up." Merilee felt comfortable letting go of Riana as the brothers reached her triad sisters and took over the argument.

Merilee was pretty sure the guys would win, so she went to meet Jake, who was finally emerging from Freeman's office, Glock secured in his holster. Just the sight of him still human and seeming so normal, so in control, gave her a measure of relief.

Still, as she made her way down the hallway, she was uncomfortably aware of the increasing conflict in the hallway, with the OCU officers on one side of the space and Sibyls on the other.

Grim faces. Rising voices.

Not good.

Without Freeman, this carefully woven collaboration was coming apart quickly.

Technically, as Freeman's second in command, Andy should be in charge now, but that didn't seem likely any time soon. Merilee thought Creed and Nick were next down the hierarchy, but Nick clearly had his hands full, hauling his pregnant, flame-spitting wife toward the stairs to the stone basement, as if he planned to lock her in the fireproof space for the night. Creed wasn't in much better shape, urging Riana toward the stairs, perhaps intending to take her to their room and convince her to stay behind.

Besides, when the captain of a unit that wasn't even officially supposed to exist got torn apart by a mythical demon—well. Was there any such thing as standard police procedures to cover this situation? Probably not. Somebody needed to step up and get the OCU officers and Sibyls back on track—and back on the streets.

Merilee glanced from them to the divided forces, then at Jake.

At first, Jake didn't take her meaning.

He stopped in the hallway and looked to his right and left, and seemed to note how the force was beginning to divide. Then he checked all directions, probably seeking his brothers, but finding nothing.

When Jake's gaze shifted back to Merilee, she saw his shock and worry. He went back to studying the unrest around him, and his shoulders sagged a fraction.

I know you can do this. Merilee said nothing, but she hoped her face conveyed her message. *You* have *to. For us. For Freeman. Trust yourself.*

As if hearing every unspoken word, Jake stared at her with an intensity that made her stomach flip. Resignation colored his expression, replaced quickly by determination.

"It had to be a power play," one officer near Merilee shouted to another. "The Legion's desperate. Scared. We need to move now and wipe them out."

"Off the face of the earth," another agreed.

"Freeman deserves that," said a third.

A Sibyl disagreed, pointing out that she had heard Freeman's murderer had significant power, and that he might have hostages—including Sibyls. "It's too much risk. We can't go blasting in without planning, without consideration."

"Fuck that," said the first officer who spoke. "That's Sibyl thinking. We can plan this raid in the van on the way. It's a takedown, not a tea party."

Jake stuck his fingers in his mouth and whistled, the sound earsplitting despite all the noise and motion in the hallway.

Which stopped, immediately.

When all eyes turned to Jake, he announced, "We do have a suspect, and, yes, he's dangerous in ways we don't even understand. It's Bartholomew August."

Angry whispers hissed like one of Cynda's fires, burning up and down the ranks of officers and warriors.

"Are you saying he's the ancient demon we've been trying to find?" Bela Argos asked, her dark eyes skeptical. "The Old One?"

An officer shook his head. "But he stopped the riots. That doesn't make any sense."

"Yeah, he leads the Peace Warriors," said an earth

Sibyl armed with daggers like the ones Riana carried. "They were way helpful during all the fighting."

A second officer raised his hand. "I heard a rumor that he's joining forces with Jensen's camp this afternoon. There's a press conference."

Merilee twitched at the mention of the conference, remembering the note asking her to meet the heinous bastard after it was over. Jake's frown was monstrous, too, as he obviously was thinking about the same thing.

After he let the Sibyls and officers talk a little more, Jake interrupted with, "We have good evidence from the Mothers and August himself tying him to Freeman's murder, but not the kind of proof that would stand up in court." He kept his arms loose at his sides, sounding more authoritative with each word. "August is a major player on the political scene. With the media scrutiny and the city ready to explode over even the hint of paranormal involvement, we have to move carefully."

"Why?" The question came from Bela, though she was starting to look too battered and exhausted to keep standing much longer. "That's what he—it—wants, isn't it? For us to think he's invulnerable. Unapproachable. He killed Freeman to paralyze us, didn't he?"

And to force us to strike at him so he can get to me, Merilee added in her mind. The truth of that stabbed at her, just as painful as her worries over Jake, but she had no time to dwell on it.

One of the air Sibyls Merilee had patched up during the riots lifted her bow. "Let's see how well an arrow approaches his skull."

Murmurs of agreement broke out among the youngest officers and Sibyls, but Jake tamped them down by holding up his hands like Freeman used to do. Then he gazed at his own outstretched fingers and seemed to realize who he was imitating, and the lines of his face tightened with sadness.

Merilee's heart twisted. She wanted to walk the last few steps to him and put her arms around him, ease his pain—but she knew she couldn't.

"We've suffered a brutal loss." Jake's quiet, dignified voice eased the darkness hanging over the townhouse. "But we can't let that divide us or send us off in crazy directions. We must be a unit. We must act together, or more of us will end up like Freeman—torn apart on a table, leaving our friends and loved ones to grieve. And leaving us one more warrior down in a battle we can't afford to lose."

This time, nobody called out or argued. A few officers and Sibyls looked at the floor.

Jake moved forward, a fraction more confident. "I need everybody to cooperate, and I've got three or four jobs we need to split up to accomplish."

For one bad moment, Merilee thought the challenging and grumbling might start again, but the air in the hallway shifted. The three Astaroths Jake had been training materialized beside him like an honor guard, still in jeans and T-shirts, muscled arms folded, pale faces stern.

"We are ready for assignment," Darian said, and Merilee was gratified by the expressions of surprise she saw on the faces of officers and Sibyls alike. "What would you have us do, Jake?"

Jake gave Darian a grateful look. "The only way to bring August down is to get him alone, so we need to cut off his support. Discredit him and isolate him from his followers. And for that, we need evidence. Bartholomew August is connected to Derek Holston's murder and the disappearances, but we have no proof to show people. Can you get us evidence—something concrete—anything that would tie him to these crimes in the eyes of the human public?"

Darian nodded, and immediately, the three Astaroths vanished before Merilee could tell them to be careful.

Jake turned back to the gathered crowd. "I need a group of officers to stay here at the townhouse—four, maybe five—to look after the housebound Sibyls and inform and assign any officers or warriors who arrive and haven't been briefed."

On the OCU side of the hallway, several officers stepped forward, then several more, and Merilee told them that they could use the kitchen for a base, since the M.E. hadn't arrived to retrieve Freeman's body from the conference room.

Behind her, Jake was speaking again, telling the remaining forces, "I need a couple of pairs of OCU officers to roust the D.A.s and judges sympathetic to us, the ones used to our kind of—well, paranormal evidence. Get me warrants to search August's properties in New York." He kept his expression firm but hopeful as a number of officers nodded. "We suspect he has hostages, but we don't know where—so we can't claim exigent circumstances and bust down his doors without attracting a shitload of attention."

Jake scrubbed a hand across his chin, and Merilee knew he was thinking on his feet, making this up as he went—but doing a fantastic job. "When we get those warrants, we'll need raid teams to move hard and fast and hit all the locations at the same time."

"Use the library as a staging area." Merilee pointed to the steps. "Plenty of room, tables, and telephones, too, to coordinate the teams."

About two thirds of the Sibyls and officers present immediately headed in that direction, leaving ten officers and five Sibyls, including Bela Argos, in the hallway with Merilee and Jake. As Merilee took stock of their reduced group, Jake said, "I need a team to double-time it to Carter's headquarters, find Andy Myles and bring her in—without telling her the bad news about Freeman. She might be a danger to herself and others, and we need to help her."

He glanced at Merilee, as if hopeful she would go for that assignment.

Damn him.

He knew she couldn't, that she wouldn't—but still, duty pulled against affection so hard Merilee wondered if she could tear in half. She wanted to find Andy, needed to locate her and be with her, but she knew, as Jake knew somewhere in his heart, that she was their best ticket to an immediate audience with August.

Jake frowned.

Anger and frustration passed over his face like clouds, but he wasn't stupid enough to forbid her or try to talk her out of what they both knew she had to do.

Merilee felt a little swell of appreciation for his respect, for the fact that he really did grasp that she was a warrior and not some fragile flower he had to protect.

Thankfully, when Merilee didn't volunteer to go on the search detail, Bela did, and Merilee gave the earth Sibyl a grateful look.

"Even if Andy does piece things together, I think I'm strong enough to balance and contain her water power long enough to get her here." Bela straightened her leathers and smoothed her hair, and Merilee hoped the little bit of energy shining from Bela's dark eyes wasn't bravado. "I'll bring her back to the townhouse as fast as I can. That'll be the best thing."

She immediately picked two Sibyls and two officers to assist her, and they headed out the front door.

"Okay," Jake said to the eight officers and two Sibyls still in the center of the hallway. "The rest of us have a little call to pay on our friend Bartholomew August."

"We can't kill him," Merilee said immediately,

though she itched to draw her weapons, charge out of the townhouse, and do just that. "The Mothers don't know what will happen when he dies. We need to capture him, then figure out a way to contain whatever power he might release when we do put him down."

"Kill, capture, contain—yeah, right." A singed, blistered Nick emerged from the basement stairwell and pulled the door closed behind him. Merilee noted that he didn't lock it, and wondered if he might be nuts. "How are we even going to get close to him?"

"August is hot and huge in this political race now." Creed's skeptical voice matched his twin's as he finished descending the stairs after his apparently successful persuasion of Riana on the staying-home issue. "We'll have to go through his people's people's people unless we're ready for the press frenzy of declaring him a person of interest, or admitting that he's essential to our investigation. I've been through that circus before. It's a bitch."

Jake gazed at Merilee, obviously not liking what he was about to remind Creed and Nick of—what he'd have to admit to the officers and Sibyls who hadn't heard about the note found on Freeman's body.

"We have a time, a place, and an invitation to get us through the door," Jake said, slowly, as if every word was heavy labor. He sucked a breath through his teeth as he kept right on staring at her, so intently she could feel his eyes like a powerful, protective embrace.

"Or at least one of us does."

30

Jake, his brothers, Merilee, and their team, all dressed in civilian clothes, stood in front of a line of orange-shirted Peace Now workers. They were at the center of a long alley at the back door of Martin Jensen's New Deal–New Day headquarters. Jake's Glock was holstered but ready, his badge in his pocket, and a pair of elementally locked handcuffs dangling from his belt.

He knew he should keep both hands free, but he had a tight grip on Merilee's fingers. He didn't care if touching her was appropriate or not at this point. He didn't want her here, and he damned sure wasn't letting go of her until he got her out of this place in one piece.

Her pretty face was tense, and she kept glancing upward.

"The Keres," she said to Jake in response to his questioning expression. "They've been bothering me since we left—not surprising since we're headed straight for the Stone Man, right?"

Jake itched to get hold of the bastard. Forget everything else the psycho had done—Jake was ready for Merilee to be free of her fear, her nightmares. He wanted no more doom hanging over her head.

As she struggled with her fright, she looked so soft in the afternoon sunlight that he wanted to sweep her into his arms and carry her away forever, threat or no threat. No matter what, he would *not* let August harm her in any way. Just the thought of August so much as looking at Merilee brought Jake's demon essence screaming forward, and he had to keep every muscle clenched to hold back his shift.

"Steady," said Nick, who was standing beside Jake's left shoulder. Creed was on Merilee's right, and the eight OCU officers and two Sibyls stood behind them.

The line of Peace Now workers continued to hold them back, just as Jake had seen them holding the press at bay at the front entrance. Only at the front entrance, he had caught glimpses of guys in black suits with sleek little headsets coming onto the scene. FBI or Secret Service—or both. Any second now, a few would probably make their way to this entrance, too.

Whatever was going down here, it was big news. Huge news. With major implications for the presidential race. The workers had acknowledged the presence of Jake and Merilee and their party, since they were listed as expected guests. Just as soon as the monumental announcement was completed, the workers promised Merilee that she and her entourage would be admitted and shown to August's new office.

Jake would have watched it on somebody's handheld or phone, but with three Sibyls close by, that wasn't possible. Nothing electronic would get clear reception, especially wireless devices. He was forced to listen to it like the campaign workers had to, on the outdoor speakers fastened to the corner eaves of the headquarters.

"The time is now for unity." August's oily voice slid all over Jake, setting his teeth on edge. "The time is now for peace. In the face of the unrest and tragedy we have experienced in this city, and with the threat of paranormal terrorism realized, we can no longer afford division and petty competition."

The Peace Now workers seemed to swell with each word, pride shining from their faces like some strange rapture. Jake pulled Merilee a little closer to him, and she didn't resist. Her expression told Jake that this scene made her skin crawl, too.

"It is in this spirit," droned the voice of August over the outdoor speakers, "that I join my campaign with that of Martin Jensen, a fine man who possesses the vision and foresight to take this nation in a new direction. I humbly request that all my supporters offer him their utmost loyalty and service, and I will work closely with him in the coming weeks as our convention approaches."

"Son of a bitch," Merilee said through her teeth, giving Jake's fingers a squeeze. "He's taking a side seat so the attention will stay on Jensen—but he'll be right there, watching everything, controlling everything."

Nick raised a fist like he wanted to punch something. "With Jensen's lead in the polls and the way August has come up in the last few days, this makes Jensen a certainty for his party's nomination."

"He'll pick August for V.P.," Creed said, "and the bastard will be in the White House with hardly anybody watching him at all."

"He won't be free that long," Jake muttered, so that only Merilee and his brothers could hear him. "He might not even be alive come November."

Merilee twitched and looked at the sky. "They're getting louder," she whispered to Jake. She bit her lip and glanced over her shoulder in the general direction of the townhouse. "I keep feeling like . . . like maybe this is a mistake. Maybe we should just go look for Andy, or go back home for now."

Creed let out a slow breath. "I know you're worried about Andy. Hell, she used to be my partner—I'm worried, too. But Cynda and Riana will take care of her until we get back."

"I know." But Merilee's discomfort was palpable. She looked toward the townhouse, then at the sky, and Jake realized she was shaking.

Fuck, but it was hard not to change, drift invisibly into that headquarters, and bite off the murdering fucker's head right on national television.

That would fix everything, wouldn't it? Assuming August didn't have some kind of high-tech Legion-designed demon alarm.

Only the gentle sensation of Merilee's grip kept Jake human—and a cop. Only her presence reminded him that there were things more important than vengeance.

Protection.

Love.

Justice.

He wouldn't let her down.

For right now, though, they were just going to talk to him. Get close to him, see him face-to-face, and discover what they could learn—and stall for time while the warrants were executed. If they were lucky, they'd rattle the bastard and something valuable would slip out.

As soon as the speech was over, the freckle-faced Peace Now worker closest to Jake broke ranks and gestured to the back door.

"Since you're expected," Freckle-Face told Merilee, "come right in. Mr. August will see you in a few moments."

Jake would have slugged the guy if Nick hadn't grabbed his arm.

This time it was Creed who said, "Steady," and Jake thought about punching him instead.

As they stepped inside, he kept Merilee's hand firmly in his and made sure she walked behind him, between the shield of his body and the fighting skills of Nick and Creed. They threaded down a hallway, past busy, ringing phone banks, offices full of posters and stickers and papers and bustling workers, and a room full of copy machines and printers that would put any business to shame. Jake noted the scent of toner, new carpet, and overheated machinery, mingled with the ever-so-slight stench of sulfur.

August.

He managed not to snarl, but barely.

Merilee tugged against his grip, and when he glanced at her, she was staring at the ceiling. He knew she must be hearing the cries of the Keres, louder than ever. "I'm worried," she said.

"I'll take care of you," he promised, even as Nick and Creed assured her they'd take care of her, too.

Jake frowned as Freckle-Face led them into a bright, windowed conference room with glass walls and asked them to take a seat at the big round table. This wasn't like Merilee, to be so unsettled about anything—even a natural demon who could kill them all with a wave of whatever fucked-up power it possessed. Her face had gone totally tense. She was drawn and trembling, and even the other OCU officers and Sibyls looked worried about her.

Jake sat her down as far from the door as he could get her and stood behind her, Nick and Creed once more flanking him.

"Are you okay?" he asked Merilee.

"No, but let's get on with it, damnit." The edge in her voice wasn't personal, and it only made Jake's gut tighten a little more. She was *really* rattled. And he *really* wanted to pulverize the asshole responsible for it.

None of the other officers or Sibyls sat down, either. They all stayed on their feet, barely breathing, hands on their hidden weapons, as a lone figure strode toward the conference room.

Jake jammed his teeth together at his first in-person sighting of the being that had killed his friend. His fingers curled against the back of Merilee's chair, and a rogue claw punched straight through the black leather.

Creed and Nick didn't tell him to be steady this time. They were both stock-still, breathing heavily, and glowing slightly around their heads and shoulders.

About six foot six with broad shoulders but a thin build, August looked like a pro basketball player as he approached. Jake could tell the guy was wiry. Deceptively strong. He wouldn't be a pussy in a fight.

I wonder what his demon form looks like?

I wonder what Freeman saw right before he died?

The image of Freeman's torn-open ribs flashed through Jake's mind, along with a memory of the Vodoun Loa he had battled at Fresh Kills. Fresh anger burned through Jake at the images. August didn't look like he had a monster that size living in his skin, but looks could be deceiving, too, as Jake well knew.

August had dark hair, dark eyes, and slightly tanned skin, and as the man pushed open the conference room door, Jake was struck by how totally . . . normal he looked, height aside. He guessed women would find August handsome, so long as they never looked too deeply into his eyes.

Black ice.

Not much there other than a total lack of conscience and the complete absence of humanity.

There's the murderer, right there in his eyes. Jake studied August's face, taking in the sight of those empty black pits. Another one of his fingers grew a claw that punched through the leather upholstery of Merilee's chair. *I can see the heartless bastard who killed Freeman right in there.*

"Welcome, welcome," August said in that same smooth voice he had just used in his press conference, only this time he was speaking to Merilee, ignoring everyone else in the room.

Jake gripped her chair even tighter, trying not to pull back his lips and let his fangs show.

Merilee shuddered as August spoke to her, but got hold of herself quickly.

"There are no recording devices in this room, and none will work if you turn them on." August kept smiling. Beaming, actually. All for Merilee. "But then you've some experience with that, since there are Sibyls amongst you."

No one spoke. Jake and everyone around him simply glared at August.

Jake kept himself as calm as possible with a little mantra, his own form of a prayer, which he offered as he did his best to study August, memorizing every detail of his appearance.

You murdered my friend and you want my woman. I'm going to tear off your head.

August stood across the table from Merilee and rested his hands on the polished wood. "Have no fear. I have no intention of exposing your little secrets. We've had enough chaos for now, don't you think?"

You murdered my friend and you want my woman. Jake kept his face as free of any expression as he could. *I'm going to tear off your head.*

"What do you want?" Merilee asked, her voice absolutely icy.

This surprised Jake. Not in the script. They were supposed to let August do all the talking unless it was absolutely necessary to speak to him. Creed and Nick both shifted beside him, as if they expected Jake to control Merilee's mouth, and two of the OCU officers grumbled to themselves.

August didn't seem to notice or care. "I want what I've been campaigning for since I arrived." He stood up straight and opened his hands as if to embrace the room. "Peace, my dear. I want peace."

As the words spilled from the man's mouth, Jake's

demon senses growled at the lies—but damned if a few of the officers and one of the Sibyls didn't look . . . what? Relieved? Hopeful?

Shit.

Was this more of the bastard's talent, to pump harmony when he wasn't pumping discord?

You killed my friend, and you want my woman. . . .

"Let's not stand on pretense and formality." August lowered his arms and kept his words directed at Merilee. "I know you're investigating me, hoping to tie me to that awful killing at the Carter headquarters—as well as other crimes."

This time, the grunts of surprise couldn't be missed, Jake's included. He didn't make it all the way through the part about tearing off the fucker's head this time.

August glanced at him, then at Creed, Nick, the OCU officers, and the other two Sibyls. Jake couldn't shake the sense that they were being probed and examined, checked for weaknesses, as if this were all one big fun game for the ancient demon in man-skin standing in front of them.

"Of *course* I know about the warrants." August sounded like a parent being indulgent with his children. "Go on and serve them wherever and however you'd like. You'll find nothing because I'm completely clean—and completely innocent. You don't even need warrants. Just knock on my door anytime, and I'll let you in. I have nothing to hide."

The bastard's smile would have lit a cathedral, but Jake didn't buy it. When he glanced down at Merilee, she was paler than he'd ever seen her, and he wanted to snatch her and run out of the room before August could do any more damage.

August was busy talking now, droning about truthfulness and how he valued life, how life was his purpose on

Earth, and Jake could swear some of his officers and now both of the Sibyls other than Merilee were actually considering some of his garbage.

August produced a piece of paper, and he handed it to the OCU officer standing nearest to him. "My own investigators have developed this list of potential suspects, criminals and perverts who were in the area at the time of Derek Holston's savaging. Perhaps it will be useful to you?"

The officer with the list looked at Jake, who gestured for him to put the paper away. The officer folded the list and tucked it into his pocket.

"Thank you," Jake said, the words actually causing him physical pain. He started to launch into their own planned spiel, about timing and coincidences, about the warrants and what they suspected they'd find, but Merilee interrupted him suddenly with the same four words she had used before.

"What do you want?"

August's smile faded, then blazed brighter than ever as he made eye contact with her. "Why don't you send your companions on their way to check out my list, and we'll discuss that, shall we?"

Jake's shoulders tensed, and the muscles in his arms bunched. They had expected a move like this, for August to try to isolate Merilee, and they had a ready response. At a nod from Jake, the OCU officers and two Sibyls filed out of the room and made as if to leave the building, but Jake knew they would hit the alley, split up, walk less than a block in all directions, and establish a makeshift perimeter. They'd be ready to swoop back in at the first sign of trouble, and they'd also be able to call for help if help was needed.

Jake remained behind with Nick and Creed. No matter what August said or tried to pull, the three of them would not leave Merilee's side.

The murdering psycho who slaughtered Freeman didn't seem flustered by this. He kept his cold gaze on Merilee and Merilee alone, and once more Jake had the sensation that August was probing. Testing out theories about Merilee, and maybe about Jake and his brothers, too.

Had it been a mistake to come here?

Were they giving August more information than he was giving them?

I should just kill him now.

But what if he explodes or some shit and hurts Merilee?

Jake punched a third claw into Merilee's chair back and had to hold his breath to stay human. His vision prismed and swam, bursting into full Astaroth awareness. For the briefest moment, the image of August darkened. Turned black. Turned huge. Then Jake's demon vision receded again, until the room looked normal to his human-form eyes.

As the door closed, leaving the five of them alone in the big glass conference room, Merilee flinched and almost looked upward toward the ceiling. She caught herself, controlled the urge, but every muscle in Jake's body went so tight his skin burned.

August gazed at Merilee and nodded. "Yes. Your friends. Those black winged creatures who have been blocking my attempts to communicate with you more . . . privately." August glanced toward the ceiling, as if he could hear the monsters shrieking just like Merilee. "Even now, they're making this meeting quite difficult. What are they? Can you summon them at will?"

Merilee straightened and went as rigid as Jake.

Jake stared at August.

He had been under the impression that the Keres belonged to August—or at least that he was using an approximation of their images to scare the shit out of Merilee and other air Sibyls.

Merilee's posture suggested that she had been assuming the same thing.

August shifted his attention to Jake, Nick, and Creed. "And you three. The demon-brothers who have risen above their makings. The unholy trinity itself, here in my office. I must say I'm honored. Your mother was a powerful biosentient. I would have liked to see her work."

Jake answered with a low growl, and he felt the instant heat of his brothers as their Curson energy surged forward and their skin began to glow gold.

August focused on Jake. "Why is it you are so different from others of your kind? Do you know? Have you even bothered to explore that question?"

Jake ached to hurt this bastard. Saw it so clearly in his mind he could almost feel the blood flowing over his fingers, but somehow he managed to stand behind Merilee and do nothing. Let him keep up his I-know-more-than-you-do game. Who knew what other tidbits he'd spill by accident, and never even realize his mistakes?

Merilee leaned forward, elbows pressing hard against the table, and repeated her earlier question. "What do you want?"

August seated himself at the table across from her, in front of the door.

Between us and the exit. Jake almost stopped breathing, cursing himself for his tactical error. But they were four against one—and he didn't care what the numbers were. If it came down to it, he would get Merilee out one way or another.

August never broke eye contact with Merilee. "We have a long and terrible history, your people and mine—but the time of the Legion is ending. I can accept that. Can you?"

Jake jerked from shock, and saw the surprise on his brothers' faces as their golden glow slipped away.

Merilee didn't react at all.

"What do you mean?" Nick asked, his voice low and quiet in the stillness of the conference room.

"I mean, the Legion is my creation," August said to Merilee instead of Nick, "but it's finished. I'm through with that way of life, and I want nothing more than to make treaty with the Sibyls. Find common ground."

He stopped. Waited.

Merilee breathed in, breathed out, and Jake felt the slow rise of hot wind from the back of her shoulders.

"You filthy, murdering bastard," she whispered. "We will never find common ground with the likes of you."

August's beatific expression never changed except for a flash of deeper coldness in those already-frozen eyes. "You misjudge me. I assure you, I haven't killed anyone—at least not recently. I'm weary of violence, Merilee. I've seen too much of it in my many centuries."

For a moment, the man seemed to have different faces, all colors, all ages. Jake thought he caught the ibislike countenance of the Egyptian god Thoth in that mix, but he wasn't certain. The effect was dizzying and hypnotic, even to him, even with all he knew.

"I'll help you bring to justice those who are guilty of the crimes you seek to redress." August's voice sounded so sincere, but Jake's skin kept right on crawling. "All I ask is that you work with me, you and your Sibyl sisters. Join with me to make a better world."

Fancy words. Fancy suit. Jake's ribs felt like they were cracking as he held back his shift—and his fists, and his Glock, too. *Fuck, can't I just kill him now? Lying asshole.*

Merilee said nothing, but she had stopped shaking. In the reflection of the glass walls, Jake saw that her expression was absolutely unreadable. The way she was staring at August, Jake wouldn't have been surprised to see her conjure a bow and arrow and shoot the bastard right between his icy black eyes.

"Leave me in peace, and I'll help restore order in this city." August smiled at her, seeming unaware that his little seduction routine was falling flat on its smelly ass. "I'll help in your search for the people who have disappeared, and I'll make certain they're returned unharmed. Work with me, Merilee."

Jake heard the sound of Merilee's teeth grinding, then the hiss in her voice when she asked, "Do I have a choice?"

August actually managed to look offended. "Of course you do." He sat back in his chair and opened his arms again. "If you don't wish to work with me, you're free to leave."

Merilee stood so fast the top of her forehead almost caught Jake in the chin.

"I understand," August said, sounding phony-sad. Sweet, but with a flinty edge that made Jake go back to thoughts of ripping off his head. "Trust takes time, my dear. Sooner or later, though, you may need me too much to turn me down."

Jake was about to discuss how cold the temperature in hell would need to be before that happened when Merilee let out a choked cry, climbed over the table, shot past August, and bolted out of the room.

Nick reacted at the same time as Jake, following the same path Merilee took, over the table and past August, who just sat in his chair smiling that television smile.

"What's going on?" Creed yelled as he caught up with them and they tore down the headquarters hallway, knocking people out of the way.

Merilee wasn't even in sight.

They heard the door to the alley bang shut before they even got past the big copy room.

"No idea," Jake said between breaths as they ran.

As they broke into the alley and shoved past the line of Peace Now workers, Nick got on his radio and barked instructions for the OCU to get the Sibyls and fall back another block, and wait for more orders.

Jake let his demon essence come forward as much as he dared, his acute senses picking up Merilec's scent on the wind she left behind. He immediately realized she was heading back to the townhouse, though he had no idea why.

Damn, she was moving fast, using her wind energy to speed her progress until she'd be nothing but a blur to human onlookers. He caught a deep whiff of her fury and terror and the kind of worry he had always associated with family fearing for their own.

Or . . . a Sibyl fearing for her triad sisters?

Jake fought not to stumble, then fought harder not to grow wings.

Oh, fuck.

His gut caught fire.

Oh, shit, no, not this.

Jake cut his eyes left and right, taking in the determined faces of his brothers as they ran.

"Send everyone to the townhouse," he yelled, adrenaline pouring through him. He strained deep inside his human form, doubling his speed to keep up with Nick and Creed once they shifted. "It's Riana and Cynda. We need to get there *right now*!"

❨31❩

Merilee covered the last two blocks to the townhouse in only seconds.

Why hadn't she listened to her instinct earlier, damnit, why?

Tears blinded her. She felt like her heart might explode.

The Keres weren't some bullshit August had been throwing at her. The second he'd asked her about them, she'd known that, felt it deep—along with the truth. That the death spirits were trying to get her attention. For some unknown reason, they had been trying to warn her, maybe even help her.

Now that her mind was open to the Keres, she could sense their meaning more clearly. The message still clanged in her brain like a warning Klaxon.

Get home.

You're in danger.

Your people are in danger.

Home. Home. Home!

Oh, fuck, she hoped that message was wrong, that it didn't mean what she thought it did.

All the gods of Olympus, let Riana and Cynda be okay. Please.

Merilee vaulted over the metal fence around the townhouse, then threw herself up the steps. She blasted her wind ahead of her so hard even her blood cells felt the pull.

The front door slammed open and shattered into so

many boards as she hurtled into the entry hall—and stopped, screaming.

Dead.

Ah, sweet goddesses, they were all dead!

She clawed at the sides of her face, scenting fire and blood and terror all at the same time.

The five OCU officers who stayed behind to watch the townhouse and help Riana and Cynda lay in broken heaps on the hardwood floors. Shot, stabbed, clawed—fuck! She couldn't tell.

"Cynda!" Merilee ran forward through red, slippery puddles, her wet footfalls slapping in the otherwise quiet house.

Too quiet.

Too still.

Nobody else here—or nobody else alive.

No!

"Riana! Cynda!" Merilee hit the stairs and hammered up one flight, then two. "Riana!"

No one answered.

Shit!

The third floor looked like a war zone. Chairs busted. Bookshelves overturned. The plaster had been cracked, and one of the support beams sagged at the center as if an earthquake had almost torn the space apart.

Riana . . .

Merilee sucked a gulp of air and ran down the hallway to Riana's open bedroom door.

One of Riana's daggers protruded from the splintered doorframe.

Inside, more broken furniture. Torn draperies. The mattress lay half off the bed. A streak of blood marked the cream-colored sheets, and the dark red pattern burned itself into Merilee's mind.

She wanted to vomit, needed to scream, but she didn't have any air left, or any time.

With no real thought, no connection to reality at all, Merilee wheeled out of the bedroom, ran back down the stairs and through the hallway. The conference room door was open, but when she looked inside, the space was empty. Sal's body—gone. But no Riana. No Cynda.

The basement door also stood open.

"Cynda. Cynda!" Merilee ran forward, yelling the word over and over again.

The wood on the basement door had been scorched black.

The bulb in the stairwell had been shattered, but Merilee plunged into the darkness and down, down to the gym where Nick left Cynda. Where Cynda often stayed when she was too agitated to control her elemental fire power.

The pungent odor of melted plastic and charred flesh almost choked her as she stumbled into the big stone room and looked around, desperate to find Cynda there, alive, okay.

Hecate help me.

Merilee shoved her palms against her own chest to contain the ache as she looked around. Blood rushed in her head so fast, so loud it made her mind spin. In the dim light she could see there was nothing left of the gym but twisted lumps of metal, scorched and exploded exercise mats and balls, and bits of ash.

Two dead bodies lay at odd angles against the gym walls.

Males, burned to death. Probably part of August's raid.

Merilee didn't give a shit about the dead men.

Her mind registered the only important fact.

Not Cynda. Not Riana. Thank all the goddesses. Not one of mine!

Go, she thought to Cynda, and sent a fierce hope into the universe that her triad sister would burn all of her kidnappers to crispy black shells, before or after Riana crushed them with molten boulders from the center of the earth.

Breath coming in jagged, painful gasps, Merilee peeled out of the basement, running harder than ever. She called wave after wave of her air energy to shove her up the steps even faster.

She had to go after Riana and Cynda. She had to find them. Save them. If she got back outside, maybe she could pick up a clue, a scent, some kind of trail. There had to be a way to follow them. She refused to consider any other possibility.

She made it to the stairwell and launched herself into the hallway, and slammed face-first into a steely, muscled chest. Hands grabbed her, steadied her. She hit whoever it was with enough wind to blow the fucker through the opposite wall—but whoever it was held on tight. Didn't even move.

Part of Merilee registered the face. The familiar scent.

Jake?

He was talking.

Words were coming out of his mouth—but what was he saying?

Merilee's mind buzzed. Agony and loss seemed to batter her whole body. She scratched at Jake's face. Tried to punch him. "Let me go!"

"Are they here?" he demanded, his voice louder as he gave her a brief shake. "Focus. Focus, Merilee, and tell me. Now."

The sound of his voice, the shake, the pressure of his grip on her forearms, and his stormy gray-blue eyes brought her back to this world enough to process his question. She stopped moving and sagged, but he held her up.

Are . . . they . . . here . . .

Riana. All the goddesses and gods, too. Cynda. Help me now, Olympus.

Are they here—

"No!" The word tore from her depths in a loud wail, and she started fighting Jake's grip all over again. Wanted away from him. Wanted away from everyone and everything except Riana and Cynda and whoever had snatched them away from her.

"Stop it," Jake said, his voice soft.

Merilee thrashed at him. Threw enough air at him to move every sand dune in the Sahara. Pictures blasted off the wall. Shelves rattled and smashed to the floor. She couldn't help herself. Couldn't make herself stop. "Let me go. I have to get out there and look for them. Goddamnit, Jake, take your hands off me!"

But he didn't.

He pulled her to him, then forced her behind him, between his back and the wall. Using his weight and greater height, he crushed her into the plaster, ignoring her kicks, her punches—not even twitching when she sank her teeth into his neck.

Then, over Jake's shoulder, Merilee saw the two hulking golden forms approaching.

Slowly.

Growling.

Fists doubled.

Eyes white with fury, the Curson forms of Jake's twin brothers bore down on them like the wrath of Olympus itself.

The nearest and largest—Nick, Merilee knew—growled, the unearthly sound so low and loud the walls seemed to shake with it.

Then it spoke.

Just one word.

"Where?"

The sound crashed through Merilee, more painful than any punch. She tried to answer him, tell him she didn't know, but a sob tore out of her throat instead. Damnit, she was crying now, and she'd never ever stop. How could she stop? Her triad had been stolen away, right under her nose. What kind of broom was she? How could she let this happen to her family of the heart?

Nick lunged forward, his blazing golden face only inches from Jake's. He was still wearing his own talisman, so somewhere in all that bulk, there was still a hint of humanity—though Merilee couldn't see a bit of it. He looked like seven feet of pure rage, out of control. When the demon opened his mouth and showed the huge, jagged teeth inside, Merilee caught her breath and tried to make herself be quiet.

Jake didn't move even an inch.

After a second of facing down dangerous Curson-Nick, he answered his brothers for Merilee, his voice so calm she had an urge to bite him again. "Riana and Cynda aren't here. August had them taken."

From behind Nick, Creed let out a roar that really did shake the walls.

The sound shook Merilee, too, letting out some of her rage and panic in a way she couldn't manage without blowing the townhouse down to its stone foundation. Her tears kept flowing, but now more anger and determination mixed with her pain, sharpening her thoughts.

The huge Cursons turned away from Merilee and Jake and thundered past the bodies of the dead officers, out of the townhouse, straight into the streets of New York City.

Jake immediately stepped away from Merilee and released her from the wall. He turned and caught hold of her arms again, keeping her close, and she saw that his face was bruised and bleeding, probably because of her.

"Are you okay?" he asked.

"No. Yes." Damn it, she would *not* start sobbing again. This didn't seem real. She was going totally numb, and maybe this wasn't real at all. "But, no."

The OCU officers and Sibyls from their team poured through the front door, pulling up short and swearing when they saw their dead comrades.

Merilee jerked away from Jake.

Slow down. Just slow down. Think it through. You're a broom. It's your fucking job to think!

Her mind shifted into a more deliberate, determined gear. She called out to the fire Sibyl in the group. "Riana and Cynda have been kidnapped. We need the Mothers. Now. Get them and send them to the fourth-floor library."

The fire Sibyl's eyes widened. She hesitated for a second, looking at all the blood in the hallway, then ran up the stairs toward Cynda's communications room and the big platform she used. Merilee had no clue how one scrawny, marginally experienced fire Sibyl would manage to open the ancient channels and bring the Mothers to the townhouse, but she had to trust that it would happen.

Her stomach heaved, and she almost broke down all over again.

Hold it, hold it, keep it together. She breathed through the sickening crush of emotions she couldn't even sort out. Her hands were shaking, so she folded her arms to steady herself.

Behind her, Jake choked out instructions to secure the scene and call back the other teams. "I'll tape it off. It's a crime scene. Tell them to come in through the kitchen and—"

"The conference room." Merilee met his eyes, then turned her face away because she couldn't stand the sorrow she saw. "It's empty now."

Without looking at Jake again, she left him to manage the officers and the scene and ran out of the townhouse, air spinning around her shoulders in fast little gusts. She jerked it back with fierce effort, worried she'd blow away some thread or bit of dust that would tell her what she needed to know.

Which way.

Which fucking way?

Her eyes bored into the porch, then the steps, then the ground as she moved all the way to the sidewalk, searching every inch, every crack and pebble for anything that would tell her which direction the kidnappers took.

For long, painful minutes, Merilee circled the outside perimeter. Twice. Three times, then four, winding up back on the sidewalk again, just inside the fence's gates.

No indication of her triad sisters. Not even a whisper of a trail, or a single clue.

Merilee knew that meant Riana and Cynda were unconscious by the time they got outside, or there would be a burn mark, a torn bit of earth—something. She would not allow the other alternative.

Dead . . .

No.

Absolutely not.

She started around the perimeter again, concentrating so hard that each step felt like an electric shock.

Riana and Cynda weren't dead.

Merilee's hands kept balling into fists so tight her nails cut into her palms.

They are not dead.

She moved to the side of the main walkway until she was standing on natural stone, a much better conductor for elemental energy, and faced away from the house and the road, too. Due north, toward the source of all wind. Then she clenched her fists and closed her eyes and let her consciousness seep into the breezes, into every bit of wind around the townhouse.

Sounds grew more intense.

Now smells.

Merilee willed her mind and essence outward, her ventsentience expanding, feeling the air, *knowing* it, touching it and following the currents to wherever they might lead. Heartache competed with burning, acidic regret at not being here when Riana and Cynda needed her most, at first clouding her awareness, then shoving it forward, forcing Merilee's mind deeper into the familiar exercise. Her thoughts sharpened to fine points, and her archivist's skills took over, sorting familiar sensations, logging them and identifying.

Strangers.

Traffic fumes.

Sewage.

Pizza from around the corner. Hot bread from up the street—and cooking sugar from a nearby bakery.

But Riana?

Cynda?

*Damn*it.

Nothing.

Merilee let her mind go farther, but she still found nothing. Frustration coiled inside her, rising and rising until it threatened to burst from the top of her head in a bashing, bruising air funnel.

Then—there. A few miles away. Mingled sulfur and fire—but not Asmodai. No, this was too familiar. It was Creed and Nick, radiating malice and terrifying a crowd of onlookers as they stormed the Jensen headquarters to get at August.

They aren't there, boys.

Neither is he.

Because she had already sensed August. South. Toward Wall Street, giving off a deeper, more malignant stench, a cross between the poisonous gas in the Carter basement and something wet and moldy, like stagnant seawater. He was on the move, seemingly calm and unconcerned, no trace of anxiety in the air or smells coming off him as he walked.

Merilee imagined his lanky frame, his insincere smile and the lies he spewed.

You bastard. How could you have been so prepared? How could you know exactly when and how to strike—and how did you steal two of the most powerful Sibyls ever trained?

Her teeth clenched so tightly her jaw and temples throbbed.

Pulling her awareness back from August before he sensed her, she breathed in the hot, shimmering breezes emanating from the townhouse's third floor, flowing down across the front entrance to the sidewalk. The fire Sibyl was dancing on Cynda's communication platform, opening the channels, reaching out to the Mothers.

A fresh, spicy scent edged out everything else, and Merilee opened her eyes to see Jake standing in front of her.

She shook her head and whispered, "Nothing."

Jake's devastated expression mirrored her own feelings. When he spoke, his voice sounded flinty, barely controlled. "If you want to grab your bow and hit the streets, I'm beside you. I'll go until we both drop."

His voice broke, and Merilee pressed a hand against her mouth and swallowed a sob.

She couldn't stand this. She couldn't get through it. No way. If anything happened to Riana and Cynda, she'd rip out her own heart.

A few breaths.

A few more.

Pull it back in. Come on. You can do it.

Jake gazed at her like he wanted to fold her in his

arms, but thank all the goddesses he didn't do it. If he touched her right now, she'd shatter, and she loved him for knowing that.

When she trusted herself enough, she said, "I want to do what Creed and Nick are doing. Cynda would run every street and alley in the whole goddamned city to find me. Riana would shake down every building in her way."

Strength seemed to flow from Jake like a steady shimmer, touching her even more gently than his hands would. She could swear that something inside him was reaching out to calm her, almost like a direct infusion of light and warmth.

"You're a broom," he said. "Earth and fire Sibyls charge in—but it's an air Sibyl's job to wait, to watch, to sweep up whatever mess they make, right? You fight differently."

"I fight differently." Merilee ran her fingers through her hair. "I do. I'm supposed to see what nobody else sees and use it to finish the job. To win the battle."

Jake remained still and calm, but his eyes flared with urgency. "What is no one else seeing? What can we use to outthink this motherfucker, to get to his next move before he does?"

Merilee's body ached as her muscles tightened all over again. Her bones hurt—but her mind whirled over every fact, every detail, every tiny piece of information. Images flashed through her brain, especially of the meeting with August. What he said. What he did. What he knew.

And . . . what he didn't know.

She glanced at the sky.

Jake had his Glock drawn before she knew what was happening. "Are you hearing those things again?" He turned before she answered, looking at the street, searching for threats. "Are those monsters screaming?"

"No, no, it's not that." She let out a breath as he came out of his wary stance. "There's no immediate threat. But August—those creatures—I thought they were his, didn't you?"

Jake holstered his gun and looked confused. Merilee chanced her own self-control by touching his arm. "The Keres. I thought August controlled them, that they were somehow tied to him or his wishes—but he didn't know what they were."

Jake covered her hand with his and seemed grateful for the chance to comfort her more directly. "August called them your friends. He said they've been blocking his attempts to communicate with you privately."

"He had to mean mind-to-mind." Merilee let Jake's touch steady her even more, and she tried to keep her mind cleared, working at full speed. "I bet that's what happened with Charlotte and Phila. He invaded their minds first, found their weaknesses, tracked their actions, then picked his moment to attack."

Jake nodded. "With you, though, the Keres have been alerting you to his approaches and his intrusions."

Merilee felt a burst of energy from the townhouse.

The ancient communication channels that had been opened were now closed. The Mothers had arrived.

She extracted her hand from Jake's and wiped leftover tears off one of her cheeks. "Let's get to the library and get some help. I know we've tried and failed, but this time, we have to succeed. We've got to figure out what my creatures are—and see if they can help us find my triad sisters."

Jake, however, didn't move.

He was staring past her, toward the steps of the townhouse.

Merilee turned and followed his gaze, and the tears she had been fighting started all over again. The brief respite from her agony ended abruptly, shattering the calm center she had managed to find while searching the wind and working with Jake to figure out which direction to take.

Bela Argos was standing on the townhouse steps with a couple of Sibyls and OCU officers, cradling an unconscious Andy in her arms.

"I'm sorry," Bela called to them. "I had to knock her out. She blew up all the water pipes over at the Carter headquarters and flooded the entire neighborhood—we couldn't get through to her. It was this or drown."

Merilee wanted to run to Bela and snatch Andy right out of her grasp.

Fuck!

Another person she loved down.

Damaged.

Andy looked so pale. So tender and wounded.

Merilee couldn't begin to imagine how hearing the news about Sal Freeman had torn Andy apart—and Merilee hadn't even been there to offer comfort, maybe soften the blow.

Jake moved up the steps and took Andy from Bela's arms as Merilee stood below and cried. She heard him say Andy was okay, saw the truth on his face as he tried to reassure her that Andy would wake, and that they'd help her.

Her chest squeezed and ached. Her tears kept flowing, and her brain was trying to switch off.

Too much.

Absolutely too much.

She didn't want to hear anything else.

She couldn't face Andy—or Bela and Jake or anyone else. Not another second. She definitely couldn't withstand Jake summarizing the disappearance of her triad sisters to Bela and the rest.

Merilee's legs moved, then her body. Her awareness

didn't catch up until she had elbowed past the crowd on the steps, skirted the taped-off crime scene, and reached the stairs.

By then she was running.

Still crying and running, and she wished she could run forever.

32

Worrying about Merilee so fiercely it made his chest ache, Jake carried Andy into the townhouse with Bela and her party following behind. He tried not to look down at the woman in his arms because her ghost-pale face tore him up even worse. He didn't know if he had ever felt sorrier for anyone in his life.

He had encouraged Freeman to tell Andy how he felt, encouraged the relationship itself—and now look what had become of it.

Death and loss and misery.

Freeman. Man, I can't believe you're gone. Andy's all I've got left of you now, and I swear, *I'll look after her.*

As they entered the townhouse, the Sibyls and officers following Jake gasped and shouted when they saw the dead OCU personnel in the entrance hallway.

Jake tried to keep thinking like a cop, like a cop in charge. If nothing else, the responsibility would keep him sane. "Bela, will you and your people stay downstairs to assist the incoming teams and the M.E.?"

Bela told her team to remain, but followed Jake another few steps. "You'll need help with Andy when she wakes."

"Merilee had the Mothers called back," Jake said as he started up the stairs. "They're here. The scene needs to be secured so you can help with the search, because Riana and Cynda are missing."

Bela froze for a three count, horror claiming her aristocratic features. Then she spun toward the entrance hall and started placing her team and arriving officers at intervals to protect key areas of evidence until the crime scene techs could arrive.

Damn, he'd hated saying those words out loud—but it seemed to settle the issue.

Jake carried Andy to the only place that seemed reasonable and safe, and the place he hoped to find Merilee. The door to the fourth-floor library already stood open, and he edged inside, careful not to slam Andy's feet against the frame.

The moment he entered the room, he knew Merilee wasn't there. The large space felt too flat and lifeless to contain her, yet almost as fast, he sensed the familiar, powerful presence of Mother Anemone—and friends.

Jake eased around the bookcase, dodged a precarious stack of books, and stepped through the curtains separating Merilee's private area from the rest of the room.

Mother Anemone and three other Mothers garbed in the blue robes of the Greek air Sibyls had managed to cram themselves between Merilee's piles of paper. Jake noticed that a bunch of Merilee's clothes had been yanked from behind the farthest bookcase. The street clothes she had worn to meet August lay in a heap.

He figured she had put on her battle leathers. His pulse spiked, and he lowered Andy gently onto Merilee's sheets, resting her lolling head on the pillows.

Mother Anemone stood nearest, her face devoid of color, her misty blue eyes wide. The other Mothers had arranged themselves in a straight line on the far side of Merilee's bed, anxious gazes now riveted on Andy.

Mother Anemone nodded her thanks. "Wait for me on the other side of the bookcase. We must set up containment to hold her water energy in case she wakes, at least until we've found our missing warriors so everyone can help manage her."

Jake gave Andy one more miserable glance, wishing he could do more for her. "Where's Merilee? I'll just—"

Mother Anemone's expression shifted from concern to hard, polished steel as she interrupted him with, "Wait for me, Jake."

Jake stood beside the bookcase and stared at the woman, feeling the instant push of claws against the tips of his fingers. He had to bite back a snarl, and he barely kept his fangs from emerging. "Tell me where Merilee is," he said, his voice deadly quiet and far outside the parameters of the respect he usually showed Mother Anemone.

The Mother went from looking angry and harsh to seeming tired, then worried. "*Agapitos*. Please trust me, we're keeping her safe. She's tired and overwrought. You have been close enough to us to realize how it devastates Sibyls to lose one of our own—Merilee more than most, because she's so very sensitive, and lets so few people truly close to her heart."

"Where is she?" Jake squeezed the edge of the bookcase and felt the wood give against his partially demon grip.

Mother Anemone's eyes fixed on Jake's hand, which shimmered from pale white back to fully human. "Be careful," she whispered. "Jake, Merilee could not withstand another loss this day."

Jake ground his teeth together hard enough to snap a molar, but he stopped shifting between human and Astaroth. Man now. Human now. No way he'd let Merilee down. Mother Anemone had to see that—and she damned well better cough up where she had Merilee hidden.

As if reading his mind, Mother Anemone gestured toward the library door. "Downstairs in Cynda's communications room. Yana and Keara are containing Merilee for her own good and everyone else's. She needs sleep. A few hours to gather herself. Then we'll welcome you to join her—and allow her to join the hunt for her missing triad sisters."

Jake shook his head. "I want to be with her. She needs me now, not later."

"I'm certain she does, but she wouldn't forgive herself if she harmed you or her surroundings with her uncontrolled energy." Mother Anemone's blue eyes dulled with what had to be fatigue and distress. "There's significant risk she'll harm herself as well, like your Andy here." She looked over her shoulder to where Andy lay, and where the other Mothers waited with impatient expressions. "Please, *agapitos*. Let this be for a moment, and allow me to assist in the containments for the water Sibyl before she wakes. As soon as I'm finished, we'll go to Merilee together."

Jake wanted to refuse, but he let Mother Anemone turn back to Andy. As soon as the Mothers seemed absorbed in the task of setting elemental locks around the bed to hold back Andy's water power, he started to walk out of the library as quietly as he could.

Wait, hell.

Not happening.

Merilee wouldn't wait. She was too upset. She was damned near desperate. Containment or no containment, the second the Mothers turned their back on her, she might do something totally insane, and he needed to be with her to stop her. Or *help* her if it came to crazy plans or desperate actions.

A barely audible sobbing in the far corner of the library brought Jake to a stop at the doorway.

His chest squeezed like somebody had hold of his heart.

Merilee?

He hadn't sensed her here, and she was supposed to be downstairs, but—

He turned and scanned the rows of bookshelves, the tables, and the chairs, but he didn't see anything.

"Merilee?" he asked aloud, and the crying grew more forceful. Loud hitches and jerks.

Jake walked back into the library and tracked the noise, moving from shelf to shelf until he found a small, crying woman huddled at the end of the farthest row, clutching a big, leather-bound volume that looked like an ancient compendium or encyclopedia.

Delilah Moses.

She had pulled herself into such a tight ball that Jake might not have seen her at all, except the ghost of his mother was standing right beside her.

Shit. Not this *again.*

Jake's stomach churned with revulsion at the sight of that dagger, that red dress, and his mother's flat, vacant eyes.

"You can't hurt me," he said aloud, wondering if real words would finally banish the spirit. "If you could use your biosentience, you'd have blown up every cell in my body by now. So whatever you want, you aren't getting it."

Delilah Moses twitched with each sound, but she didn't look up.

The response from Jake's mother was swift and vicious and instant. She bared her teeth, raised her dagger and plunged it downward, straight into Delilah's head.

Jake's gut lurched as the phantasmal tip disappeared into the old woman's skull—but Delilah didn't so much as twitch.

His fists clamped together. He wished he could choke his mother's ghost to death, but that wasn't reasonable or possible. She was only a shade, nothing more than a vestigial flicker of—

He went cold.

No . . . way.

Was it . . . could it be?

No.

But—*oh, shit.*

The knowledge came to him as clearly as if the words were spoken aloud.

His mother was the vestigial representation of the snake in the gift box. The unexpected threat from within.

Jake's skin went from cold to frozen as realization covered him, clear as a thin sheet of ice.

His mother's manifestation wasn't a personal thing at all. It wasn't even her, for shit's sake. It was Jake's own Astaroth instincts trying to tell him what he needed to know.

He stared at the sobbing old woman on the floor, the woman who saved him once—the woman he owed, the one he promised to help.

Delilah Moses.

The source Bartholomew August had likely been using to gain information on the Sibyls and the OCU for who knew how long.

From the corner of his eye, Jake saw the apparition beside the old woman break apart and drift down to the floor, the books, the shelves like so much silvery dust.

He wanted to pound his fists into the bookshelves, pulverize every volume, every piece of wood.

I'm such a fucking idiot.

"Delilah," Jake said, forcing himself to keep his tone calm even though he wanted to snatch her off the floor and shake her. "Look at me."

Something about his word choice seemed to wound her. She convulsed and gripped her book tighter, but a few seconds later, she did as he asked.

Jake noted her unkempt hair. Her pale skin. The tears in her eyes and the livid bruise under her right eye.

He still wanted to shake her, but he didn't move. Couldn't. He'd commit murder if he took a single step.

"I know what you've done," he said, rage creeping into every slow, overly articulated word. "I know you've betrayed us to him. To August."

"Good." Delilah's voice shook, but it held more power than Jake expected. She sobbed once, then caught herself and managed to get to her feet. That bruise was worse than he thought. Somebody had really knocked the hell out of her. "Then I won't be leavin' this townhouse alive, and I'll be free of him. I can't take another minute. Not even another second."

Confusion made Jake hesitate, slowed his reaction time just enough for Delilah to say, "You owe me, cop, and now I'm collectin'. Kill me. Kill me right now, then do whatever you can to save my boy."

She held her book and looked at him, like she was waiting. Truly wanting what she had just requested.

Jake's insides heaved. He wanted to grant her wish, but he didn't kill women—especially not women he owed.

But why had she done this?

Why spare his life then, help them all—only to betray them?

"What turned you, Delilah?" He ground out the words, still doing his best to keep the fury out of his voice. "And why do you want me to kill you now?"

Delilah blinked. "I had no choice, cop. It was this or my boy's life, but I know now I can't protect him anymore." Tears slid down her cheeks, and she suddenly looked twice as old. Frail and weak in ways Jake had never seen from her before. "No matter what I do, my boy and I, we're both done for, so kill me. I know you'll do it fast. And maybe if I'm gone, he'll lose interest in Max and let the boy live a bit longer."

"Max Moses." Jake kept himself planted between

Delilah and the end of the bookcase where she might escape. The pieces were all there, he knew it, he just couldn't slide them together.

"His son. Our son. Goddess save me." Delilah's gaze shifted from Jake to the volume she clutched. "I didn't know what he was, you see? When I was younger. He was handsome. A rogue. I thought he was a witch, or maybe a changeling. I never guessed—"

Air left Jake's lungs in a rush, and his muscles went slack from the shock.

Delilah and August?

Max Moses . . . their son?

"I never guessed his true nature, cop. Or how cruel he'd be. How he'd . . . use us, whenever he wanted." With both hands, Delilah thrust the leather-bound compendium toward Jake. "I've been lookin' every day, but I've never found his like or his picture in this library to learn his true nature and find a way to have at him. I did find what's plaguing him though, what he sent me after. Maybe it'll help you instead. Help you save yourself—and Max, too, if you can."

Jake didn't want to touch the book, and at the same time he wanted to grab it out of Delilah's hands and order her to get out, never come back, never let him see her face again.

But her face. It was bruised. Her whole soul seemed bruised, and she was clearly terrified—and of more than Jake's wrath.

She saved my life once. She saved all of our lives.

"These are the spirits helpin' your Merilee and keepin' that bastard out of her mind." Delilah came toward him, still holding out the book. "He doesn't understand them. I think—I think he fears them."

She sounded so earnest.

Jake stared into her wrinkled face and tried to see the lie, the trick, but found nothing.

But he hadn't seen any of this coming at all, had he? So what good were his fucking instincts, especially where Delilah was concerned?

Senses on high alert, he jerked the book from Delilah's hands and opened the yellowed volume to the spot she had marked with a strip of paper. The thin, aged pages revealed a full-color print of the Keres, fangs glowing white in the moonlight, the fog of their mountain wrapping their long, deadly bodies.

"He's scared of them," Delilah repeated. "But I don't know why. I'd tell you if I did." She brushed her palms against her skirt and swallowed. "Now, demon. I expect you to pay your debt. I'd prefer a broken neck. Always heard that doesn't hurt, except for a few seconds."

"Clearly, I've missed something," Mother Anemone said as she came to stand beside Jake.

He didn't answer.

He couldn't stop staring at the Keres, wondering why they had been making such a point to reach out to Merilee, and to help her.

Delilah, talkative as always despite her obvious exhaustion and wish to die, began explaining her treachery to Mother Anemone, who seemed to grow more stiff and angry with each word. Jake figured he might not have to carry out the old woman's death sentence. The Mothers were probably more than up to that task.

The picture of the Keres called him more deeply, and his senses spread out into the oils, seeking their essence, seeking an answer—and he became aware of a vibration in the energy of the library.

Was it them?

Was he hearing a hint of the screaming that had so disturbed Merilee?

But . . . no.

From behind him came the voices of Mother Keara and Mother Yana as they entered the library.

It must have been their approach he sensed.

That was all.

Jake frowned.

"She's sleeping now," Keara told Mother Anemone, who had moved forward and taken hold of Delilah by one arm and her collar. "We've left Bela to guard the door, and to come for us when Merilee wakes. The remainder of our New York Sibyls are combing the city. Shall we join them?"

Jake noted how unhappy the Irish Mother sounded, and that Mother Yana didn't speak at all. No doubt both women were profoundly distressed at the kidnapping of Riana and Cynda, Sibyls who had been, essentially, daughters to them.

"We can't leave this place as yet," Mother Anemone growled as the others came forward, clearly confused by her response and what they were seeing.

Mother Anemone laid everything out for them in quick, terse sentences. The remaining Greek Mothers joined the conversation, and the women discussed what in hell to do with the traitor they had trusted and allowed so deeply into their ranks.

Jake heard them, but didn't hear them at the same time. He kept his attention firmly on the dark spirits of death.

Who are you, really?

What's your angle with this?

A new ripple of energy came again, whispering through the library like a quiet wave.

It felt familiar to Jake, but strange, too.

The Keres in the picture seemed to move, and his head snapped up. He lifted his hand to his neck and touched the spot where his talisman would have been, before he gave it to Merilee.

Did she touch it?

Had she taken it off?

Jake turned to the Mothers. "Can Merilee open the communication channels?"

Mother Anemone turned her gaze on him, looking surprised. "No, *agapitos*. She cannot. She's secured in Cynda's communications room with elemental locks—absolutely contained, absolutely safe."

Jake gripped the book tighter. "Are you sure?"

"Completely," Mother Yana said. "The channels can only be managed by fire Sibyls. Vhy?"

"Because . . ." He glanced over his shoulder, to the empty library, as if he might see the energy glowing red like a sulfur trail. "I think I just felt them open, only not like they usually do."

He touched his neck again, sensing his talisman somehow, feeling it and yet not feeling it, as if some connection had been irretrievably severed.

When the Mothers gazed at him, obviously not believing him, he growled. "I've sensed this kind of energy before, many times. Here. At the Motherhouses. I'm telling you, the channels opened in some weird way. I'm positive they did."

He glanced down at the picture of the Keres, and a seed of dread bloomed in his gut.

Jake held the book toward Mother Anemone. "If Merilee can't open the channels—can they?"

Mother Anemone handed Delilah to the smoking Mother Keara, then took the book from Jake's hands and stared at the death spirits. "Foul, vile creatures." Her fingers grew white as they curled against the book. "I can't imagine they would be concerned by our means of talk and travel."

"But they are very old," Mother Yana said. "Very powerful. And they may have been communicating vith your Merilee, no? There is no telling vhat they vould be capable of doing, should they decide to attempt it."

A burst of energy exploded through the library.

Jake slammed against the bookcase shoulder-first, pain blasting his senses clear as the Mothers and Delilah all dropped on their backsides.

From somewhere below them, glass shattered.

"The channels were opened," Mother Keara said as they all managed to get upright, her words thick with wonder and anger. "Now they're closed—and not by us."

Jake righted himself, let out a roar, and bolted out of the library, desperation surging through every vein and sinew.

Down the hall. Down the steps.

He had to get to Merilee. He had to stop her.

Fuck. I'd do it in her shoes—but no. Merilee, please no.

He was aware that the Mothers were following him, dragging Delilah along for the ride, but he didn't wait. He ran straight to Cynda's communications room, where Bela was shaking her head as if to clear cobwebs from the rush of energy she must have just endured.

Shoving past her, Jake grabbed the door handles and threw open the wooden doors.

The communication platform was charred a brittle black—and the largest projective mirror had been blown apart. A few black feathers lay on the floor beside the platform, next to . . . Jake's talisman.

His body went still, from his mind to his heart. No movement. No thought, no beat. Nothing. All of his emotion dried to nothing as he stared at the talisman, not wanting to accept what he was seeing.

When he went for the gold chain and ring, his legs were heavy, unfamiliar, not quite within his command.

As he knelt and picked up the jewelry, he started feeling again, and what he felt was pain. Everywhere. Inside and out. He still didn't want to believe Merilee had taken it off.

But she was gone. Disappeared through the mirrors, into the ancient channels, who knew how—or *where.*

The talisman, though.

The talisman was here.

Jake squeezed the gold chain so tightly the links crushed and bent in his palm.

This is how you think it has to be.

He could still smell her here, still feel her—but the room was empty except for himself, and the Mothers, who were now running in behind him and around him. Mother Keara, the last one through, shoved Delilah toward Bela. "Take her to the basement. Do not let her out of your sight."

As Bela left with the old woman, Jake put on his talisman, the gold as heavy and cold as his heart.

Merilee . . .

He bent toward the broken mirror and grabbed pieces of its frame. A thousand bits of glass sifted through his fingers. Almost sand again. No putting it back together—but there were several more mirrors.

One of them might work, right? One of them might get him to Merilee, wherever she had gone.

"Dear goddesses of Olympus." Mother Anemone held out a black feather in one hand, away from her body like it might be dangerous or poisonous all on its own. "She's gone to the Keres."

Mother Yana and Mother Keara moved to her side, long-faced, looking older than their many, many combined years. "Ve have all lost the daughters of our heart."

"Lost?" Jake's senses revved back to full alert as he studied the women. "She's in danger, right? I get that—but why do you think she's lost?"

"The treaty." Tears crystallized in the corners of Mother Anemone's eyes. "By law, when she went to them, she became a suicide. Lost to us. Even if she intended to bargain for her triad's life, the price they'll demand—Merilee. It will be my Merilee."

She lowered her head, but Jake grabbed her by both shoulders and shook her until she looked at him. "Fuck the treaty! Merilee's not a suicide. She's *not* lost. And what price? What will those monsters do to her?"

"Ve cannot know that, demon," Mother Yana answered as she, too, stooped to collect a feather. "They are death spirits. If they offered to help her, it vas for their own reasons. They live for blood and battle and madness."

Jake let go of Mother Anemone. His claws tore out of the ends of his fingers. His fangs jabbed through his gums and grew, punching into his bottom lip. No way he could hold them back. He wanted to snarl like a mad dog, bite something, claw it to bits.

"Whatever the Keres do, it won't involve Merilee's survival." Mother Keara sounded flat and bleak. "Likely, she will indeed try to trade her life for the lives of her triad. In her position, given the same opportunity, we would all make the same sacrifice."

"They'll glory in possessing the blood of an air Sibyl." Tears rolled down Mother Anemone's face. "Our conflict is older than time and deeply bitter. Because of the treaty protecting both our races, they couldn't act against us—but Merilee has gone to them of her own request, her own will. They played this situation perfectly."

Jake wheeled on the fire Sibyl Mother. "Open the channels again. To wherever these Keres are—where Merilee is. These other mirrors work, don't they? Use one of them."

Flames licked across Mother Keara's shoulders, and her sharp face grew shrewd. "Káto Ólimbos is closed to us. I could attempt it, force the issue, but the journey would likely kill you."

Jake clenched his fists. "Do it."

"*Agapitos.*" Mother Anemone's gentle hand came to rest on Jake's wrist. "Even if you survive the transport, you are not a Sibyl, and not human. It would strip you to your basic nature. To your Astaroth essence." She broke off, choked by her crying.

"It is the same dilemma you have been facing," Mother Yana finished for her. "Ve vould not be able to help you regain your human form. If you do this, you vill be a demon evermore."

Jake turned to Mother Keara, his wings already emerging, his skin turning paler by the moment. "I don't care what happens to me as long as Merilee lives through this."

The Mothers didn't move or speak. They stood around the charred communication platform staring at him, each looking sad—Mother Anemone the saddest of all.

"I can't fly to Greece fast enough to do this myself," Jake yelled, the demon resonance in his voice echoing around Cynda's communications room. "Send me to Merilee, goddamnit. Send me now!"

33

Merilee stood on the moonlit mountaintop straight out of her nightmares, teeth chattering in the cold wind and mist. Her heart pounded against her ribs, too fast yet too weak, almost fluttery from the sudden change of altitude. Her head swam from getting jerked through the projective mirror, and her leathers felt like no more shield from the frigid air than thin black paper. She clutched her bow and wished she could draw an arrow, but that might offend the creatures watching her with empty black eyes.

I can't believe I called for them in the mirror.

I've got to be out of my fucking mind.

She swallowed and shuddered as the chill got deeper, stabbing into her joints and bones and leaving her lashes crusted with frost. When the Mothers had locked her into Cynda's room to force her to rest, Merilee had known how it would go. Seen it in her heart and mind. The Sibyls would regroup, plan, and search—and find nothing. They'd be too late. Riana and Cynda and their babies would die just as surely as the sun rose and set each day, and that simply wasn't acceptable to Merilee.

So she had taken off Jake's talisman, gently, carefully, sobbing as she did it, and placed it on the floor where it wouldn't get damaged, and where he'd be sure to find it. Then she had climbed onto the platform. She had pressed her hands against the most powerful of the projective mirrors, and she had called out to the death spirits.

They had been helping her. They had some interest in this situation—so she had grasped at the longest of long shots.

She had offered herself to the Keres if they would meet her price.

And they came.

I can't believe they brought me here.

Gods and goddesses, I don't even have a roof to jump off—can't jump—can't run away.

A few yards from where she stood, the Keres ringed her, ten of them in stained red robes. They were taller than she remembered or imagined, but just as gaunt. Almost skeletal—though definitely, definitely female in shape and form and energy. Black feathers drifted from their ragged wings as they flexed their shoulder muscles and clawed fingers. Matted black hair hung in their pale faces, and their hooked fangs gleamed in the unearthly, almost black moonlight of Káto Ólimbos. The dark place. The forbidden place.

The last place I'll ever see.

If it hadn't been for her superior Sibyl vision, she probably wouldn't have been able to see anything at all in the strange darkness that seemed to deepen every few seconds.

Merilee choked back a sob, caught between regret and fear, but still resolved to do whatever she had to do to save her triad sisters and their babies. It had to be this way, so it would be this way. She didn't call her wind, or even try to stir the air to protect herself. From her previous dreams, she knew her elemental energy wouldn't work anyway.

Her chest ached at the thought that she would never see her sisters of the heart again, or Jake. Oh, sweet Aphrodite, Jake. Merilee touched her neck, feeling the empty hollow where his talisman had been.

How she'd love to kiss him just one more time.

Please understand. She closed her eyes and sent the thought toward him with all her energy. *Please know I love you.*

But she was her triad's broom, their last line of salvation, and she would *not* let them down again.

Merilee lifted her chin. "I'm ready," she said, her words issuing through the quiet cold in a rush of white steam.

She braced herself, waiting for the onslaught of shrieking, for the monsters to leap forward and shred her with those claws and fangs—but they just stood there until Merilee's blood pressure shot so high her brain malfunctioned and her mouth started working without her consent. "I told you my terms. My life for the safe return of my triad sisters to the townhouse and to those who love them. You agreed—and you came. So kill me and go save Riana and Cynda."

The Keres spoke. Some of them. Maybe all of them. The answer raked across Merilee's consciousness, making her whole body bend and tremble.

"We cannot rescue the Sibyls. They are not our province."

"*What?*" Merilee hugged herself and forced herself upright. Her eyes widened despite the brutal cold. "Then why am I here? Why did you answer me and jerk me through the mirror?"

This time it was several of the monsters that talked, she was sure of it. "You are special amongst your kind. Sensitive enough to hear us and understand our warnings. We can speak with you. Your energy has drawn us before."

Merilee did manage to snatch an arrow from her quiver even though her hands shook. In her mind, all she could see was that moonlit night at Motherhouse Greece, when the Keres had taken flight and one of them had come toward her.

It did happen. Exactly like that. One of them flew at me.

She got the arrow nocked, surprised the winged monsters didn't charge at her. She didn't know which to aim at, so she picked the one closest to her, dead forward. "I don't want to *talk,* and you know it. I want to save my triad sisters. That's the only reason I called you. The only reason I offered myself to you!"

The Keres all spoke at once then, the noise of their harsh voices blending into the mind-stabbing sounds Merilee had taken for shrieks every time she had heard them. She shook her head, then cried out with them and had to drop her bow and arrow. To save her hearing, she clapped her leather-clad fingers over her ears. "Wait! Stop. Stop it!"

Were they listening? She didn't want to move her hands to find out. Shit, what had she been thinking, drawing weapons on death spirits as old as time itself?

"I can't survive all of you making noise at the same time, so take turns, okay?" She risked lowering her hands, but didn't bother with the weapons again. "Maybe pick someone to speak for you."

The Keres shifted slightly, then turned their scary faces to stare at one another.

The silence soothed Merilee's aching ears, but she had an uneasy sense that the Keres were speaking mind-to-mind. Taking nominations. Maybe even voting.

She knelt slowly, making as few movements as possible, retrieved her arrow and slid it into her quiver, and picked up her bow. She couldn't use the weapons, no, but she could have them with her, on her. If she died here, she at least wanted to die armed, the way a Sibyl should.

A moment later, the death spirit at whom Merilee had aimed her arrow broke the circle by stepping forward. The creature walked a few feet, then stopped an arm's length from Merilee.

Against all of her instincts for self-preservation, Merilee held her bow but didn't raise it.

Was this the death spirit that had flown at her all those years ago, sending her screaming and flailing off that rooftop?

Somehow, she thought it was.

Merilee tried not to gag at the stench of rotting meat rising off the spirit's robes, her skin, her hair. Even in the icy air, it seemed like enough to kill a person outright if she breathed too deeply.

They're like walking corpses. Zombies with wings. And they can't help me. What the hell am I doing here?

Maybe she ought to raise the bow and shoot as many of the things as she could.

Tears pressed into her eyes, turning icy almost immediately, stinging and burning as she tried to blink them back.

That would be vengeance, wouldn't it?

But vengeance against what? Fate? Awful luck—or maybe stupid choices?

Her chest ached from holding back screams and curses, and a bleak hopelessness covered her like the mountain's cold, creeping fog.

Cynda. Riana. I'm so sorry. I thought this was the answer, but I've gotten myself killed for nothing. I've failed you both.

And Jake.

Jake . . .

The creature in front of Merilee tilted its disgusting head as if listening to her thoughts, then spoke slowly, almost too carefully, pronouncing each word as if she might be teaching an infant something of dire consequence.

"I am Nosi, daughter of Nyx, sister of Fate and

Doom, and many others, released to freedom by Pandora, to whom we owe never-ending allegiance."

Merilee's mouth came open.

What—they were into formal introductions with their dinner? They liked to know their food on a first-name basis, and its lineage, too?

Well, whatever.

Merilee didn't know what else to do, so she cleared her throat and said in the strongest voice she could manage, "I am Merilee, daughter of Sibyls, granddaughter of Hecate. We have no further ties or designations. To our Motherhouse and triad we remain ever-bonded."

The thing that called herself Nosi gave a slight bow, then straightened and once more regarded Merilee with empty black eyes. "We have no love for creatures of light and life." She raised her hand as if to indicate the superiority of the dark mountain around them. "But we have common purpose with you this day, this time in the world."

The cold was getting to Merilee almost as much as her agony over not being able to help Cynda and Riana. Through her teeth, she said, "If you can't help me save my triad sisters, we have no common purpose at all. Just eat me and get it over with."

The Keres remained silent, but Merilee could have sworn a few of them moved with what looked like laughter, or maybe even approval.

Clearly, they didn't like weakness and preferred prey with a little spirit.

"We desire the destruction of the Leviathan," Nosi said, still speaking slowly like she was addressing a small child.

"A . . . Leviathan?" Merilee's full attention riveted on the death spirit in front of her. "That's what August is?"

Oh, fuck. In her mind, Merilee saw an image of a massive, merciless sea serpent, large enough to swallow ships and destroy islands with a flick of its barbed tail. Mother Yana had been right. An Old One. Maybe the worst Old One ever known—and it had survived over the centuries, with the depths of the ocean for cover.

"He has crawled from his salty prison too often." Nosi produced an expression like disgust. "When he establishes the world he plans, there will be no humans remaining. No noble battles. No true wars and conflict."

Merilee eased her grip on the bow, her fingers throbbing with relief. "But won't that make you happy?"

The chittering-screaming-shrieking started from the nine Keres surrounding Merilee and their elected speaker, but Nosi silenced them with a raised hand. "If the Leviathan succeeds, we would be . . . without."

Understanding dawned inside Merilee with a rush so hot it chased back a fraction of the cold. She shouldered her bow, then faced Nosi directly, hands at her sides. "Without human death from violence and battles, you'll have nothing to feed you."

Nosi nodded. "A glut, and then nothing. We would pass into nonexistence."

"Starve and die." Merilee wasn't sure that was a bad thing, and her face must have shown her thoughts because Nosi leaned in close and bared her fearsome fangs.

"We could kill you now, air Sibyl." The creature's frigid breath seemed to stick to Merilee's face like leftover gore. "You know very well that by our ancient treaty, you belong to us. You asked to come here of your own free will. Irrespective of your reasons for that request, you are ours. We are not bound to honor any terms with you, or accept any bargain."

Merilee tensed and clenched her fists so tightly she was surprised she didn't draw blood in her palms.

No weakness.

No weakness.

"Right. Look, fuck off. If you were going to eat me, you'd have done it already, so what do you want from me?"

Nosi remained close for a moment, then backed away, lips parted.

Was she smiling?

The thought almost made Merilee physically ill.

The creature folded its arms in what looked like a gesture of defeat, or maybe just surrender. "We have a bargain of our own, air Sibyl."

Merilee kept her fists tight, and her rising anger heated her skin.

No weakness.

"Then spit it out, death spirit, because otherwise, you're wasting my time."

"We will set you free to find your triad sisters and give you what aid we can." Nosi gestured to the ground beneath her bare, filthy feet. "In return, you will bring the Leviathan here to us before the next sunrise behind your home on Áno Ólimbos."

Merilee worked out the time difference quickly. When the Keres sent her back, she'd have until roughly midnight, New York time, to find Riana and Cynda, rescue them, then get August back here to Káto Ólimbos.

Seven hours.

Fucking impossible.

No way.

"I need more time."

"There is no more time, air Sibyl." Nosi shook her ugly head. "If you do not accomplish this task in these few hours, the Leviathan will set in motion destruction that none of us can stop, least of all those of us who are trapped here in body, on this mountain, for all eternity because of a treaty with *your* kind."

Merilee set her jaw and refused to show any panic. So it wasn't their deadline, the seven hours. The Keres couldn't change it. Merilee flexed her fingers, hoping to fend off frostbite. "And if I fail?"

"If you fail, your life is forfeit, as it will be in any case if the Leviathan succeeds. We will eat your flesh and enjoy what time we have left to us. Break the treaty and feed at will." Nosi turned her fierce face toward the hidden slope above her, to Motherhouse Greece. "Beginning with the nearest and closest."

Nosi gazed at Merilee again and a horrid, dark energy flowed forward, slamming into Merilee like a black wall of hate and despair.

The vision pummeled her with so much force it drove her to her knees.

In her mind, she saw the Keres descending on the Mothers and adepts, shredding them, eating them, spilling their blood across the crystal hallways.

Merilee pitched forward, her face striking the frozen earth as her body writhed from the force of the images. She shook and screamed as her body burned from the cold, throbbed from it, and she envisioned the death spirits moving outward like a black cloud of pestilence, consuming the City of Gods and all of Greece.

And more.

And forward.

Onward. All over the world.

Merilee screamed until she felt like her throat was tearing, shook until she thought her bones would come apart—but she couldn't stop, couldn't push it back, couldn't help herself.

She was witnessing a contest between August and the Keres, to see who could kill more people, before the

Leviathan established his new world order—and the only true losers were the people of the world. All of them. Oh, sweet Olympus, all. All!

Almost every human life-form on the planet's surface.

No.

No!

Her soul started to come apart.

Her body started to die even as she fought for breath, for sanity.

The world shook.

Something exploded nearby, and Merilee feared it was her body, that she had frozen solid and shattered into a great mass of frozen blood and tissue, leaving only her consciousness behind to suffer and know how badly she had failed.

A loud, furious roar split the pictures in her mind, dividing them, shoving them sideways and restoring enough awareness for her to realize she had been lifted from the cold, cold mountain earth.

Warmth flooded over her skin.

Light blinded her.

The scent of spice drove the mountain's suffocating miasma of death out of her nose, out of her mind, and she felt the slight sting of cool metal against her cheek and shoulder. A chain. A ring.

Something powerful and warm was cradling her, and the Keres were backing away, shielding their black-nothing eyes, hissing and spitting and snarling like a pack of rabid cats.

"Jake?" Merilee's lips were numb. Her eyes clumped shut with melting ice. When she moved, she felt like needles jabbed her skin in a thousand places, but she managed to slip her arms around Jake's neck.

Even with her eyes stuck shut, Merilee could tell Jake was glowing. He held her even closer, somehow giving her his heat. She felt it flow through her veins, strengthening her, rebuilding her as if his presence was an elixir. He breathed into her hair, pressed his lips against her head, and kissed her, melting away the cold and the frost until she felt almost herself again, able to stand, to fight if she had to.

Then his deep, demon-resonant voice said, "After we get out of here alive, and after we've rescued your triad and killed that fucker August, I swear to all your goddesses, I'm going to spank your ass for scaring the living shit out of me. And I'm going to spank it hard."

Merilee heated up even more and opened her eyes as Jake shouted, "She's mine. This woman is *mine,* and she leaves this mountain with me. Whatever bargain she's made, I take it for her. It's mine, too. Which of you would challenge me?"

None of the Keres moved, but Merilee's heart and mind lurched against Jake's words.

"Jake. No!" She struggled to get out of his grasp, but he held her so tightly she couldn't move no matter how hard she tried. "He doesn't mean that. He doesn't understand. He doesn't know what he's agreeing to!"

Jake shifted his grip until her mouth pressed into the rock of his muscled shoulder and her words became nothing but muffled garbage. She bit at his glowing skin, but he didn't even twitch.

"I think the demon understands," Nosi said, still using that slow, deliberate voice. "I think he knows exactly the bargain he makes."

The death spirit repeated the terms of their deal, including the time limit, and once more, Jake accepted.

As Merilee did her best to free herself from Jake's powerful embrace, she heard the Keres laughing together in a low, spine-clawing shriek.

Nosi's voice rose above the din. "So be it. Now leave us and tend your bargain. Bring us the Leviathan. We can manage his death energies here. Deliver him, or pay the blood price at sunrise."

Before Merilee could twist against Jake one more time, they both jerked backward—and hurtled straight off the jagged edge of Káto Ólimbos.

Merilee screamed against Jake's flesh as his arms tightened around her until she couldn't breathe at all.

Her belly dropped as they plunged down, toward absolute oblivion—and even the darkness disappeared.

34

Jake's mind fractured like brittle stone.

One second he was holding Merilee and falling. Fast. Too far.

The next second, his body jerked and stretched like he was being sucked through time and space itself. Like the projective mirror, only a lot worse.

Merilee!

Pressure jammed against every inch of his skin. Spikes of agony hammered into his muscles and bones.

He burst. Exploded. Came apart, lost his thread of thought—

In a screaming rush of wind, Jake came back together again.

More like pulled himself back together—head and legs, essence first.

Then slowly, the rest of his body, his form.

His . . . Astaroth form.

Aching. Freezing and burning at the same time.

But alive. Not falling anymore. No.

Standing.

He was standing on a stone floor, in a stone room, wearing a pair of jeans or something like jeans.

He wasn't on the dark mountain anymore.

The townhouse?

Yes, he thought so.

The townhouse in the basement, and there were people in the room with them, but for the moment, Jake didn't give a damn.

The only thing that mattered was that he still had Merilee in his arms.

Jake gazed down at her, his demon senses registering the flush in her cheeks, the scent of her fear, and her even, regular breathing. Her eyelids fluttered, and she groaned.

Thank whatever gods or goddesses give a damn.

Jake held her to him, buried his face in her hair. He felt the warmth of her life in his own flesh, his own heart, in the breath in his own lungs. For a moment, he didn't care that she had left him and his talisman behind, that she likely didn't feel the soul-level connection that bound him to her more firmly than any physical tie. He was Astaroth now, and he could tell he'd never find human form again, never have her again—but she was alive, alive and whole, and Jake had never been so grateful for anything in the history of his existence.

Light poured out of his skin, covering her, bathing her, stroking her, and Jake imagined the glow feeding his love directly into her body to soothe her. He'd give her anything she'd take, anything she'd accept.

Jake lowered his head and brushed his lips against hers, careful not to harm her with his fangs.

She gripped his neck fiercely, pulling him to her, holding his mouth against hers.

Demon or not, Jake's entire body responded to her. Every bit of his mind, every bit of his flesh. He ached to take her, to make love to her here and now. If he hadn't been scared to death he might harm her, he would have taken her to the stone floor and—her sweet smell of white tea and honey almost blocked the hints of burnt rubber and plastic and the odd remnant tang of melted metal, but not quite.

We're in the townhouse, some part of his brain reminded him. *In the basement where Cynda was taken. And we aren't alone.*

Jake raised his head to see Bela Argos dressed in battle leathers, daggers drawn, gazing steadily at him. Beside her stood Delilah Moses, arms folded, the bruise under her right eye an ugly blue-black.

Behind them hovered Darian, Quince, and Jared, along with five other Astaroths Jake didn't know. The demons had papers, books, and what looked like cassettes and videotapes in their pale, clawed hands. From the corner of his eye, Jake also saw crime scene tape and white markings where the M.E. had recorded the positions of the kidnappers Cynda must have fried before the root took her away.

"The Keres sent you back through the channels." Bela sounded amazed. "Without a mirror. Goddess. How? Why? And why here?"

Jake pulled Merilee against his chest as she stirred, careful not to rake her with his claws. Good questions, but he couldn't cope with the lengthy explanations it would take to answer any of them.

They were sent back to do a job, or die. And probably sent to here, to this spot, because it was where they needed to begin.

"What time is it?" he asked.

Both Bela and Delilah seemed surprised by his question, and neither answered.

Jake's pulse accelerated. "Damnit, what time is it? *What time is it?*"

"Five," Darian answered. The Astaroth glanced at the windowless walls, then the stone ceiling. "Waning sun, if that's important."

Jake let out a fast breath. Five in the evening.

He had seven hours to make sure Riana and Cynda were rescued, find August, fork the bastard over to the death spirits on Káto Ólimbos, and save Merilee a second time.

"Jake." Merilee's voice yanked his attention away

from everything else. The rest of the basement and its occupants faded away as he gazed into her sea-blue eyes.

Tears waited in those blue depths.

She whispered his name again and touched the talisman around his neck.

The hot, delicious shock of her fingers on the gold that controlled him registered in every cell of his body.

My demon body. I'm Astaroth now. Forever. That's what she sees. That's all she'll ever see.

Her hands moved over the translucent pearly skin of his bare chest, and the misery in her eyes told him that she understood what he had done, and why, and where that left them.

"I'm so sorry," she whispered, those tears threatening to flow and tear Jake's heart in half. "I had no idea that you would follow me, that you even *could* follow me. I never meant—"

"I know," he said, his voice hoarse with grief, but absolutely without regret. He didn't want to hear the rest—why she didn't wait for him, or why she left his talisman behind. He couldn't bear that, and it didn't matter anyway. Not now. What was done was done. "We've got to find Cynda and Riana and make sure they're safe from August, then get to him and take him down."

Merilee's expression sharpened, and she tensed in his arms. "The blood price. Shit. Why in the name of all the goddesses did you join that bargain with me, Jake?"

Jake set her on her feet, then steadied her with both hands on her shoulders, his heart breaking because she didn't know, couldn't understand something so basic.

"My fate is your fate," he whispered, and it sounded like a vow.

Hell, it was a vow.

Merilee drew his promise inside her with a slow intake of breath and her air energy.

Did she feel it?

Did she take it as deeply as he wished?

How could she? Shit. Look *at me.*

For a long moment, she did look, and he looked, and they couldn't stop. They stared into each other's eyes, and it hurt Jake, killed him inside, to know what met Merilee's eyes. His pale hair. His white skin and golden eyes. Fangs and claws and wings.

He waited to catch the flicker of revulsion, but it never came. Merilee's face reflected guilt and unhappiness and worry and a hundred other things, but she didn't seem disgusted with him, or what he had become.

She lifted up on her toes and pressed her body into his, the sensation like raw electricity over every inch of Jake's skin. Her lips brushed against his cheek, and Jake's heart squeezed until he had to push her back.

It'll hit her later, he knew, even as he made himself look away from the sudden burst of love in her eyes. *She'll react when the crisis has passed.*

Fuck.

So will I.

Merilee turned toward Bela and the Astaroths, her voice still unnaturally soft and anguished as she said, "August is a Leviathan. The Keres told me."

The Astaroths reacted with frowns and hisses, and Jake felt a primal urge to snarl along with them. He didn't, but then he wondered why.

I'm them now, and they're me. We're one. I might as well get used to it.

Bela whistled low, palming her daggers and sheathing them at her hips. "We're fucked, aren't we? That's the largest—and the oldest—demon ever known."

Merilee crossed her arms and seemed to be trying to

shake off the last bit of shock over the transport from Káto Ólimbos. "He must have survived because he had the sea for cover. That's all I can figure. And like most demons, he can take a human form. Probably many human forms."

"How do we possibly kill something like that?" Bela rubbed her palms against the hilts of her daggers.

"We don't." Jake tried not to react to the demonness of his voice. So loud, vibrating the air around all of them like a bass guitar note. "We capture him and take him to the death spirits. I think they know what to do."

Bela leaned back, eyes wide. "And you trust those monsters?"

"Not one friggin' bit," Merilee said, "but they need him dead as badly as we do. Besides, I don't have a choice." She looked toward the basement door. "Where are Andy and the Mothers?"

"Andy's still out cold, but the rest of them are looking for Cynda and Riana and the other missing Sibyls." Bela pointed toward the ceiling, as if to indicate the streets of New York City above. "I'm here to guard Delilah, and in case Andy wakes up, I've got two earth adepts in the library to watch her. The OCU search teams that hit August's properties with the warrants—they came back with nothing."

"He has other places." Delilah's words cut into Jake's mind as cleanly as any surgical knife, trimming away all distractions and bringing his attention fully and squarely to her.

Once more she seemed old and burdened. In pain, both physically and emotionally, but her eyes gleamed with what he hoped was the truth of her words. "I can show you, cop. Demon. Whatever you are. I can take you, if you'll try to do right by my boy."

"I won't make promises about Max," Jake said, no

longer caring about the Astaroth resonance in his voice. "But I'll do what I can for his safety."

That seemed to be enough for Delilah. Merilee frowned, and Bela explained to her quickly about Max and Delilah, and their connection with August.

That changed Merilee's frown to a horrified scowl, and Delilah cowered away from her. Still, Jake knew Merilee would do what she could to help Max, if they found him alive.

Darian stepped forward, moving between Bela and Delilah to stand in front of Jake and Merilee. "We raided police and library archives, and . . . frightened information out of many sources," he said as he extended a thick stack of papers. "I am not certain it is the type of evidence you require, but we have documents tracing the Leviathan's age back at least four hundred years."

Quince came forward, too, and lifted the books in his hands. "Photographs. Ledgers of illegal business dealings."

"And tapes." Jared remained in his place, but showed the collection of videotapes and cassettes in his hands. "Not of recent crimes, but past crimes, when he did not know he was being observed by security systems."

From the soft but lethal snarling of the Astaroths Jake didn't know, he figured they didn't understand why they shouldn't just attack August and have done with it. Darian must have exerted influence over them, reasoned with them. And Darian must be a decent leader, to have gotten so many demons to follow him into a battle in which they had no stake.

Jake gestured for Darian and Quince to keep what they had collected. "It's enough for now. Where are my brothers?"

"In jail," Bela said.

Merilee let out a slew of curses as the words sucker-punched Jake.

He breathed in sharply, then coughed, still not quite sure he heard the Sibyl correctly. "Jail." Jake tried to shake that off, but he couldn't. "You're not serious."

Bela sighed. "Sorry, but they tore up the Jensen head-quarters trying to get at August, got shot, and ended up having to shift back and forth between demon and human forms to heal themselves. Some regulars got elemental cuffs off an OCU officer and took them in."

Jake's demon muscles rippled as he made eye contact with Darian. "Stash that stuff someplace safe and spring Creed and Nick. Show it to them so they can get a judge to act—and Darian, don't hurt anyone. If we slash a bunch of throats, no one in the human world will care what we have to say."

Darian nodded once before he vanished, taking Quince, Jared, and the other five Astaroths with him.

"Damn." Bela shook her head. "Whatever precinct they're about to visit—that place won't ever be the same again."

Merilee agreed, her voice still a little shaky, then asked, "What about August, Bela? Do we have a fix on him yet?

"The bastard has a rally scheduled tonight at Central Park, for 'his candidate.'" Bela glared at the far wall like she wanted to use her earth energy to yank it down just at the thought of August. "Galling. But it starts at seven."

"Get some Sibyls to track the Leviathan at a safe distance," Jake said. "Keep him in your sights. When the time comes, we'll need to know his exact position—and it won't be easy with the private and federal security. Get Andy taken care of, and Merilee and I will meet you by Strawberry Fields fifteen minutes before his big event begins."

"All right." Bela caught Merilee's hand in hers, then let it go. "But where are you two going?"

Jake bared his fangs, releasing the snarl he'd been holding back since the other Astaroths made their feelings known. He took Delilah by her elbow as gently as he could and pulled her against his left side. With his right arm, he gathered Merilee to his right side and spread both sets of his wings.

"Open the basement door," he growled to Bela, who ran to do as he asked.

Jake snarled again, temporarily just fine with his Astaroth essence.

More than fine.

He flapped his wings and lifted himself and Merilee and Delilah off the stone floor, into the open air of the large basement. Good thing the door was arched and wide, or he'd be taking part of it with him.

Merilee released some of her wind energy to assist him.

"Stay clear," he warned Bela, who moved to the far corner of the basement as Jake started to fly. "We have Sibyls to find."

35

Merilee guided her wind beneath Jake's wings to help them stay aloft while Delilah directed them south, toward Wall Street. Manhattan bled by beneath them, rush-hour taillights and headlights gleaming in the dusk. The air smelled like exhaust and concrete, with a sweet, hot splash of electrical wiring.

Her bow pulled tight against her back and shoulders as they flew. Her heart pounded at the prospect of rescuing her triad sisters even as her mind and heart ached so much she could barely see straight.

He's a demon.

Jake's a demon forever—and it's my fault.

She pressed into him, one arm around his back as he held her to his side and flew.

Merilee tried to keep breathing normally as they hurtled through empty sky, but her chest was too tight. Air stung her eyes and nose. Her ears got so cold they throbbed. Everything ached. And everything—everything was her fault. Jake came through the ancient channels to Káto Ólimbos to save her, and joined in the bargain with the Keres.

If she and Jake couldn't snatch August and get him back to Greece by midnight, Jake would die with her—and everyone else would follow. Motherhouse Greece. The villages. Ultimately, the world.

All the goddesses of Olympus, help us now. Please, please help us.

"Over there." Delilah lifted her arm against the rushing air and pointed to a penthouse balcony.

Jake zeroed in on where she pointed and flew them fast, faster, straight toward the spot.

Merilee's belly dropped as they did. She blinked against the blast of air in her face, and she let her senses flood outward, searching for any hint of August.

Of the Leviathan.

Oldest. Largest. Most powerful. Shit.

She came up with only bits and traces, next to nothing—but did that mean anything? Could he hide himself from their senses?

She was about to ask that question when they touched down inside the penthouse railing, and Jake said, "I don't feel the bastard. He's been here—but not now."

Delilah was already pushing through the glass doors. "Max? Boy, are you here? Max!"

Blood surging, Merilee readied her bow and an arrow, then tailed Delilah and Jake into the large apartment. The place was modern, pristine. Like, totally spotless and immaculate. Unnaturally so.

Wiped? she wondered, but couldn't dwell on it. Breath catching roughly as she turned loose her ventsentience, she sucked in the aroma of cleanser and seawater.

Merilee's fingers curled on her bow.

That can't be all.

She pushed her mind harder, breathed deeper, combed through the air around her, seeking Riana's signature, that earthy smell, or any sign of Cynda and her fire and smoke.

Please.

Her gut ached.

Please, please . . .

Damn*it.*

Merilee almost sobbed.

They weren't here. They just weren't.

Instead of the scents she so wanted to find, Merilee's

ventsentience brought her whiffs of blood and rage, radiating from a room far in the back.

"Jake. There." She pointed with the tip of her bow. "The room in the back. The left, on the left!"

Delilah was opening all the doors in the place looking for her son, but Jake folded his wings and slipped past her, moving with an ethereal grace almost too beautiful to bear. Merilee's gaze fixed on him and she followed him down the short hallway, hoping, praying, breath catching harder in her throat with each step.

Maybe she had been wrong. Maybe her senses were just off, and they were in this room, Riana and Cynda, right here waiting for her.

Her heart was beating so loudly she could barely concentrate, but she kept her bow raised.

Jake palmed the door handle and rattled it. Locked.

Merilee readied a blast of wind to knock it down, but Jake touched the handle again, closed his fist around it, claws lapping over to his knuckles as he seemed to will the metal to obey him.

Merilee felt a steady flow of elemental energy emanate from Jake, mixed in form, but very effective.

With a groaning creak, the handle wrenched sideways and Jake opened the door. He glanced inside, then stepped back into the hall, fangs bared. "Not them—but you better go first." His claws clicked as he curled his fingers into fists, then released them and pointed to her bow. "You won't need that. I'll call for an ambulance."

A muffled groaning met Merilee as she entered the room, sheathing her arrow and slinging her bow back over her shoulder. Her gut pitched at what she saw, but she ran to the bedside anyway.

The dark-skinned woman, naked and bound to the four posts with strips of sheets, thrashed and moaned against the gag in her mouth.

"Phila." Merilee reached out, but she didn't dare touch the Vodoun priestess. She could tell from the woman's wild, frantic gaze that she wasn't seeing anything real, anything present. Phila was lost in her own mind from the horrors and violations she had endured.

Desperate to do something to ease Phila's suffering, Merilee let her wind spread over the woman's bruises and cuts, sending what healing she could to the wounds. As for Phila's mind—another matter.

Merilee heard Jake speaking as he used the apartment's landline to call for an ambulance and OCU backup. She could tell he was doing his best to keep the Astaroth resonance in his voice at a minimum, but it wasn't working.

Phila.

Hecate, ease her.

But Hecate might not help the emergency personnel on their way to treat the priestess, so Merilee did what she had to do. With soft words and quick gestures, she placed elemental locks around Phila's formidable powers. Not permanent. They'd wear off in a few days, but hopefully that would be long enough for Phila to get treatment and care, and regain her senses enough to know friend from foe.

With each binding, Merilee's heart ached worse.

Her jaw throbbed as she ground her teeth. She *hated* what she was doing, trapping another living being's power, and a woman as wounded as Phila—but there was no choice.

All our choices have been taken, haven't they?

She wanted to quit. Maybe scream—but folding under pressure was not an option, so Merilee finished binding Phila's powers, then went back to sending the priestess healing wind and soothing air.

It was all she knew to do. All she could do.

That, and worry like hell about Riana and Cynda, and what might have happened to them. What might be happening to them right this very second.

Just letting her thoughts drift in that direction scalded Merilee inside. She felt raw, like somebody had burned out everything that made her whole and real.

"We're getting you out of here," she said aloud, hoping Phila could make sense of her words, and hoping she couldn't hear the tension lacing every syllable.

"Nobody else here," Delilah said from the bedroom door in a flat, defeated tone. "Maybe the warehouse next. I know that place and a handful more. So long as he didn't take them someplace new, we'll find Max and your friends."

Merilee heard the bravado and knew the old woman didn't really know, that she was frantic to find Max, grasping at any straw. When Merilee glanced at the woman who had been spying on her and her fellow members of the Dark Crescent Sisterhood for almost two years now, she saw the same desperation on Delilah's face that she felt.

There was no spark in Delilah's eyes. No hint of hope, despite what she had just said about finding Max and Cynda and Riana. *She thinks her son may be dead, or dying, or suffering at the hands of his father.*

Despite Merilee's anger over Delilah's betrayals, she had to feel some sympathy, then revulsion as Delilah's expression let her know that Delilah had seen Phila in this state already.

Merilee's muscles tightened with disgust. "Did you help keep her captive?"

"All of them except your two friends, the most recent ones he took." Delilah sounded deeply ashamed and kept her eyes on the floor. "He would have beaten me. Killed me. And Max. He's not like your demon. There's no good in him, you understand? And I can't best him." The old woman sniffed, then let out a quiet sob. "I understand that now. Would that I had seen it sooner—or found my courage before I did."

Merilee's mind had snagged on the "not like your demon" part.

Merilee wanted to sob with Delilah, but she forced herself to keep her attention on Phila.

Sirens rose on the streets below, and Jake came to the bedroom doorway.

"We've got people on the scene already. I've warned the OCU officers accompanying them about what they'll be dealing with and unlocked the door, and they're coming up in the outer elevator now with some beat cops. We need to leave."

Merilee bent close to Phila, who was still staring into faraway nothingness. "Help's here, honey." She ruffled the priestess's hair with a soft gust. "Help's right here. You're going to be safe, and you'll be able to use your powers again in just a few days."

She would have said more, but she could already hear footsteps thumping down the hallway toward the penthouse door.

"Six hours, fifteen minutes," Jake said as he moved back to the balcony with Delilah and spread his four wings against the moonlight.

Merilee ran to him and grabbed hold of his glowing, muscular arms. Wind rushed across her face as he flew them away from the penthouse just ahead of the onslaught of officers and medical personnel coming to rescue Phila.

The warehouse next.

Delilah was directing them.

Merilee couldn't concentrate on the lights Jake blazed past, his whole body jerking with the force of his wing beats. She couldn't process the traffic below, or even the flow of air around them. All she could think about was Riana and Cynda. Getting to them. Ensuring their safety so she and Jake would be free to launch at August with everything they had left.

The warehouse.

Her triad sisters had to be there.

Please, let them be there.

Cynda and Riana are *at the warehouse.*

Merilee clutched that thought as tightly as she clutched Jake, and as they flew, she did what she could to pray to Olympus she was right.

"Energy—earth and fire," Jake said as they faced the metal door of the rundown waterfront space. A streetlamp flickered out from the rush of Merilee's ventsentient power as Jake moved Delilah to his left, to keep her out of the way.

"Do you feel it, too?" he asked. "Contained. Probably with elementally locked cuffs."

"It's not them." Merilee kicked at a concrete post beside the door, welcoming the flare of pain in her toes as she sucked back her air sensing. She focused on the ache in her foot so she wouldn't start screaming. "Doesn't smell the same, not right—and Cynda and Riana could never be contained by just cuffs for very long. Fuck!" She kicked the post again. "There's air energy, too, but I don't sense August. Let's get inside."

Jake gripped the metal doors and Merilee wrapped him with wind, increasing his power as he bent the old steel enough to pry it loose. It gave with a loud *clank,* and a gust of terror and anger blazed up Merilee's nose.

Sibyls. Definitely Sibyls, but damn, damn, damn, *not mine.*

She hurried inside behind Jake, and Delilah followed her, once more heading off to search side rooms and storage areas for Max.

It only took a few minutes to locate the small back

storeroom where August had stashed the young ranger triad, the first Sibyls who had gone missing.

Beaten. Brutalized.

But alive.

Merilee's mind buzzed as she released them from their elemental cuffs using one of her arrow tips, while Jake broke into an office next door to phone in the location.

These were barely more than adepts, just on their own, and sobbing so hard, already begging her to stay—shit, it was hard to leave them, but they were alive, and in one piece, and help was coming for them.

"I'm sorry." Merilee fought her own tears as she finished her work on the cuffs and pried the little air Sibyl's fingers off her battle leathers. "I have to go. The OCU and ambulances will be here any second."

When the young woman tried to grab her again, Merilee grabbed her wrists instead. "Be a broom, honey. That's what I've got to do."

Her words came out too fast, too harsh, and she regretted them immediately. Trying to be more gentle, she said, "I'm so sorry for everything you've been through—but you've got to collect yourself and soothe your fire Sibyl. Help her call the Mothers."

The air Sibyl nodded and let her go.

As the young woman headed back to her wounded, crying triad, Merilee couldn't help but wonder if any of the former captives were pregnant, if August could force a Sibyl to conceive. And Phila. And how many others?

Merilee actually wondered if her blood could boil. Felt like it.

Shit!

She tried to get hold of herself, and started walking away.

Damn, but these poor women will have to face so

many brutal decisions on top of the trauma they've been through.

She needed to kill August twice. Three times. She needed to make him hurt.

When she reached Jake and Delilah at the warehouse door, Delilah wouldn't meet Merilee's eyes.

No sign of Max, Merilee presumed as Jake took hold of both of them.

"Five hours, fifty minutes," Jake said as he swept Merilee and Delilah out of the warehouse and above the scattering of glass where he had smashed into the office to use the telephone.

Merilee couldn't answer him.

She was crying too hard.

Even as she gripped Jake's neck, she clenched her teeth until her head hurt.

We rescued a triad. That's something.

But not enough. Dear goddesses, I've got to find them!

Her air energy ripped from her chest and she had to fight it, force it to aid Jake's flying instead of spreading wild all over the sky.

Delilah was pointing west now, yelling about a storage facility.

This time, Merilee didn't even spare the energy to pray.

Seconds turned into minutes, and minutes into a long, exhausting blur.

The storage building.

Another apartment.

Another warehouse.

Sibyls, pagan witches, other elementally powerful female practitioners.

More victims of August—alive, rescued, but with each passing moment, Merilee's heart darkened.

Where *were* they?

At the sixth site they visited, a remodeled apartment near the home Riana still owned at Sixty-third and Fifth Avenue, the smell of death knocked them all back at the door.

"Shit," Jake managed between coughs. "No. Merilee, wait—"

But gagging, eyes watering from the stench, Merilee flung herself through the door Jake had shouldered open. She was sobbing as she threw herself toward the awful smell, past the living room, toward the back bedroom—

A dead woman tied to the bed.

Blond. Slight. Merilee couldn't make out the features.

Not mine.

Oh, thank Olympus, not mine.

From behind her, she heard Jake getting on the telephone and Delilah calling out for her son.

Merilee stared at the dead woman and her gut wrenched another turn.

She despised herself for the relief she felt.

To make up for not grieving the lost life, Merilee rested a hand on the woman's icy forehead and whispered a blessing for her loved ones as Jake finished his call and Delilah knocked open the last few doors in the place, hunting for Max.

"Did this girl not meet your standards?" Merilee whispered, her voice nearly gone. Her throat was so sore from holding back screams and sobs that she couldn't even get the words to sound right, make sense. "Did she displease you somehow, you sick, psychotic bastard?"

They were running out of time—and Delilah was out of locations. Hope was draining away so quickly Merilee couldn't capture it, couldn't hold on to even a glimmer of it. Her tears dried up even as she stood there.

Just stopped. She didn't have any left, but by all the goddesses, she had rage.

No, not rage.

Pure hatred.

It seethed inside her like a brewing maelstrom, and Merilee wondered if she couldn't take out August herself. No help at all.

An uprooted tree to the head—or maybe an F5 tornadic burst, right in the face.

She saw him crushed by flying cars, broken from being hurled off the Empire State Building. She even imagined what he might look like if she filled his groin full of elementally locked arrows, then fired one through his temple at close range.

No, wait. He was probably eternal. Wouldn't it be better to lock him in a cell beneath one of the Motherhouses and make him suffer forever, across generations and generations of Sibyls?

She shook her head.

"A cell is way too fucking good for that monster." Her words sounded like hammer strikes in the silent, death-filled space.

Even the Keres might be too gentle.

Her hands flexed.

She *really* wanted to be the one to kill August. She'd take him back to Greece, to the death spirits, so the world would be protected from his dying energy—but she wanted to be the one who took his life, one fucking arrow at a time.

Her mind flexed along with her fingers at that thought, and all of her senses, too—and she caught something slipping through the nose-numbing odor of death all around her.

Slight.

Faint.

Almost . . . not there.

But it was.

Merilee's eyes widened.

"You know the drill," Jake said as he came into the bedroom leading Delilah behind him. "The NYPD is laying down tracks to this address."

Merilee walked around Jake, trailing her fingers along his bare, pale side for a moment. She passed him up, and Delilah, too, not really hearing anything else he said—but she caught Delilah's expression.

Startled. Then . . . satisfied.

Merilee's chest clenched.

Has she done this on purpose? Led us on this friggin' nightmare of a chase all over New York?

Only to bring us here last . . .

Why?

Merilee walked out in the hallway, to the stairs, to give herself a little distance from the dead woman and all the distracting smells.

She sucked in a deep breath of air, trying not to hack at the stench of rot still permeating the space.

And . . . there it was again!

So, so weak.

The barest hint of earth.

The slightest whiff of smoke.

Close—yet not close.

Her own words nudged into her thoughts as she hurried down the stairs, leaped down them, using her wind energy to keep her from breaking her legs.

A cell is way too fucking good for that monster.

Yeah, it was.

But it wasn't too good to hold a couple of Sibyls. With the right reinforcements, the right modifications, they wouldn't be able to use their power or call for help, not at all.

Something like fireworks exploded in Merilee's brain. Her pulse exploded, too. She couldn't quite get her breath.

Even two very powerful Sibyls could be contained in a cell of elementally locked lead, and Merilee knew exactly where such a jail cell was.

In Riana's brownstone, at Sixty-third and Fifth.

"Jake!" she cried, blood rushing against her eardrums. "Keep hold of that bitch and don't let her go!"

She didn't wait for his response.

Merilee was already out of the remodeled apartment and on the street, running as fast as she could make her body move.

The scent of earth and fire was getting stronger.

Merilee poured on the wind and shot forward, turning the corner by Central Park, streaking past all the cars on the road. She dodged pedestrians who seemed to be moving no faster than fire hydrants and mailboxes.

Riana and Creed had been staying at the townhouse because of Riana's pregnancy—but they still owned the brownstone where Riana, Cynda, and Merilee had begun their work as Sibyls in New York City. Riana had a lab downstairs in that brownstone.

And in that lab, a well-crafted elementally locked lead cell.

Son of a bitch.

You hid them in plain sight, right where we'd never look.

Merilee's whole body hummed with certainty, and blood pounded in her ears with each step.

She was going to find her triad.

By all the goddesses of Olympus, she *would* save them, and she would do it right now.

Then she was going for August, and if it was the last thing Merilee ever managed to do, she would slay herself a Leviathan.

36

Merilee reached the door of Riana's brownstone and blew it open so hard she ripped the wind chimes off the ceiling in the entryway.

The little pipes smashed to the floor as she ran through the otherwise undisturbed living room, aware of Jake touching down behind her and leading Delilah through the front door.

Oh, yeah.

Definite earth smell here. Definite fire. And not remnants. Fresh. Muted, yes—but current. Here. Now.

Joy flowed through her like wild spring winds.

No August—no, no trace of him yet, not that she could sense.

Hands out, Merilee smashed her way through the swinging door of the kitchen. She'd spent years here. The place was so well known she could navigate it in her sleep, so familiar it made her heart ache.

"Riana!" she yelled as she reached the step to the basement and leaped downward, riding a blast of wind straight to the floor.

Nobody answered.

Merilee's heart was beating so loud she was afraid she wouldn't hear her triad sisters call out even if they did. Nerves humming, she swept her ventsentience through the space as fast as she could.

No demon tang.

Some nasty-scented sweat.

And raw elemental power, her triad's power, *everywhere.*

On her right, Riana's bedroom door was closed. Down the hall and to the left, the lab door was closed, too.

Merilee's wind acted almost without her conscious thought, blasting both doors to nails and splinters.

The bedroom was empty.

She ran into the lab, leaped through the ruined door—and came to a fast stop, face-to-face with Max Moses—

Holding a pistol leveled at her chest.

Merilee shrieked like one of the Keres, gathering her wind so fast, so strong the microscopes in the lab started to shake. She drew back her fist to fling a burst of wind at the pistol, but from the corner of her eye, she saw them.

Gods and goddesses.

Riana. Cynda. In the cell.

Both of them were down on the stone floor, covered with stained sheets.

Merilee lowered her fist.

If she hit that gun with a wind blast, it might go off—or Max might squeeze the trigger out of reflex. The bullet could fire anywhere, or ricochet—too risky.

Max's entire lanky frame trembled. His face was badly bruised, new marks and the shadows of old beatings, too, and his gun hand was shaking. He used it to gesture to the far side of the lab. "I'm supposed to—but I don't want to, not unless you make me. They had a rough time of it. I . . . I cleaned up. Gave them some water, but they need . . . more. Help them and we'll go—but do it from here. I know you can send them energy."

Merilee risked turning away from Max.

They were right here, yes, right here, her triad sisters. Right in front of her in the cell. She had found them. Jolts of triumph racked her exhausted body, but she couldn't even enjoy the victory, because Riana and Cynda definitely weren't okay.

And, oh, sweet goddesses, Riana was holding babies. Two tiny, still little bundles rested in her arms, cradled tight against her chest.

Merilee almost shrieked again.

Riana and Cynda had delivered.

Merilee reached out with her ventsentience, and the coppery reek of blood filled her senses. Soiling and weakness. Muscle tissue, wasting.

Oh, sweet goddesses of Olympus, her triad sisters had given birth right in that jail cell. Somebody had done a shit-sloppy job of cleanup—yes, Max said that. And he gave them water.

But food? Medical care?

Was Cynda even breathing?

All of Olympus, let her be breathing.

And the babies . . . oh, the babies!

Merilee tried to speak, but her words hung in her throat. She choked. Coughed. Pushed out, "I'm here, Riana. Cynda, I'm right here."

It was all she could manage, along with a little cry as she took in the amount of blood on Cynda's sheet—and the floor around her.

Riana didn't seem to hear when Merilee called out. At least she didn't change positions, or look toward the sound of Merilee's voice. Cynda didn't move, either—or the babies.

Fuck the little twit Max. Let him shoot me.

Merilee put her body between Max and her triad sisters, ran to the elementally locked bars, and grabbed them. Cold metal scraped her skin. Little humming currents shocked her fingers and palms, and the sticky-sweet scent of blood made her want to sob.

"Riana. Honey. Look at me. Where's the key?"

Riana's head didn't move and her eyes stayed closed.

She held the babies to her chest and murmured. "He has it. August. Saw the cell in my mind . . . brought us . . . and Max. . . . Supposed to cuff you. Shoot you, too . . . kill us, I think."

That little bit of talking appeared to exhaust her, and she sagged against the back cell wall. The babies in her arms stirred a fraction, then went still again.

Merilee smashed her fists against the bars. Pain echoed through her knuckles, to her elbows, through her neck—and the shocks from the elemental locks, too.

So close. Right here—and she couldn't even reach her triad or their infants, touch them, offer them any real help!

She beat her fists against the bars again, absorbing each shock, and screamed her frustration.

"Back off!" Max bleated, but Merilee ignored him. She knew she was still between him and any shot at her triad, and he could cram that gun up his asshole for all she cared.

"Move, Merilee. Move *now*." Jake's command filled the room, so intense and primal that Merilee literally jumped out of the way before she could second-guess her instincts.

Wings folded, fangs bared, Jake strode across the room holding Delilah in a headlock.

"I've called for help," he said, his voice still sounding beyond dangerous.

Max let out a little wail and raised his gun toward Jake, but he didn't fire. Merilee knew he couldn't, not without risking a hit to his mother. She was beginning to think Max didn't want to shoot anyone anyway, that he didn't have it in him.

Jake seemed to tower and glow in his Astaroth form, and Max lowered his gun altogether. He took out the clip and placed it on the floor at his feet.

As soon as the gun pointed at the floor, Jake shoved Delilah toward Merilee. She caught the woman, moved her up against the back wall, and motioned for Max to join his mother as Jake grabbed the cell door in both powerful hands.

The crackle-shock of elemental locks shook his arms. It shook the whole room—but Jake didn't let go.

Max flat-out ran to get beside Delilah, and Merilee let loose enough wind to bind them tightly to the wall.

With a roar that might have been heard in New Jersey, Jake leaned backward, ripped the cell door off its hinges, and threw it across the lab. It smashed into the far wall, sending a spray of paint and rock and dust spattering across the floor.

Merilee tore into the open cell and dropped to her knees between Riana, the babies, Cynda, and the bars.

The babies made fretting, mewling sounds at all the noise and banging, and Merilee's heart surged with relief.

Merilee reinforced her binding on Max and Delilah, but the rest of the room, the rest of the world faded to nothing as she touched each baby. Weak, dehydrated, but strong heartbeats. Riana must have been focusing all her healing power on maintaining the little ones.

Merilee gave the babies a burst of her own warm wind energy, then shifted one palm to Riana's arm and the other to Cynda's chest.

Riana's breathing was shallow, but her heartbeat was steady.

As for Cynda . . .

Thready pulse.

Uneven respiration.

Her triad sister smelled wonderful and awful at the same time. Fire and smoke and ferocity—but it was muted. Cynda had lost too much blood. Merilee exhaled all the healing air energy she had left in her body, willing it into Cynda, leaving herself almost too dizzy to think.

She shook herself to stay upright, keep her focus on maintaining her binding on Max and Delilah, and concentrate on Cynda—but for all the energy Merilee poured into her triad sister, there wasn't much change in return. Not much improvement at all.

"I don't think she's going to make it," Riana said in such a quiet voice Merilee barely heard her.

Riana's eyes fluttered and came open, a dull green, totally not Riana, almost lifeless. "I can't heal her. I've tried. I c-can't." Her pale face grew even more ghostly white. The babies in her arms whimpered. One of them smoked.

Merilee let go of Cynda and steadied Riana and the infants. "We've got to get you out of here."

"No." Jake's tone was firm as he came to stand at the open end of the cell. "They can't be moved. Take the babies and get out of the cell."

Merilee's mouth came open. She turned toward him. "Jake, you can't—"

His golden eyes blazed, killing her words in her throat. He seemed to grow a foot. A terrible, angry, menacing foot that made her heart go absolutely still and quiet. Her eyes fixed on his talisman, as if to be sure somebody hadn't snatched it and sent him on a murder mission to finish off her triad.

Jake growled, raising the fine hairs along Merilee's arms. "If you don't trust me, they'll both die right here, right now. Get. Out."

Trust.

Merilee swallowed, her throat so dry she coughed with the effort.

It's Jake.

But he's a demon, and he's pissed.

It's . . . Jake.

And that decided it.

Merilee clenched her teeth to keep from saying anything else. Hands and arms shaking, she coaxed the infants out of Riana's failing grip.

"Ethan," Riana whispered, reaching white, trembling fingers after the listless, dark-haired infant Merilee took first. The little boy's life force flickered at the movement. Merilee was sure both Sibyls had tried to breast-feed, but without food, without enough to drink—

Gods and goddesses.

Her rage at August doubled, and swept wider to include Max and Delilah. Merilee wanted to kill them all.

When she got the second baby, the smoking one with the patch of red curls, Riana said, "Cynda wanted Neala, because it's a champion's name—tell—tell Creed and Nick."

Merilee gazed at the little girl, surprised at the energy in her thin, scowly little face.

A fire Sibyl born.

The girl gave a weak kick and wave, and more smoke rose from the pieces of her mother's leathers covering her tiny body.

Was there anything stronger, even at this size, than a fire Sibyl?

Merilee's jaw worked as she held back a new wave of emotion, and her wind energy spread over the two children in her arms. A second blanket. An extra cover.

"You'll tell Nick and Creed their names yourself, Riana. You and Cynda." Somehow, despite the dried, used-up feeling trying to claim Merilee's consciousness, she started to cry. "We *are* getting you out of here."

Riana smiled at her, then closed her cloudy green eyes and slipped into unconsciousness.

"Ri!" Merilee would have grabbed her triad sister's arm, but she couldn't, not while holding the babies.

"Merilee," Jake said, sounding so calm his tone bordered on cold. "Now."

Merilee stood on rubbery legs, eased herself out of the cell and past Jake, and carried the babies as far as the nearest lab table. She took two seconds to reinforce the wind prison holding Max and Delilah, and when she turned back toward the cell, Jake gazed at her briefly.

His inhuman golden eyes flickered with an emotion she couldn't name.

Then he walked into the cell, knelt, and put one hand on each of her triad sisters.

The air in the lab buzzed and shifted, seemed to get thicker—and Jake started to chant. Words Merilee didn't understand, but she could swear she had heard them before.

A while back.

When—

Jake started to glow. At first a soft yellow, then brighter and brighter, until he seemed to be made of white, glittering light.

His chant continued, and Merilee remembered times she thought she had felt Jake's energy flowing into her. Times when she needed it, when he seemed to heal her with that light.

Her muscles tensed with each passing second. The infant in her left arm burned through her leathers and scorched the inside of Merilee's forearm, but she couldn't tear her eyes from Jake, or stop listening to that chant.

Two years ago. In the townhouse basement. I heard Jake's mother chanting like that.

Right before she tried to explode our bodies and murder us all with her biosentient abilities.

Merilee almost dropped the babies.

"Jake." The word came out a strangled whisper, but

Jake didn't react. He kept chanting and kept glowing, and all that white light flowed out of him, covering Riana, washing Cynda, moving into both of her triad sisters like a glowing, brilliant wave.

Of all the improbable memories, Merilee fixed on August's face when they had met the bastard at the Jensen headquarters.

Why is it you are so different from others of your kind? he had asked Jake. *Do you know? Have you even bothered to explore that question?*

Well, Merilee knew now.

She watched Jake's light shine, watched it bind him to Riana and Cynda and her, too. Her more than ever. Deeper than ever.

He's a biosentient.

Jake's a biosentient.

Only, he doesn't blow up living things like his mother did. He's putting them back together.

Jake inherited his mother's elemental talent. That must have been how he survived her abuse—all those scars. *Hecate help him.* He healed himself from what she did to him, as best he could.

No wonder he was so different from other Astaroths. He had almost healed himself from that perversion of his life force, too—but he couldn't. Not all the way. Merilee doubted Jake understood what he was, what he was doing, even now. He was just following what he had seen and learned, going where his heart led him, and trying to do the next right thing.

Live.

Help.

Heal.

Merilee's tears flowed freely now, and she hugged the babies tight to her chest even though little Neala was busy trying to set her on fire.

Riana moaned and opened her eyes. A second later,

she sat up and pulled away from Jake and blinked. Shook her head like she was dazed or coming out of a stupor.

Even as Merilee watched, strength seemed to return to Riana's body and color rose to her cheeks as she adjusted the sheet to cover herself.

Jake shifted both hands to Cynda, his light growing so bright Merilee had to squint, and Riana turned her face and shielded her eyes.

Jake's essence shimmered.

Merilee squeezed the babies and gasped as he started winking in and out of visibility.

"Be careful!" Merilee's heart pounded impossibly faster than it had over the last several hours. "It's costing you, Jake. It's got to—don't go too far."

Jake faded slowly.

Came back.

"Jake," Merilee said, louder, making the babies shift in her grip. "Jake!"

Jake's concentration remained fully on Cynda as he faded again.

"Stop!" Merilee clutched the babies and reached out with her wind, first snuffing Neala's little blazes, then extending outward to brush against Jake's face and get his attention. . . .

But Jake was gone.

Just like that.

He vanished to nothingness, his light shutting off so abruptly Merilee had to blink against the stars and streamers it left behind in her vision.

Cynda thrashed and cried out, then sat straight up and started to smoke from her bare shoulders. She looked around at Riana, then at Merilee and the babies. Relief claimed her features. She started trying to get to her feet, no doubt to come and claim her fiery little daughter.

Sirens wailed outside the brownstone, and a few seconds later, Merilee heard voices upstairs.

All of this played through Merilee's head like a movie.

She couldn't move.

She felt like her body had vanished right along with Jake's.

She couldn't feel anything or think anything coherent.

Jake had vanished.

He hadn't just turned invisible, either, because her wind couldn't find him.

No.

He had disappeared.

As in gone.

Used up?

Gods and goddesses, no.

That thought brought a wave of misery so strong that her wind energy faltered and died away. Delilah and Max moved immediately, but Merilee couldn't bring herself to care.

Two OCU officers and some paramedics were in the basement now, rushing toward Riana, helping Cynda, gently prying the babies from Merilee's grasp, and still she couldn't move.

"I'm fine," she told a first responder trying to check her out, then said to the OCU officers trying to get through her wind to Delilah and Max, "They're mine. I'll take care of them."

She released her wind energy, and Max and Delilah sagged to the lab floor.

For a few seconds, Merilee just kept staring at the spot where Jake had been, whispering his name in her mind.

"He's expectin' you," said a marginally familiar voice.

She turned her head enough to see Max Moses standing beside her. Delilah was on her other side. "We know when we're bested, don't we, Max? It's not shame, to make a change in plans."

Max's right hand was covered with a jacket. In his left hand was a pair of handcuffs. Elementally locked, by the smell and feel of them, even at this distance. Max shook the cuffs. "I was supposed to kill them, shoot you in the leg, cuff you, and bring you to him."

Merilee processed the words, but they made very little sense to her, and didn't loosen her limbs in the slightest.

Jake.

Where is he?

How do I get him back?

She had to find him, had to talk to him, touch him, hold him, give him her entire heart and all her gratitude for saving her, for bringing Riana and Cynda back from the brink of death—and just because. Because he was Jake, and he was hers, and she didn't care if he had wings or fangs or claws, or ten heads.

Jake!

Max Moses was still talking, even as bedraggled Sibyls and more OCU officers began to crowd into the lab and take over. She waved everyone away from her, and away from Max and Delilah, wanting Cynda and Riana and the babies to have all the attention.

"Only I couldn't hurt the women and the babies, see?" Max nodded toward Riana and Cynda as they passed by on stretchers, hooked to bags of fluids. "Babies. How could I do that, now? But he's waitin', and I'm supposed to bring you to the rally, and you have to do me this square, for letting them out of this alive."

When Merilee didn't respond, Max said. "The rally. You gotta. At least make it look good or he'll kill me. We'll be—yeah. We'll be your ticket in. You want to get at him, don't you?"

Rally. Rally . . .

That word touched off recognition in Merilee's exhausted brain.

Delilah tugged Max away. "She's done for. Leave her. Let's get as far away as we can."

Something about the rally, which should already be started now, shouldn't it? Athena's teeth, but every inch of her body ached, and she needed to sleep.

Needed to, but . . . couldn't.

Max and Delilah were heading out of the basement.

Another little voice intruded, far back in Merilee's brain.

It sounded like her own, from forever ago, when she was rested and intelligent and sane, and not torn into a million little bits. A Sibyl's voice, strong and authoritative, keeping track of detail as only Sibyls could do.

This was the voice that finally got her moving. Running, in fact, toward Delilah and Max and his idiotic elementally locked handcuffs.

It said, *Four hours, twenty-two minutes.*

And counting.

(37)

Bartholomew August got out of his newly refitted limousine at Tavern on the Green without waiting for his driver to come around and open the door. Orange-shirted Peace Warriors lined the drive, keeping back the hansom cabs and onlookers, members of the media, and rally-goers who had strayed from the main event. The NYPD was on scene as well, and August had been notified that a Secret Service detail would be joining him before he went onstage in an hour or two.

Nothing like respect.

Nothing like a good crowd to whip into riot mentality.

For now, though, a glass of wine and a decent meal.

Some human habits August more than enjoyed.

The night was warm, and Tavern on the Green glowed so beautifully, like a jewel of hope, a beacon of new beginnings. The loneliness inhabiting August's core eased a fraction, enough to allow him a true smile.

Tonight would be a big step toward August's new beginnings. Already, the rally in Central Park was reaching a fever pitch. Jensen would ride the wave of their combined efforts directly into a position of leadership. Jensen, code name *Klaus* to August's people, would direct the free world. For his part, August would have unprecedented access to the weaponry and forces needed to effect a rapid resolution to the nagging problem of the earth's human infestation.

Access—and relatively little supervision, compared to the president.

By the time anyone, Klaus included, realized August's true aims, he would be impossible to stop, and nearly finished with the task of destroying the bulk of the human race. He would sire many babies with his genetically superior mates. Accelerate their growth. Then watch the race get stronger as each generation bred the next.

"Do you need anything, sir?" the driver asked, stopping near August and folding his hands behind his back.

Nothing like respect.

"No. Thank you." August ran his fingers across the gloss of the limousine's back door, admiring the paint job that concealed the elementally treated lead now lining the passenger section of the vehicle. "Keep the engine warm. As soon as the rally's over, we're pulling out for Philadelphia to meet up with the rest of the campaign staff for the nationwide phase."

"Stumping. Yes sir." The driver smiled.

August thought *stumping* was an idiotic term, but such was the American political game. "I'm expecting a guest and his . . . ah, grandmother and sister. Please seat them comfortably in the car and notify me on the cell when they arrive." August patted the pocket of his dinner jacket that held his phone. Human contrivances for human purposes. Effective, if annoying. "I have it on vibrate in case it's during the speech. I might not answer, but I'll know you've called."

The driver nodded and moved toward the front of the limousine.

August swept his gaze over the crowd once more, waving to a few people who shouted and reached toward him.

Where *was* Max, after all?

They should be here by now, all of them, or a few minutes from now at the very least.

August had no delusions about his son's capabilities. He knew the boy could never carry out the task he had been assigned, and August wasn't counting on that at all.

No.

He was counting on Delilah.

Let those black winged creatures block his mind from Merilee's. Let their energy shove him back from approaching her at every turn. Delilah was his intermediary now, and August was certain the black winged menaces would pay the woman no attention at all.

But where the hell *were* they?

He'd make her pay for being late.

August glanced toward Sixty-third.

By now, Merilee would have located her triad sisters, or what was left of them after Max did his dirty work—assuming he was competent enough to manage killing two defenseless, unarmed pregnant women.

Either way, the captive Sibyls would be in bad shape, and Merilee would be devastated. Vulnerable. It would be nothing for Max to complete the leg shot as they had practiced, cuff her, and bring her here, to be placed in a limousine every bit as fortified as the cell that contained her now-dead triad sisters.

But he'd fail.

Failure was in Max's nature.

And when Max couldn't subdue the air Sibyl, Delilah would find a way to get Merilee here anyway. A con, a lie, a trick—something, anything to make sure the job got done and protect her boy.

Delilah was resourceful like that. Always had been.

August smiled again as he separated himself from the limousine and headed into the restaurant to join his fellow candidate for a bit of fortification before they addressed the masses.

The night was just too beautiful to worry about anything, and too perfect to stay angry for long.

38

Jake sped through a great gray nothingness, though he couldn't quite remember where he was trying to get to, or why he was trying to get there so fast.

A blazing light ahead of him caught his attention and he changed course, flapping his wings and using his feet for a rudder as if he had been flying every day of his life, maybe for centuries.

So rapid.

So free.

Why hadn't he done this more often?

Air rushed over his body, feeding him, making him stronger. He glanced upward, wondering when the sun would rise. How splendid it would be, to fly toward that bright yellow orb as it burst free of the far horizon.

For now, though, he approached what appeared to be a massive castle rising out of a silvery-white mist, a structure so big he couldn't take in its complete dimensions. Left, right, back to front, the damned thing went on forever.

The stone walls didn't seem quite . . . solid, either. More phantasm than corporeal, yet Jake was able to land in one of the arched windows. The stone felt real enough beneath his bare feet, smooth and cool and pleasing in its own way.

He slipped inside.

His muscles relaxed, and his mind, too, as if he had always meant to come here, should have been here a thousand times or more.

This was . . . home?

"What an archive," he said out loud, amazed by the massive room before him. "I've never seen anything like this—felt it, maybe, in my head, through my vestigial memories, but seeing it . . ."

Shelf upon shelf, book upon book.

Damn, but he could spend the next thousand years going through all of these books—and what if the entire castle was nothing but rooms like this?

"I'm pleased to meet you here, Leader." The voice startled Jake into spinning around, and he found Darian standing behind him dressed in jeans like the ones Jake usually wore.

Darian's arms were folded across his chest, and his wings were half-extended.

There was plenty of room for wings in this place. Nice.

Jake extended his, too, and relaxed again. "Do me a favor, okay? Tell me—where is *here*?"

Darian tilted his head as if considering the question. "Here is . . . where we come to think. *Here* is where our memories live. We use it to strengthen, and sometimes to do what you're doing—move quickly from place to place."

Jake glanced around the massive library. Was it bigger? He could swear it was bigger, as if books were being written minute by minute, and placed on newly grown shelves inside newly expanded walls.

Losing it. No doubt. He rubbed his hand across the back of his neck, surprised that his own flesh felt as real and solid as it did. "What are you talking about—moving quickly from place to place?"

"You can relocate from this central point, from one physical, tangible location to another." Darian gave Jake something like a smile, Astaroth-style.

Jake cocked his head. For some reason, right now, that moving-place-to-place thing would be a valuable skill.

But why?

"How does that work?" he asked.

"Once you're here, you can go anywhere." Darian unfolded his arms and tapped his temple with one long, pale finger. "Just by a thought."

"Damn, I suck at this part of the game." Jake shook his head. "I know a lot about fighting, about being a cop, but you know a lot about being an Astaroth. All this time, maybe you should have been training me."

At these words, Darian appeared to be truly shocked. When he recovered enough, he said, "But I have no human left in me, Leader. No special abilities beyond my Astaroth gifts. You have both natures—human *and* demon. You are . . . more than we are."

It was Jake's turn to gape. "Human—more—? No, wait. I'm stubborn, not more. I was changed to an Astaroth, just as you were. My human body was put to rest years ago." He was starting to feel antsy, though he couldn't yet grasp why. Maybe all this admiration. Jake never was much on admiration.

Darian's golden eyes remained fixed on Jake's face. "But you have your ability, the light within you—what you can do with cells and the essence of life itself. What is the term—biosentience? You retained some of your human essence through sheer force of will, and for that, all Astaroths admire you and wish to learn from you."

Jake stepped back from Darian, his internal agitation cranking up a notch. "I'm not biosentient. My mother was, but she's dead."

"Look at yourself, Leader." Darian gestured to Jake's midsection.

Jake glanced down, half expecting to see the spectral image of his murdering mother rising up from his gut, complete with her gleaming dagger.

Instead, he saw his own body, pale, translucent like

Darian's—yet, somehow more concrete. A shade darker than the other Astaroth. More . . . real than the castle in which he stood.

"You see?" Darian's voice was thick with respect. "Even here in our place of the mind, your body has a solid character that the rest of us may never achieve. You are special amongst our kind, Leader. We look to you for great things."

Jake doubled both fists and kept staring at himself. Something about this place—no, not the place, the situation, it was all wrong. He was confused, somehow. Not thinking straight.

"Darian, why am I here?" Jake looked up at the other Astaroth, hoping for a quick answer before he crawled out of his barely real skin.

"Because you used so much of your energy in healing the wounded Sibyls that you degraded, lost your tangible form." Darian pointed to Jake's legs, which were only just now gaining the same solid quality as the rest of him. "You came instinctively for restoration. The first time you've needed it, I suspect, since your biosentience allows you to heal yourself and others so completely."

I was healing Sibyls.

Who was hurt?

Why had he spent so much energy healing anyone?

Jake focused on Darian again. "Why are you here?"

Darian bared his fangs and let out a long hiss. When he pulled himself to his full height, wings extended, Jake couldn't help but think of generals and battlefield commanders he had read about and, yeah, admired.

"We completed the mission of rescuing your brothers from jail, but they checked in with the OCU and went straight to the hospital where their wives and children were taken. So I came to get reinforcements." Darian snarled, low and dangerous. "We'll need them if we're to save your woman, Leader."

Reality came whistling back to Jake like somebody set off a bomb in his brain.

His thoughts caught fire.

His claws grew longer and his fangs, too.

"Merilee!" He let out a hiss to rival Darian's.

If Riana and Cynda and the babies are already at the hospital and my brothers are already out of jail—what time is it? How long have I been here?

"How does time work here?" he asked Darian. "Compared to, uh, there. The other world."

"Below," Darian supplied. "We call it Below. The time Below runs faster, though I've never attended to how much faster." Darian pointed to the stone floor beneath Jake's bare feet. "You can see for yourself, if you'd like."

Jake stared at the stones, which had become translucent now, like glass, or a movie screen.

Jake squinted at them, feeling his demon senses swell, delving into the sights and sounds unfolding for his viewing.

In the picture, Jake saw the splendor of Manhattan after dark, spread beneath him like jewels against a field of black velvet.

Times Square flashed by, and he caught the numbers on the clock. Eight something.

Fuck!

The view grew sharper, more focused, then narrowed to a smaller area. Trees, grass, rocks, and paths.

Central Park.

Closer again. Even narrower in focus.

Tavern on the Green. The sounds of a crowd rose and fell near the restaurant, in front of the bandshell, and Jake knew it was the political rally, probably at full tilt right about now.

Merilee.

There she was, face grim, eyes flat.

His heart surged at the sight of her.

She was cleaned up and dressed in fresh leathers that looked a bit too large for her. Probably Riana's, from the brownstone. She was unarmed, and she was walking stiffly between Delilah and Max Moses, with her hands hidden beneath a black jacket.

The sight of Merilee so close to Delilah and Max made Jake want to chew on lead. His fangs gnashed at the image.

Why was she walking so slowly?

And her hands—did they have her cuffed?

What the fuck?

Jake's fists flexed, his claws extending until they dug into his palms, then his wrists.

Delilah and Max and the chauffeur guy marched her past another group of security officers, toward a big black limousine that felt . . . wrong. Smelled wrong. Was wrong.

Elementally locked.

A cage.

Jake let out a louder hiss.

That car was a trap just like the cell in Riana's lab.

"How do I get out of here?" Jake bellowed to Darian.

Darian touched the side of his own head again. "Think it. Will it. Go to her, and we will join you soon, Leader."

Darian shimmered, then dissipated, leaving behind nothing but a silvery afterimage.

Jake squeezed his eyes shut and threw every ounce of his energy into where he wanted to go.

Merilee.

Take me to her.

He imagined the feel of her wind, the gentle signature of her elemental energy. He imagined her scent, that tantalizing white tea and honey, and the soft, quiet sounds her leather-clad feet must be making as she walked toward her doom in that limousine.

He felt himself getting less substantial. Lighter.

But, shit, he was still in the castle. Above.

How much time was passing here? Below?

Seconds?

Minutes?

Jake thought about the joy of holding Merilee, kissing her, touching her. He imagined touching her right now, grabbing her away from Max and Delilah and flying her out of Central Park before August got within a hundred feet of her.

Merilee.

He couldn't see her anymore. The stones below his feet had gone solid again. He gripped his own talisman, ordering himself to reach her, sending his demon senses toward her like an arrow fired dead center at the bull's-eye.

Jake sensed himself disappearing—starting to sink through the castle floor.

Yes.

Merilee.

That's it.

Hold on.

Merilee, I'm coming!

39

Streetlamps and flashlights and news spotlights turned night into day as Merilee walked into Central Park, but thanks to the elementally locked handcuffs, her vision was so dulled she still couldn't make out too many features of her surroundings. With each step she took toward the limousine where she was supposed to meet the Leviathan, more anger built in her depths.

Max and Delilah Moses, cleaned up from sink baths and spot-dabbing their black pants and Peace Warrior orange shirts, flanked her like well-trained guard dogs.

They had the good sense not to speak. If they had, elementally locked cuffs or no, Merilee would have killed them on the spot.

They had to know she wasn't doing this for them.

They were, as they had noted back at the brownstone's basement, just her ticket through all the modern security surrounding the ancient demon.

Her wrists ached from the bite of the elementally locked lead, and waves of nausea made it hard to concentrate. Her hearing was as dulled as her vision. Her nose was absolutely numb. She couldn't smell anything. She felt disoriented without being able to tap the air, draw the wind, move freely through her element and feel it moving freely through her.

But it had to be this way.

August thought the cuffs would hold her, would make her helpless, and she needed him to believe that. If her elemental energy wasn't somewhat contained,

August would sense it, and everything would blow up in her face.

Like it hasn't already?

Jake . . .

Somewhere, somehow, he had to be alive, and she intended to keep him that way—and herself, too, if she could.

Three hours, fifty-nine minutes, said the Sibyl voice in her mind, keeping up with the basics, always attentive to the details.

From deeper in the park, she heard the roar of cheers and magnified voices as the rally proceeded.

Without putting so much as a finger on her, Delilah and Max showed identification and orange passes, then guided her through the third and final line of orange shirted private security workers. Merilee had threatened them about touching her, and they'd believed her. She hadn't let them put their hands on her weapons when she left them at the townhouse, or put the cuffs around her wrists, or even wrap the jacket over her arms to hide the cuffs.

Delilah and Max were filthy to Merilee.

Filthy, and treacherous, and she could find only the barest shred of sympathy for either of them—if that.

Heat swirled inside her, growing, swelling, and burning until she thought she might finally understand what it felt like to be Cynda. To explode with flames and fire and burn down anything that got in her way.

Thank all the goddesses my triad is alive, that their babies are alive.

That thought fueled her as the limousine came into view, sitting at the far end of the turnaround outside Tavern on the Green.

Like thoughts of Jake, memories of Riana and Cynda kept Merilee moving.

One day, she wanted to fight with her triad again. She *was* their broom. Nobody else would take care of them like she did.

As they closed in on the limo, darker images flashed through Merilee's mind, of Charlotte Heart, driven to suicide rather than face capture by the Leviathan. Of Sal Freeman dead on a conference room table, torn open by massive, merciless hands. Of Phila Gruyere, abused and strapped to that bed. Of the terrified, battered young Sibyl triad sobbing for her to stay with them. Of the poor, dead girl who wouldn't even have the opportunity to heal from this bastard creature and the evil he perpetrated.

It went so much deeper than that, too.

The Leviathan and his Legion had been murdering people at their own whim for a century. And before that, how many had he killed in various forms, various guises?

Merilee bared her teeth and wished she had fangs like Jake.

This world had definitely had enough of Bartholomew August, or whatever name he chose to use. Eventually everything came to an end. Every creature went back to its maker.

Tonight, the Leviathan would meet his at the top of Káto Ólimbos.

They reached the limousine, and a man dressed in chauffeur's black hurried around to meet them.

"Mr. August told me you would be coming." The man, who looked completely normal, if a little on the small side, beamed and pulled open the back door.

Merilee flinched back a step.

Even with the dulling from the cuffs, she sensed the horrible, powerless void inside that car.

She had been wondering when she'd find the first trap, and here it was. A limousine that doubled as an elementally locked cage.

Delilah and Max swapped worried looks.

"After you," Merilee said to Max.

The man frowned at his mother, but Delilah jerked her head toward the car. "Go ahead."

Max slid onto the seat and moved over to give Merilee and his mother room.

Instead of getting into the limo, Merilee faced the chauffeur. "Where is Mr. August?" she asked, trying to keep her voice light even as her fingers curled tight against her palms.

The chauffeur pointed away from Tavern on the Green. "At the main stage, ma'am. He's speaking now—or soon—but I'll call to let him know you've arrived."

"Oh, don't." Merilee widened her eyes and flashed the chauffeur her best, sexiest smile. "Let me surprise him at the stage."

Delilah went rigid, clamping her fists together, but the chauffeur's eyes moved slowly from Merilee's face to her leathers and back up again, obviously appreciating what he saw.

"He wanted us to wait here." Delilah gripped the limousine door. "He told us to meet him at this car."

Merilee changed her smile to indulgent and winked at the chauffeur. "Give us a moment, would you?"

When the chauffeur moved away to a discreet distance, Merilee fixed her gaze on the old woman. "Is that what you really want, Delilah—to play his game on his terms?" She kept her voice low, so only the two of them could hear what she said. "Where has that gotten you so far? Think carefully, because this is your last chance."

The old woman's eyes narrowed, and her grip on the door tightened. Her throat worked as she stared at Merilee, then at Max in the limo. For the briefest moment, her features softened enough to suggest a flicker of hope.

When she raised her eyes to meet Merilee's, there was an honesty in her gaze Merilee had never seen before.

Her only question was simple. "Can you take him?"

Merilee measured Delilah in her mind, weighing all her betrayals against her one consistency. Max. Always Max. This was the woman who used Cynda's sword to take out a major Legion ally two years ago. The woman who had survived a long and involuntary relationship with a bloodthirsty demon, perhaps the most dangerous creature on the planet, and she was still right here, willing to put her life on the line for the one and only thing she cared about.

Her son.

Merilee lifted her cuffed hands, letting the jacket fall back just enough to reveal the elementally locked arrow tip peeking out of the sleeve of her leathers.

She lowered her hands, letting the jacket fall back into place. Without ever breaking eye contact with Delilah, she said, "To protect what *I* love, I can take him."

"Stay in the car," Delilah said to Max, and she slammed the door.

The chauffeur came back over, gripping his hat in both hands. "Um," he managed as Merilee smiled at him again.

"The boy can wait in the car, but I'll escort this one to the back steps." Delilah's jaunty grin impressed even Merilee. "I know Mr. August will be so glad to have her support. Directly, if you know what I mean."

The chauffeur's cheeks flushed. He stepped out of their way, and Delilah and Merilee walked away from Tavern on the Green, crossing the West Drive and heading for the cheers and shouts and speeches of the rally, which sounded like it had to be at the Mall area in front of the Naumburg Bandshell.

Three hours, thirty-two minutes, Merilee's brain informed her, her Sibyl time-sense keeping careful track of the disappearing seconds. I can do this. *He won't have Asmodai—no time to make any, and I doubt he's got any stashed or stored, since they only last a day. All the Cursons and Astaroths aren't fighting anymore, or they're on our side.*

She went over everything again just to keep her mind clear, but she still felt like her head was stuffed with cotton. *If I can get him away from his security officers, he'll be alone. He'll underestimate me. I can do this.*

They cut northeast across Sheep Meadow, closing in on the lights and noise. Delilah led her around the nearly frenzied Mall crowd, keeping to the left-hand side of the bandshell. The stage had been extended with temporary wooden reinforcements, and the whole half-bowl-shaped enclosure was packed with men in suits, sound techs, security personnel, and what looked like a band quickly setting up behind the speaker.

Her blood chilled when she made out the fuzzy lines of August at the microphone, holding out his hands in a beatific, embracing gesture.

"Peace," the bastard was saying. "Peace for a new day, and a new deal. It's our *only* option."

And the crowd cheered, and cheered, and cheered, until Merilee was glad her hearing was a little muffled.

August stepped back to make way for the band, which kicked up loud, punchy theme music.

Merilee and Delilah walked faster, staying at the fringes of all the banners and balloons and cheering people waving signs and placards. They skirted the left side of the bandshell until they drew even with the front columns and escaped into the green area behind. Most of that space had been cordoned off, and they slipped past a distracted guard.

"There," Delilah suggested, indicating a deserted spot on the red-brick terrace surrounding Bethesda

Fountain. The tiered fountain wasn't under guard or restricted by tape or barriers.

They came to a stop in front of the fountain, and Merilee's dulled vision took in the way the lights played off the water sheeting down from the tiers. At the bottom, a pool. Short columns rose to support another bowl, this one crested by a group of four cherublike figures meant to represent the virtues of Temperance, Purity, Health, and Peace. Above that, the crowning piece, the Angel of the Waters, an eight-foot bronze winged woman holding a lily, blessing the water below her.

Merilee wished the statue could come to life and bless *her*.

Goddesses of Olympus, she needed it now.

Because she was shaking like an adept before her initiation into battle rites.

She moved her arm, letting the arrow inch down until its sharp tip pressed into her wrist.

One arrow against the largest, most powerful demon ever known.

Should I hit him in the throat? The eye? How do I begin to disable a Leviathan enough to take him to the Keres—and even if I do, how will I get him past the security here, and all the way to Greece?

Behind the big fountain, Central Park's lake twinkled in the moonlight. To the left lay the route to Strawberry Fields, and to the right, the exit to Fifth Avenue.

"He'll come this way," Delilah was saying. "I know, because he's plannin' to meet the limousine at Fifth when it's over—and he'll notice you, like you're wantin' him to. Here. Outside the car."

Three hours, twenty-three minutes.

Yeah.

Who the hell knew if Delilah was telling the truth, even now?

Merilee clenched her teeth.

It didn't matter, really, because she was about to make damned sure the demon noticed her and came to her. Right now.

She cleared her mind again, then threw her entire focus into her suppressed air energy. She knew she couldn't stir it much, but enough . . . maybe enough.

The sluggish wind inside her tried to rise to her call, but dropped back in sickening waves.

Merilee summoned images of her triad, healthy and happy and in full fighting form. She reached for the memory of combining her power with Cynda's, with Riana's—and pulled.

Hard.

Down deep.

Until her insides quivered.

The wind rose in her depths again, and this time, Merilee thought about Jake. As a human. As an Astaroth. Jake, alive and well, in any form he chose to take. Her mental picture of him heated her all over. Her wrists bucked and strained against the elementally locked cuffs. Her muscles burned with the effort, and her chest—every part of her—and she poured herself into the swell, giving it her smell, her character, her joys, her strengths—*this is me, it's who I am, I'm air, I'm wind. No cuffs can hold me.*

No . . . cuffs . . . can . . . hold . . . me—

A wild gust of everything that was Merilee escaped from her shoulders and shot toward the bandshell to find its target.

She sagged and would have fallen if Delilah hadn't caught her and shoved her to her feet.

"You should go now," Merilee murmured as she fought to regain her balance. The jacket fell away from her cuffed hands, and her chest squeezed so fiercely she almost puked up enough bile to fill the fountain behind her. "You should hide, Delilah."

Her Sibyl vision, freed for the briefest of moments by her battle against the cuffs, flashed an image of a tall man striding around the bandshell, turning for the fountain and picking up speed.

"He's coming."

Delilah didn't have to be told a second time.

Merilee heard the old woman's shoes flap against the bricks around the fountain, then whisper into the grass.

She was alone now.

Waiting to face her nightmare.

Her own breathing sounded like sandpaper rasping in her ears, and she bit her lip until the pain made her clamp her eyes shut.

Hold your ground.

Get ready.

She opened her eyes again.

Merilee expected August to show up with fifty or so of his security personnel, but he came alone, closing in on her with frightening speed.

Her blurry, elementally impeded vision saw him first as a man-shaped monster. Then a walking snake. Then an ibis. For a few seconds, he seemed like nothing but a shadow, endlessly long, endlessly tall, and wider than the entire park.

A sensation like a storm of iron bugs took off in her belly, stinging and banging and bashing until her knees wanted to buckle, but she kept standing.

You're a broom. You will *finish this.*

For your triad. For every Sibyl. For every human being he's hurt, or might hurt.

August reached the red bricks of the terrace, paused long enough to gaze at Merilee and turn what was left of her guts into Jell-O.

Then he came forward more slowly, keeping a more stable shape, until he stopped directly in front of her. Tonight he had chosen a black Armani suit, making his dark hair seem even darker. His black eyes were bright with fascination, and if Merilee hadn't known exactly what he was, she could have taken him for a Kennedy-esque man of rhetoric, intelligent, maybe even possessed of some great destiny.

Three hours, fourteen minutes. That's all the destiny he has.

Using every bit of will and strength left to her, Merilee forced herself to smile at the demon, just to keep him guessing.

August tilted his head, then smiled back at her. He raised his right hand and closed his fist, and from somewhere nearby came a choked strangle.

Something heavy, maybe something body-sized, splashed into the lake.

"She's dead," he said, with no emotion in his voice, but for a moment, the Leviathan's human face actually looked pained. "That was . . . easier than I imagined it would be. And necessary. Delilah will never betray either of us again, my dear."

Another smile.

It was all Merilee could do not to start screaming. She worked the arrow lower. She had the tip fully in her palm now. A little farther, and she could grip the shaft.

"Why kill the woman now, after all this time?" she asked, still not quite sure she believed Delilah was dead, but feeling the truth of it winking darkly at her center.

August shrugged. "Because I don't need her anymore. And because I told her to keep you in the car." His next smile was enough to freeze the Great Lakes. "I should have counted on your cunning, I see. You sensed the elemental barriers I installed in the limousine?"

Merilee swallowed and nodded.

Almost . . . got . . . the shaft . . .

August shifted his weight and moved closer to her.

He lifted his nose and turned his head, like he was scenting her, head to toe.

The gesture brought back her urge to puke, in full.

"The barriers are distasteful to me as well, but necessary." August grabbed her left forearm. "We can't stand here forever getting to know each other without attracting attention. Come, my dear. It's time to go."

Merilee recoiled from his cold, slimy touch, ripping her arm free even though she had to lift her cuffed hands to do it.

August's eyes widened. Fuck. He was getting an erection.

This time, Merilee did wretch. Hot, bitter bile surged into her mouth, and she spit out a mouthful, letting it spatter at August's feet.

"I like spirit," he murmured, and reached for her again.

Merilee choked back the acid taste on her tongue and planted her feet so firmly it would have taken a crane to lift her off the terrace.

A crane, or an ancient demon.

August grabbed the chain linking her cuffs and yanked her forward, rubbing himself against her body like she was no more than a plastic sex-toy doll.

Heart hammering, Merilee threw her weight backward, jerking August into her.

Shit, he's so slimy and cold!

She twisted her wrists as hard as she could, trapping his fingers in the elementally locked chain.

He snarled at her—and snapped the chain as he freed his hand, as easily as if the lead links were made of paper.

The left cuff opened and clattered to the bricks, and the heady rush of wind through Merilee's mind almost addled her. Not all of her power, but some of it—gods and goddesses, yes, some!

She stumbled back from him a few feet, then a yard, sucked a huge breath, let the air fill her, all her senses sharpening at the same time.

Seawater. Rotten. He smells like ocean dregs.

The arrow came free into her right hand and she held it just out of August's view as he charged her again, this time frowning.

"That's enough, my dear." He thrust out his hand to catch her, but Merilee snatched his wrist instead.

With as big a burst of wind as she could manage, she used the air and his body weight to launch herself forward, her face against his, her arms at the level of his neck.

With all her strength she drove her arrow directly into the demon's ear.

"What's that, my dear?" she growled as the arrow met resistance, then plunged into the soft nothingness at the center of August's skull. "Your sick-fuck brain?"

August roared, grabbed her at the waist, and hurled her away from him.

Merilee's shoulders crashed into the fountain cherubs.

Bone cracked.

White-hot agony blazed through her neck, her shoulders, her back. Like the worst electric shock. Like a lightning strike.

Had her fingers just blown off the ends of her hands?

Had she snapped in half?

Hecate, save me—

So much pain!

Fire claimed her back and shoulders as she fell limp into the basin, her head just out of the water—and her body went numb.

Just . . . numb.

Nothing ached.

No part of her felt anything at all. And absolutely no part of her, not even her lungs, moved.

Dimly, Merilee saw August grip the sides of his head with both hands.

She tried to get a breath.

Couldn't.

Her chest was crushing in, crushing her, the weight of her own ribs killing her second by second.

The demon's next bellow shook the fountain, sloshing water into Merilee's paralyzed face.

From the direction of the bandshell came screaming and shouting. Male voices calling out orders.

When the demon reached up, yanked the gore-spattered arrow out of his head, and threw it at her so hard it lodged into the metal beside her cheek, Merilee was pretty sure she was dead.

But when August started to change, started to grow and writhe and roar so loud it sounded like he was pulling the heavens down around them, she was certain of it.

Jake.

Riana.

Cynda.

Merilee let herself have the happy images instead of the reality of the Leviathan swelling to the black, scaled proportions of a building in front of her. She tried to hear their voices instead of the ever-louder screaming and shouting closing in around the fountain.

Sorry.

I did my best . . .

I hope I was . . . I hope I am . . .

Your broom.

40

Jake yanked his body into solid form so hard and fast he felt like his brain would burst right out of his Astaroth head.

His perceptions swam.

Fuck, but something smelled like a barge full of rotten seawater and untreated sewage.

He gagged.

Bricks scraped his bare feet.

Behind him, people shouted and screamed, but the noises seemed to be moving away from him, not toward him.

Something massive and dark and slimy was writhing and expanding on his left. When Jake looked squarely at the thing, his skin crawled as the creature shifted and stretched and grew, adding scale, adding horns. Shit.

Air rushed in and out of Jake's lungs. Blood pounded in his ears as his senses tightened, his mind focused.

It's huge.

It's too big.

Was that a tail with big, ugly spikes?

Grass ripped beneath the thing as it twisted. Trees slammed to the ground as the creature's body made contact.

Definitely too big.

When he shifted his gaze to the right, Bethesda Terrace and the fountain with the Angel of the Waters came clear to Jake in one blazing rush. No humans close by. Jake sensed everyone involved in the political rally, security and spectators alike, running like hell, bailing out of Central Park like the end of the world had come to visit in that very spot.

Maybe it has.

Jake growled and analyzed the situation, his heart thudding and his blood boiling with anger and fear. Fear for the woman he loved.

Where is she?

One life sign close by grabbed hold of his senses.

He focused his mind on it, and his heart almost stopped its manic pounding when he saw Merilee's broken body.

She was in the fountain, sagged against the lower basin.

Merilee looked like a sad, discarded, beautiful doll. Roaring, Jake flapped all four wings and lunged to grab her—

A heavy scaled talon bashed him sideways.

Jake flipped through the air and wheezed as he slammed into a set of concrete steps. His hip snapped and pain blasted through his leg and back. Fire-coated sticks stabbed in his chest, too, making him shout. Something tore inside him. Popped like a balloon full of scalding oil. He opened his mouth, but blood bubbled out on his chin.

He tried to get up, but doubled over and fell on his knees, barely able to lift his head as blood gushed past his lips and puddled on the bricks in front of him.

The sight of Merilee in that fountain, maybe drowning, drove Jake's awareness deep inside his own body. Light blazed across the terrace darkness as his biosentient power grabbed his bones and jammed them back together.

Jake rolled forward as his hip and chest sizzled. But he could see the bones in his mind. Forced them to knit even though he felt like he was cramming his body in frothing acid.

Next, he sealed his lung tissue. Gasped as it inflated.

Lurched to his feet, throbbing everywhere.

Jake knew he had healed himself, but everything still burned like ever-loving hell. His chest ripped and ached like the ribs he had just fixed might burst right out of his white skin. He didn't care. He just had to kill—whatever that thing was—and get to Merilee.

The thing with the scales shook a head the size of a brownstone and seemed to be trying to get its bearings. It had horns like thick, sharpened trees, and some kind of scarlet membrane flared out from its neck.

Shit.

The fucker was as big as ten city buses, end to end and top to bottom. And it seemed like it was trying to get bigger. Long, clawed arms. No feet, but a massive spiked tail.

It bowed its immense body as if it intended to slither toward the fountain. It dwarfed the eight-foot angel like the fountain was no more than a child's toy. If it got one of those man-sized claws on Merilee—

Blood hammering through his veins, Jake spread his wings and hurtled toward the Leviathan, fists out, clenched together like a club.

Remembering the battle with the Vodoun Loa at Fresh Kills, he aimed straight for one of the thing's big red eyes.

The Leviathan might be big, but big meant slow.

It saw Jake coming. Tried to blink.

Not fast enough.

Jake bashed into the membrane, bounced sideways, and grabbed the thing's leathery lid to swing himself back toward his target.

The beast raised its massive claws toward him—too slow again. Jake's claws ripped through the membrane, plunging his hands into hot, viscous fluid. His sharp demon senses registered coal-black blood running out of the demon's giant ear—like something had already stabbed it a good one, right in the brain.

Probably made it slower.

He flailed in the creature's eye, then jerked himself out of the fluid, flying hard toward the stars, fighting against the heavy liquid. Below him, the creature swept its massive head back and forth, back and forth, roaring so loud it made Jake's ears ring.

It turned away from the fountain, tracking Jake.

He sucked air, and flew farther, leading the thing past the fountain to the edge of the lake. As fast as he could he shook off more sticky, rotten liquid and turned in the sky, intending to drop at the thing's other eye.

The Leviathan swept its claws across Jake's chest, ripping him right out of the sky.

Jake slammed to the bricks behind the fountain and Merilee, breaking ribs all over again, and a shoulder, and an arm. Pain blinded him. He couldn't do anything but yell and kick until blood spewed from his mouth again, and his chest, too.

He was burning alive.

Throbbing.

Blood pulsing out of him with each beat of his heart.

He lifted his clawed hand and pressed it against the torn, screaming flesh. His legs didn't want to work, but he kicked anyhow, getting himself upright, forcing his tissue back together as fast as he could.

His light blazed out, but this time, he couldn't do it, couldn't make the bones in his ribs and arms and shoulder knit.

Not fast enough at all.

The Leviathan bellowed and turned its good eye on Jake. It opened its mouth. Drool pooled and dripped between pointed teeth bigger than cars.

Fuck! It's coming back toward the fountain.

Jake dug his claws into the bricks and flapped the

two wings that would still work. With his good arm, he dragged himself away from the basin, away from Merilee. A few inches. A foot.

Got to get farther.

More blood bubbled between his lips.

He tried to crawl and heal himself at the same time. Had to do it. Had to get himself back on his feet.

Not working.

Merilee—

He pulled himself with every bit of his strength, but his body collapsed even as he fought for one more foot, just another damned inch so the fucking thing wouldn't get close to her when it ate him.

The Leviathan let out a bone-scraping roar, but it didn't attack.

It was standing still at the edge of the lake, about ten yards from the fountain, its head swiveling around to turn its good eye in the direction of the bandshell.

Groaning, half-choking on his own blood, Jake rolled in that direction.

His wavy vision picked up movement.

He squinted.

Squinted a little harder.

A woman—a very angry-looking woman—decked out in an NYPD raid suit was storming down the path, a SIG gripped firmly in her right hand.

And she was leading what looked like every last one of the OCU officers still fit for duty. Thirty, maybe thirty-five, in full-dress riot gear.

They were coming hard and fast, weapons hot, deploying in a surround pattern Jake had seen Freeman diagram a thousand times.

Right behind the officers came almost as many Sibyls in battle leathers, all that was left of the New York triads, and a few extra Jake recognized from New Jersey and Pennsylvania, too. Like the OCU officers, the Sibyls had weapons drawn, faces sharp and tight, eyes focused on only one target.

The air Sibyls dropped back for vantage shots even as the fire Sibyls lit up swords and the earth Sibyls palmed shining daggers, all waiting for the woman in front to call the order to attack.

With pain blinding him, halfway to passing out, Jake almost didn't recognize Andy with her red hair pulled back into a tight bun, moving with such authority. That, and Andy's clothing was completely, spotlessly dry—though it looked oddly bulky on her slender frame.

"Now!" Andy shouted with a resonance just like a furious demon, louder, even, like the force of the sea itself flowed through her command. She aimed her SIG at the behemoth by the lake and squeezed the trigger.

Instantly, the night filled with gunshots and swinging arcs of fire, whistling arrows and flying daggers. The ground shook. The wind kicked up to hurricane level, sending trees and benches and rocks slamming across the grass.

A few yards from Jake, the one-eyed Leviathan bellowed and started swinging claws and its head and its tail—and Jake turned away.

Crawling toward the fountain now. The world bucked underneath him as he moved. Jets and blasts of fire scorched over his head. Water sloshed from the fountain as he got closer, chilling him with each splash.

He knitted what he could inside himself. A patch job. Enough to stop the bleeding. Enough to move.

The only thing that mattered to him now was Merilee.

As the battle for New York City and the world raged around the Bethesda Terrace and its fountain, Jake crawled over the lip of the bowl and fought through the tepid water to reach Merilee.

All other sights and sounds faded to background

rumbles as he got to her and pulled her cold, wet body into his lap.

Motionless.

Totally still.

Jake felt like his chest was being torn open by the Leviathan all over again.

Desperation surged through him, waking every bit of his healing energy, drawing it together, focusing it into one massive beam. Even as he reached inside her essence to find all her wounds, his demon mind sucked in and spewed forth every vestigial memory available since the dawn of time about healing and medicine and human bodies.

Shit, so many places I need to fix!

Her neck. Her spine.

She wasn't breathing. Her muscles had failed. Her heart was trying to fail, too.

Not happening.

Jake closed his eyes and willed air into her lungs. Willed the faint beat of her heart to continue, to strengthen. He focused into her essence until he could see each tiny fracture and tear and bruise.

The battle was nothing but a dull drone as Jake focused on bringing Merilee back to him. His chest ached as his healing light built, and he poured all that energy into her even as he felt himself start bleeding and breaking all over again.

She needed it all.

She would have it all.

Like working some infinite, intricate puzzle, he healed cell after cell after cell. Breathing for her.

Then breathing with her.

Merilee.

He felt himself fading like he had when he healed Cynda and Riana at the brownstone, but no way was he stopping now.

Her heart rate increased.

Warmth trickled back through her limp body as Jake meshed bone with bone and welded the marrow back into place. It was all so clear now, down to molecules and atoms and how they had to bond and move as one, and he thought it, and he made it so.

She moved in his grip. Turned her head. Her hands twitched.

Fierce joy seized Jake at the tiny signs of life.

"Come back to me," he shouted, tasting the copper of his own blood even as he made hers flow steadily through her veins. "You feel like the wind. I need you like air."

As his words drifted between them, Merilee opened her sea-blue eyes.

Jake was certain he had never seen anything more beautiful.

"What the fuck?" she whispered as a fire bolt slashed over their heads and blasted the Angel of Waters right off her moorings. The big bronze statue smashed to the bricks behind them, bringing Jake's awareness back to the screeches and explosions of the fight against the Leviathan.

Jake flickered. He tried to keep himself present, tried to remain with Merilee, but he knew he was too far gone.

She reached up, pressed her hands against his cheeks and kissed him so deeply he didn't dare move for fear his fangs would rip her freshly healed lips. He felt the contact everywhere even as his own pain came roaring back.

He flickered again, but stayed with her.

She pulled back and whispered, "Don't you dare," and kissed him again, then said, "We've got less than two hours."

A massive, spiked tail slammed against the fountain, tearing her right out of his arms. Jake hissed and grabbed for her as the basin rocked sideways. Caught her arm as water spilled over the edges.

Merilee was scrambling, trying to force her body toward him. Jake braced his legs against the bottom of the tilted basin and held on to her, but the whole fountain pitched, and they rolled out onto the bricks of the terrace.

Jake's bones and muscles howled with each flip and twist, but he managed not to let go of Merilee's arm. As they came to a stop, he pulled her closer.

The dark forms of officers and Sibyls littered the ground.

The giant demon-beast stormed in a large circle, its scales deflecting most of the damage from the guns and knives and swords. It had some scorch marks, and it was limping, but the fucking thing was winning.

Jake snarled and tested his wings. Neither pair worked this time, and just moving the muscles attached to them made him feel like he was going to die.

Merilee tried to get up, but he held her tight and his essence shimmered.

"We have to," she said, pulling away from him more firmly. "We're running out of time. Ninety minutes."

They had no weapons. He couldn't fly.

Merilee sent her wind outward, but Jake felt how weak it was. Nothing but a breeze.

An earth Sibyl shook the ground, and they both rocked back on their asses.

Merilee let out a blast of epithets and managed to get herself upright.

Jake could tell she knew it was hopeless, but he forced himself up to stand beside her and wait for the fucking monster to notice them.

She took his hand in hers and looked at him with those otherworldly beautiful eyes. "My fate is your fate, right?"

Jake coughed a little bit of blood and wondered if one of his ribs was ripping through his gut wall, but he nodded—and he stayed solid even though his healing energy was completely tapped out.

There was no way in hell he could go to that castle in the air to restore himself if it meant leaving her here to die. That realization anchored him even as his demon essence roared against that decision. The little bit of human in Jake kept him right where he was, standing beside his woman, where he belonged.

I've finally learned to be both, haven't I? I'm Astaroth and *human, right here, right now.* The thought struck him like a fresh blow, only this one almost made him laugh from the irony. *Perfect fucking timing.*

With his one good hand, he took off his talisman and slipped it over Merilee's head again, glad for the rush of warmth when her fingers brushed against the gold.

She had time to smile at him just once before the Leviathan swung its great head around, and its single blazing eye fixed on the pair of them.

41

The ancient demon opened its massive maw and Merilee wondered if her heart would fly apart.

Those teeth were going to chew her to pieces, and Jake, too. She drew on her air, but felt almost no response. A spit of wind. Too soon after her injuries. Too weak.

The OCU officers still standing and the Sibyls still able to fight hit the beast with everything they had. Bullets ricocheted. Swords and daggers and arrows bounced against its scales and fell useless to the ground.

Nothing. No damage. No effect.

Merilee knew the Leviathan was coming for her and for Jake, and nothing could stop it.

She glanced at Jake, finally and completely registering how his right arm and wings hung useless. Dark, deep slashes marked his chest. His whole pale body seemed bruised and misshapen, like bones had been broken and badly healed. The sight of him made her ache all over, and brought reality banging home in her mind.

He can't fight.

But Jake looked the Leviathan right in its blood-red eye, bared his fangs, and snarled.

Merilee snarled with him and dropped into a fighting stance.

What the hell am I going to do? Kick it in the nose?

But she couldn't just stand still and let the demon kill them.

If they could reach one of the fallen Sibyls or officers,

they could arm themselves, but Jake could barely walk—and the beast blocked their access to the battlefield. The reek coming off the thing made her eyes water, and every time she took a deeper breath, she coughed from the stench of stagnant water and rancid, murky salt.

The beast seemed to swallow the night and every aspect of the natural world.

"I can take him," Merilee muttered to herself, remembering her boast to Delilah even as her slack muscles went even weaker from fear and dread. "Yeah, right. *That* was mental."

The Leviathan swung its head once, knocking away another bunch of arrows—and it started toward her and Jake.

A tall figure in blood-streaked leathers leaped between the monster and Merilee and Jake.

"Bela!" Merilee cried as the Sibyl swung toward them, her black hair loose and wild around her cut, bleeding face. She hurled a bow toward Merilee, along with a quiver that still had a few arrows left.

Next came a dirt-crusted French bastard sword, tumbling blade over streamlined hilt. Jake snatched it one-handed out of the air and raised it awkwardly, still snarling, now louder than ever.

Bela drew her two hand-sized saw-toothed swords from her waist sheaths and seemed to dare the beast to come another step. Her earth energy roiled outward, making the ground between herself and the Leviathan buck and bubble.

As Merilee readied an arrow, the beast stumbled and let out a thunderous roar.

"Come on, you scaly fucker!" Bela yelled. "What are you waiting for?"

Dread chilled Merilee deep in the pit of her being as she tried to get a bead on the ancient demon's remaining eyeball—but the loudest, scariest bunch of ululating cries she had ever heard fell out of the sky and rattled the cold straight out of her body.

She raised her head at the same second Bela lowered her hand swords and Jake's blade wavered, then went tip-down toward the terrace. He turned his golden eyes toward Merilee. "Is that what I think it is?"

"Gods and goddesses—yes—but how?" She gulped in a breath as the piercing noises came again, climbing all over her nerve endings, setting off a primal urge to scream with them.

Bela did.

Merilee's heart surged into her throat, then she screamed, too, the sound rippling through her body, stirring the air inside her, drawing it up, up, until she could almost feel it ready to flow from her skin and do real damage.

The Leviathan froze where it stood.

Other Sibyls on the battlefield joined the cry. Some who had fallen lurched to their feet and managed to raise their weapons.

OCU officers looked left and right, then backed away from the Dark Crescent Sisterhood, but Jake held his ground, shouting a welcome as Merilee and Bela and all the Sibyls screamed again.

Merilee turned her face to the night sky.

A hoard of Astaroths sank slowly toward the ground, wings spread wide, forming a circle around the Leviathan—and each was holding a wizened little woman dressed in brown, green, or blue robes. The robed women were packing a beautiful array of swords, bows, and daggers—and radiating enough elemental energy to topple every skyscraper in Manhattan.

"Shit," Jake whispered. "It *is* the Mothers. All of them." He raised his sword again, more of a salute than a battle stance.

The Astaroths deposited their passengers and backed away.

One of them turned toward Jake, and Merilee knew it was Darian.

Jake gestured to the fallen on the battlefield, and in seconds, just a few breaths, some of the winged demons surged outward, collected the wounded officers and Sibyls, and surged away into the dark reaches of Central Park.

Darian and the remaining Astaroths formed a second circle behind the Mothers, fangs bared, pale skin glowing like they had drawn the moon into their flesh.

The Leviathan twitched and snarled at its new challengers.

The Mothers raised their blades and nocked their arrows. Some of the swords caught fire, light playing off the beast's filthy scales.

It lunged forward, almost caught a fire Sibyl Mother in its cavernous jaws, but the little woman didn't so much as twitch. Her big Chinese sword spit a jet of flames into the air, and a shitload of earth, fire, and air energy coursed outward at the same moment, stealing Merilee's breath and catching the Leviathan mid-leap.

It fell back on its clawed feet and swung its tail.

More elemental energy slammed against the movement, stopping the huge barbs as surely as if they had struck a wall of steel ten feet thick.

The night seemed to come alive with power. Chills fanned across Merilee's neck and shoulders, and she knew her wind had come back to her, fed into her by the abundance of elemental energy flowing across the terrace.

"*Damn,* it's about time," a woman yelled, and Jake saw Andy get to her feet on the other side of the fountain. She glanced in Jake's direction. "Lowell! Get your human skin back on. You're in charge until Nick and Creed show up. Let them slug out who gets my job."

She threw her SIG into the fountain, then stripped out of her raid suit, revealing the yellow robes she had on beneath her police gear. Her Mother's robes—with a dart gun holstered at the waist.

Merilee squeezed her bow tighter as Andy whipped out her HKP-11, turned toward the paralyzed Leviathan, and approached it with long, confident strides.

"There's more power now," Jake said. "New power."

And Merilee felt it with him, felt the water energy rising, stirring the lake, pulling it toward the shore. As Andy's energy joined with the other elemental powers, Merilee's mind rocked like the Earth had just jumped on its axis. As if the planet itself had just acknowledged its masters.

"Shit," Jake whispered.

The Leviathan managed to let out a long, low groan as Andy walked right up to its massive head. She raised her brutal dart pistol until the barrel touched its one good eye.

"All right, you murdering motherfucker," she said. "It's *my* turn now."

She flung out her free hand, and the lake went still as glass. In fact, it looked just like glass.

Mother Keara barked a command, and half the fire Sibyl Mothers walked directly out onto the water, buoyed by Andy's unbelievable energy, and they started to dance.

"It's projective." Awe swam through Merilee. "Andy's turned that lake into one giant projective mirror. Gods and goddesses, I wish Riana and Cynda were here to see this."

Jake let out a quiet sigh. "I kind of wish Freeman had lived to see it, too, but then, he just would have bitched about how the Parks Department was going to give him shit for the next hundred years."

As the ancient channels ground open under the insistence of the fire Sibyl Mothers, bells began to ring all over New York City.

"Come on." Merilee put up her arrow and slung her bow over her shoulder. "It's time to go."

She gently took hold of Jake's wounded arm. His fingers curled around hers even though it made him wince, and he had almost no grip strength at all.

As Andy reached outward in the general direction of New York Harbor, Merilee and Jake limped toward the lake. They both hesitated at the edge, then walked out on the solid glasslike surface with the Mothers. Bela and a few more Sibyls, any warrior who could move, hobbled into the circle, too.

Merilee led Jake to Mother Anemone, faced the Leviathan, and joined her air energy with the power binding the demon.

Mother Anemone nodded and broke away and moved to Andy's side. Mother Keara left the fire Sibyls, and Mother Yana separated from the earth Sibyl Mothers to stand with Andy as well. They blended her water energy with their own power.

Merilee saw the fierce, hungry joy on the faces of her fellow Sibyls, and she knew she must look the same way. They were born for this. Trained for it.

Tonight, they *were* the masters of the Earth, and all its monumental power.

A moment or so later, a stream of water came slowly across the starlit sky, perfectly aligned, perfectly controlled.

Andy brought the flowing pillar down around the Leviathan, encasing the beast in its natural element.

"World's largest fish tank," Jake muttered, and Merilee would have laughed if it wouldn't have broken her concentration.

Damn, she loved his sense of humor.

Inch by inch and foot by foot, air, earth, fire, and water power floated the ancient demon off Bethesda Terrace and out over the solidified lake, hovering about five feet above its surface.

It twitched and struggled, but couldn't so much as let out a roar.

All the Mothers followed, arms out, elemental energy pulsing out from their skin in almost visible waves. This time, the Astaroths stayed back, and Merilee realized Jake was waving them off.

Sibyl business.

Probably a new concept to them, but Merilee figured they would learn.

When the monster and the Mothers reached the center of the lake, Andy turned toward Jake and Merilee. "Greece, right? Káto Ólimbos. Wherever the fuck *that* is."

Merilee leaned against Jake a little bit—or maybe he was leaning against her, she couldn't tell. They both nodded.

Andy pointed a finger at Jake, then at Merilee. "Y'all so owe me. When you can walk and shit, you're going to be spending a lot of nights working this off in trade. Just so you know."

Without waiting for them to answer, she wheeled back to the Leviathan, raised her arms, and all the Mothers raised their arms—and Merilee's mind and her body and the lake in Central Park exploded upward in one huge *whoosh* of swirling water and air and earth and fire.

Merilee held fast to Jake as the planet seemed to fire upward. Gravity pushed against her bones, racked her skeleton, shoving her skin backward so hard she was sure it would tear, but she felt no real pain. Just pressure. All the goddesses of Olympus, so much pressure!

Then a lurch in her gut, like stepping through a normal projective mirror, only magnified by a hundred. Maybe a thousand.

Sibyl battle cries rang in the void, and her skin tingled, and—

Her feet touched solid, foggy ground. So cold, so dark, and totally familiar now.

Káto Ólimbos.

A wide expanse of the mountain, from what she could make out in the gray, misty light—about the size of the area in Central Park where they had been fighting.

Jake thumped to the same ground beside her with a grunt, doubled over, and she pulled him upright and held him against her with one arm. Blood streaked his cheeks, face, and neck, and he looked twice as pale now. Probably wiped from the transport.

Water came crashing down in a great tidal surge around them, then every drop evaporated, leaving only the darkness and fog and rocks—and the Mothers, and the Sibyls, and Andy, in a wide circle around the demon, much as they had been at the lake.

The Leviathan's one eye was wide now, furious red light pouring from its empty socket and one of its ears, too. Its muscles strained. Its scales rippled.

But it absolutely could not move against its elemental bindings, which seemed twice as powerful now that they had come to this ancient mountain.

Merilee held back an urge to spit on the damned thing.

Andy didn't.

"Uh, are we on time?" Jake asked in a soft voice.

Merilee's internal clock felt haywire, but best she

could tell, they were down to about forty-five minutes and change, provided she hadn't gotten too off in her count while she wasn't conscious. "No sweat," she whispered back. "We're early."

Jake's eyebrows lifted, but he didn't have time to speak, because the air was really starting to stink, even worse than the rotten-water stench of the demon. Merilee glanced to her right and left, noting Andy's grim expression and the firm set of Mother Anemone's jaw. The rest of the Sibyls and Mothers remained completely focused on containing the ancient demon.

Shadows oozed out of the rising mist in front of the demon's head, between the Leviathan and where Merilee stood next to Jake. Tall, almost skeletal forms solidified, wearing stained red robes, their matted black hair covering their pale faces. Ten Keres came forward, their torn wings shedding black feathers as they walked.

One death spirit separated from the others and approached Merilee until she stood only an arm's length away.

"Nosi," Merilee said, and the spirit inclined its head in greeting.

Merilee's eyes and lungs burned from the stench of rotten meat, but she forced herself to keep a neutral expression—unlike Andy, who was holding her nose.

Mother Anemone spoke next. "We are not here to offer ourselves as suicides. We only assist our sister Sibyl, who has come to pay her blood price. Respectfully, we request that you honor the spirit of our visit."

Merilee's blood turned to ice as she realized that every Sibyl on Káto Ólimbos was technically in violation of the ancient treaty, and could be taken as forfeit. Jake's low snarl suggested that he realized exactly the same thing—and he wouldn't be allowing any treaty terms but their own to be fulfilled this night.

Her fingers flexed and her pulse raced as she considered reaching for her bow, but Andy coughed and let go of her nose. "What the nice lady means is, if you pull any shit, we'll fight our way off this mountain—and we'll turn this big ugly bastard of a lizard loose, too. Clear enough?"

Mother Anemone went stiff, but Mother Keara, Mother Yana, and Bela laughed outright.

Merilee found herself smiling, too.

She couldn't see Nosi's face for the hair, just the fangs, but she was pretty sure the death spirit was amused.

No weakness.

They like courage—at least they're consistent. And really, not so different from us.

Nosi glanced toward Andy. In her strange, eerie voice, she said, "You will be a friend to us, water Sibyl. For you"—she shifted her hidden gaze back to Merilee—"and for you, we will help your people to depart in peace."

Relief surged through Merilee. She wasn't sure if there were any formal words she was supposed to recite to complete the bargain, but Nosi turned away before Merilee could ask.

"Release the Leviathan," the death spirit commanded. "Its elemental energy cannot escape our bindings, even in its death throes."

Merilee knew what was coming next.

"Cover your ears!" she shouted as the Mothers and Sibyls turned the demon loose—and several dozen more death spirits popped out of thin air, filling the space between the warriors and the Leviathan.

Even as Merilee slammed her palms against her ears and stretched on her toes to press an elbow against the ear Jake couldn't cover because of his bad arm, the keening cries of the Keres tried to rip apart Merilee's eardrums.

But that was nothing—*nothing*—to what the death spirits did to the demon with their fangs and claws.

The creature might as well have had fur instead of scales, and its size and roars didn't matter one damned bit. It never even got off a good swipe of its barbed tail.

Merilee's stomach clenched, but she didn't look away from the destruction of the creature who had created the Legion and caused the death of countless members of the Dark Crescent Sisterhood.

None of the Sibyls averted their eyes.

Justice was justice, no matter how bloody.

Merilee felt the vibration in the elbow she had against Jake's ear as he hissed his approval.

Seconds later, the demon fell under the onslaught of blows and slashes and unnaturally powerful bursts of elemental energy. The thing never stood a chance against creatures who could wield magic and strength even older and more powerful than its own—and yet, when the Keres finished with it, Merilee could have sworn it was still breathing. She lowered her hands from her ears and moved her elbow away from Jake's head. Her heart rate picked up, and her fingers once more ached to grab her bow and ready an arrow.

"Fucker's still alive," Jake said, and Merilee heard the rising violence in his tone. Bum arm or not, he would take on the thing all over again if he had to.

Nosi once more emerged from the pack of her fellow Keres, who kept the Leviathan's heaving form pinned to the dark, rocky mountain.

The death spirit drifted straight toward Andy and offered her gore-flecked hand.

Andy took hold of Nosi's fingers without flinching, and the death spirit led her to the head of the Leviathan.

Merilee's heart squeezed at the sight of Andy so close to the beast without her elemental energy in full swing, but when Andy reached the thing's big red eye, she took out her HKP-11 and leveled it right at the glowing center.

"This is for Sal, you asshole," she said, and fired all four darts directly into the Leviathan's brain.

The mountain groaned and shuddered, pitching Merilee against Jake.

As she righted herself, she sensed a detonation of elemental energy more powerful than any nuclear warhead, but the air and the fog and the mountain absorbed it before it touched any living creature.

The beast twitched once, then went still.

Andy lowered her dart pistol and a satisfied expression spread across her face.

Closure.

Merilee could almost see it happening as Andy holstered the pistol, then raised her face to the fog-laced stars above and let out a long, piercing howl of mingled rage and pain and triumph.

The Keres screamed so loud in response that Merilee almost fainted.

Her body lurched.

She slammed against Jake, had time to feel his good arm circle around her, and then a powerful wave of elemental energy grabbed hold of them.

They were moving again.

Sailing away from the mountain.

Away from the death spirits.

Racing through time and space and nothingness, so fast her brain felt like it was turning inside out.

Seconds later, they jerked to a complete stop and settled into totally solid, totally normal form.

After a few blinks and deep breaths, Merilee realized they were back in Central Park, standing along the edge of the lake. All of them, Sibyls and Mothers alike.

When she glanced over her shoulder, she saw that the whole area was still deserted except for the newly returned Sibyls and Mothers, and totally torn to hell. Trees lay in piles of splinters. Rocks and dirt were strewn in piles through huge patches of torn-up and burned grass, and daggers and swords and guns and arrows littered the ground.

There were probably emergency vehicles and all kinds of personnel ringing the park, but no fucking way were they going to approach before the OCU told them it was clear—and most of the OCU was out of commission, wherever the Astaroths had taken them for medical attention.

It's over.

Thank Hecate, it's over.

She let out a breath and savored the sight of the returned Sibyls and Mothers, and drank in the sensation of Jake alive and whole next to her.

They were safe now.

She let his spicy scent fill her nose, cleanse her senses—but when she turned to face him, his pale skin and his broken expression sent tremors of worry all through her.

"Jake?" she whispered as she reached for him, but he was fading away.

Her mouth came open. Her breath stopped. She grabbed for his shoulders with both hands, but caught only air. He was nothing but a ghostly image now.

"Don't you leave me!" she screamed, her mind and heart tearing apart at every seam and joint.

"I'm sorry," he said, his voice and body breaking up like a bad radio signal. "I love you."

"No!" Merilee wrapped both hands around his talisman, and she saw him shimmer brighter from her touch.

"Like a feather on my soul," he whispered, and he smiled.

"Jake Lowell," she yelled, letting every bit of her wind power her voice as she squeezed the chain and ring so tightly it dug deep in her skin. "I *order* you not to die!"

42

"At least there's some justice in the world." Merilee put down the copy of the *Post,* knocking two discarded chip bags to the floor. The headline announced Martin Jensen's arrest for conspiracy in the murder of Derek Holston, and a bunch of other shady crap related to the late, not-so-great "Bartholomew August" and the Leviathan's defunct, dispersed Legion cult. Apparently Max Moses, facing a major bunch of trials himself and a string of potential life sentences, had ratted out on every person he had ever seen do business with August.

After attending Sal Freeman's memorial, four Sibyl funerals, and nine services for OCU officers—and after seeing the damage to the Sibyls and other women who were so horribly misused—Merilee wanted every asshole involved with August to pay as dearly as possible, Jensen included. "I hope that sneaky bastard spends the rest of his life playing butt-monkey to some huge convict named Bubba."

"Oh, come on." Cynda slugged back her espresso as Merilee slid the paper across the table to Riana, who was busy looking at the chip bag mess near Merilee like it was killing her not to pick it up. "Tell us what you *really* feel, Merilee."

Merilee tried to ignore that comment, because she didn't need to talk about her real feelings, not unless she wanted to sob for days. "I'm just glad the media's moved on from all the paranormal hysteria—and that they never got around to finding out about us or the Leviathan."

"Earthquake. In Central Park." Cynda shook her head. "I so can't believe the public was so eager to chew up that bunch of bullshit. I guess nobody noticed the big horned skyscraper demon from hell—that, or people believe what they need to believe to get them by."

Merilee blinked, then stared down at the table.

She knew Cynda didn't mean anything by what she said, but it still struck a little too close to home.

Riana glanced at the paper, then seemed to notice Merilee's silence. She moved her steaming mug of evening coffee to one side, leaned across the kitchen table, and rested her palm on Merilee's wrist. Her dark eyes reflected caring and hope, but it was her frown that gave away how much she was worried. "Darian promised Jake will come back, honey. All the Astaroths have told you the same thing—it's *fine* to believe that."

Merilee inhaled the rich scent of her French roast and tried not to cry for the millionth time. She felt her triad sister's gentle gift of earth energy flow into her veins—and Cynda's not-so-gentle singe of fire against her right hip.

"Ow!" Merilee patted out the flame on her jeans and glared at Cynda. "Way to be understanding. Bitch."

"Sorry." Cynda gripped her espresso cup with one hand and stared at her other smoking hand like it belonged to somebody else. The circles under her eyes made her look like a freckled raccoon—with steam coming out its ears. "I haven't had a good night's sleep in over a month. Shit gets away from me."

The cutest little Satan's spawn ever started to cry from the second floor of the brownstone, and Cynda leaped up to go see to her daughter before Neala burned up yet another set of draperies.

Cynda, Riana, Creed, Nick, and Merilee had all been staying at the brownstone since the battle with the Leviathan. The new mommies and daddies needed help with their infants, and the townhouse on the Upper East Side was just too jam-packed and chaotic. Every day, it seemed like they were dealing with more OCU trainees, not to mention the influx of Astaroths who had decided they wanted to be of use in the human world.

And . . . Merilee and her triad all just wanted to be together for a while. They had been talking a lot, eating a ton of chips and cookies and ice cream, fighting about the messes Merilee made, patrolling, and spending long hours repairing all the damage to the downstairs area.

It was almost like old times.

Except for the husbands.

And the babies.

And the Jake-sized hole in Merilee's heart.

She inhaled another rich breath of coffee and tried to let the delicious scent flow through her restless mind.

Six weeks and nineteen hours.

Merilee pulled away from Riana's comforting touch, and her hand rested against the talisman she never took off. Just for good measure, she mentally ordered Jake to come home to her, as she had so many times over every single day he had been missing. Or restoring. Or whatever Darian kept trying to explain about where Astaroths went when they weren't "Below."

"I think—" Merilee started. Then stopped. She took a deep breath and made herself look Riana in the eye. "I think tonight's a good night for me to go home. If you and Cynda think you can handle it from here. I'd like to make sure Andy's space is all cleaned up and demon-free."

Riana nodded slowly, studying Merilee in that deep way only a triad's mortar could do—like she was searching for cracks in Merilee's foundation, for any fissure in her logic and self-control. "Creed's hours should be getting more sane come Monday," she said, "when Andy gets back from Greece. Nick's also taking two weeks off to spell Cynda awhile." She leaned back in her chair and stretched, obviously needing more sleep herself, even though little Ethan was more peaceful than Neala. "I'm really glad Andy decided to be OCU captain *and* a Mother. It just didn't seem right, not having her in the city—but building the new water Sibyl Motherhouse on Kérkira to be closer to the Greek Mothers was a good idea."

Merilee laughed out loud. "*You* don't have to live on that island, do you?" She laughed again, then stopped before she brought on tears. That had been happening since Jake went missing. Everything seemed to lead back to tears. Aware that Riana was studying her again, Merilee shrugged off her sudden wave of moroseness with, "Oh, well. They have lots of earthquakes in the Ionian Sea. Who'll notice a few random tidal waves?"

"Water Sibyls." Riana shook her head. "Kinda cool that they came back into existence during our lifetime, isn't it—and that *we* found the first one?"

Merilee turned her right arm over and studied her revised tattoo, and so did Riana. It was still a mortar, pestle, and broom in triangular points around a dark crescent moon—only now the points were connected with subtle, slightly rolling lines, like gentle swells in the ocean. The lines symbolized water, the element that flowed between them all, and bound them ever more tightly together. Every Sibyl in the world now bore the new mark—or rather the old mark—of the Dark Crescent Sisterhood.

Yeah. Definitely cool that water Sibyls were among them again.

Young women with water talents were arriving every day at the new Motherhouse, and babies were beginning to be presented for training. They were coming from everywhere, all over the world, as if the universe understood the need for trainees of all ages.

In a generation, triads would become quads, and fighting would get . . . a lot more interesting. Not to mention wet.

"You're sure about going?" Riana's question was so soft and gentle that Merilee wanted to smack her, because it almost stirred up the tears she had so neatly tamped down just a second ago.

"I'm positive." She turned her tattoo back to the table, not wanting to lie to its face. "I think I'm ready."

Riana gave her another one of those mortar looks. "Do you promise you won't lock yourself in your library and moon about Jake?"

"No. I don't promise." Merilee finished her coffee in one long, satisfying gulp before thumping her mug on the table. "But I won't have that much time, since we've got patrol tomorrow night."

Riana groaned. "Please don't remind me. I thought with the Legion gone, we'd get to take a big fat rest, but nooooo."

"Evil never sleeps. Kind of like babies." Merilee pushed her chair back, took her mug to the sink, and came back to the table to give Riana a kiss on the cheek. "I'll keep Ethan tomorrow if you need a break before we go out. And tell Cynda that Bela and I will watch Neala, too, if you whip us up another batch of burn ointment and get another crib for the gym."

"Stone walls. Stone floors." Riana pinched the bridge of her nose and closed her eyes. Then she yawned. "Much better than all the paper in your library. I'll bring the stuff—and the babies—around two?"

"And if Andy brings all the water babies back with her, we'll have quite a gymful." Merilee grinned.

That would be pretty cool.

Merilee knew she needed to stay busy. And keep her mind off—

She sighed.

Jake.

Before Riana could start worrying all over again, Merilee plastered on a calm expression and raised both hands. "Not much mooning. Really. I swear."

Then she picked up her chip bags and tossed them, and left before her triad sister could call her a liar.

It didn't take that long to kick all the stray Astaroths out of Andy's room and get it spic-and-span for her return. Just an hour or so. Well, closer to two, and another hour to do a long yoga session and calm herself down. At least the physical labor helped Merilee burn off some of her fathomless, endless damned urges to cry.

She didn't want to face her grief, couldn't cope with it, but sooner or later, she'd have to.

Darian's promises—well, Astaroths were brilliant, but they didn't have major social skills. Merilee wasn't certain, but she thought the demon just wanted her to feel better. Keep a little hope, so she didn't fall completely into despair.

As she climbed the stairs back to her library, which no doubt needed a good dusting, she knew she had to start finding a way to handle how much she missed Jake. Every time she saw one of the winged demons drifting down a townhouse hallway—which would probably be a lot from now on—she'd think about him. And it would hurt.

But . . . he might not be coming back.

He probably wasn't coming back.

Her throat closed as she pushed through the library door—but in a big hurry, her thoughts shifted to more immediate concerns.

"Okay, guys. Out. It's after hours, and I'm home. Out. Out!"

Seven apologetic demons, including Darian, whisked toward her, paid their respects, then hurried on their way. She let them keep the books they were reading, of course. It would have been cruel to take reading material away from an Astaroth. They were like long, tall, pale demon-sponges. With wings. Always soaking up text and theory and whatever wisdom they could wrap their claws around.

Darian stopped at the door on his way out, brushed his graceful fingers against the pockets of his jeans, and regarded her with his eerie golden eyes. "Are you well?" he asked.

It did no good to lie to Astaroths, who in addition to being sponges, were also fairly decent living polygraph machines. "As well as can be expected," Merilee said, which was the best she could do.

Darian frowned. "The Leader—"

"Yeah, I know." Merilee fought the urge to slap the demon, or stick him in the ass with the first arrow she could find. "Jake will be back. So you keep saying, and I'm trying to believe you." She swallowed, feeling that ever-present lump coming right back to choke her up again. "I'm . . . desperate to believe you."

Darian's golden gaze faltered, and he looked away. "His volumes are still being written. I'm certain he's Above, just in deeper places. He had much healing to do."

"But you haven't actually seen him."

Darian hesitated and still didn't meet her eyes. Finally, he shook his head.

Merilee turned her back on him before she burst into tears.

The Astaroth left so quietly Merilee wouldn't have

known he was gone if the door hadn't closed behind him with a soft little thump.

She moved around the library, opening all the windows to let in the air, to welcome the wind and let it touch her deep inside, where she needed the comfort.

Then she dusted.

For hours.

Every shelf. Every book. Every knickknack and paperweight and bracket in the whole damned library. She neatened her notebooks, sharpened her pencils, and even restacked her stacks. By the time she was done, her forehead was creased with sweat, her jeans were a dusty mess, and her blouse was the same color as the rags she pitched in the trash near the balcony doors. She had to strip off her clothes and take a long shower to get all the layers of filth off.

When she pulled on her thick white robe and walked back to the library, to the open balcony doors, she felt better.

Aching, tired—but a little more organized than usual. And better.

And she wasn't crying.

At least until she thought about not crying.

Shit.

Merilee put her face in her hands and sobbed, feeling the yawning, all-consuming emptiness twist her insides into one big painful knot.

This was never going to get better.

She was never going to get over this. Not ever.

A soft thump behind her made her gather a burst of her wind in one fist and whirl around to hurl it at whichever demon hadn't gotten the after-hours message loud and clear.

Merilee stopped mid-pitch. Her mouth came open and her heart started a wild *pound-pound* she could feel in her neck, her face, her fingers—everywhere.

Jake.

Air energy rushed out of her hand before she could yank it back, the blast knocking over books and sending all the curtains swirling. Some even ripped off their rods and drifted, diaphanous, to the hardwood floor.

Jake.

She blinked to make sure she wasn't fantasizing, but the image didn't change.

Jake was standing in the open balcony doorway wearing nothing but a pair of sin-tight jeans. He had wings—but the rest of him was totally solid and totally human. All scar and muscle and tan and . . . and . . .

"Jake." Merilee heard herself say his name, but she still didn't believe what she was seeing, even though her whole body had started to hum.

He glanced at her upraised hand, then fixed his gorgeous gray-blue eyes on hers. "You can hit me," he said in the low, delectable bass she had been craving for so many hours, days, and weeks. "But if you slap me, I get to give you that spanking I promised you on Káto Ólimbos."

Gods and goddesses, did *that* image ever make her hotter than hell, total shock and idiotic flowing tears notwithstanding.

She lowered her hand, then lunged forward and slapped him so hard his head turned halfway to his shoulder.

"I can't believe you stayed gone for a month and a half! I've almost cried my eyes right out of my head, you big demon idiot!"

Then she threw her arms around his neck and buried her face against his chest and cried.

"I'm so sorry it took me so long." He rocked her and kissed her head, stroking her shoulders and back, massaging out the anger and pain and tension like he knew exactly which muscle to work and how hard. "I love you."

"I love you, too, so much." Merilee clung to him, trying to convince herself that the hard, sculpted flesh was real. That Jake was here. That he was hers. "I ordered you back. Your talisman—I ordered you back a hundred times."

He pulled away from her enough to look into her face and smile. "Each command gave me strength, healed me a little more. You pulled me closer."

"Do you want to wear it now?" She let go of him and gripped the necklace, and a big, rippling shudder went through him.

He covered her hand with his, pressing the necklace into her fingers and chest. "It's yours forever, just like me—if you want me, that is."

Merilee stared at him, slack-jawed, feeling every place he touched her like a blast of sweet, hot wind. "If I want you? You are kidding, right?"

Jake's expression was totally serious as he ran his fingers through her hair, then traced the small scar on her jaw. "I've been able to use my biosentience to get better with my human form again, but it isn't very consistent. I shift a lot, and I can't promise I won't wind up stuck in my Astaroth form for long stretches."

Merilee lifted her eyebrows. "You think a little pale skin and a few claws can spook me? My goddaughter—your niece—might burn down the townhouse tomorrow. Now *she's* scary."

He pulled her closer, leaned toward her mouth until her lips tingled, waiting for his kiss—then he hesitated.

Her eyes were closed, and the heat of his breath washed over her face.

When he spoke, his voice was even lower, and sorrowful. "I don't know if I can ever give you a child of your own."

"Oh, shit, Jake. Right now, all I want is a kiss." Merilee pressed her hands against his head and pulled him the rest of the way to her mouth.

He growled like he'd spent the last month and a half thinking of nothing but how he'd taste her, how he'd touch her, and she held on tight, giving herself to his fierce lips, his spicy scent, the power of his hands gripping her hips, and the simple, blissful reality of his presence.

She tasted him right back as his lips devoured hers, running her hands through his short, soft hair. The air in her body heated and howled and spun until her nipples ached, her sex ached, her very soul ached for him to take her any way he'd have her, in whatever form he could manage.

Demon.

Human.

Nine-headed hydra.

She really didn't give a damn.

Jake's hands moved inside her robe, marking her with each searing touch.

"Give me your air," he murmured as she unfastened his jeans and shoved them down over his trim hips. "I want your wind."

She wrapped them both in a wild flare of her elemental energy as she stroked his hard cock, moving him where she wanted him, pressing his erection between her legs.

Jake's wings lifted her up, up, higher, spreading and pumping, taking her to the balcony, out of the library, into the night. So fast. So high. Into a wide, dark, and empty sky that belonged just to them.

"Fly with me, Merilee."

His voice rumbled through her mind, stirring her, letting her know without question—

This is real.

He's real.

We're real.

Merilee's heart pumped like his wings as she held on for dear life, trusting him, wanting him, falling into the rhythm of his flight, feeling the unbelievable heat as he slid his cock deep into her aching center.

She arched her hips against his thrusts and let go with her arms, letting him hold her, soaring like she had always wanted to soar, completely free and open to wherever this ride might take them.

"Fly with me," Jake whispered again. . . .

And she did.

(acknowledgments)

Well, dear readers, thank you for reading this trilogy. I hope it brightened your lives and stirred up winds in your minds.

I would like to extend my thanks to the intrepid copy editors at Random House. You truly contributed to the quality and consistency of my work, and I'm both grateful and a little awed. *How* do you notice all that stuff? Amazing.

As always, this piece wouldn't have been possible without the eagle-eyed critique of Cheyenne McCray, who at least didn't have to give up a vacation for this one. More appreciation to Tara Donn—thanks for not letting me point weapons at friendlies and do utterly stupid things with my law enforcement officers.

To my editor Kate Collins—this one was all yours, and I appreciate your feedback and careful work. Signe Pike, good luck in your new ventures, and I still covet your old e-mail address. Kelli Fillingim, welcome, and I'll try not to be too big a pain in your neck. Really.

And Nancy—I got you in the dedication this time, but I know, I know . . . that doesn't apply to the endless supply of chocolate (and coffee) I owe you.